THE ASSEMBLER
OF
PARTS

THE ASSEMBLER
OF
PARTS

A Novel

Raoul Wientzen

ARCADE PUBLISHING • NEW YORK

First Edition

The song "Dark Eyed Molly" is reprinted here by the kind permission of Archie Fisher MBE.

This is a work of fiction. Names, characters, places, and incidents are either the products of the author's imagination or are used fictitiously.

Arcade Publishing books may be purchased in bulk at special discounts for sales promotion, corporate gifts, fund-raising, or educational purposes. Special editions can also be created to specifications. For details, contact the Special Sales Department, Arcade Publishing, 307 West 36th Street, 11th Floor, New York, NY 10018 or arcade@skyhorsepublishing.com.

Arcade Publishing® is a registered trademark of Skyhorse Publishing, Inc.®, a Delaware corporation.

Visit our website at www.arcadepub.com.

10 9 8 7 6 5 4 3 2 1

Library of Congress Cataloging-in-Publication Data
Wientzen, Raoul L.
The assembler of parts/Raoul Wientzen.
pages cm
ISBN 978-1-61145-891-6 (alk. paper)
1. Families—Fiction. 2. Abnormalities, Human—Fiction.
3. Washington (D.C.)—Fiction. 4. Psychological fiction. I. Title.
PS3623.I3845A37 2013
813'.6—dc23
2013016863

Printed in the United States of America

For Judy, luminous and beautiful as a constellation.
You light my life.

CONTENTS

THE ASSEMBLER
OF
PARTS

PART ONE
THEN* AS NOW*

1

ALMOST PERFECT

I forgive him. I forgive Dr. O'Brien, now*, forgive his thought as he laid eyes on me. After all, he was the very first to see me, varnished with glossy vernix and tarnished with rusty blood, worming my way out into the lance of his light, and I'm afraid I took him by surprise. I see his big hands on my head, cradling it gently like a priceless gem or a barely hot baked potato. He eased it down toward the floor a little, as if he wanted me to see something important, his blue paper shoe covers or the marbled pattern on the hospital linoleum or the drops of episiotomy blood that had collected in two intersecting pools like the symbol for infinity.

But I was allowed only the briefest look, because the perfect pair of shoulders I had been awarded by the Assembler scraped clear of my mother's springy pubis just then. They popped free, announcing their beautiful symmetry, just as Dr. O'Brien was giving me a look at the ceiling. Nothing much there to see, really, so unlike the stucco ceiling that would be in my bedroom, above my crib rails, with stars that glowed at night and animals that sprang from the ridges and savannahs of plaster during the day. The rest of me—what there was of it—was quick to come then. He lifted me out—chest and belly, arms and legs—gently as a flyfisherman easing a speckled trout from the stream.

His first thought: "My God! She'll never hitch a ride home."

I forgive him.

I was born without thumbs, the four blue fingers of my right hand even in the cold of the delivery room trying to hang on to the folds in the sleeve of his green OR gown as he suctioned my mouth of the gobs of my mother's secretions.

I forgive him, too, the slight, boneless wavering I then felt in his one-armed cradling embrace. It was just for a second as he jiggled the red rubber tip of the bulb syringe in my mouth, trolling for the bite of my breath, but I felt his arm go slack as if he'd rather not be holding me at all. I was not a sparkling trout, but an alien spider crab or scary scorpion fish, instead. The fingers of my hand tugged a tiny pleat in his sleeve just then, and even before I spit out my first mewling cry, his arm tightened. I grew used to that—how I could pull people back to me with tiny claw hands after they'd first turned away, wanting to let go.

I forgive him for that slight sag in his arm, his soul.

I knew I had cried by the look Mother gave Father—the quick turn of the head from her hard concentration on her supernova'ed perineum to smile at him. It is a good thing to have here* in heaven, the first memory of your mother smiling through the pain.

I knew I'd cried by that look of relief on her face—"My baby's breathing! My baby's breathing!"—but I could not hear in all its lionesque claim on life my roar made of baby's breath, the fierce bouquet of cries I presented the world. One needs ears to hear, ears that are more than the pretty pink spirals the Assembler had so nicely stuck to the sides of my head. One needs passageways and pearly membranes, ossicles that clang with sound in the cleft of the skull and set up tides of noise in the canals of the brain. These parts I was not given.

My newborn cry was for others to hear, not for me.

Still, I looked cute in the pink blanket and cotton cap the nurses fitted me with against the chill of the delivery room. The cap came down to the tops of my ears, each perfect as a coiled nautilus but without its sweet-salty susurrus. But, now*, watching my birth, I know the day will come at twelve weeks when my quiet conches fill with the sea's loud tumble, speech. The surgeons would see to that, slicing through my silence and fitting me with aids. Then, words would sink through gelled fathoms to reach me. "J-l-e-a-s-s-h-h!" I would hear my mother say that day of surgery. "S-h-w-e-e-t-a-r-h-h."

I would have seven years of double listening with my eyes and with my ears to the lips of the world. My glossy black eyes read the purse and pucker, my electric ears heard the pulse of lips, and words were born in my missing parts. I took them in, tasted them, and they were sweet enough to kiss. But they nourished my voice poorly. My thin newborn cry would never fatten normally on the dumpling coos, the buttery "ahs," the syrupy "sweetheart Jesses" that the lips of my world served. I could see the words leaping from mouths, could hear them thrashing like hooked fish in the dumbing weight of the sea, could taste them all with my lips. But I never could fully digest the alpha, the beta, of the soup of sound. I would grow fat on a slaw of slurred words and sunken sounds. It would be a peculiar kind of plumpness I would grow, turns of fat around my neck, lumps above my knees, clots between my tiny toes. The doctors told us it was part of my syndrome. I knew better. It was love. And my voice shared in this comic dysmorphism, words emerging from my throat with bloated middles or overstuffed suffixes or mountainous prefixes—like pastries made by psychotics. At seven, I told Cassidy, "Chewww'l ah-bya okay." It made him stop crying and put down his glass and kiss me. It really did. And he really would be okay.

*

All the perfect sounds came to me at seven, when I died. The Assembler saw to that. They came like a swarm of honeybees and filled my ears full of honey buzz, all the words, all the songs, all the laughter and sighs, speaking perfectly at once. It was good because the perfect words also brought me my new svelte voice. Which I bring to you now*. More work of that artful Assembler who replays my life for me now* so I see it all as a piece, so I hear it all with His air ears.

I would like to say I first met Him, the Assembler, yes-terday*. At least it seems like yesterday* when His bright-ness woke me. I was somewhere alone in a dark and tiny place, then here*, bathed in His buzzing bright whiteness that got in my ears like the sand at the beach. But instead of that gritty itch I'd felt before, now* there was a sweet, reso-nant, humming tickle of sound. He stood before me and smiled at my amazement. "Watch," He said, and the whole black vault above filled with the images of my birth. "Film, the First," He said grandly, "in the review of your life."

As I watch, I am here* and there*, I am then* and now*, at once observer and performer, naive child and evolving cosmic consciousness, one and the same. It makes me dizzy, watching. It makes me long for the simpler stories off the flat pages of brightly colored books I so loved in life. But I review my life with my new ears, my eternal eyes, my perfect voice, as if I am living it both then* and now*.

I am bold enough to ask, "Assembler, what is it I search for in my life? Why do You show me my birth and the doctor's faltering? Is it so I can forgive him, as I do forgive him?"

"What was hidden from the wise," He tells me, "has now been revealed to the blind!"

Blind? Dare I tell Him? No, not now*, not yet*.

"It's a girl!" Dr. O'Brien said to my parents after examining my genitalia in the light of a lamp like an exploding star. I felt as if I had eclipsed my mother, my bright sun of a mother, put between her and that blinding lamp. "Call the pediatricians," he whispered to the circulating nurse as he double-clamped my wormy cord and snipped me free to squirm in a heated blanket.

My mother had my papoosed body in her arms. Her face was flushed from the final push of placenta. But the faint pink blush around her mouth was pressed away by her wide smile, a smile that never faded, not even when Dr. O'Brien said, from the crux of her limbs, "Kate. Kate. I have to tell you. The baby . . . she has no thumbs." He stood there so tall, so still, lost in the whiteness from the light.

"Jessica. Jessica Mary," is all she said to that, to me, and her smile warmed me softly. I felt the hand of my father on my knee. His finger made tentative half circles on my blanket. I would have regarded his face then if I could have, but the transfixing stare of a smiling mother is something all-entrancing. We regarded each other—I, her sweaty pinkness, her Chiclet teeth, her crinkled eyes; she, my coal-black globes and womb-squashed nose—even as the nurse took me away to be studied.

Well, examined, really. Under the bronze glow of a radiant warmer in the newborn nursery. The nurse with her cold hands set me free of my cotton confinement, free to wiggle my ten toes and eight fingers in the exploration of face and flank and fanny, the latter graced with the briefest of my tender touch when she flexed my legs from the matting to introduce me to the rectal probe of her plastic-sheathed thermometer. To this day* I fear that kind woman mistook my thorny shriek for a cry of pain, when in fact it was pitched jubilation; the joy in the little things, holes and tubes and skin! "Rejoice," my cry announced, "there is a way in and there is a way out!" But she heard my quick exclamation and placed her free hand on my head for comfort. I felt the heat go out of me into that cold palm. I reached with my hand and hooked her thumb with my forefinger. The timer beeped, my temperature done, but the nurse stayed in my grasp until her hand glowed pink with my warmth. Then I let her go.

The doctors came. They were the first of what would become a white-coated invasion of my life, seven years of Viking raids on my body and my blood, parts of me carried off to other lands, made to work in the labs of the world in the service of science. I didn't really mind. There was so much of me to share, to spare. I let them all have their way with me.

The first was Dr. Burke. He was younger then. His face hadn't yet grown the furrows where seeds of concern would sprout, seeds planted by me and a host of other patients. He stood over me as I bathed in the warm glow of the heater with one hand behind my head. What he said tasted like a sweet, cold drink. "Well, look at you, young lady, catching the rays during spring break!" "Young lady"— I liked that so much that, when it came time, I helped him hold his stethoscope against my heart. It was near midnight when he arrived. Bedtime Listerine was still fresh on his breath.

What did he find in his half hour of poking and probing, tapping and listening? Or more importantly, what did he not find in that trove of organs that was my seven-pound, four-ounce, skin-wrapped self? My unhitched thumbs were the easiest to see—or not see. But a certain spongy "give" in the outer aspect of my forearms led him to suspect, and later confirm by X-ray, the absence of the radius bones that normally attach at the base of the thumbs, the thenar eminences. He used that word "thenar" in his rambling description of his findings to the intern standing with him. "Thenar," a word that tastes strange to me, hollow and empty rather than solid and full. Thenar. Thenar. Even now* when I look at my hands, I taste a shallow scooped hole. Thenar. Even now*, with thumbs, Thenar, you are a cave.

Other bones omitted from the box: the ossicles of the middle ear, three pair of bones the weight of a mouse pellet. Too tiny for the Assembler to see, perhaps? The end of a busy week, tired? A Friday afternoon job, bleary-eyed? Who's to say? But I do know this. Those were all that were amiss in my skeleton—a dozen bones—two in my limbs, four in my thumbs, and six in my head. Twelve missing out of a total of how many? Two hundred six in the human body. My skeleton was ninety-five percent perfect, and I was pleased.

Not so Dr. Burke. He squinted, he puckered his lips, he shook his head. "Looks like a syndrome of some sort," he told the young doctor standing now on the other side of my warmer. The intern yawned. When Burke found the blind-ending pouch that should have been my external ear canal, he scratched his crew-cut head and queried, "One of the oral-facial-maxillary dysostoses, maybe?"

Now, that's an eyeful to choke on, I thought then* (or I think now*, it's so hard to sort it all out, then* and now*). "Sometimes associated with renal, rectal, and vertebral anomalies," he went on. His hand pressed my belly— left, right, up, down, shallow, deep, deeper still. All that work to announce: "No palpable masses." He gave me my first taste of popsicle stick while he inspected my mouth. He puckered my lips with his thumb and forefinger and inserted the wooden blade. It tasted slightly sweet, but I lost that thought to the click-and-clack feel of stick on stone as his probe found teeth: four teeth to be exact! Of all things, to get some extra teeth. A consolation prize. A makeup gift from the Assembler upon the discovery of His bony lapses.

Not to be. The Assembler giveth and Burke taketh away. He pulled them, then and there, right before my first attempt to suckle. He pulled them with forceps that looked like needle-nosed mosquitoes come to suck my tongue. All to protect me from an early death, should those teeth wobble free, lodge in my airway, and close it off. Oh, the irony in his care.

I tasted blood, my own, before my mother's milk. The intern yawned again.

I confess to falling a little out of love with Dr. Burke just then. He tried to see my genitals, but I pushed my thighs against his pries, and peed. And cried, and peed again against his reprise. "Excellent," was all he said after he'd won the contest, but I was unsure what he was complimenting, my plumbing, my strength, my will. He flipped me over onto my belly and pinched my buttock. I fought with all my strength for position as that sharp press spread into me, and I cried. I rocked and flailed and raised my head. I squirmed and pushed with my four-fingered hands against the taut bedding, trying to roll my rump from his next attack. I managed only to turn my head from left-looking to right, where I could watch out of my upper eye for the next descent of Burke's rude pincer grasp. Instead came a gentle pat, a soothing rub, on my small round mound of rear, and the words, "Sorry. Sorry, little baby. . . . Excellent motor response," he added, turning to catch the intern in another gaping yawn.

So there I was when Burke had finished with me: blood on the tongue, urine on the tush, and twelve bones short of perfect. (The next day a kind lady would rub warm cream over my belly and collect pictures of my kidneys. A sweet irony here: the kidney is a bean-shaped organ, and my left one was barely a nubbin of tissue the size of a bean, a kidney somehow damaged during assembly. Such good news, though, because the other was perfect, one million nephrons bundled together like an endless collection of

roller coasters for my urine to ride until it found the exit.
All you need is one kidney, and I was blessed with it.)

I wonder to this day* where those four teeth went, if
they missed the slippery swipe of my tongue and the syrup
of my gums. I know where that left kidney wound up. Or
the half of it not put on slides for the pathologist to gaze
at. It sat in formalin, in a black-capped jar in Burke's office,
next to my picture when I was almost two, the photo taken
on the day I was discharged from the hospital after my surgery to remove the dysplastic renal tissue. It was the best
way, the doctors told us, to treat my high blood pressure.
And it worked. I wore a new red sweater the day I went
home, a gift from Dr. Burke.

When Dr. Burke was done, a warm-handed nurse
wrapped me tight in a baby blanket and wheeled me away
to my mother's room. The hall was hushed and dark, but
the nurse's lips moved a song my way as we went. It was
too dim to catch all her words. Something about Tom
Thumb and a plum.

My mother was sitting in bed, crying, when I was
wheeled in. Dr. Burke was at the bedside speaking, and
my father stood opposite him with a look on his face that
could only be called grave, though here I was, alive and
happy to kick, if someone would merely unwrap me. But
Mother was crying in the room's blue fluorescent light.
She dabbed her blue-stained tears with white Kleenex.
I was struck by the reversal in the order of things: from
joy to sadness, from whitest light to dull blue glow, from
radiant smile to limp, handheld flags of defeat. She wept
in pain before her jubilant baby daughter. Crying, sad,
because of me.

Dr. Burke was telling her of my missing parts and of the plan afoot to search for other errors in assembly. He paused for a moment so Mother could blow her nose and unfold another hanky from the packet she held pressed to her right breast. Before he could resume his discussion, I began to cry. I listen now* to that cry. It was a looping cry that began low and rose in pitch, hovered there and swooped back down only to rise again, my "hold me" cry, rude and crude for lack of practice. Back then* in that dim room I couldn't hear its songful beauty, but Burke's good ears deciphered it immediately. He walked over, his neck-hung stethoscope swinging like a metronome to my rough music, and scooped me up from the bassinet. He laid me on the pillow where my mother's head had lain and unwrapped me. I could smell her sweat, and the warm honey-scent of my mother's hair, as if it had hived a hundred bees. He made a show of my hands to Mother and Father. He had her press my forearm like I was a cake tested for doneness. I was spongy to the gentle press, and her tears only increased through this inventory of missing parts. When Burke slipped her pinkie tip into the blind pouches that should have been ear canals, her sadness became a moan. Father was stoic, his back straight, his arms fixed at his sides, a man with a stiff upper lip and a stiffer skeleton, bone on every bone. He cleared his throat and asked, "Does this mean she can't hear?"

"Probably it does," said Burke. "We can do some hearing tests to be absolutely sure, but most of the time this external anomaly is associated with absence of the bones that conduct sound. So I'm sorry, but yes, there is a very good chance Jessica is deaf. But ear surgeons can do wonderful things now to correct some of these defects, to restore some hearing, so let's wait and see what they have to say. I think they'll figure a way to give her some auditory capability. And with the new generation of hearing aids, well, there's a lot of hope here, is what I'm trying to say."

Father's bones seemed to age as his shoulders sank. He took Mother's free hand in his. "Kate," he said. "This isn't what—"

Burke interrupted. "Look at her eyes, Kate. Look at them. They're looking right at you, and they are beautiful. Really beautiful."

Well, I was, and she did. My black eyes locked on to my mother's blood-shot browns, and we stared at each other for a while. Her tears stopped, and her moans. I reached out with my right hand and scraped the blue air. She offered me her index finger, and I perched my fingers and hand on it like a bird on a branch. "Aren't they the most amazing coal-black eyes?" Burke asked. "There's so much strength in them. Don't you think?" In that instant Mother managed a weak smile, a shadow of the one I'd seen after delivery, but a smile nonetheless. I forgave Dr. Burke his every transgression, his pinch of my skin and his pinching of my tiny teeth, and fell in love with him all over again. He made my mother halt her tears; he lighted her with smile. I never could hold a grudge very long.

But I could hold a finger. I squeezed Mother's with all my neonate might and tried to coo. It was even more imperfect than my "hold me" cry, but Mother smiled again. She looked at Father and dropped the words, "Jessica is beautiful, don't you think, Ford? Even with everything, she's beautiful." She looked back to me and I kicked with my legs.

Father's frame lost even more of its bone. His head hung down like a shamed child's. Without looking at either of us, he whispered, "Yes," and released Mother's hand.

I hung on to the other with four fingers.

In the newborn period the mouth is dry as baked clay, unless made moist from the plucking of teeth or the sucking of teat. By that moment in my mother's room the thin roots ripped away had ceased their bloody seep and again my mouth was all sand and talc. It is a circumstance, I think, well intended by the Assembler whose aim is to fix us with a constant thirst, to pucker us always for the wet sweet weep of mother's milk. She put me to her breast. My mouth seemed me, all of me, more than me, as I tried to latch on to the milk nubbin she cradled me against. But at my first attempt, my lips closed before my tongue had settled. I squirmed and sucked but managed not a drop. She gently pulled me off and brought me back, but my tongue would not stop its useless flick, and my lips lost the way to a perfect seal. Away again and a pat on the back. A third attempt came so very close—a drop of colostrum before my tongue lost its way. My mouth seemed me, all of me, more than me—it was all thumbs.

We switched sides and tried again. This time, it was a piece of cake. I nursed her to sleep on this second sweet breast. Her heart tapped me kindly to keep me awake all the while I sucked. She awoke to find my black eyes studying her face. Such a beautiful face, my mother's. She smiled.

I left my droopy-eyed mother a little while later after I had mastered her other breast and had lain warm and content with my cheek on her chest. The nurse entered the room and watched me watch my mother's slow breathful rise. She took me up and placed me in the bassinet, leaving my mother content to rest after her labors.

In the nursery I was reintroduced to the rectal thermometer. Not to be outdone, my infant bowel presented the world its first stool. Meconium, as sticky and greeny-black as that dark name suggests. My nurse withdrew her slender probe and said, "Well, aren't you the best little one!" Something inside me deep as the roots of the rose knew I was. I slept well that night in the silent nursery.

There were more tests and examinations in the next days. Many more. I helped the lady cardiologist listen to my heart. I held still and tried not to breathe too fast as she positioned her cold stethoscope and colder hand on my chest. She had words for all the sounds of the heart. They fell from her lips to my eyes and to my mouth, and they were so hard they hurt: aortic, mitral, systole, diastole, shunt, murmur. I tried to help her hold the metal disc of her stethoscope, but she moved my hands away. Her quick touch was like ice. Then she wiped her hands on her nursery outer gown. It stung to see her do that. But so ardent was she for the sounds of my heart, so much did her eyes register nothing, for her ears were her full self as she stood with black tubes in her face and caught my noises and dropped them back out of her slack mouth, that I forgave her wiping and tried not to breathe. She was the first to hear the sounds of my true heart, its leaky swirl and swish, and was true enough herself to whisper them to me. So I rolled my fingers into bird fists and lay on my back. I waited for the shape of words from her lips to fall at me. My hands unfurled like flowers to catch them. I knew not then the fruit of those sad blossoms. It was a good thing, really, not to know.

The pictures she later took with her echo machine told the story of my sounds without words. The holes not given to my ears had somehow been mounted in my heart. Ventricular septal defect, atrial septal defect. The Assembler napping on the job again, not quite finished with the knit of tissue to quarter my heart to chambers, upper, lower, left, right.

The tally grew: two thumbs, twelve bones, one kidney, and two holes in the lace of the heart.

The news she gave my mother, though, was excellent. The heart would likely heal itself, knit up those tiny leaks and silence those puny squeaks, and if not, at age seven the nimble surgeon would sew me up. Until then I would carry a noise like a shout in my heart, one I could not myself hear but which, in quiet moments as I fell to sleep, I could often feel athump and aswish.

Good news, very good news, indeed, what the heart lady said. But in the end, the news was not wholly true. The telling was a kindness told so she, or we, would not lose heart.

In my newborn life, sound traded places with scent. I couldn't hear my own belly rumble or the rocket burst of a good burp or the fresh squish of a seedy stool. They come back to me now*, those thousand intestinal voices, in a grand chorus of music that takes my breath away. But then*, in noiseless life, those functions of the body announced their presence in the world with their own perfumes. But my noisy, soundless heart's perfume I did not, could not, share. It lay furled inside my chest like a flower

never bloomed, a petal case for fragrance only I could
breathe. It was there as I fell to sleep, that scent pulsed out
into my nose by the soundless thump, the quiet swish of an
imperfectly quartered heart. It smelled like earth, rich and
damp and deep. It smelled like the tunnels worms make.

It is a game we play up here*, at meals or on walks or
before the movies start: rank your doctors in order of pref-
erence. We all had doctors in life, some more than others,
but all of us well acquainted with the disciples of life and
living.

My list: Burke, Garraway, Marshall, O'Neil, Law, Mar-
tel, Zarur, Stein, and Shaw.

There were many others, but they played small parts in
my life, my death.

Sean Burke and his kindness for my life was first, and
Eileen Marshall of Cardiology, kind too, but in third place
if only because her hands were cold, summer or winter—
and she never let me warm them—and because it was her
error that took my life at seven. But she ranks ahead of
Pat O'Neil of ENT and Carmen Law of Nephrology, and
Arthur Stein of Urology and all those others, because she
made my mother and my father untroubled, at least for a
while. Thank you, Eileen Marshall.

The doctors trailing Marshall, they were all fine. More
cut and dried than the first three on the list, perhaps (especially that urologist Stein who took my kidney and left it
in a jar like a pig's knuckle in a saloon), but all fine enough.

Then there was Vincent Garraway, my geneticist. I
loved him so, my number two. He knew so much and was
so wise, had the softest of words and the sweetest of kisses.
He was the only one, of all my doctors, who ever kissed

me. He kissed me every visit. He opened my eyes with his kiss on my lids, but he opened my heart with his kiss on my fingers. "Good morning, my pretty little lady!" he'd say and take my hand to his lips. One, two, three, four would go his pecks. Only then, in the wish for a fifth touch of his lips, did I ever long for missing thumbs. Only then.

But if I kicked enough with feet and legs, he'd sometimes nod and smile and bend low to blow on my toes, to the blessed number ten. It made me scream, giddy with joy.

And if this were not enough to win me, here is what else he did: he made it possible for Mother to have another child! Through him, a sister to come out into the limelight, to watch over the stars and animals of the ceiling, to feed and sleep and stool and coo and be and be in love.

But that was not for some time to come. There was that first visit to me in the nursery well before there was little baby Jeanine. That first visit, not long after the inventory was nearly complete, organ by organ, system by system, exam by exam. It is all recorded on Tape #2.

I was on my back taking in the evening shadows spread out on the nursery's far wall when he came through the door. The shadows were made by the sun's push past the bird cutouts taped to the large western window to dissuade real birds from attempting to visit us babies.

I first noticed him when he stood with the shadow of a parrot on his shoulder. He was very tall and gangly and appeared in a sleeveless hospital gown with his slim arms at his side. The arms were bare and shiny and curved like cutlasses. He needed only a black patch over one eye to be a pirate. He waited by the wall, watching me watch him, until my mother arrived.

They talked for a few minutes before they approached my bassinet. Mother wasn't smiling then, but there was a confidence in her eyes, a cross between acceptance and anticipation, maybe, or relief and determination. "Good morning, my pretty little lady," he said taking my hands in his for the first time. It was a long way down to my stubby arms from where his mouth had dropped those syrupy words, but he came down like a graceful stork, regally closer second by second, and with his thin straight lips, he deposited his octuplet of baby kisses. I squealed and kicked and couldn't control my roving, raving eyes until I was so out of breath I had to quiet. He began his exam just then and did again what all the others had done before, a search for holes denied or oversupplied, for bones amiss, unmatched and matchless. But more than any of his predecessors, he searched for something else, something in my eyes. Well, not *in* my eyes, but somehow *through* my eyes. Maybe good Dr. Burke had seen it too, that first night. But Vincent Garraway's watery blue globes fixed themselves on my lumps of jellied coal until I thought they'd ignite in flames. I refused to turn away from his face with its long sharp nose and not-too-pretty ears and tarnished red skin and a mark like a splash of purple wine on his forehead. I wanted to study that stain because its shape promised a new and unusual landscape (in time I would find there a tiny salamander whose tongue was stuck to a frozen lamppost, but not that first visit), but I held his eyes with mine until he was done.

The upshot of his examination: my uvula was missing! Ha! The useless uvula missing! Very good news from Dr. Vincent Garraway. Apparently only the finest of singers suffer by the absence of the uvula. And that made no difference to me.

Final tally before going home from the hospital: two thumbs, twelve bones, one kidney, one uvula, and two holes in the heart.

Final words to my mother before Dr. Garraway left that night: "She's a keeper, all right."

He made me feel almost perfect.

2

OF RITES AND WRONGS

The main advantage to a February birthday was the range of sweaters I could be dressed in. Mother had received at least a dozen baby outfits that included a sweater. Some were heavy and warm, made of scratchy wool; others were light and pretty, made of cotton or silk. The morning we left the hospital, on my fifth day of life, she dressed me in a bright red one that had tiny roses embroidered on both sleeves. She covered my head with a matching red bonnet and, heedless of my kicks, managed to stuff my fat baby hams into a pair of white tights.

Father took a picture of us that morning just before we left to go home. The room was festooned with flowers and balloons. Mother was holding me cradled in the crook of one arm, and in the other rested a bouquet of red and white roses. Her head was inclined toward me and she was smiling, with sunlight on her neck. It became our family's Christmas card ten months later. I studied it many times as I grew older. I was five before I understood its powerful message. The sleeves of my sweater are pulled up to the mid-portion of my forearms. My baby-pink skin shines against the bright red silk. The looking eye notes that contrast immediately. The eye is drawn also to the hands, the four-fingered hands, the thumbless hands. There are two bouquets in Mother's arms, her message to the world.

I was fast asleep the entire car ride home. The vibrations of the car's engine were like a tactile lullaby, a vibratory hymn that tranced me and made me droop with sleep. I passed from car seat to crib this way, and not even a brief stop for a diaper change on the cold tabletop in my room could rouse me.

Hours later I awoke, rediapered, refreshed, and reflective on my back, facing the dollops and swirls of the yellow cream seas and ripe savannahs on my stucco ceiling. It would be eighteen months before the first elephant would materialize out of that primordial wavy landscape and months more before the lions and egrets chose to be seen. But now I had an ocean of waves, a plain of grasses, to scan. On the waters, I saw crests and caps, canyons and barrels, peaks like breasts—the only items of my newfound world that called me back to the hungry here of crib and home.

That first day home, my mother came to my call, looked into my large black eyes, and said, "Oh, so hungry from your baby dreams!" She put me to her breast. She rocked me slowly in the green-plaid chair while, all mouth and eyes, I took her in. She was wrong, though, in her view of baby sleep. There were no dreams back then when I slept, just the pounding dark and the faint wormy whiff of tunneled earth in my nose. I awoke from this nowhere five or six times a day, and went with my eyes wherever I could. There were so many worlds in my mother's face, a dozen at least in her round brown eyes, a hundred in her smiles.

The day after discharge Mother dressed me in a tiny pair of denim overalls and zipped me up in a sort of burlap bag for transport to the office of Dr. Burke. I cried during the thirty-minute car ride because my chin was scratchy from the rough brown weave and my arms were held to my sides by the sack.

"What's the matter with her?" Father asked, careful not to take his eyes off the road ahead except to glance anxiously in the rearview mirror at Mother and me in the backseat. His eyes progressively narrowed in discomfort as the noisy ride proceeded.

"Maybe I overdressed her," Mother finally said as we entered the gloom of the hospital's underground garage. She pulled down the casing's zipper and my crying stopped at once. She looked at me with a face so full of self-reproach that I wished for an instant I had been born cry-less as well as deaf. Her index finger swept softly under my jowl and cooled my rough red skin.

"I'm sorry, baby," she cooed at me. "I'm sorry," and her fingers brushed away my pain. Father's eyes in the mirror winced.

The visit was more than a simple follow-up with Dr. Burke. He had assembled the others in the tiny conference room that smelled like burnt rubber from the new tile floor (and still smelled faintly of that acrid melt seven years later at my final visit). From where I sat propped on Mother's lap, the room itself held my interest only in the lattice of acoustic squares that made up the ceiling. Each taupe tile was punctured by thousands of holes and cuts and nicks. There were no breasts in this flat expanse, but as years of meetings went by in this same cramped room, I would stitch hole to hole and scrape to scrape to spy a horse, a crab, an archer, the ceiling having become my horoscopic heavens.

Burke spoke. The words are with me now*, but then* all I could do was note the face of my doctor as his lips moved and the augury of words dropped onto the shiny conference table for all to see.

He began by clearing his perpetually mucousy throat with a long, drawn-out "Knnnnnnn" that elevated his Adam's apple toward his razor jaw. He said a word or two—"Mrs. and Mr. Jackson, good afternoon"—and repeated the cleansing grind of tonsil on tongue, palate on adenoid, and jiggled again the crab apple in his neck. "Thank you for coming." Eileen Marshall wrote on a yellow pad, Patrick O'Neil yawned, and Carmen Law looked at his watch. Vincent Garraway stared at me and every once in a while wiggled his eyebrows or rolled his eyes. "We've all had an opportunity to evaluate little Miss Jess and we've discussed our findings as a group. We are pretty certain Jess has Hilgar syndrome. It's a rare form of a larger group of congenital malformations called the orofacial-maxillary dysostoses. I've shared with you already Jess's features that are part of Hilgar's—her missing bones, her hearing defect, her heart murmur, her kidney problem. Today I want each of the disciplines involved in Jess's evaluation to review for you its plan of care—what tests or treatments need still to be done.

"As Jess's primary care physician, I'll tell you that she's going to need all the routine care any healthy baby will need—a lot of baby shots, good nutrition to foster growth, close tracking of her developmental milestones, and therapy for intercurrent illnesses—the colds and flus and intestinal stuff all kids get.

"My second role is to be the coordinator of her subspecialty care with the kidney, genetics, ENT, heart docs, and others. My main role is to be sure we don't lose sight of the big picture of Jess as we go about caring for her blood pressure or murmur or whatever."

I couldn't see my mother's face for my position on her lap, but I could feel the increase in pressure of her hands where they lay on my thighs. And I could feel through her dress her heart's tattoo tick faster and her breaths grow shallower as Burke went on. Father sat stoically with his elbow propped on the table and his chin supported in the base of the L made by his extended thumb and index finger. It bothered me not at all that I would never be able to imitate that posture of nonchalant studiousness. I doubted my head would ever feel that heavy.

I brought my hands to the midline of my body for Dr. Garraway to see. He stuck his tongue out at me and flared his nostrils and winked. That did it. My tongue began to dart and dance inside my open mouth like the clapper of a church bell, and my arms and hands flapped and slapped in a shameless display of flirtation. He shook his head and chuckled. "So I'll turn it over to the group here to make short presentations and then answer any questions you might have," concluded Burke. He extended his palm toward the four physicians seated to his left.

Garraway made an effort to begin but Arthur Stein interrupted. "Do you mind if I go first? I have a patient in the OR in a few minutes." Garraway nodded his assent. "Well, what you've got is a dysplastic kidney on the left. Her renal function is okay because the right is normal and unobstructed. But the left side has a duplicated collecting system and eventually will have to come out. We can hold off for now, waiting for her to fatten up and grow, as long as her blood pressure doesn't go through the roof." Stein stopped there to elevate his right hand over his head and to give my mother a quizzical, uncertain look. It struck me then that of all my physicians he was the only one who had never put his hands to my flesh in an examination, relying instead on the gray images his technician had recorded with an ultrasound machine. "If that happens, then we go. No questions asked. We go." He checked his watch and looked to Burke. "You going to get into contact sports? Lacrosse and whatever, you know, with only one kidney?" Burke nodded gravely. "Good. Any questions?" he asked as he stood to go.

Father removed his chin from its cradle. "Well, how big or how old should Jess be before you do the surgery? I mean, is it something you would normally consider in a few months or are we talking years here?"

"Things go well, we'd do it electively at about age two. About two." He took a step back from the table. "Everything okay?"

Father nodded and Stein left. "So," said Sean Burke, "that's the kidney. Dr. O'Neil, would you go over the issues about Jess's hearing?"

Patrick O'Neil was my youngest-looking doctor. He had the boyish face of any number of comic book characters I would later have crushes on. It didn't seem right to me that such a fresh-looking man would be so dour in his speech. He told Mother and Father that he would try to construct a middle ear that would transmit sound to my brain; that he would fit me with "acoustic amplifiers" to boost what sound made it through; that he was doubtful I would ever be able to master normal speech; that we,

the entire family, should enroll in the state-sponsored pro-
grams for the deaf and learn American Sign Language. He
shook his head as he concluded, "But it's worth a try for
the surgery when she's a few months old. Assuming her
general health permits it. That's Burke's call." He scratched
the tip of his nose with the eraser of a pencil and nodded
in Burke's direction.

Both my parents had known this before we had left the
hospital—Garraway had said as much to Mother after he
examined me. But the news coming from this surgeon's
mouth—that there was little hope of bringing sound
into my brain to prompt the development of intelligible
speech—seemed somehow harsher, more final, than the
geneticist's earlier remarks. Father looked to Mother and
put his hand on her shoulder. Mother's heart raced against
my head, and I could no longer feel the separation of her
staccato beats. Her heart moved like a fast-running river,
waveless and solid, pouring itself out into some unmoved
delta. She bobbed my head, though, with her sighs.

There was quiet in the room after O'Neil finished. It
went on for a minute. Finally, Vincent Garraway turned
his head to ask his ENT colleague, "What about the rest of
the upper airway? Any problems with that?" It was a question to which he already knew the answer. He asked it out
of kindness, in the way of many of his questions. Though
the question was important because one of the dangerous
conditions associated with Hilgar syndrome is a malforma-
tion of the upper airway—the larynx and the trachea. Narrowing can be life-threatening and in need of aggressive
reconstructive surgery.

"Oh, thank you for reminding me, Vinny. It's fully clear,
the upper airway. The trachea is in the normal range but

on the small side. But it shouldn't pose a problem and probably will grow relatively larger over time. So that's good news—her defect is limited to the auditory apparatus only. Her CAT scans are good, perfect really."

As if the word "perfect" were a gong or the report of the starter's pistol, Vincent Garraway began to roll his eyes again, but now with a cyclonic fury. Round and round they went in his narrow sockets, quickly round and round. I was so excited my legs stiffened like bands of taut rubber before releasing themselves in a dyskinetic barrage of kicks that practically dislodged me from Mother's lap. "AAAAGHNNNN!" I proclaimed through the self-jostling. "AAAAGHNNNN!" Garraway gave me his crooked, coy smile.

Father asked about the process of learning sign language. Mother wanted to know if she could use Q-tips to clean my ear canals until the surgery. Even now* as I watch the tape's images flash by, I can't follow O'Neil's answers very well since Garraway wouldn't stop making faces at me. Even now* my legs twitch and tighten and twitch again. When finally his turn came to discuss my case, my legs were aching and limp from a baby marathon.

I would be smart, very, very smart, he said. "Already, Jess is doing things—motor and cognitive skills, the use of muscle and brain—at least four to eight weeks ahead of schedule. It's like she was born with the developmental level of a two-month-old."

"AAAAGHNNNN," I replied, trying to make his eyes roll again. But I think he was tired, too. Mother felt not fatigue, but relief, just then. The pressured clasp of her hands relented. But when Eileen Marshall began in on my holey heart, once more I could feel on my skull the discrete tap-tap-tap from within her breast.

They were to watch for signs of heart failure, my parents were. Hard breathing, fatigue with feeds, soaking sweats. Other than that, there was no problem with my cardiovascular system. The Assembler had hooked up everything quite properly.

Properly, perfect, smart, the residues of my day.

On the way home I sat in my infant car seat under a borrowed hospital blanket, quiet except for an occasional couplet of hiccups, and watched the sun compete with long winter shadow. Mother laughed as we drove, amused by the startled look that took my face with each surprise attack. My scratchy sack had been stuffed into the baby carryall, never to be seen again. The hiccups passed in a while, and the light and shadow flecked my eyes hypnotically. I sat most of the trip in a trance, content to breathe the splashing light. In a near whisper, Mother said, "I think we will be real glad to have the doctors we have for Jess. They all seem to know what they're doing. Especially Dr. Garraway. He has such a nice way with Jess. It's like he already knows her as a person." Father nodded and drove. "Dr. Burke is nice, too. I think they'll make quite a pair of doctors for her." She swiveled to face me. "You like that nice Dr. Burke, Jessy baby? He your favorite, little girl? Hmm?"

Father drove on, letting his eyes occasionally glance into the mirror to see us. He started to say something twice, but each time his lips moved a little and stopped. Mother began to hum. The song reached him in the front seat, and "Mary Had a Little Lamb" began to saw into his brain. He wanted to tell her to stop, that I couldn't hear any of her notes now, or her words when she pushed her face into mine and spoke. He wanted to tell her to stop because he couldn't stand to see her treat me as if I could. He wanted to tell her to stop because she was wasting her breath. He wanted to tell her to stop and to listen to him, how *uncertain* he felt about it all—the missing parts, the future surgery, the need to learn sign language, a family burdened with a defective baby. And not just uncertain. Scared. Scared and angry both. And often more angry than scared. And that his anger spun around from place to place like the finger of Final Judgment, sometimes pointing to God and fate for making his baby so goddamned imperfect, and sometimes to himself for being so goddamned imperfect that he couldn't accept her life, and sometimes to Mother, simply for bearing the thumbless, deaf mutant child. And when this last thought blackly coalesced in his brain, he returned to being angry at himself for his own failings, the greatest of which was to blame the woman he loved for the baby they made. He wanted to tell her all this, but the tranquility in her song stung his reeling heart into silence. Let her be, he said to himself. Let her be.

Finally, he remembered what the geneticist had told them, twice now. He asked, "Do you think Garraway really knows how to predict if a baby with a genetic syndrome is smart? I mean, was he just saying that to cheer us up or did he sense something in Jess that's special?" He turned his head partway to look at us directly. His gaze lasted only a second, but I could see by the arch of his eyebrows the earnestness with which he wanted an answer. It was the one good thing about me that he could hold on to. He was wearing his ski cap in the car, the red one with white reindeer on the sides, and the movement of his forehead seemed to rattle their antlers a little. I felt Mother's hand caress my head through my cap.

"I think doctors have an ethical duty to tell the truth. I believe he meant what he said," she replied, nodding. Then she strained against her shoulder harness so her face was right in front of mine. "You a smart little girl, my angel Jess? Are you, baby?" and she ruffled my cheek with the back of a finger. "You have a little head full of thoughts, child of mine?" My hands and feet were wrapped so tight, I couldn't move them at all. So instead, I fixed her eyes with mine and watched the pulsing of the light coming onto her face. She was so beautiful, in light and in shadow, so beautiful. Father drove on, silent and sad, in sun and shade, trying to hold on to Garraway's augury. I see his thumbed hands gripping the wheel knuckle-white tight as Mother hummed.

As a week-old newborn I had few waking hours, but those that managed to bob on the calm dark surface of sleep were fully pleasurable. Awake all at once, as if from a dry rebirth, I came out of the depths of sleep to engage the world with my senses. Much of the world was my own humming machinery and much of that was my mouth. At first, it explored itself like a captive animal in its pen. My tongue liked to count the papery ridges of the hard palate's plateau, and to glide over the floor of the mouth to feel its tether, the sharply lined frenulum, and to milk a little saliva from the glands that hid on its either side, and to search for the miracle of erupting teeth in the newly emptied pits along my gumline. It found the frenulum attaching my upper lip to the dental arch one day and worried it sore between two feeds. It licked my lips like a friendly dog, and I am sure would have slathered my cheeks, chin, and nose in happy slobber if only it could have reached. What it could reach now was the frequent offering of my

mother's breasts, and it grew to know the shallow corruga-
tions of each nipple and every soft subcutaneous tubercle
in both dark areolae, bumps to slow my sucking progress.
Speed bumps.

And the day came when it made the acquaintance of
my fingers. It was not a planned visit of digit and mouth.
No, it was all chance that brought my right hand to my
face where it groped my nose and found a lip to pull and
from the lip a cavity to enter and within the cavity a happy,
hungry dog of a tongue to play with. Other fingers followed until all four were red and boggy from the licking
and sucking. It was my general sense that day that a thumb
could never have been accommodated in that small and
busy place. So there, all the better.

If my mouth had the character of an animal, my skin was
pure heavenly soul, intent on softness, lightness, tickles,
and caresses, and indeed as I lay on the changing table to
receive dry diapers and a dusting of talc, my skin was my
organ of conveyance to the future respite of heaven where
all is skin lighted from within, a soft warm lamp of skin
aglow with quiet peace. My skin was just like that back
then*, and never more prickled with joy than when in the
yellow plastic tub, lapped by water warm as the liquor I
knew before birth, but water I could set now in motion
to catch the light. I splashed to make lenses of the waves,
to focus the light on my submerged integument, on the
ceiling of the bathroom, against the vanity mirror whose
height from ground level would never, in all my life, permit
me a view of myself unless I stood tiptoed on the toilet
seat or bathtub rim. I threw wet light at that mirror even
as bright streaks shot down my body and returned in the

water's recoil from the bath basin's walls. Light, then*, was my plaything. Now*, it is me.

*

I wonder about thumbs. They are, after all, what most makes us human. Had the Assembler screwed mine in place, would I have been ennobled in some way? Made more human? Everyone agrees, to err is human. So perhaps those stumpy digits would have offended, would have perfected hands that might have strangled the spirit. So I wonder, as I see myself playing with light, did He make me a little imperfect to preserve me from some greater imperfection? Did He number my bones to improve my soul? Yes, as I watch my life, I think I begin to see. More tapes arrive. I watch, the past*, the present*, the here*, the there*, all blending like the parts of light to a single bright whiteness. I feel so clean.

The few wakeful hours of those first weeks rarely involved Father. In the evenings, yes, home from work he held me against his shirt and let me breathe his breath as he looked down on me with whiskered face and eyes as soft as water. He cooed and smiled and called me "Jessy Baby" and held me stiffly in his basket arms. There was a spot on his chin near the center cleft where his beard refused to grow. When I was four months old, I finally got my hands to it. Even though his beard was not too bushy, when my index finger slipped down that hole, it was like exploring the nest of some exotic bird. He circled his head a little so my finger was brushed by his beard. I shrieked and he laughed. "Jessy Baby's big adventure," he said loudly so Mother could hear.

He shaved the beard after Jeanine was born. My nest was gone, but not the bald patch of skin on his chin, which looked just like a thumbprint, ridged and wavy, lined and unique. I could touch it with the side of my hand and pretend, whenever I wanted.

But I knew he was pretending, was in fact the first to pretend. In those new evenings home from work, he took me up and held me while Mother prepared their supper. He had the words and the gestures, the smiles and arched eyebrows of the committed loving father. But in the gloaming's weak, lingering light, February's timid affront to winter, there was a hollowness to the words that formed from his lips. They came into my eyes, they melted in my mouth, like the false fluff of cotton candy—so much that was all so little, sweetness that was no more than stale air. What gave them away—gave him away—was the force of the words. They were overblown, shouted, not spoken. I could feel the word-rumble in his chest as he called out. The vibrations were thick and gluey through his sweater. Even before the word was born—"Jess!"—I could feel the empty center of it against my cheek. "Jess!" again he'd yell so Mother could hear. "My baby Jess!" Words like bubbles from the inner machinery of a man, a father, not yet sure of his love of a child with missing parts. My father, the first to pretend, the third to be tugged back with time, third after Dr. O'Brien and Cassidy, the man with the guitar. I pulled extra hard on Father's sleeve, his sweater, nose, beard, and lip. Time and again I pulled and would not give up. For the man had wanted, first with his bitten silence and later with his loud and shouted words, nothing more than to protect my mother's heart. "Baby Jess's Big Adventure!" he boomed with my finger in his beard as he held me in the doorway to the kitchen where my mother stood frying onions, smiling.

I grew used to the pretenders and their trussed words. I tried to tug them all back, and most I did.

My father worked in the post office, a mile from our house. He weighed parcels and envelopes, sold stamps, sealed boxes, doled out packages. He held the records for daily stamp sales and heaviest single item shipped, a barbell set going from Rockville, Maryland, to Nome, Alaska, for Christmas. Three men carried it in to the post office, a single box weighing three hundred twenty-five pounds. Father stayed late that night to help load it onto a truck. He routinely apologized to people who had to wait in line even briefly, and he watched the street for the parking police through the large window opposite his counter, announcing their presence with a low, loud, "Whoa! Who needs dimes? Dimes for sale. Cheaper than a stamp!" He never charged for dimes. His third record—most free dimes, nineteen, unbroken to this day*.

His friend Joe Cassidy worked a slot at the counter with Father. He accepted two cigars and returned as many back-claps when Father returned to work after my birth. "Show me a picture of this Jessy Jackson," he teased. "This, I gotta see!" Father showed him the one he took the morning we went home. The unlighted White Owl had just been clamped by Cassidy's yellow teeth when he saw the thumbless baby surrounded by the thorned roses. He bit through the thick end and the cigar dropped to the counter. "Beautiful," he said with a thumb-sized chunk of tobacco unspooling on his tongue. "Really pretty."

In the silence that followed, he picked the cigar tip from his mouth and thought of what more to say. Father added, looking down on the photo, unable to take his friend's gaze, "She's deaf, too, they say."

Cassidy retrieved the rolling stogie from the counter. He pushed it like a knife against Father's heart. "I meant it. She's really pretty." He added, a second later, "Anything. Anything at all. You let me know, and I'll do it."

Another pretender of the kind kind. Their numbers would swell to the size of a chorus.

I was all in white for my baptism at two weeks, except for pink mittens Father insisted I wear against the cold of the church's vestibule. New snow lay smooth and cold as blue skin on the streets that Sunday when we drove to the church. The baptismal font was in the back, and it was chilly and dark out there. But the church smelled sweet from the melt of beeswax and stir of ladies' talc and the old settled incense of a thousand High Masses. Aunt Miriam and Uncle Jack, Mother's younger siblings, held me and laughed as my nose twitched to the new smells like a rabbit's. Cassidy hovered nearby.

His hands and arms jumped out as if to catch me every time Aunt Miriam adjusted my position in her arms. He was worried because she was only eighteen. His concern was even more valid because the pink mittens had stolen my grasp. Even before Father Larrie had begun the service, Miriam tilted me backwards over the baptismal font. I stared up at the ceiling lights. There were only two in that large space, but the glare prevented me from seeing the artwork painted up there—the golden lamb hung round the shepherd's neck, a fleece I would study endlessly on

Sundays as I grew older, finding in that swirly coat images of apostles and saints and at least three renowned baseball players. By the age of six I vowed someday to find a stepladder so I could climb close enough to read the artist's name. But it is hard to come by a fourteen-foot ladder in a Catholic church.

The priest opened the book and asked the questions. The standing group of relatives and friends recited the answers for me. Apparently, I rejected Satan and his work and all his pomp. Cassidy's eyebrows went high as his receding hairline at that word. I saw him shake his head and look up to the reading priest. I caught his eye, and he squinted as if in pain. At that moment I passed a seedy stool with a long, loud grunt and a fishy swish. My impudence made Father Larrie stumble over his words and lose his place. He looked up from his book, flustered and cross. Before he could resume his incantations, Cassidy began to laugh. Then Aunt Miriam's head turned away and she held her breath. In the next moment, she withdrew her right arm, the one cradling my bottom, to look for leaks, and I began to slip into the waters of rebirth. Cassidy lunged and caught me. "No more pomp for you, missy," he joked as he handed me back to Aunt Miriam. My spit-up towel now hung on her dry arm. Her face was as green as old copper.

At the party in our house, Cassidy wouldn't put me down or hand me off to anyone except my mother when I loosed my "feed me" cry or, much later, when the guests pressed him for tunes from his guitar. He held me like a football tight in the crook of his left arm for hours, and drank rye whiskey on ice from a glass in his right hand all the while. "Naw, naw, we're good" was all he said when a friend offered to relieve him. "We're good, me and her. We're good." He smelled like wet wool, black licorice, and cheap cigars at the joint of his shoulder. He looked down on me every few minutes and smiled and whispered wryly, "Pompous ass that Father Larrie, and you showed the likes of him. Showed him good. You see what I'm sayin'?" His gapped yellow teeth filled his mouth and looked not at all out of place against his grog-blossom nose and weak gray eyes. He breathed his whiskey breath on me. "I think you do. Think you see it all," he said after another nip and a chaser of my gaze.

There were forty or more guests that day, and their bodies heated our house better than the oil burner in the basement ever could. Men took off jackets and sweaters, removed ties, rolled up sleeves. Women sweated and fanned faces and busied themselves about the tables. Toddlers walked and fell, laughed and cried, while older children ran in packs from room to room and no one said, "Slow down." The morning's frost on the windows turned to slush and slipped slowly down the panes in thin sheets of white lattice.

Food was served—a huge ham, navy beans baked with crisped hunks of salt pork, potato salad, coleslaw, and a big pan of corned beef hash brought by Cassidy and handed to Mother with a wink. "It stretches. Feeds a crowd," he whispered at the door.

Cassidy sent Mother to the dining room with the guests to get her plate. He sat on the couch holding me and talking with Father about the pending increase in the cost of first class stamps, the burden of junk mail, the new U.S. Postal sealing tape they'd started to use. Cassidy was recalling the days of "good old cotton string" when he looked down to my face and saw the sheen of sweat on my skin.

I tried to bat my sweaty nose with my hand, but the pink mittens disrupted my accuracy, and I managed only to stir a little warm air across my brow. I squirmed and fretted and batted again.

"You heatin' up too much, Jessy? You gettin' to be a spud in the oven all dressed up like that?" He took his whiskey glass and pressed its bottom to my forehead. It was wonderfully cool, and I ceased my search for comfort immediately. He slid the sweating tumbler across my brow, down my left cheek, over the bridge of my nose, and down my right cheek. I watched his face.

"Her black eyes sure bore inta ya, don't they, Ford? She's not missin' a thing with them eyes." He looked over to Father. "I think she's too warm with them mitts on, Ford. How's about we take them off?"

Father hesitated. His face clouded over, he licked his lips. "Ford," Cassidy said, "Ford, she's hot. And with them eyes of hers, she's not missing a thing."

Father untied the thin white ribbon on my left wrist, Joe Cassidy the one on the right, setting hands free to roam the weave of his jacket, the bumps of vein on the back of his hand, the thick ridges on his fingernails.

"Hey, go in and eat with your wife while I finish my booze. We're good here right now."

"Joe," said Father, his finger ringing his shirt collar, "it's . . . she's . . ."

"I haven't held one since Joey was born, ya know. So it feels real good. Real nice, just to sit here with this little load in my arm. Ya know? Thirteen, almost fourteen years now. Ya know?"

"Yeah. Sure, I know. Thanks," said Father. He took his cocktail napkin and blotted my face. "You be nice for your

Uncle Joe," he told me as he left. It was the first time in my life he spoke to me the way Mother always had from birth, as if it mattered, and was somehow communicated to my consciousness. Solid words, words not missing parts. Cassidy's concern and affection had touched his troubled heart, made it beat right if only for a bit. That was the first time Cassidy did so, but not the last.

Cassidy held me silently for a while, staring off into the mid-distance of the empty room. The ice was full off the windows now, and the afternoon sun made the snow hurt the eyes. Cassidy's welled up a little, but the tears were gone in a few blinks. He hefted me with his arm as if he were trying to guess my weight or see if I made a sloshing sound when shaken like a ripe melon off a pile at the grocery store. He sighed and said, "He was a little fatter than you, I expect. Maybe a few ounces more, Joey was." I slipped my right hand into my mouth and, while my tongue darted over and around the fingers like a crazy puppy, I curled the fingers of my left hand around the thumb of the hand holding me, and squeezed. He took my eyes again then, and smiled. "You don't miss nothin' with them eyes of yours. See what I'm sayin'?" He blinked away the last trace of tears.

I saw.

"Such a big box they put him in. I always thought it would have been better if they coulda put him in with his ma. You know, tucked up against her like he'd just fallen asleep after takin' a feed. It was like he was lost in there, alone in that big box. But Father Larrie wouldn't have it. Too much pomp. Two people in one casket. Not 'conventional,' he said. Borders on heresy, he said. Heresy for a ma ta love a baby son, is it? I ask. Joseph, the ass replies ta me, you just don't know all the *rules*. Rules? Love is the rule!" He paused for a few breaths and his eyes looked far away, old and far away. "But you showed him today. You did." He sipped his drink and swallowed. My hand came out of my mouth. He looked at the glistening fingers. He studied the spot missing the thumb. He looked to the room's entrance to be sure we were alone, stood, placed his drink on the coffee table, and lowered my slick hand into his whiskey, withdrew it, and put it to my lips. "In memory of little Joey and Rose Mary Cassidy," he whispered. "A toast ta them." He drank from his glass as I inserted my liquored fingers into my mouth. The burn of the alcohol tamed my tongue's wild thrusting. Instead, it slid slowly over the digits, one by one, tasting the toast a knuckle at a time.

I hear his songs now* whenever I want. All I have to do is think his name and the music plays. That day, Charlie Warren asked for "My Wild Irish Rose." Cassidy strummed his guitar to find his low key and began to croon. He walked to where Mother held me, and he sang right at me. I watched his words, easy words they were, so deliberately cadenced, and I could feel the thrum of his music in my bones. I kicked a little at this marrow harmonic, and Mother began to dance with me. Half across the carpet, Paddy Murphy took me from her and spun to the wall. His wife Peggy relieved him. She put me in burp position, high on her shoulder, so I could see the four corners of the room as we twirled. Children in conical party hats came onto the carpet and danced like chickens walking on hot coals. Peggy sang as she moved. I couldn't see the words she sang as she held me hard and close, but I felt them rise like waves from her chest. I danced this sea of words with

everyone that day, and everyone sang a marrow song,
even Father, to the shivering notes off Cassidy's fingers.

The hours passed. Cassidy's voice grew raspy, and
his face was in desperate need of the bottom of his iced
whiskey tumbler. When finally he put down his guitar, he
held his left hand—the one that had dutifully fretted the
strings without reprieve—in a tight claw. Paddy Murphy
poured him a stiff one from the bottle on the table. Cassidy
hoisted it in his right hand and drank it down in five gulps,
each swallow accompanied by the miraculous incremental
opening of the frozen hand. People clapped.

You really don't need thumbs to play guitar. Or clap.
And four fingers of whiskey is plenty for me.

*

The more I watch the Assembler's tapes of my life, the
more I see my purpose. Cassidy, set free of the bonds of
his sorrow by his love for me. My imperfection the key
to his heart, my missing bones somehow whittled by the
Assembler to fit precisely into the hole of his loss. Thumbs
that are keys, bones that heal, give life, give love. Yes, I
really begin to see now*. Cassidy unties my bonds with his
hands, I unlock his heart with mine. My life, a life of purpose and intent to liberate the captive from the prison of
his sorrow. Isaiah. The Assembler makes of my life Isaiah. I
see it now*. But the films continue.

The night of my baptism, Mother developed the flu.
She wasn't very sick, but Father demanded she stay in
bed through the night so she would be well rested for the
day. He fed me bottles of pumped breast milk. I woke at
two and again at five. The ceiling loomed over me with

the green-glowing stars like angel eyes staring down at
me. I tracked them left to right across my crib, waiting for
a blink or a wink, and then I cried when my hunger grew
hard. Father came with milk just too warm and rocked
me in the chair. He sang "Amazing Grace" in his song
voice that had marbles in it while I sucked. He burped
me twice and each loud eructation took his quiet blessing. Quiet blessing. Twice again, no loud, hollow cast-
ing of words for Mother to hear. Simply a soft and full
"Bless you, Jess" for each bubble I brought. It was good to
see the solid quietness come off his lips. Unbidden that
night, he took my hand. By the light of the corner lamp,
I took his eyes and, unbidden, he took my hand, the
whiskeyed one. I burped again. For three nights Mother
rested and Father's grasp and stare grew stronger in the
semidark.

I feel a debt of gratitude to influenza for giving me
Father's hands and eyes, even though at seven, it would
steal my breath.

"How did she do?" Mother asked when he returned to
bed at two thirty that first night.

"You should be asleep," he said. "Four ounces and a
smidge," he added proudly.

"Did you burp her?"

"Jesus, naw, I held her upside down and squeezed the
gas out. Did I burp her!"

They lay quietly for a full minute, and he said, "I
shouldn't have put those mittens on her for church. I,
you know, all the people going in and out, gawking . . .
I thought it would be better. And the guests and all." He
sighed in the dark.

"Ford, it was cold in the church. And back home you took them off. And look what went on. Everyone loves her. I felt so . . . so good when they were passing her around, stepping out to Cassidy's songs."

"It was him that suggested we take 'em off. She was sweating and hot, he said. So off they come. I did one. He did one. And now everybody's seen it. Seen them."

"Yes. Yes, they have." She lay quiet again for three breaths and moved her hand to his chest. His hair fit between her fingers in thick rows. "Thank you for that," she said tugging a little. "It's not *what* she is. Just *how*. They all know that, Ford. We do, too."

"Just how," he repeated. But the darkness in their bedroom, the place of my incomplete conception, again got him to thinking, "Just how is she going to learn a trade or make friends or wipe her own ass? Christ, just how?"

He awoke at five for the next feed and again he spoke in a half whisper, and I sucked and burped and presented him with a stool the size of a twenty-dollar roll of stamps. "Whew," he said at the changing table. "What did Uncle Joe feed you at the party, missy? Whew-ee!" I stared at him with my hand in my mouth.

My father's hollow words were a full year in filling in. The words at two and at five in the dim room grew solid night over night as if we only built in blackness with the dark as cement. Softer grew his song, and solid too, in those hours of passing dark rocking. He had a fair voice for a tune, if rough and grumbly and not as stretched as Cassidy's, which could pull a note taut till it seemed to break and then wrap the torn ends around your heart and pull that to a tear. Cassidy sang "Dark Eyed Molly" at my funeral mass with not a drink in him to steady his nerves, and in the end Father Larrie had to wait until the noise from blown noses had settled before he could proceed. "Peace be wit' you, too, Father," Cassidy mumbled when finally the priest could continue the service.

But Father's voice, what I could feel of it, was nice in the nights. He never made me cry and his rendition of "Toura-loura-loura" cured my hiccups more than once. Days were different, though. On weekends and in the evenings, home from work, he sometimes fell to the forced high volume that emptied words of meaning, shouting when I began crawling at five months, "There she goes! There she goes!" and at seven months when I cruised between table and couch in the living room, "Off to the races! The filly's off to the races!" It was as if any progress I made brought forth his fears for my eventual failure. He loved me timidly in that first year. There were nights when he was content in our quiet feeding dance, and even occasional days when his noise held solid affection. But often that year his empty words tried to knock me down, push me back, steamroll me into submission to some concept of inevitable failure that he could only slowly vacate.

I made my first sign at seven months right after I'd eaten my first bite of mashed banana. "More," I signed. And he yelled loud enough to wake the dead, "My Chiquita girl! My Chicky-Chiquita girl!" as if to announce my deafness against my development. Mother signed back, "Good."

I ate a whole banana that feed and didn't even need to burp.

3

THE DEAD OF ALL THE DAYS

Advancing age and bad weather had prevented my only grandparents, Mother's parents, from traveling to Maryland for my baptism. By the end of March the yellow forsythia had faded, the crocuses had come and gone in purple and mud, the grass was new green and tight on the skin of the yards, and they arrived to meet me. By then I was six weeks old and sleeping, Mother would joke, like a baby: sleep for an hour, wake up and cry; sleep for an hour, wake up and cry. I was ravenous for her milk, her sleepy milky eyes, her creamy smile, for the lotions she spread on me at odd times, for the feel of the wet wipes cold on my bottom, the solid pats of her hand on my back, the sights of the wall behind her burping shoulder where the painter—Father—had left a pink stippling of paint drops at the bottom of the doorframe (which later, when I was just past two, I would connect with a marker and reveal a flamingo taking flight). And I ate her every slow, soft word that dropped on me when she looked down. "Thunder thighs," "Butter butt," "Chubby cheeks," "Rosebud lips,"

and "Auger eyes," her articulations of my developing articulations.

But Nana, my grandmother, spoke only of my hands.
She met me in my crib, awakening at noon from an hour's
nap, content to babble and coo at the waves of the ceiling
while my hunger crested. She came in with Mother. She
watched Mother scoop me up and begin a diaper change. I
watched her watch my hands as they scrabbled my round
belly while my bum was raised and lowered, washed and
dusted, diapered and done.

"Jess, I would like you to meet your grandmother,"
Mother said, wrapping my lower half in a blanket and
handing me off. Nana held me in the crook of her left
arm. Her right hand clasped my wrist and held it still. My
grasp reflex was triggered and all eight fingers clutched for
purchase. My right hand found only the smooth knuckle
of Nana's restraining thumb, while my left caught the
starched end of her shirt cuff.

"Can she hold a bottle with them?" Nana asked.

"Ma, she's only six weeks. We haven't even tried yet."

"Does it hurt to touch where the thumb's not at?"

"No, Ma, nothing hurts anywhere in her body. Except
her insides when she's hungry. Let me take her and get her
going."

Nana watched my fingers caress her knuckle, wave after
wave of tiny fingers on her slippery bony ridge. "Looks like
a big old spider taking a stroll," she remarked. She shifted
her attention to my face, and I stared back. Her features
were plain and unadorned as a child's crayon scribble. Her
eyes were gray dots and her eyebrows gray lines and her
hair a gray cloud. The pink tip of her tongue slipped out
of her mouth when I scratched her. "You need to cut her

nails, Kate, before she scratches us all up. At least it won't take long to do," she said handing me back to Mother. "And she'll never need an orthodontist, either," she added confidently. We went downstairs to the living room where Mother fed me on the couch. Nana watched.

My grandfather emerged from his rounds of the basement as my feeding ended.

"Everything seems shipshape," he allowed when he entered the living room. "Furnace is holding up. Hot water heater, too. No problems. No problems the rest of this winter. I might decalcify the humidifier pad. It's gotten a mite crusty." He sniffed the air to check the house's humidity. "Not working bad, though. Probably like forty percent."

Mother had me in her lap for a burping. "Dad, this is Jessica Mary. Jessica, your granddad."

He came to his knees and studied my hands for a second. He took my right hand in his big, calloused paw and shook it till my head bobbed and he became a blur with a beard. "Call me Ned, young lady. Ned will do perfectly well." He finally stopped his pumping and encased my hand between his two palms. He looked like a priest at prayer, with his hands held together and his red Irish face bowed and his copper hair slicked back and smelling of pomade. He was staring at my feet, which were covered by pink booties, gifts from Mother's coworkers at the preschool she used to staff. He raised his head in a snapping motion. He asked excitedly, "Kate, she have big toes?"

"I wouldn't say big, Dad. Normal size toes. For a baby."

"I meant 'big toes,' you know, the two big ones." He uncovered my hand and moved his thumb to the digit-denied side of my palm. He pressed in once, twice, a third time. I caught his thumb with my fingers before he could raise it again and held on tight. He looked surprised and said, "Well, now!"

"Yeah, sure she does. And all the other toes, too," Mother said with a hint of exasperation in her voice.

"Maybe somebody could do a switch. Put her toes where the thumbs should be. Who needs all those toes down there anyway? Thumbs are what make us human." He slipped his own human thumb from under my fingertips, and held it wide in the plane of his palm. "See, this is how she is without thumbs. Like a little critter or a bird. Her fingers are near useless. And this is what they could change her to." His thumb moved out of the plane of the palm and did a little dance with his other digits. "See?"

"I'll mention your idea to the doctors, Dad. See what they think."

"Well, let's all just call you Doctor Ned O'Brien from now on. You who spent forty years operating a bulldozer and a crane on the roads of Maryland. Girl's got no thumbs, Ned. Never'll have thumbs. Your tinkering around life is not going to change that." Nana rose from the couch and stood over her kneeling husband. "I'll go start the lunch. I could use a good hot cup of tea."

Ned sat next to Mother and watched Nana walk off. "Mom will be okay after a while," he said. "You know how hard it is for her. Give her time, Kate, and she'll come around." They sat silently for a minute while Mother blotted an eye with her sleeve. "Can I hold her?" he asked. Mother nodded. "Well, Jessy, you sure seem to be taking all this in. Someday we'll tell you all about your early months." He settled me in his arm, just the way Cassidy had done. He felt the same, Ned did, like his arm was some solid shell around me, but he lacked the earthy odors that came away from Cassidy's torso. Ned used deodorant and men's cologne and smelled like a florist shop in the summer.

"Dad, how old was he when he died? Billy? Do you even know much about him?"

"She showed me pictures once just before we got married. I think she wanted me to know what I might be getting into. He was, I'd say, maybe three or four in the picture. Remember, now Kate, this was fifty, sixty years ago. There was nothing for children with birth defects back then, and he had this really bad heart condition as well as those other defects. But I do remember he was smiling in the picture, at some zoo or park where there were cages of animals. His face was . . . was sort of puffy and bloated, but he was at this place enjoying himself, it seemed."

"And Mom, how old was she?"

"Just a young girl. Ten, twelve maybe, when he died. But you know back then, the family carried it all on their shoulders. The home care, the financial burden, the . . ." He paused to rub my head with his big palm.

"The shame," Mother added quietly.

Ned sighed and moved his hand from my head to Mother's. "Kate, sixty years is a real long time. People had different ways of looking at things like this, back then. Mom will work it out in time. I'll help her. All we have to do is give her time and let little Jess blossom." He leaned down to stroke the top of my head with his scratchy beard and to kiss its crown. I squealed.

"Were there thumbs in the picture of Billy, Dad? Did he have thumbs?"

"No, Kate, Billy did not." Ned looked at Mother with a face set for the hard work ahead.

I squealed and kicked.

Nana and Ned stayed for two weeks. The weather turned unseasonably warm. Mother pushed me in my carriage for hours each day. Often Ned was busy with a project—an oil change for the car, a new coat of paint for the two bathrooms, an overhaul of the central air conditioner. Nana always came with us, though. I could see her from where I lay on my back. For such a stern-looking woman, her stride seemed young and free. She moved her hands and arms in such wide arcs with each step, she looked like a jockey whipping her mount as it came furiously down the stretch. The outdoors made her smile, too, especially if we were passing a spot that evoked a memory of her own life as a young mother. We lived in what had been their house through all those years of raising a family. Mother and Father, newlyweds, had purchased it from them eight years ago, as Nana and Ned went off to Florida with a pension from the state of Maryland. Even so, Nana would always consider the neighborhood her own, though the house no longer belonged to her.

On the first day, I watched them talk of the things mothers and daughters always discuss. Their husbands— "Your father is getting on in years, I'm afraid. Some mornings it's all I can do to get him out of bed by seven." And "Ford's up for a promotion at the post office. They're thinking of making him branch manager." Their roles as wives and mothers—"Ned couldn't wash clothes if his underwear got brown as a nut. It makes me so mad!" And "I miss my girlfriends at the preschool. When Jess is asleep, sometimes I go a little stir-crazy, listening to the creaks in the

staircase, the hum of the refrigerator." Their relatives—
"Your Uncle Emmett has diabetes." "Eric, cousin Eric, shot
three deer this season. He wanted to send us the third's
antlers as a gift for Jess! He's so weird!" Their friends—
"Millie Casserton had triple bypass." And "Sara Scott has
had her closets professionally organized. Just because of
her shoe collection. Can you imagine?"

"Tell me about Billy, Ma," Mother said on the morning of the third walk. We were barely two houses away
from home when she spoke. The look on her face was set
so tight her eyes could have belonged in a church's stone
angel. Her request put Nana's arms to rest and parted her
mouth an inch. "You can start by telling me how he and
Jess compare." Mother stared straight ahead. Nana's arms
resumed their arcing. She closed her mouth and swallowed
hard enough to wiggle her ears.

"Billy was a mess," she began. Her eyes searched the
sidewalk at her feet.

"His heart was full of leaks.

"He wasn't allowed any salt.

"In the summers he'd try to lick my skin just for the taste
of salt.

"His arms and legs—especially his legs—all puffed out
so they split open at the ankles and wrists. They were like
slits in pie crust.

"They wept pink ooze till they were sticky as a used
sucker." She looked up from the pavement to Mother.
"Then I had to wash him in his wheelchair, run the damp
cloth over his hands and feet and legs while he tried to get
his tongue to my neck or face." She shook her head. "He
was a mess." We crossed Buchanan.

"And he was my brother, Kate. My brother with no thumbs." She sighed at the flash of memory.

"He liked to lick his fingers after he'd held some food to his mouth. It turned my stomach when he did that. Finger after finger going in and out of his mouth with loud sucking sounds.

"I had to push his wheelchair around when we were out. At the end he couldn't walk at all. He just sat in his chair and turned his head and smiled at me when someone we knew passed, or a dog or a cat.

"A mess."

Mother waited for a few seconds. "Could he hear? Did he speak?"

Nana shook her head at the sidewalk. "Not a word. But he had sounds, noises, he'd made up for some things. A different grunt for me, one for our father and mother, one for the neighbor's German shepherd. His own language."

They both looked at me then as they trudged on. "You were ashamed of him," Mother finally said. There was no tone of accusation in her voice, simply a soft acknowledgment.

"I was eleven years old when all this was happening, Kate. The kids teased me at school about his claw hands, his elephant legs always crusted with ooze. I could never have my friends to the house. Even my teachers at school seemed to treat me . . . differently than the other girls. I didn't cry when he died. I remember that. I didn't cry a single tear."

We crossed a street. I felt the front wheels bump down and then the rear. The sensation made me laugh.

"I couldn't bear it if anything happened to Jess," Mother said. "But it won't. Her heart has a murmur but it will either mend itself or get fixed by surgery when she's seven. The cardiologist did all the tests and told us so." Nana's face registered surprise, and she stumbled a little coming off the curb.

"How do they know that?" she asked.

"They have all these tests—EKGs and echocardiograms and X-rays. Her heart's not going to be a problem for her. It's going to be her hearing and her learning to speak, to communicate. She's going to have an operation on her ears in six weeks. We'll work with the speech pathologists. Then we're all going to learn sign language. We're going to do it, Ma. Her geneticist is convinced Jess is smart. Real smart. And we believe him."

Nana's eyes drilled into mine. "Well, she looks smart, if you don't notice her hands. Not like Billy, I'll give you that."

"Ma, Ford and I have talked. We'll take whatever it is we got with Jess. We hope you and Dad do, too."

Nana looked at me again where I lay under a pink blanket. "I thanked God when every one of the four of you were born normal. Fingers, ears, toes, hearts, all normal. I thought I'd gotten free of the shame and the memory of Billy. But now . . . Now Kate, I know I didn't. It's in our genes like a spoiled spot on an apple. It's in our genes, whatever condition this is, and it's skipped a generation."

Mother took hold of Nana's arm. "Dr. Garraway, Jess's geneticist, told us it's a lot more complicated than that, Ma. And he told us that Jess isn't the syndrome she has. She's a baby girl. Jess is a baby girl, Ma, just like any other baby. What's more, she's my baby."

Nana wouldn't take her eyes from mine. "Yes, she is, Kate," she finally said. "She's yours." They walked a silent

route down Macomb, through the community gardens
stitched straight with the bright spring green of new-
sprouted onion, radish, and lettuce, and back home along
Quince. Now* I listen and hear what they heard—the brittle traffic noises, the faint squeak of the carriage chassis,
the birds' daysong in the branches, footfall too heavy for
the spring.

As we came though the gate, Mother said, "I'd like it
if you'd come to the doctor's with me for her checkup. It
might help you see her differently."

"I'll go. But I don't see what it could change." Mother
took me up out of the carriage and carried me up the stairs.
"Ned should come, too," Nana said to her back.

On the fifth day of strolling, Nana mentioned Joe
Cassidy. She had been close friends with Carina, his
mother, had watched her raise him alone after her husband had run off. Nana had attended Cassidy's First Communion, his confirmation, his high school graduation, his
leaving by train for a stint in the army, his marriage to
Rose Mary, the baptism of their son Joey, and, sadly, the
wakes and funerals of mother and baby. And in the years
following that terrible event, she had gone with Ned and
Carina to retrieve Cassidy from police stations, saloons,
alleys, emergency departments, and, once at midnight, in
the midst of a blizzard, the deserted St. Anthony Church
where, drunk again, he had taken a baseball bat to the
stands of votive candles flanking the sanctuary. The three
of them, Nana, Ned, and Carina, had used all their con-
nections with the county police to keep Joe Cassidy out of
court so he could keep his job in the post office. Then, five
years into it, Carina died of stroke, and he lost his taste for

violent behavior but not for his drinks. To the world, he became a happy drunk, backslapping and singing and pawing his way through crowds at bars and parties and family gatherings. But to Nana, he was a heartbroken man who never missed a day of work, or a night of loss.

"How's Joe Cassidy getting along?" she asked Mother as they strolled home along Macomb. None of the trees had leafed out yet, giving the streets a sun-washed look that she always associated with the light at the beach.

"If you mean is he still drinking, the answer would be yes. If you mean do we love him dearly, also yes. But he overdid it at Jess's christening party. Ford had to drive him home. Joe had him pull over twice on the way."

"Cassidy, alright," Nana said with sad eyes. "All that drink in his system but he'll not vomit in your car." They walked in silence, regarding the tulips for a block.

"Would you like him over to supper, Ma?" Mother finally asked. She already knew the answer.

"I could make my beef stew," Nana replied. "It's not too hot for that quite yet. And a nice bread pudding for dessert."

"I'll call him, then, at the post office." Her sides were beginning to itch from the rub of her plumpness—her nursing girdle, the OB called it—against her blouse. The last thing she needed was stew and bread pudding. But Cassidy was like an older brother to her, so often had he been at the house while she was growing up. Two drinks, she thought, I'll limit him to just two drinks.

Two days later on Saturday night Cassidy arrived out of the rain, carrying flowers in one hand and his guitar, wrapped in a green plastic garbage bag, in the other.

He didn't bother to ring the bell. He just opened the front door and walked right to the kitchen, where Nana and Mother were trying to find five unchipped dessert plates from the stack on the counter and Ned was holding me.

Nana hugged and kissed him and held him by his wet shoulders for a few moments to study his face. "I see your mother in your eyes, Joseph," she said. "You still carry her kind eye."

He handed her the flowers and cleared his throat. "I know the one who's kind, Mrs. O'B." He faced Kate. "Kate, lovely as the sun on the cliffs, as usual." He kissed the top of her head.

"Thanks for coming, with the rain and all," Mother answered. She took the flowers from Nana and started searching for a vase.

"Joe," said Ned, shaking Cassidy's hand and nodding to the sink.

"Mr. Ned, a pleasure," Cassidy replied, reaching to lay the dripping wrapped guitar on the white porcelain.

When Father entered, Cassidy added, "Ah, Kate, your grandfather with the leprosy. A pleasure ta see you again, sir."

"I'll mail you the part you're missing if mine ever drops off out there on Molokai," Father said in reply.

"Boys, we got ladies here present," Ned said.

Cassidy and Father both laughed, but they bowed to Nana and nodded to Mother. "May I?" Cassidy asked, proffering his hand toward Ned and me. "May I take her?"

"If there is no more of that wild talk, you may," Ned said with a smile. He passed me to Cassidy and began to untie the knot that sealed Cassidy's guitar. Gone were the smells of licorice and wet wool and cigar from the crease of

Cassidy's arm. In their place, nothing but the sharp brace of Old Spice. My nose worked the fabric of his jacket for more of him, but there was nothing but his aftershave to catch. What he didn't do for my baptism—shower and shave and freshen—he did for his visit with Nana.

"Whoa!" he exclaimed as he hefted me. "What a load you're becoming, little miss. A regular double-stuffed, I'd say. Kate, what ya feedin' this one with? Must be getting half her daddy's lunch pail every morning before he goes. The *density* of her, Kate. Good job!"

Mother blushed the cutest pink and smiled. Ned led us all to the living room. Cassidy's nose had lost its bloom.

"Beautiful flowers, Joe," Mother said as she placed the vase on the cocktail table. "Can we get you a drink?" She sat on the couch next to Nana and Ned.

"Rye rocks would be nice," he said, looking at the carpet. He sat with me in the pale green wing chair in the corner, careful to lean a little forward to prevent his head from resting on the ancient lace antimacassar that looked like an exploding star.

"Ford," Mother said. Father rose from his chair and walked to the kitchen.

"Really, Kate," Cassidy asked, "how's it all goin'? Jess really does look the thriving lass, and you do, too. You getting enough help from Ford? I got a two-by-four at my station ta work him over with if he's been slothful. Ford," he called into the kitchen, "sloth ranks right below envy on the list of cardinal sins. Good Father Larrie was instructin' me on them just yesterday. You hear me in there or are you asleep?" He winked at Nana. "Envy, Ford, like every time you see me wrap a package all tight and neat, neat and tight."

"You did say club soda, Joey?" Father yelled from the kitchen. Even Ned laughed.

"Ford has been great these past weeks. He takes one, sometimes even both, of the nighttime feedings. When he gets home the first thing he does is to wash his hands and take her for a while. And Mom and Dad have been here for more than a week already, helping out. I'm up to my ears in help, really. I'm spoiled."

"And you, Joe, how are you doing?" Ned asked as Father returned carrying a peacock tray with drinks.

"Meanin'?" Cassidy replied with his head atilt.

"Meaning, how are you doing?" Ned said without the slightest trace of impatience in his voice.

"Very well. Very well, indeed." Ford handed him his drink. "Better and better all the time." He sipped. Beads of sweat already glistened on the bottom of the tumbler. He swiped the glass on the coaster Father had set down on the table and held it just over my head. "May I, Kate?" he asked.

"Drink it?"

"No, cool her forehead a little. Like this." He ran the cold glass over my brow and down my nose. I kicked and cooed and shrieked. The house was warm whenever Nana visited, and that night the oven had added hours of fragrant heat to the rooms. He moved it down my cheeks, to the side of my fat neck, up and over my chin. I lost myself in the sensation, and flapped my arms, moved my feet, roved my eyes to the cold. And began to pool saliva on the floor of my mouth in anticipation of another toast. Nana laughed like a child.

"Joseph Delaney Cassidy, you always did have a way with a baby!" she said from the seat of memory. "You made all mine laugh with your tricks."

"To laughing babies, then," he said, raising his glass, "and to the ladies that bore them!" He drank down half the brown liquid in two swallows and set the tumbler on the table. To the silence that followed—no, not silence, really, for now* I can hear the gentle feet of rain on the windows and Mother clearing her throat and Ned scraping the side of his shoe on the carpet under the coffee table and Nana breathing a single deep gulp of air and slowly exhaling— Cassidy added, "Those here and those departed." I felt his arm around me tighten, make a smaller circle. He looked across the room to the legs of water walking the glass outside. He reached for his drink, hesitated a second, and took a tiny sip. "Kate," he said, "hold this load for me while I go get my picks from the car. Something about this wet night calls for a song."

His picks were in an envelope in the glove compartment of his Taurus. A pint of Seagram's shared the space. He braced himself with two long belts. It would be the first of three trips to the vehicle that night—now for the picks, as the food was served for a new string, and when the plates were being cleared to check if he'd left the dome light on.

During the meal I was passed like a basket of rolls from person to person. Each cradled me in an arm or held me on a lap and jiggled me while eating bites of meat or potato or carrot with a free hand. When Cassidy's turn came, he put down his fork, tines piercing his gravy, and watched my face until it was time to hand me off. His eyes had that easy look, like a pond without a ripple or wave, and his nose was in full bloom. He played with four fingers and smiled. I sucked the other four, ever hopeful. Before he passed me on, Nana said, "Joe, would you have the time to visit their

graves with me while we're in town? We could say a little
prayer and leave a nice bouquet for spring."

He handed me to Mother. "It's a date," he said in a low
rumble. "Next Saturday, if it's dry?"

"It'll be dry," Nana said with finality.

He passed on Nana's hard sauce that went on the bread
pudding. Mother limited him to two drinks. He sang for an
hour before the meal and for two with the coffee. By the
end, the rain had walked off the windows and the wind was
blowing dry as chaff.

Three days before they were to return to Florida, Nana
and Ned accompanied Mother and me to Dr. Burke's office
for my two-month checkup. Ned drove Father's car with
both big hands at the top of the steering wheel. When he
turned a corner, both elbows shot up and out, the right
invariably jostling Nana's left shoulder. She looked back to
Mother. "He still does that when he drives. All the time,
no matter what it is, he drives like he's struggling with a
twenty-ton monster of a machine." Her eyebrows arched.
"Even a bike, Kate, he rides like that." She laughed and so
did Mother, and Nana patted Ned's right elbow.

We checked in at the desk and sat in Waiting Room
One. There were eight other mothers with their infants
already there. Some of the babies slept, some squirmed,
and some cried. They all looked overdressed. More than
half had on floppy bonnets and all wore sweaters, even
though the April weather was warm and sunny.

I was dressed in a diaper, tee shirt, and pull-on sack that
Nana had bought especially for doctor's visits. The sack
was big enough to fit me until I would be two years old.
"Why go to the bother of dressing them up at home when

all they want to do at the doctor's is to get them naked for the weighing and the shots?" she explained to Mother in the morning as they got me ready.

"I see your point, Ma," Mother said with little conviction as she slipped the top back onto the gift box she had just opened, the one that contained the pretty green sweater, the matching tights, and a hat. Instead, she slid me into the sack and zipped me up. Only my face showed.

Ned took me to see the fish in the office's little aquarium. Then his eye caught sight of the bench in Waiting Room Two, and he brought me there to study it with him. It was old and long and gleaming against the far wall. The few patients in that room sat with their mothers on regular chairs, leaving the bench unoccupied. His hand slid down three feet of its fifteen-foot length. He rapped his knuckles on it four times, cocking his head to read the sound's report. He let the tip of his index finger cross the grain of the wood. He pressed it with his nail, and his breath caught in his throat. He looked down at me with a face full of wonder and said sacramentally, "Red pine." He dropped to his knees and placed me gently on the floor under the bench, where a second later he joined me. We both looked up to the bench's underside. "Not a screw, not a nail," he said appreciatively. He looked my way and said, "Dovetail fit, from mortises and tenons." His hand caressed a joint. "And here, dowels, perfectly shaved, perfectly spaced." He unzipped my sack and extracted an arm. He held me up over his chest, supporting my head in his palm, took my hand and let me feel the handiwork. The wood was slick, even the joints cut so tight, if you closed your eyes to the design, it felt like a single block of wood. The board showed the same, tight, wavy grain as the top side of the seat. The ridges tickled my fingertips. "Not one single screw," he said when we had finally stood.

The mothers in the room watched us as we walked out. "This is a real good place," Ned said to their quizzical looks.

Nana was miffed when Ned returned to his seat next to her. She looked quickly around the room and saw it was too late to return my arms to the sack's secrecy. Ned said, "We checked out an old wood bench on the other side. It's a beauty." Nana stared at him. We were called after a few minutes of silent waiting.

The nurse slid the rest of me out of the casing, removed my shirt and diaper and put me on a scale. I had gained almost four pounds. She wrapped a tape around my head and wrote a number in my chart. She slid a ruler under me and stretched out my legs and wrote again.

"Growing like a weed, Mrs. Jackson. You're doing a real good job." Then she looked at me. "We've got something special for you today, baby girl." She winked at my mother and said softly, "Shots." She wrapped me in a pink blanket, handed me to Mother, and brought us to the examining room where for fifteen minutes I studied the cartoon forms of animals painted on the walls. In real life, only monkeys and porpoises smile. On Dr. Burke's wall, the lips of every species—aardvark to zebra—curved up into big expressions of glee. On the way home, both my thighs aching from that nurse's promise of something special, I saw those smiling rabbits and puppies and fawns and mice. For the remainder of my life, I would be wary of happy animals.

Burke wore a backwards baseball cap and a pin-striped Yankees shirt. He greeted Mother with a "Kate," Nana with a "Mrs.," and Ned with a "Hmm" when he heard him blurt out, even before their handshake had concluded, "You ought to look into switching her two big toes to her hands. Seems like the thing to do. To me, anyway. Shouldn't be that hard."

Nana groaned and Mother frowned. Burke said, again, "Hmm." He tugged the visor of his cap and added, "Well, that's not such a bad thought." In those few seconds when everyone in the room arranged themselves around the exam table to watch Burke's investigation of my growing body, I caught his eyes darting repetitively from my feet to my hands. Finally, the lids narrowed and he nodded a little. "I'll mention it to Dr. Garraway and see what he thinks."

He asked about my development and tilted his head in disbelief when Mother told him I was holding objects up to my line of vision and on the verge of turning over from belly to back. "Let's try this," he said. He put his hand under my head and neck and brought me to a sitting position. He waited a second for me to stabilize, then he removed his support. I swayed for a moment, first left, then right, then steadied long enough to drip a sticky streak of saliva onto my belly and shriek at its wet tickle. "Very good, Jess," Burke complimented as his hand went to my back again. "She's way ahead in her development. Doing things at two months we usually see at four to five. Dr. Garraway's prediction seems right on." He eased me carefully down and began his exam. For ten minutes he looked and he listened, pushed and pulled, and pronounced, "Heart's doing fine. No change in anything there. Kidney's not palpable. Very advanced in milestones. She's fit as a fiddle. We're all expecting big things from her."

Mother smiled. Ned smiled. Nana smiled. Those cartoon beasts on the taupe walls smiled. The nurse came in with her tray.

Ned drove, so proud of Burke's endorsement that his elbows jutted wide as swan wings. Nana hugged the passenger-side door and hummed. Mother sat next to me with her eyes half closed. I cried all the way home. It didn't bother anyone.

Nana carried me into the house and gave me a diaper change. Her gray face was soft as silk and there was a sheeny creaminess in her eyes. She whacked the bottom of the talcum can a second time. "An extra dose of dust for a day well done," she said. She taped the diaper at the corners. She slipped her hand under my tee shirt and felt my chest over my heart and nodded.

It was the only time I went to a cemetery with Cassidy while I was alive, the Saturday I went with him and my family. I'd return yearly with Nana to visit the grave of her friend, Carina, but Cassidy never again went with us. The Saturday we all went was two days before Nana and Ned flew back to Florida. We were all dressed for Sunday, everybody in black except Cassidy and me. But even Cassidy wore a suit jacket. The next day, Easter, he would come to our home for dinner in a ketchup-wounded sweater and a day's growth of beard. But that Saturday his face was smooth, and he wore a brown shirt under a bright green jacket. He looked like the sod on the graves in that jacket.

He met us in his car at the entrance to the place. The graves were close enough to walk to. Robins hopped the grass in spurts, came to proper attention, and watched us with single dead-still eyes as we passed. It was nearly ten o'clock, too late for their singing. The low sun stretched their shadows to arrows on the grass. When, startled, they flew away to the budding trees, it looked as if they were being hunted.

Mother pushed my stroller. Father and Cassidy carried flowers. Nana held a prayer book. Ned, empty-handed, was the only one who spoke as we walked. "You're getting a little bit of a squeak in your brakes, Ford. Let's check 'em when we get back." Father nodded his agreement. Cassidy sniffed his roses and looked at me grimly.

We found the plots easily. The headstones were on a slight hill just off the paved drive, under a maple tree that dripped red pollen onto their granite shoulders. From left to right, there were Carina Daley Cassidy, Rose Mary Ferraro Cassidy, and Joseph Delaney Cassidy Jr. There were dates on the stones. Numbers occupied almost all of the space on Joseph's small stone: 10-23-1984 and 12-22-1984. There was room only for a single additional word, chiseled in tiny letters: Joey. Rose Mary's bore the same date of death as her son.

Ned lifted me out of my stroller. At first we stood in a line facing the graves. Nana walked up and laid her lilies on Carina's grave, just beneath the headstone. Cassidy put his flowers on Rose Mary's. They stepped back to our line. Nana said to the deceased, "I miss you, Carina Dee. I remember all those years. Your smile and your tea. Your laughter and your soda bread. May God bless you in peace, Carina." She quieted for a moment and then went on. "And God bless Rose Mary and little Joey. We had such a short time to know you, but loved you in full measure still. Rest in peace." Ned shifted me to his other hip while everyone stared straight ahead. After a while, Father said, "Amen to that, Lord." "Yes," said Mother. Ned shifted me again and coughed a little before he added,

"Well said, Mae. Well said." They waited in silence a while before Nana asked, "Joseph, would you add your prayer to ours?"

Cassidy looked down to his feet and ran his hand over his bristly gray hair. "Ta the dead of all the days, good and bad, mother and son and mother, God grant you rest." Even before he had finished his declaration, he was moving to the headstone. He bent down and reversed the position of his flowers. Now the blossoms lay between Rose Mary and Joey, and the stems, cut by the florist on a sharp angle, touched the fringe of Carina's grass. Nana sighed and opened her book of prayer. She led us in the Act of Faith and three Hail Marys.

We walked silently back to the cars. As Mother began to arrange my car seat in the back, Cassidy asked excitedly, "Kate, maybe you'd like ta ride with me back ta your place. You and Jess? Give the old folks a little peace on the way. Room ta stretch."

Mother looked at Nana with an expression half between sorrow and annoyance. But Ned said, "Aw, Cassidy, if it's about the brakes don't go on about it. They're fine. A little dust in the pads is what it'll be. Don't go worrying about it."

Cassidy stepped close to him. "Worrying lasts but a minute, Ned. What can come after goes on and on." Cassidy's face was black in the hollows in the bright spring sun. "And not just the grief but the anger. The anger, that's what strikes the heart, Ned. All for want of worrying." He turned his blank eyes to Nana. "I've not had a drink today, Mae. You can believe that." She touched his arm and tugged the lapel of his jacket, moving it on his shoulders as the wind shrugs the grass.

"Kate, you and Jess ride with Joe. We need to stop at the bakery on the way anyway. We'll have a nice cake with our tea."

In the early morning hours of Easter, Mother came to my cry to feed me. We settled in the chair and she rocked as I nursed. Between the first and second breast, she grew taut in her frame and said absently, "He needs to stop blaming his dead ma for it. It wasn't her fault. She was just driving the car." She burped me and sat me on her lap. "There was no call to move those flowers. None at all." Her second breast held on to its milk that Easter morning. It resisted the force of my hungry mouth. She put me down and I slept again. Scarcely two hours later I woke to the Resurrection hungrier than ever before.

There was early Mass in the damp church. Nana had dressed me in my new green sweater and tights. In the pew lying on my back, I watched her pray. She'd turn and look down on me every once in a while, her mouth moving in short bursts like she was chewing words. At one point her lips said, "Maker of Heaven and Earth, all that is seen and unseen." I held up my hands and clasped them. It made her smile, pinked her cheeks.

She fed me sugar water from a four-ounce bottle when I squirmed during the long procession to Communion. I helped her hold the bottle. For a step or two down the aisle, she took her hand away. I held the bottle steady between my palms. It was very light. She turned her head to Mother processing behind her and whispered.

*

I wonder now* if there weren't multiple purposes in my unique construction. The Assembler never really told me I'd find only one reason to explain my life, after all. So, yes, why not, then? I was put on Earth to heal both these victims of pain, Cassidy and Nana. A thumb for each, then, and other bones to spare as the need may arise. Truly, there was so much of me to share, to spare, in life. The miracle I see in the making, the Assembler's miracle with me, through me: He shared even what I did not have. What was not given was what I gave. I see, I see.

4

THE RED SINK

The evening Nana and Ned left, a teacher came to our house to instruct Mother and Father in the art of communicating with the hearing impaired. She came three times a week at first, and later added a Saturday visit to make it an even four. Posture, gesture, eye contact, facial expression, body language; this was their initial curriculum. I watched them practice with Miss Lamb for an hour in the living room. They arched their eyebrows till their foreheads ached for the press of their palms; they squinted and widened, rolled and crinkled their eyes for Miss Lamb's emotional demand. "Be happy!" she giggled, instantaneously lighting her plump, childlike face with joy as if it had just been plugged in. "Now, disapproval!" she growled and scared me with her countenance cold and clouded like a day of winter rain. "Surprise!" she exclaimed and ran her eyebrows up the masts of her elastic forehead. Halfway through the exercise, Mother said she was dizzy; Father had a rumbling nausea. Miss Lamb allowed a quick break. While Mother and Father boiled water for tea, she looked at me and waited for some action to attack with her quick gimmickry. I passed gas. She sucked her eyes deep into their sockets and tried to blow them out of her flaring nostrils. "Not nice, lady girl," she said with the close of her lids and a shake of her head.

The lesson resumed. They practiced their stares. Mother and Father locked each other's eyes so tightly it seemed to draw their faces closer. They forswore the blink until their conjunctivae itched with urgency, and then they blinked a single blink of capitulation only to start the stare again when Miss Lamb ordered, "Again!" Near the end of the hour, Father said, in the midst of a stare that lasted minutes, "You're beautiful, Kate," which made her laugh, which made her blink, which made him laugh and blink, to which Miss Lamb said, sternly, "Not now, you two." The blinkless gazing resumed with a passion.

She *was* beautiful, my mother. Her face had an eternal softness to it. No sharpness anywhere. Her nose was small and rounded, the bony rims around her eyes thin and flat as sand dollar shells, her chin uncleft and modest. Her brown eyes held a dollop of gray in them, as if they were too shy to boast of their richness. Milk chocolate, they said, not the fancy dark. And when she laughed, they turned almost a terra-cotta color, like those tiny pots used to hold sprays of flowers. Yes, there were flowers in her eyes. I saw them every day.

Father wasn't so much handsome, as reliably rugged. The beard, when it was there, was bristly and dark, as if he had just stepped off the deck of some old sailing ship. He had that look of a sailor even after he shaved his beard— the deep creases at the sides of his nose ran down toward his broad lips, looking like they had been etched by the millennial run of river water. And there was that patch of baldness on his chin, not a scar's legacy, just a hairless spot. When I touched it with the thumb-poor side of my hand I felt as if we both had just been rejoined with something missing. It always made him laugh when I touched him there, connecting us both to things we never had. But for all the rips and marks on his face, his blue eyes were pristine as an unruffled lake, clear and sparkly. Those eyes now grappled with Mother's again at Miss Lamb's command, held her eyes for another minute, and Miss Lamb had to repeat, "I said, not now, you two!" when Father moaned, softly.

They tucked me in early that night after she'd left. A quick feed and change, tired faces pushed into my eyes, a soft pat on the head, and they were gone.

I stared at the new mobile hanging over my crib, a gift from Nana, a carousel of colored ponies with forelegs bent in flexion. I fussed and cried a little, hoping to stir them into motion. Father came, shirtless, and turned the key. The ponies pranced.

For that month before my ear operation, Mother and Father seemed never to have their faces, their eyes, to themselves. Hour upon hour they gave me looks of approval, of love, of concern. If I cried out of diaper discomfort, Mother's face would ask what's wrong, her eyebrows bunched and her forehead furrowed. When I cried for hunger, her face was different, full of supplication but with her mouth agape and her tongue flapping like a matador's red cape. When I lay quiet, fed, content, her face would beatify the moment with her simple beguiling smile spread straight across her mouth like the sea horizon. Father, in the evenings, was less perfect but no less persevering in his gestures. He had a way of bunching his beard to convey dismay at his defeat in deciphering my mood that always made me laugh. I'd be cold or hot, or wet or hungry, or even sometimes just bored, and he'd try his "What's wrong?" look. Less adept at intuiting my needs than Mother, he'd at first panic at my persistent screams. The panic torqued his beard clockwise ten degrees. Another cry, pitched and piercing, would reverse the twist of facial hair, and another would rotate that black mass clockwise yet again. I had him in my power, running him in circles with my little imperfect voice. That's what made me laugh. I began to laugh at fourteen weeks.

Miss Lamb added sign instruction to her sessions. I still was subject to my parents' undivided attention, but now I'd see them shape their hands to accompany a particular facial expression. Hungry? Okay? Sleepy? Wet? Go? More? Hurts? began my sign vocabulary.

Nana returned a few days before my ear operation. She took me on long walks in the mild May air. Her face was not so sternly set anymore. It was still gray as a rain puddle, but now at least there were no dark clouds reflected off her pewter skin, just the dull sheen of age and slight hope. As we went she told me stories of her brother Billy, and not all of them were sad.

She'd found a blue-jay feather once and brought it home to him. He wore it in his hair.

She let a neighbor's dog lick his feet until he cried from the tickle.

She would tilt his wheelchair backwards. It was his favorite thing.

A week before he died she went to the movies, not to see the film but just to buy the popcorn. Extra salt and extra butter. She fed it to him in his hospital bed, piece by piece.

He was too weak to use his hands.

She let him lick her fingers.

He was her brother, she said, her real brother.

"I should have cried," she told me quietly the morning she pushed me all the way to the post office. "I wanted to," she added.

They all came from behind their counters and from the back shipping rooms to see me. Nana warned them all against giving me a cold. Father picked me up out of the carriage to show me around. Hands that smelled of glue and ink, of tannic brown paper and cardboard boxes, of clean cotton cord, adhesive tape, and of the dust on old parcels, touched my brow, my chin, caressed my fat neck. Cassidy took me and blew air in my face, dropped his head to my belly, and nuzzled. My hands found his short, spiky hair and tried to grip it so he'd never leave. I squealed and kicked. Nana said, "Alright now, Joseph. Don't rile her too much. She'll never go down for her nap."

Father walked us to the corner and thanked her for coming. I watched him run in an easy lope back to the building. Meanwhile, Mother marketed or cooked or cleaned as a liniment to her anxiety over my looming procedure. The freezer became a cornucopia of stews and casseroles. There was enough milk in the refrigerator for a Boy Scout troop. Enough bread for the five thousand of the Gospels. Every towel, every sheet in the house was washed and folded away against the possibility of a prolonged hospital stay.

I went in to the hospital at six in the morning on a Tuesday, had my surgery at ten, and was sent home the next afternoon.

O'Neil reconstructed my middle ear cleft. It became a space large enough to accommodate his array of tiny plastic tubes and platinum transmitters. Thin gray wires attached my new acoustic apparatus to baby hearing aids that hugged the helices of my ears like bees on blossoms.

I awoke from anesthesia in my mother's arms. "You Okay?" her face asked me. Father's face looked pinched and pale. I felt like someone had struck matches and was holding them, flaring and hissing, against the sides of my head. It burned and ached with an incessant spitting sound in my ears. Mother put me to her breast—it had been the previous midnight since my last feed—but each hungry suck sprayed gasoline on the flames. I cried and pulled away and cried again, each shriek producing a tiny distortion in the anatomy of my new middle ears that in turn brought even more hot, throbbing pain. A nurse put cold cloths to my ears and injected me with morphine. I could hear the fire in my ears slowly die. The hiss softened to a warm swish, and the swish cooled to a lukewarm hum, and the hum did not hurt. I slept and woke and ate to the crackle noise of my hospital room, every monitor beep, every nurse footfall, every shuffle of cover converted by my new electronics to a modulation of shattering glass. Mother looked down on me. "J-l-e-a-s-s-h-h, s-h-w-e-e-t-a-r-h-h," the first perfect imperfect words I heard anyone speak.

In time that night the crackle would brace to clicks and the clicks would sum to a swish and the swish would ignite to a hiss. My nurse knew that cry of flaring pain and was ready with her needle. Mother and Father stood by the side of my crib and watched for quiet to settle my face.

Nana came with Cassidy for evening visiting hours. I was in the third-hour twilight of my most recent dose of morphine and received their touches, their eyes, like a sleepy dog. I remember Cassidy's strong cologne and his sad eyes, helpless sad eyes, and Nana's brave smile. After a while Nana sent the three of them to eat. The nurse put me in Nana's lap. She knew better than to rock. My twilight soon lengthened to full daylight, and for twenty minutes before the pain resumed we watched each other quietly. "Going to be okay," she said in a voice full of tiny wet sparks. H-o-a-k-a-y-a.

"It's time," she said to the nurse in her no-nonsense tone when I started to fret and to bat the side of my head. "It's time now."

In the morning Dr. O'Neil visited. He brought a machine on wheels that attached by wires to my scalp. He turned it on and told Mother to say something, anything, to me. "I love you, Jess," she said. A-h-h l-o-o-a-v-a-o-u-u-h-l-e-a-s-s-h-h.

He pointed to the machine's green screen. "See," he said, "they're working."

The nurses stopped the morphine and gave me codeine by mouth. It blunted the pain, but I could still feel the flame of a torch touching my brain from the sides. We were sent home at five.

It was not an easy evening. I nursed poorly in my room. Mother laid me down and wound the mobile. I heard the music, but my growing discomfort prevented me from enjoying it. The pain robbed me of sleep and I cried. Father brought me downstairs to where supper was being eaten. He gave me medicine from an eyedropper. I cried in his lap, and Mother's and Nana's. The codeine was like a cage around a snarling wild animal, nothing more than a container for the pain. Cassidy walked into the room as I was in my third circuit of holders. They all had been patient and kind with me, but the unremitting shriek of a three-month-old baby can erode even the thickest armor of forbearance. Cassidy saw the unpracticed, drained look of exasperation on their faces.

"I'll take her for a ride," he said to Nana who sat before a plate of uneaten chicken and broccoli casserole. "That'll help soothe her. Works like a charm every time." He had an unlit cigar between the first two fingers of his right hand that he pointed at Mother. "And the answer ta Kate's unasked question would be no. Not yet." In the end it was all they could think to do. It was too soon for more codeine, and they didn't want to bother Dr. O'Neil. Why, I don't fully understand, but it had to do with his station in life relative to theirs. They were that way with all my doctors, reluctant to call for advice or help unless it was during normal working hours. It's part of what killed me. They also said, "Thank you" to diner waitresses who brought more bread and toll-booth attendants who took their quarters and paperboys who threw the *Post* onto our covered stoop. It's part of what made me love them.

Father put my car seat in the back of Cassidy's car. "I'll go with you," he volunteered.

"Naw, go back in and eat your supper. Take a break from this." His cigar swept over the racket I was spewing forth in his backseat. "I'll drive around fifteen, twenty minutes until she settles. If she don't, I'll drive some more and then get her back. Go in ta your wife." He clamped the cigar between his teeth.

Father put his hand on Cassidy's shoulder. "Thanks for this, Joe." He handed over my pacifier and a bottle of pumped breast milk. "She may be a touch hungry."

"Go on in," Cassidy repeated.

There was a throaty rumble to Cassidy's old car, like a
rocket vainly trying to go up and up. That and the pulsing
of light through the canopy of trees that lined the streets at
first distracted me from my pain. We drove a mile and my
cry became a whimper. The long red light at Van Ness put
an end to the trip's trance, though, and my cry resumed in
all its booming force. He swiveled in his seat to look at me
before the light turned green. I spit the pacifier out of my
mouth. It dangled on its tether like a dog on a leash.

"If I had an earache and the pills weren't doing the job,
I know what I'd take," he said matter-of-factly. He drove
to the parking lot of Calvert Woodley Liquors. He took
his bottle from the glove compartment and sat beside me.
He nicked the tip of the pacifier with his pocket knife.
He poured a small amount into the hollow end of the
rubber nipple and put it in my mouth. "Whiskey nipple,"
he remarked through teeth clenching his spot-wet cigar.
"Good for what ails ya."

The heat on my tongue sapped the strength of the
flame in my ears. My nose burned a little from the vapors.
I sucked down the whiskey, and my hot breath bore away
more heat. My stomach warmed. From my car seat I saw
the sign of the liquor store flash on and off in the fading
evening light. The red-lettered word "Liquors" pulsed and
faded and seemed to snatch the light from the dying sun.
He gave me a drop or two more before he held the milk to
my mouth. "Not my idea of a chaser," he said with a wink.
He held his whiskey in his other hand, regarding it like it
was something new, something just now discovered. He
shook it to a light froth. "Not right now," he mumbled and
replaced the bottle in the compartment. We drove an hour

in the car's embracing rattle, the only sound I heard as I slipped shimmeringly to sleep.

When I replay it all now* I can see the gentleness with which he replaces the bottle into the dashboard box. He holds the glass lightly, as if it could shatter like an egg in his hand. He rests it on maps and folded repair receipts, first bottom, then middle, then top, as if its geometry was unfamiliar, or changeable, or simply imperfect for the space. He regards the laid-down whiskey with his head to the side, just like Mother sometimes looks at me in my crib. He waits till the sloshing liquid settles; he takes measure of the measure left. He closes the door to the compartment slowly, pushing gently until the lock catches with a soft click. His hand lingers on the door for a moment, then taps it twice the way one would say good-bye to a friend.

He said, "no, thanks" to the coffee they offered when I'd been tucked away. Nana made him take a slice of cake on a paper plate. She tapped his arm twice when she walked him to the door.

Now* I watch what he does later that night in his house, what had been his mother's house where he was raised. When the bottle from the kitchen runs dry, he staggers to his car and drinks what is left there. He lies in the backseat taking pulls at the bottle. He falls asleep with his head on the spot where my seat had been secured, his long legs bent at the knees, extending through the open door, his feet resting on the driveway, a body uncontainable by the space, like his sorrow.

Wednesday's ear pain was Thursday's dull ache, belittled to a mild annoyance by three doses of codeine. Friday came painlessly into my ears with clicks and sounds like fish flexing slowly through a sea of molasses. "Tired?" Mother asked me after a series of midday yawns, the word barely able to shimmy its way through the gelled medium of my new, raw middle ears before my eyes closed. In those few transitional seconds from stupor to sleep, I could still sense the riotous gallop in my chest, still could not hear the various thin jets and leaky sprays of each heartbeat, but the sensation of faulty motion brought me back to Cassidy's car ride where, in the light-headed swoon of his whiskey nipple, that wormy scent from my eddy heart had never been so strong.

Ned arrived Saturday, four days into my recovery from surgery. He went with us for my post-op check on Monday. He never left O'Neil's waiting room, trapped by the dozens of pamphlets describing the latest in gadgetry for the deaf, including the system now in place in me. "Not all that complicated," he said to O'Neil when it was time to go.

Nana was glad to have her strolls with Mother and me. Father went to work each day, walking in the early mornings, always with a pocketful of eight-minute dimes to defeat the parking police. I could hear him now: he jingled.

Miss Lamb intensified her curriculum of language training when my recovery was complete. Each hour was devoted to perfection of facial expression, eye contact, and body movements now delivered with progressively more complex hand signs and slow repetition of clearly spoken words. Each session concluded with the reading of a story book. I sat propped in her lap as she turned the pages of *Pat the Bunny*, *Goodnight Moon*, and a dozen other works as

Mother or Father sat before me forming signs and pronouncing words like prophecies. I studied the pictures of
rabbits, puppies, pigs, elephants, hippos, and bees, heard
the words, saw the signs, watched the lips mound, round,
and flatten the sounds. In a few months my own hands
moved in gibberish imitation of theirs.

Even if I had known what I wanted to say, even if I
had known how to say it in sign, I was thumb-tied in
sign language. I lisped and stumbled over thumb-twisters
like "shoot" and "sacrifice," which, without those oppos-
able digits, came out like "short" and "soil." It would be a
bother to me to the last days of my life, when, in preparation for my coming First Holy Communion, I listened to
Father Larrie read the Gospel words meant to give comfort and hope. "What Father when his child asks for a fish,
hands her a snake instead?" That seemed all too frighten-
ingly possible in my case. Be careful what you ask for, I
told myself that day, because you might get something
else.

Had I lived, I would have grown more thumb-tied with
each passing year, would have relied on speechreading
and imperfect phonation for all my communicating. If I
had lived. That had been O'Neil's plan all along. Create
the noise and let me figure it all out. His recommenda-
tion for ASL was more to help with my receptive language
learning than my expressive communicative skills. So the
broad training went on. I mastered those signs my anatomy allowed and reproduced speech in the manner of a
deep-sea diver repeating words shouted down to her from
a boat bobbing on the sea. When at eight months I began
repeating what I had heard, Miss Lamb was there to wring
those sounds dry and press them flat. I can't begin to tell

you how difficult it is to remember to reassemble the forms of a heard word before repeating it. It is something quintessentially contrary to the language circuitry of the brain. It's as if I had to insert an additional synapse at each nerve junction, one that would interrupt what is evolutionarily the great pulse of the brain, the electric urge to replicate the "in" perfectly as an "out."

At first, "Uamm" was my Mama. "Uamm," I would call when I saw her eyes. "No," she would sign and shake and say, "Mama." Three days of trial and error, cutting and pasting, ripping and sewing those four simple letters before "Mama" emerged off my tired tongue and Mother smiled and nodded and said, "Yes, Mama." Three days the gestation of a new, proper word risen up from the floor of the sea like a bubble clear and eye-bright. So it went with Dada, milk, bottle, go, Nana, Ned, car. I took the sounds, split them with my tongue, parsed them with my lips, assembling the words for what my world contained.

But Cassidy, Cassidy was pleased with his watered-down name, his name with a wet chaser that came from me at a year. I sat in my high chair, my family around the Sunday dinner table. "AceyDee," I called him, for that is what I heard whenever his name reached me down there, and "AceyDee" he became, no assembly required.

I had follow-up visits with my doctors. Burke's nurses kept giving me injections. I wouldn't grace the stenciled menagerie on the walls with even the briefest glance. O'Neil fiddled with the gain of my aids. The sea of noise grew calmer but was eternally close in my head. Voices, telephone rings, music, traffic, birdcalls washed in these more well-rounded waves with each adjustment he made.

Finally, it was as if each sound dove into the chop whose skin was continuously punctured by shoals of darting, clicking silver fish. The words, the notes of music, the jolts of telephone rings swam around and around while I dissected and reassembled them. Out they came, first as solos, then as struggling duets at fifteen months, and finally, at a year and a half, fully assembled sentences.

My first word: "Mama," at eight months.

My first practiced phrase: "Want more," at a year.

My first sentence: "Where is AceyDee?" at eighteen months.

Eileen Marshall had continued confidence in my heart. The leaks were no worse, she told Mother and Nana after repeating my echo tests, and the lungs were handling the increased blood flow quite well. Patience. Time. Wait.

Garraway made me laugh and scream with his tickling kisses. He drew blood from Mother and Nana on the first office visit and gave them a report that made them beam at the second. The gene Mother and Nana shared had "weak penetrance." The odds of another pregnancy complicated by the syndrome were roughly one in a hundred.

Arthur Stein took my blood pressure five times each visit. At fifteen months, the numbers all of a sudden skyrocketed. He tried a drug that tasted like the smell near the oil burner in the basement—rancid and cloying at the same time. He put me on a low-salt diet. At eighteen months, my blood pressure continued to rise. He admitted me to the hospital to remove my kidney.

"Where is AceyDee?" I asked as we drove to the hospital that early morning in August of my second year. He had told me he would come to the hospital with us that day.

"He will meet us there," Mother said and signed. Her face was tired and worried. Her anxiety was in her hands, too, as she used the sign for "leave" instead of "meet."

I looked from her hands to her face and gave the sign for "meet." Mother touched my head. "Yes, sorry, meet," she gesticulated.

He came into my room minutes before they wheeled me away. I could see on his face how hard the previous evening had been on him. His red dragon eyes, his puffy cheeks, his formaldehyde breath, a fine snow of dandruff on the shoulders of his rumpled blue shirt. "Are you sure they need ta do this, Ford?" he asked as he watched a nurse squirt something into my buretrol. "A kidney operation on a baby. That's not nothin'. Maybe they should wait."

"We been through it all before with you," Father said with a note of exasperation in his voice. "It's her pressure they're worried about and this'll fix that. Take the strain off her heart. Stop from needing the pills. It's the right thing, Joe."

"Her heart's fine," he said. He fixed the sock on my left foot.

"It is for now," Mother said. "But it's got to close those leaks, and the high pressure will prevent that from happening. And this kidney operation at least isn't open heart. We're here to try to put *that* off, Joe. Think of it like that, if you can."

"And she'll be fine. This is a good place, Joe, and Stein has a lot of experience." Father took him by his elbow.

"Stein," said Cassidy. "Stein."

The nurse unplugged my IV setup and unlocked the wheels of my bed. Cassidy bent over me in a hug. His

familiar essence—breathy rankness from the drinks of
the night, stale tobacco smoke caught in the weave of his
clothes—was at least as calming as Mother's kiss and Father's
parting pats, as the aides wheeled me away. The medicine
in my drips made me sleepy. My eyes closed. Even the
peculiar incense of Joe Cassidy could not church the scent
that rose with sleep in the back of my nose. The worm-
scrawled earth, bitterdamp fug of decay, blew through my
every breath.

It was a very different sort of pain I had after kidney
surgery. More like a deep, deep ache that kept changing location. First I felt it in my side. It was as if I had
fallen hard on the small of my back against the point of a
wooden stair. The first ten minutes after a fall like that was
the pain I had for a day and a half. Then, all of a sudden,
I felt as if someone had tightened his grip on the tissues
in my lower belly and wrenched it clockwise. I was keen
to double over in an effort to lessen the discomfort, but
the stitches in my back yanked me in recoil before they
tore through their bites of skin. For a day and a half I
flexed and returned between doses of morphine. On the
fourth day, the pain was gone. In its place I could feel the
hot thrust of blood beating at my wound eighty times a
minute. I lay on ice on Cassidy's chest and listened to the
stories he read from the new book he brought as a get-
well present. I liked the one about the king penguin chicks
on the winter ice. Penguins have no ears. Cassidy pointed
that out to me.

The last night in the hospital I kept him reading until
late. His eyes were closing over. He kept rereading the same
sentence. Even the ice pack on his belly couldn't keep him

awake. Nana was in the room with us. Mother and Father had gone home, and she was to spend the night. She sat watching us. When Cassidy would startle awake, I'd say, "Please, AceyDee, more." Pah-ees, AceyDee, mah-oh-ah. Then he would reread, "The Wooly Penguin looks like an ugly duckling now, but in the warmth of summer. . . ," and droop his chin to his chest. After the third or fourth time, Nana rose, found a piece of paper and wrote him a note. She took her little overnight bag, kissed me on the head, and signed, "Good-night." She closed the door gently.

I sat feeling the ice pack press my wound each time Cassidy breathed. In four or five minutes, he awoke and looked around the room. "I tired," I said and gave the sign for sleep. "Good thing," he said huskily. "Let's find Nana." "Gone," I said. Gah-on-a. By then he'd found the note. "You looked so peaceful there asleep, I thought you might like to spend the night. Be back first light. Mae." He scratched his head with the hand holding the paper. "Ty-ud," I repeated. He eyed the door, then the fold-out cot next to the window. I could feel the breath come into his chest and stay there a while. The cold press of it felt good on my incision. Finally, he exhaled and rose to get me ready. When he had me comfortable in my crib, he looked at the door again for a while. Then he looked at me, smiled weakly, and said, "Sleep tight, Jess." He turned out the light and lay on the cot. I had rarely before been as grateful for the gift of hearing as that night when I lay awake listening to the snores and snorts, the restless shifting, the toss of bed covers, the occasional muted shouts that came from a sleeping Joe Cassidy. Sober and asleep, he was reason to ignore the burning pulse in my back, to doze and await the light of new day that seeped through the imperfectly fitted window drapes, before calling for my codeine with a shriek.

Next morning, Mother, Father, and Nana arrived to pack me up and take me home. Cassidy was beside my crib drinking coffee he'd gotten from one of the nurses. He stood watching me pick dry Cheerios from a pile on my breakfast tray. I nabbed them two and three at a time, between the index and middle fingers of both hands. His hand shook when he brought his cup to his lips, but his face lacked the cracked-leather appearance it so often had in the mornings. And his eyes were somehow bright, an effect perhaps of sclera a faint muddy brown color instead of crimson red. It was Friday, a working day, for Father and him. He stared at Nana when she came through the door. Mother and Father said good morning and came to my bed.

"Slept well at home, did you, Mae?" he asked.

"That I did, Joe. And yourself?"

"Passable," he replied, sounding annoyed.

Nana took my new red sweater from the box.

"Wouldn't it be a bit warm for that outfit?" he asked. "August days."

"It was just too cute to pass up," Mother interjected. Cassidy shook his head in disagreement. "And in a few months she'll have outgrown it, Joe." He shook his head again, unconvinced of the wisdom in it, sipped his trembling coffee, and shuffled his feet.

"Ride with me to work," Father suggested after I had been dressed.

Cassidy checked his watch. "Thought I'd stop by my place ta clean up a bit first," he said. All three of them stopped to stare at him. His hands shook the surface of the coffee to a little squall. A few drops of brown liquid sloshed over the side of the white Styrofoam container and dripped to the floor. I heard the first and fourth splats.

"I'll drop ya off, Ford, and then I'll go home a bit," he said quickly.

"Wash up quickly here, Joe, and we'll go in together," Father retorted. "You don't need anything from home."

Cassidy straightened his back and took a jerky step toward the door. His eyes narrowed. "I do, Ford, and I'm going ta get it. You can wait in the car on the street if ya want, but I'm stopping by my house. I know what this is all about, but just leave me be." In the silence that followed I watched his face charge with pain. Back now was the morning's etch of lines in his forehead and around his eyes. It was quiet for a long time. No one moved. Another silent drop fell to the floor from his cup.

It was Mother who spoke next. "So be it, Joe. But you've got to come to supper tonight to celebrate Jess's discharge. And to thank you for spending the night so we could get everything ready."

"Book," I said. "Read book." I gave the sign for "bird" and clapped my hands.

"Sure," Cassidy said. "I got ta finish the story anyway." He signed "good-bye" to me and walked out of the room.

"It's a start. One night's a start," Nana said.

"Let's hope," said Father.

"Not much of a start if he goes at it hard this morning. What kind of start is that?" Mother asked.

"Well, I don't know what kind of start it is, Kate. Just that it's a start," Nana said.

"Book," I said. "Read book."

We left at eight. It was warm in the car in my sweater.
I thought of ice and whiskey in a sweating glass and penguins on frozen seas.

Now* I see him in his kitchen, drinking tap water till
his belly aches, and he must bend over the sink. The door
of the kitchen cabinet holding the liquor is open. The bottle rests on the shelf untouched, until he's drunk five huge
glasses of water in rapid succession. His stomach is so distended he can't straighten out. I can hear him moan over
the splash of water from the tap. He stands there flexed
at the waist, his face only a few inches away from the red
porcelain sink. In a moment his right hand reaches up to
the shelf and finds the bottle. Without looking he takes it
down and unscrews the cap. He tilts the bottle back and
takes a single long pull. Before he swallows, he stares at the
red sink, replaces the cap, and slides the bottle back onto
the shelf. The liquor goes down his gullet with a moan
that could be pain, could be pleasure. His hand finds the
cabinet door and slams it shut.

He doesn't shave or wash. He comes straight to work
and is only a little late. His supervisor tells him to get
checked out by a goddamn urologist the fifth time Cassidy
leaves his station to use the bathroom. "Gladly I'd go," Cassidy says, "if only the insurance would cover a visit ta the
horse vets. Them's the only ones with instruments ta fit my
size." He winks at Father, who chuckles.

My high blood pressure was cured. My body's defective tissue will stare out of a glass jar until Dr. Burke dies at
seventy-three and a junior member of the practice inherits
his office. That young woman will hold it up to the light

and marvel at what modern genetic testing has been able to prevent since the early days of that discipline. Then she deposits me in the trash.

It was in those few months of my recuperating from kidney surgery that Father finally abandoned his loud empty words. What had been so instinctual and effortless for Mother, the graceful indulgence of her flesh for my flesh, both through the watery miracle of her womb and the milky feast of her breasts, bound her to me in love. I was her creation, unseen and then seen, through days hidden and then revealed, and she loved me like a jealous god. Father, though, had had the smallest of parts in that endeavor. I became, I was, I grew, beside him, not through him.

In the fall of my second year he began to paste more stars onto my ceiling. There were already a few flung glowing specks up there when I had come home from the hospital as a newborn, part of the predelivery ritual of readying the room for their new arrival. But on that night in late October, he climbed the stepladder as I read in Mother's lap, and he began to affix a few dozen more fluorescent stars to the flat valleys in that corrugated terrain. His hand went out and stuck a star here and there in no particular pattern. He climbed down, moved the creaky ladder a few feet, and reascended to do more pasting. He moved through the room for twenty minutes until he was done. Mother changed my diaper for bed and kissed me goodnight, signing "Love you" with her hands, and passed me to Father. She turned off the light, closed the door, and left.

Father sat rocking me for a few minutes, trying to remember the words to "Camptown Races." His song lapped imperfectly by as my eyes scanned the new, green, glowing spots on the ceiling. At the middle of his third rendition of the song, the stars coalesced. There above us, just over our heads, stood a horse. Not a nag with a cropped tail and certainly not an everyday reddish-brown steed, such as Father's song was made of. No, this animal was green and glowing and proud and bushy-tailed, his body and legs and tail clearly delineated by the recently placed stars. "O-arr-sa," I said over his song. "O-arr-sa." He went on singing, now with a nod to my apparent endorsement of his tune. "O-arr-sa!" I yelled, this time pointing with my right index finger to the scene above. He looked up, moved to do so more by the sense of motion of my rising arm than his ability to see it in the dark. A few more notes fell from his mouth, and then he stopped at "all the do-dah" and stared with me. "Sweet Jesus, it is," he muttered. I could feel his head swivel on his neck to align the glowing dots more perfectly. "It most surely is."

He took me downstairs to the kitchen and held me while he thumbed through the *Encyclopaedia Britannica* on astronomy. "Pegasus," was all he said as he pointed to the illustration of the Autumn Constellations.

"Peg-shush o-arr-sa," I echoed back.

"Yeah," he said with a shake of his head. "You're right." He gave me a half-quizzical look and turned to study the illustration again. Then he wrapped me up in his old green army jacket and took me outside. We lay on the cool, dewy grass in the backyard looking up at the night sky. It didn't take long to find what we were searching for. He held my arm outstretched and traced the outline in black space with my fingers. There are seventeen stars in that horse, and we found them all with my fingers. Then we found more.

He said the names reverently, quietly, that early fall night. "Aries." "Pisces." "Aquarius." I spoke them back as well as I could. "A-rees." "Py-see." "Kar-y-oos."

I whispered, too.

Mother came into the kitchen and saw the open door. She looked out. "Ford, what are you doing out there with her *laying on the ground?!* It's cold and damp and she's going to get sick. Now come back in here with her. She should be in her crib by now. What's wrong with you? Don't you know she needs rest after her surgery?" She folded her arms across her chest.

"We're studying the stars, is all," he said. "She found a constellation on her ceiling and we're just tracking it out here. We got us a pretty smart little one, this girl here," he said nodding toward me. "What her docs have been saying all along about her, well, I think they're right." He pointed my fingers at Pisces and asked, "This, Jess?"

"Py-see," I whispered again.

"See what I'm saying, Kate?"

Mother softened a little and uncrossed her arms. "I didn't need all the stars in heaven to see," Mother said. She waved us inside with her right hand, saying, "In. Now."

It was the end of the hollowness in his words, the start of his unreserved love of me. We would lie together on that same spot of fescue and weeds hundreds of times in the coming years studying the night skies. The grass would be green or brown, dry as dust or wet as rain, covered with snow or still warm from the day's sun. It didn't matter. We'd lie there once or twice a week in the dark and look at what the Assembler had made, and marvel at its beauty. We found the constellations of the seasons: winter's Orion and his dogs, Taurus the Bull and brave Perseus,

Gemini and Cancer the Crab and Cassiopeia; spring's Ursa
Major the Great Bear, Leo and Virgo and Corvus the Crow
and Boötes the Herdsman; summer's birds, Cygnus the
Swan and Aquila the Eagle, all the parts to the Serpens the
Snake, its head and tail, and, Scorpius and Sagittarius and
the perfect Northern Crown, Corona Borealis.

*

We became our own constellation on that patch of sod,
the two of us pressing our weight down into the earth like
stars pressed into the black vault of the sky. Now* I can look
down from here* and see our contours still there, percep-
tible to my new eyes for eternity, his heels, elbows, shoulder blades, and head, dark dots on the dun earth, and my
smaller ones next to them. My marks are less distinct than
his, made scattered and fuzzy by my growth through the
years. It almost looks as if my contour was shaded in to
give flesh to my form. I wonder, now*, if this is what the
Assembler wants me to see, how I brought that man to
love me through the assembly of a horse, how I created a
pattern fixed for eternity on the soft crust of the world the
same way He hung the stars on the velvet void. I think,
The girl with hands useless as a bird's begat a constellation
of love. This is the meaning I am meant to see in the tapes.
I am certain of it.

5

THE NINE IN JEANINE

At age three I became perplexed by the groups of things so randomly categorized in my reading. How many zebras, a herd? Wolves, a pack? Seals, a pod? Crows, a murder? Oh, the books all cast out their declarations of names, but never would they commit to an honest integration of individuals into a group. Cassidy chuckled each time I brought this topic up. He was reading me his newest gift—*The Big Book of Animal Groups*—most nights of the week. Even when Miss Lamb had her evening sessions, he'd stop by after dinner to learn sign and, later, to read me to sleep.

We opened the book, exposing the luminous blackness of the crow that both frightened and fascinated me. "Haw ahn-y cro-aws?" I asked after he'd read the page's caption about a murder.

"Five crows, that's murder. Gotta be," he said with authority.

We turned the page. The next bird was the owl. Its squat shape and bulbous head somehow reminded me of a

thumb. "Why?" I asked Cassidy. "Why no thumbs?" I shook
my hand over the brown-speckled bird. It seemed strange
to me that there would be a bird that looked exactly like
what I didn't have. Then I remembered the book about
penguins. "And why no ears?" I circled the rims of mine
with index fingers. "Why in penguins no ears?" A-wha ahn
pahn-kans na ah-res?

Cassidy closed the book and took a deep breath.
"Damned if I know. Could be the Man upstairs just plain
forgot. Screwed up, you know. Or maybe He was just
braggin' through His work. You know, 'Look what I can
do, even when I throw away some bones.' Like someone
showing off, sealin' a box with hardly no tape at all. But
whatever, it was Him, the Assembler, His doing," he said.
"He puts the parts of everything together. Just the way He
likes." He took my hand in his. "These are good hands.
Good as any, Jess. The Assembler made 'em, and He don't
make junk. You got enough fingers for two kids. Enough
voice for ten. He makes everything just to please Himself.
The bones and the skin, the meat and the sap, just the way
it suits Him." He let go of my hand and tweaked me on the
arm. "Bones and sap."

I nodded. "He makes things like I make cookies?" I stud-
ded cookies with raisins—three eyes, or two, or one and
as many noses as I wished—just for my own pleasure, and
then gave them to Mother or Nana to admire. Then I'd get
to bake them and eat them.

"He got everything together in one place and glued
you all together and there you were, and you made Him
happy," he said nodding.

"Nails, screws, glue and whatnot," I added casually.
"The Assembler did it."

"He did," Cassidy said. "All the little parts became you, a human being little girl."

"Ah-lls," I said, satisfied about my origin. "Read the ah-lls."

He opened the book and found the place. I patted the page with my right hand, letting it rest briefly next to the bird that was a thumb with feathers and, when I looked carefully, with the tiny ears of a mouse.

It was not an idle thought, the grouping of things into one unit. I had a growing, evolving world on the ceiling above my bed. The sea had been there, primordially, since my earliest scanning of that stuccoed space. Through the months the waters receded in places—over there by the corner windows, and to my right in the space above the doorway, and to my left where my changing table had been and where my orange dresser now sat. The islands dried when I was eight months old. Wavy stands of grass appeared at a year and, later, palm trees and bushes with hanging fruit. There was no logic to the evolution of the animals for my Eden. When I was a year and a half, the first creature to walk the savannah grasses of my new world was an elephant. We watched each other in mutual adoration for several months. Then one bright winter afternoon I awoke from my nap and an egret had alighted on his island. The next day, a lion. Just as in my books, there was no squabbling. They all stood their ground regally, gracefully, and let the light play with them.

The light. The ever-changing light. That's what seemed to put this burgeoning world into motion. On rabbit island, next to the western-facing window, three rabbits stood on hind legs, each slowly waving a curled forepaw goodnight in the waning evening glow. Enough for a warren, three rabbits? I do not know, even now*. Above my door, the swirled plaster fashioned two zebras. The early slanting sun moved through the swales of pale grasses where they stood. Their tails seemed to twitch in the morning, their lancet ears in the western evening light, as if a slow shudder had passed with the day through their skins. That same transit of sun tusked my elephant in the morning, flapped his rogue, rug ears at midday. It was this that stirred the dust in my room.

It was in ardent following of a particularly massive suspended speck that my eyes were first drawn to him. The clown. There he was, all of a sudden, as if he had popped out of a speeding miniature car that had zoomed away leaving him stranded there on my ceiling. Short, dumpy, face broad as a shovel, eyes wide as a syndrome, nose bulbous as a doorknob, lips fat as sausages. It was the day after Cassidy had taken me to my first circus, my birthday present from him even though it was two months late because the circus didn't come to Washington in February. When I saw the clown on my ceiling, I immediately smelled again the sharp urea of moist sawdust, the warmed peanuts, the tangy cocktail of all those manures deposited by carnivore and herbivore alike, the breath of lions. The breath of lions, especially, for some clown not unlike the one there with me in my room had inserted his head—his whole head—into the mouth of one of those roaring beasts. I sniffed ferociously that day in my room. As the sun went behind a cloud, the light waned. The clown winked.

People laugh at clowns for their antics. I applaud their courage. I was convinced, too, that one clown was a circus.

It was good to have the clown to talk to. He under-stood my flawed speech perfectly. And if Mother, standing at the bottom of the stairs, shouted for me to quiet down and take my nap of an afternoon, I'd simply switch to my equally imperfect signing and carry on with that.

I introduced him to the waters, the trees, the animals defying gravity all about him. I told him about Mother and Father, Nana and Ned. I told him about me. I told him I didn't like green beans or squash or Velcro or metal snaps. I told him about my operations and about how I heard and spoke and tied my shoelaces and buttoned my buttons with the index and middle fingers of both hands. I told him about my friend Cassidy from the post office. I think he already knew about him. How, I don't know. But a slight shift in light from a passing cloud or a wisp of birds—five at least in a wisp, but certainly not more than twenty—made the clown's face darken like a shadow. I put my fisted right hand to my chin with my index finger extended and drew it down. Lonely, I signed. The clown's eyes widened as the light returned.

I began going to preschool when I was four and a half. There were six other kids in my group. None of them wore hearing aids, but none was particularly good at hearing, either. They all had attention deficit and learning disorders. The four boys liked to wrestle and fight and take the things the girls were playing with and try to make us chase them. Poor Ms. Whitney had her hands full. Jeremy was the worst. He even looked the worst. The skin of his face had a patchy look like the bark of a peeling sycamore. He had a crew cut just like Cassidy, but there was something strange about the pattern of his hair. It was all in intersecting whorls, like tornadoes touching down everywhere on his head. Even his brown eyebrows seemed to spin. He made me dizzy just by looking at him. And he couldn't even sit still long enough to finish eating a cookie. One time he started running in the very middle of a long burp he was forcing from his mouth. But for me, the most remarkable thing about him was that when the phone on the desk rang, he'd startle like he'd just received an electric shock. His hands would fly out and his legs would skip a step and his head would twist around. You could get hurt just by standing next to him when Ms. Whitney got a call. And the second ring would produce the same wild jerking response, albeit with a little less vigor. As would the third, and so on.

One day, just two weeks into the school year, Ms. Whitney was attending to the spurting bloody nose of my friend Tina—Jeremy had snatched her doll and thrown it at her, hitting her square on the bridge of the nose—when the phone began to ring. Caught in disposable plastic gloves and with the teacher's aide gone to fetch ice, Ms. Whitney had no option but to let the phone ring. Except for Jeremy, we were all sitting on the floor waiting to start a song. Jeremy jumped and jerked like a loose-limbed puppet on a string for the first six salutes. Then only his shoulders and arms went into spasm, going up two inches or so as the caller persisted. Seven or eight rings later, only Jeremy's neck responded to the sounds. The long muscles in front, under his jaw, tightened like snapping leather belts, and his head jerked forward and downwards. I watched until finally his eyes closed and he slumped to the floor where he lay across my legs like a dead boy. He felt so heavy lying there on me. Ms. Whitney continued to attend to Tina's bloody nasal mucus and tiny clear tears. I put my index finger on

Jeremy's head, tracing the swirls of hair from place to place. It was slippery under my finger and sort of silky. My finger went all over, from tornado to tornado, spinning easily against his skull. It was as if his bones were without a single groove or bump, polished smooth as old wood by the spin of the storms. Jeremy began to snore like a fat old dog asleep. It was the first time I had seen him quiet in the weeks I had been in school with him.

We didn't learn much in that class. In part, it was because Ms. Whitney had to spend most of the time trying to control Jeremy and the three other boys. Some days she'd get them quieted down long enough to read stories or wash baby dolls. Some days if the boys were especially bad— Mondays, usually, it seemed—we got to go outside and play on the playground. I'd climb the monkey bars or slide down the twisting slides. This often was the best option for the morning—it seemed a waste of time to sit and wait for hours while the boys disobeyed Ms. Whitney or just began to roll around with each other, wrestling and trying to break things. I soon realized all I had to do was get Jeremy to chase me around the classroom, and Ms. Whitney would declare our need for fresh air and exercise and take us to the playground. I'd wait until she wasn't looking. Then I'd grab Jeremy's sleeve and tug. "Get me, boy!" I'd whisper in his ear. Ah-gt me, ba-oi! And, unless he was tied to his chair, he'd be after me in a heartbeat. I'd run around, wobbly, and scream in pretend panic. Ms. Whitney would abandon her plan for finger-painting or a rondo of children's songs and usher us all outside. I needed practice on the monkey bars.

But the sad thing about Jeremy was that sometimes he was tied to his chair. His parents had given the school permission to use broad, soft restraints that caught by Velcro to hold him, bound at the legs and chest, in his seat. It was sad, really sad, to watch him when they did that. He was like those caught wild animals I had seen on TV. He threw himself at the table, banged his hands, screeched like a wolf pup with a trap-crushed paw. The third or fourth time they tied him up, we were trying to draw sailboats on a lake. The phone rang. Jeremy, caught in the early part of his tantrum, jerked, and jerked, and jerked again. On the fifth ring, Ms. Whitney made for the phone from where she stood bent over Tina's drawing.

"No!" I signed, too excited by my thought even to speak. But then I did shout, "No! No, Ms. Whitney! Ett a-hit wing!" I rose and went to the phone. I put my hand on the receiver to block hers. "Let it ring so he'll sleep."

Ms. Whitney looked at me the way some adults do the first time they meet me, caught between pity and revulsion, between the command, "Get your paws off that!" and the compliment, "You're so thoughtful!" She had never looked at me like that before. I said, "It makes him tired," and I pointed to Jeremy who by then had settled to his shoulder-shrug with each ring. Ten seconds later, his head bowed repetitively like a priest in prayer, and then finally his eyes closed and he lay asleep on his folded arms atop the table. Ms. Whitney watched as Jeremy began to snore. "When he wakes up, he'll be quiet," I added. "Could we read a book then?" I asked.

"If you'd like," she said with a far-off voice.

A few days later they moved me to a different class. It was a lot bigger—fourteen in all, counting me. In this class the boys didn't run and fight. But they weren't nice to me, either. They stared at my hearing aids all the time. One of them refused to touch anything I had touched. He was a fat boy with a face like a big pink cake, and he smelled like wet ashes in a fireplace. Timmy was his name. During lunch period on my first day he watched me eat my peanut butter and jelly sandwich. Mother had cut it into quarters, as she always did, so I could hold each small square between my index and middle fingers.

"You eat like a chimp," he said to me from across the table. "Monkey hand. Monkey girl." A few boys laughed. My face got hot and my mouth got dry.

The teacher's aide went to Timmy and put her hand on his shoulder. "We don't call people names here, Timmy," she said. "Jessica was born without thumbs. Other than that she's the same as you." The aide was about Nana's age. Her face was the color of coffee, and kind.

"No, she's not. She's deaf, too," Timmy said and then defiantly sipped his chocolate milk through a straw. The aide opened her mouth to say something, but before she could speak I said, "I have only one kidney and holes in my heart." Ah huve uwny un khadny ahn howza ahn mah hahr. "I'm not like you at all." I dropped my sandwich on the table and brought my fisted hands to my face with the index fingers pointed up. I crossed them quickly, then uncrossed them and curled the index fingers down.

"She gave me the finger!" Timmy shouted. A brown clot of mucoused chocolate milk unexpectedly oozed from a nostril, and he began to choke and cough.

"No, I didn't," I said.

The aide clapped Timmy on the back to settle his cough. "Yes, you did!" he said hoarsely. "I saw you."

"What was that sign, Jessica?" the aide asked, none too pleased with our behavior.

It was the first time in my life I considered lying. My inclination was to say that I had given the sign for a surgical operation. But I knew how easy it was to look up signs in the manual. "I said he's ugly." Timmy started to cry.

I finished my lunch seated at a separate table in the corner, where I quietly read a book on whales, thinking I was the only one in class who knew Timmy had been wrong when he called me "monkey hand." Monkeys have thumbs, even though they don't work exactly like human ones.

There were six girls in my class. We got along alright if we were doing individual activities, like finger-painting or writing our numbers and letters or stringing beads into necklaces. Sometimes a few of them would stop what they were doing and watch me. For some it was the way I held a brush or pencil between my middle and ring fingers that fascinated them. For others, it was the way I used my mouth and teeth when stringing beads or tying a cord in a knot. I had already learned the whole alphabet and could count way past a hundred and could write those letters and numbers down. None of my classmates had learned half of what I had at home. I was proud of it all, but especially proud of my printing. Cassidy taught me. He was a great printer. It came in handy when he had to help customers fix addresses on letters and packages. I tried to make my letters just like his. It made me feel good to catch one of my classmates studying my *H*'s or *G*'s and then regarding their own scribble with a look of surprise on their faces. I always offered to help.

But it was group activities that brought out their meanness. They took after the boys in that regard. If we played a game with a ball, many refused to catch the one I threw.

And that game where you pass from person to person a red apple held against your neck with your chin—that was always an embarrassment for me. It was always boys against the girls, each group standing in a line facing the other. There wasn't a girl in the class who allowed me to put my face against her shoulder to receive or transfer the apple. The teachers tried everything—having me go first or last, offering prizes for the winning team, giving heartbreakingly beautiful expositions on the dignity of the handicapped. Not a single girl bought it. The first time my turn came to receive the transfer, the boys whooped and hollered, Timmy especially, and shouted, "No way! Don't do it." Dorcy with the tucked chin looked at me. Her eyes fell on my ears, bowed down by the weight of my hearing aids. And then those eyes dropped to my hands. "Go, Dorey, go! Pass it on to Jess," the aide exhorted. At this she started toward me a little. She positioned her neck and torso to align with mine. But then she straightened, raised her head, and let the apple drop. The boys laughed. I wanted to kick them all—apple, boys, and Dorey—but I saw the aide take Dorey roughly by the elbow. I reached out and took the aide's hand instead. "A-hit's okay," I said. She let Dorey go.

After a while they only started that game if a boy was absent and the lines would be unbalanced. Then they'd make me the official timer, handing me a stopwatch with the instructions on how to arrest the sweep of the second hand when the object had finally passed all the way down the winning line. Everybody laughed and shouted so much I had to turn my hearing aids off. The seconds swept by in silence.

I asked the clown one afternoon if he thought they played the game the same way when I was absent. Was

Timmy made the timer, or Gary or Josh? He didn't really know. I never told my parents or Cassidy about it. I just kept practicing my printing and my numbers; kept learning new signs; kept reading and listening to stories; kept putting all the new sounds into proper shapes before letting them out; kept scanning the ceiling for friends.

None of the girls in my class ever invited me to their house to play. That didn't bother me as much as the way they went about making their plans to visit each other. They started, usually, during the lunch break. We sat together at a long table in the back of the classroom. Marci or Courtney or Dorey or Sasha or Lexi or Lacy would announce their new present. Dorey would say, "I have a new sheepdog puppy with a diamond collar!" The other girls would stop eating and stare at her in wonder. In a few seconds she would say, "Lexi, would you like to come over today to play with him? We can feed him cupcakes! He *loves* cupcakes!" Then she'd look at me and smile a little before continuing, now in a whisper so I, theoretically, wouldn't hear, "His name is Bo Bo! I named him that!" "A puppy!" Lexi would reply. "I love puppies!" Then it would be Lexi's turn to give me a wan and knowing look. In a whisper that hollowly echoed Dorey's feigned concern, she'd add, "I'll ask my mom if I can."

I sat, quietly chewing my finger sandwich, reading their foul lips, never letting them see how sad they made me feel by pretending their whispers worked. For something so soft, a whisper can sting like a whip.

Most lunch periods I took to quietly counting numbers in my head. I went slowly, trying to see how each number looked when it was spelled out, stumbling over the eighties for weeks, somehow the alignment of letters never looking quite right, but eventually I could get way into the two hundreds before it was time to clear our trays and sit in a circle for a song.

I did have one friend, Tina, from my first classroom. She didn't have as much trouble sitting still as most of the other kids there, but it was very hard for her to speak. She stuttered. It made Jeremy laugh. Even Ms. Whitney smiled a few times. "What is your name?" she asked her that first day of class. "T-T-T-T-T-T-T-Tina," came the rat-a-tat reply. Jeremy rose from his seat, streaked to her chair, and stole the ribbon from her ponytail. "T-T-T-Tina!" he yelled, running and waving the ribbon so fast it seemed to blur to a pink cloud above his head.

Soon after I went to my new class, Tina's mother called mine to arrange a Saturday playdate. Father drove me to their house. It wasn't far from school. Close enough, in fact, that we sometimes walked there with Tina's mom to play on the swings and climbing sets if the weather was nice. But that first day, we just stayed inside her house. Tina's mother was a big woman with so much black hair I could see only the very center of her face. Her eyebrows and ears were hidden in a ringleted wave of shiny black. She reminded me of a raven with a smile. She had the warmest hands of any human being I have ever touched. She took my hand in hers as we walked from Father's car, and it was like holding a hot bun right from the oven. "Are you a nurse?" I asked on the second step of the brick stairs going up to the front door.

"No, honey," she said with a big smile of very white teeth. "I'm just Tina's mommy." It was an early October day, the kind that spreads sky blue on the city every autumn.

The light was clear and made the fallen leaves shine yellow and orange. Every window in the house was open to the mix of scents from the earth. Tina's father was in the backyard mowing the grass. It all smelled sweet as a bakery.

We played a while in her room. Her ceiling was flat and painted pink. There were no ridges in the plaster, but the overlapping roller marks left by the painter made dark rhomboids that looked like a puzzle to be assembled. We gave her dolls a tea party. Tina said very little. She let me do most of the talking. She did say once, "M-M-M-More t-t-t-t-tea?" to Raggedy Anne. And then she frowned and moved her lips quietly, "More tea? More tea? More tea?"

"You said it! You said, 'More tea' three times!" I spoke as slowly and carefully as I could, somehow warned by Tina's tongue to be gentle with words. Still Tina had an innate talent in deciphering my voice and was able to understand me. Chew ed a-hit! Chew ed, 'Umure tya' tahree tayumes!

"N-N-No I d-d-d-d-didn't!" she stammered. "I d-d-d-d-didn't s-s-say any-th-thing!" Her face drained of color and tears welled in her eyes.

"I saw your lips say it. 'More tea' three times went your lips."

She looked at me blankly and lipped again, "More tea."

"You did it again!" I exclaimed. Tina started to cry. She covered her face with her hands. "Tina," I started, "don't cry. You don't even have to try to talk to me. Just move your lips and I'll know what you said. I just need to be looking at you." I put my hand on her arm. It was warm like her mother's, but tears had dripped down in wet streaks making it a little slippery. Somehow I thought of Jeremy's head. "Is Jeremy still wild?" I asked, hoping to break the spell of sadness that had been cast. She uncovered her face and nodded.

"He's c-c-c-c," she tried.

I shook my head and lipped, "He's crazy."

"He's crazy," she lipped back. "Really crazy."

"Really, really crazy," I mouthed with my eyes spinning like crashing moons. It made her laugh.

We went downstairs. There was a jigsaw puzzle under construction on the dining room table, a Halloween jack-o'-lantern that was bigger than my bathtub. We worked on it for the remainder of the afternoon. When she wanted to tell me something, she tapped the tabletop with a piece so I'd look up. Freed of the need to talk, of the fear of her own uncertain voice, Tina didn't leave her seat for two hours. Her mother looked in on us fourteen times. I counted.

"Good-bye," Tina lipped in the driveway when Father arrived to pick me up.

"Good-bye," I lipped back.

It was the start of my only real friendship with another child, one that would last the three years until I died. I'm pretty sure it was Tina who gave me the flu that December. She gave it to me when she shouted, spraying a little spit in my eyes, "I'm sick! I have a c-cold." She said it with pride and near perfection. We were coloring Santas at the kitchen table in her house. Her mom had baked brownies for us. We ate them before they cooled, with the chocolate chips still mostly liquid. "I love brownies," she declared with her mouth brown and full.

I never tire of watching that tape.

Father was the god of my nocturnal firmament. He expanded it year on year. In the beginning, there were single stars so lonely in the void they could have been the eyes of cast-off angels looking down on me. If, in the dark, I let my own eyes pass from glowing point to glowing point, sometimes it seemed one would blink. Then the rapid movement of my eyes back to the signaling star would seem to start others twinkling. Next, Father came with constellations. Before I fell asleep, I was content to lie on my back and decode the shapes he was gradually pasting there, trying to remember what had been present before and what new star had appeared in my heavens. In the bright light of day, the stars transformed the ceiling's savannah to a rocky plain where egrets stood on boulders and rabbits threw stones from raised paws. It all made the clown laugh.

I was born in February, the month dedicated in antiquity to purification. I am Aquarius, the Water Bearer. My symbol glows above my bed, the two jagged parallel lines like tight waves in the sea. Father used a fluorescent paint for that. He tinted it the exact color of the ceiling so I couldn't see it in the light of day. But I had no need to. In the day, my whole ceiling sloshed like the eternal ocean. It befitted me.

When I started kindergarten at five and a half, Father wanted me to play sports with the other kids. He saw how lonely I was in school. It didn't seem right to him that I was always and only with Tina during breaks. He favored soccer over T-ball because of the bat, over bowling because of the ball. Mother went along mostly because she was so swollen with her pregnancy.

Cassidy was dead set against it. He was against it right after he asked me if I wanted to play "in the cold and the rain and the suckin' mud."

"It's not the rain or the mud or the cold," I truthfully answered. I extended my index fingers from my fist and brought them together side by side I cupped my right hand, palm down, and brought it up and down at waist level four times.

Cassidy scratched his head and struggled a moment with the sign. Then he said, "Same kids as in your class right now?"

"Yes," I said. "Tina and home are better."

"Ford," he told Father, "it's not the best of times ta start this soccer stuff with Jess. With Kate and the baby coming soon, ya know, it'll be a real chore getting her to practices and games. What d'ya think, put it off a year? I mean, five is still real young for starting in on soccer." It was the sign-up weekend and he had come over to sit in on my morning ASL lesson.

"We'll manage, Joe," Father said, not even looking up from the form he was filling out. "About how tall are you now, Jess? Do you know?"

"No."

"Do you know how much you weigh?"

"No."

He eyed me up and down. "I'll put forty-four inches and forty-four pounds. Nobody'll check it." He jotted the numbers and mumbled, "Brown. Brown. No. No. Yes." He looked up again. "You've had your TB shots and measles, haven't you?"

"There's no shot for TB," Cassidy said with a medical finality I'd rarely heard from my physicians.

"Says here there is," Father said tapping a line on the form. "I'm sure you had all this stuff. I'll write down a date when you were, like, one and a half. Nobody'll check it."

"Ford," Cassidy said, "it ain't right."

"Joe, I told you: nobody'll check it. And if they do, we'll just correct the dates and numbers. I mean, Jesus, this stuff isn't like zip codes or anything."

"Not the dates and stuff, Ford. Soccer. It ain't right. She don't really want ta do it in the first place. And it's the same group a kids as in her class right now. They don't get along in school and kickin' a soccer ball around isn't going ta change that a bit. I think she'd do better visiting with Tina or being here with us than running around in the cold with a bunch of kids who . . ." He stumbled for words for a second, before concluding, ". . . who she don't like."

"Well, Joe, sometimes you just got to try something new." He signed his name to the bottom of the third page with a flourish. "Let's go!" he said like one of those soldiers in the movies when they begin to attack and die.

What really soured me on the enterprise was my clumsiness. I had terrible balance. I was okay if I walked slowly, like in school, but as soon as I started running, I would start lurching and listing. Then my arms would start to thrust wildly, like a tightwire walker desperately trying to prevent a fall. Running, I looked as strange as Jeremy in the presence of a sounding phone. I worried about the merciless teasing certain to come from the kids. They had never seen me run before. Really, only Tina and her mom had, when we went to the empty school ground to play. Then, we'd chase each other, Tina in those early months joyously stuck in the shouted first groove of my name, "J-J-J-J-J-J," as she tried to catch me in a two-person game of "a-a-a-a-a-it," and me barely out of her reach, flouncing like a windmill mounted on a boat sailing herky-jerky in a gale. Tina, exposed to crazy Jeremy day after day, thought nothing of my spastic sprints. What my classmates would think, and more importantly what they would say, would be something else entirely.

As we drove to the first practice that Saturday, I imagined how the girls in my class would look running on the field. All I could see in my mind's eye were their six shining ponytails, gracefully rising and gracefully falling with each lope, perfect tails going up and down with each perfect stride. My hair was cut too short for a ponytail. It didn't even cover my ears.

Everyone in the class showed up to join the team, the fourteen of us. Our coach was Mr. Lester, the third grade teacher. He had a thin mustache that made him look like he was always smiling. Which was good, because he never really did. But he never yelled, either. He let the parents do that at the games. They hardly needed his help. Mr. Lester was nice.

We practiced that day. There were cut-up oranges and water so cold it gave me an ache in my eyes.

We kicked the soccer ball to him a few times and he kicked it back. Then we did some drills. Timmy was made the goalie. His parents clapped and cheered, "Timmy! Tiiiimmm-eeee!" when he stepped in front of the net. They were eating potato chips from a big bag and were sharing a Diet Coke from a can. Timmy's mother wore shorts. Each of her legs was bigger than my whole body.

I had been right about the girls. They ran beautifully. Marci was the best. She was so fast and could stop so easily and just as easily dart off again. All of their ponytails were well behaved, even Sasha's, whose hair was kind of curly.

My turn came to run in the drill. Mr. Lester stood thirty feet away next to a brown rubber cone that looked like a toy volcano. Halfway between us, Courtney stood facing me. All I had to do was run, kicking the ball in front of me, past Courtney, all the way to Mr. Lester. He had a stopwatch in his hand and said, just like Father at home, "Let's go!" I kicked the ball and ran after it and kicked it again and ran again. Then I kicked and missed far left and almost fell. I came back to the ball and kicked it hard, but it squibbled away to the right. I ran to it fast as I could and tried to kick it towards Courtney because she was in line with Mr. Lester. The ball rolled past her, and I had to run hard again. I kicked it three more times before, panting and dizzy, I got to the brown volcano.

"I think you'd make a good defender," he said, looking at his watch. "Left side."

My face was stinging hot from the running, and I was out of breath and still dizzy. I looked to the side of the field. Father stood smiling with his fist raised in victory salute. Cassidy looked down at the foot-worn grass with both hands in his pants pockets. Courtney passed me going to the starting point. "Dumbo. Your ears flap like baby Dumbo's when you run." She jogged past me, her ponytail burnished by the midday sun. The sight of the brown volcano made me want to vomit.

That night I stood on the toilet seat in my bathroom at home so I could see myself in the mirror, and I jogged in place. With each pounding step, my ear flapped down and a little forward due to the weight of the apparatus behind it.

I had seen the movie. Cassidy had brought it over when I was three and we watched it together a dozen times over the months. I loved that baby elephant, so brave and pure. What Courtney had said about me wasn't untrue. I did look

like him when he waved his big ears and tried to fly. Seeing
that truth somehow took the sting out of Courtney's snipe,
and the anger out of my heart. On the coming Monday in
school, when the new taunt from the ponytail herd began,
"Dumbo, Dumbo, Dumbo," I smiled at them and flapped
both ears with my index fingers.

I counted all the more furiously during my soundless
lunches. I was into the thousands now. The numbers, the
words for the numbers, came in flocks, in herds, in droves
that seemed to cover the backs of my eyes. I could make
them whatever colors I chose. There were so many in my
eyes I could see nothing else.

"What's Dumbo thinking about?" Lexi asked me Tuesday. She had gotten her very own soccer goal for her
backyard on Sunday, the day after first practice. "Are you
thinking about flying?" The other girls giggled. "It would
be faster than your running," Courtney added.

"Fly, Dumbo, fly!" said Lexi.

I flapped my ears, flicking the switches that turned off
my aids without looking up from my lunch tray. I said quite
softly, "One thousand four hundred eleven." I decided to
call any group of five or more girls with ponytails a "lash."

We had practice every Tuesday and Thursday afternoon.
We played five Saturday games against other teams. It
rained on three of the practices and two of the games. The
field was muddy where I was positioned every game and
practice. It was windy and freezing cold in mid-October
the fourth game, and I had to wear a sweater and a wool cap
to keep warm as I stood, motionless, for the better part of
an hour. I was so cold that day, the water I drank from the
yellow jug at halftime didn't hurt my eyes.

Timmy was an even worse player than me. He could barely move when the ball came his way. He blocked only two kicks the whole season, including during practices. The girls laughed at him almost as much as at me. The boys were a little better. I think they were afraid to make him mad. He had a temper. Lexi told him her opinion every time they were close on the field and away from the hearing of Mr. Lester. "You stink," she said. Since I was positioned on the left as a defender, I was always pretty close to where Timmy stood. I could smell his damp creosote odor in the air all the time. It really didn't stink. It reminded me of going to the beach in the summers and visiting the boats at the marinas. Timmy stood in front of the goal and looked like a moored boat—a tug or a ferry— ever so imperceptibly moving left, right, left, right to the swells only he could feel. His pink face got red just from the exertion of standing and rocking with the tiniest of excursions. "Next time," I yelled as encouragement the first time the other side scored.

"You shut up, Dumbo," he shouted back, rocking, rocking, relentlessly rocking. "You stink, too."

I asked Mother to let me grow my hair longer like the other girls. She said it was a cute cut, like a pixie. Besides, I didn't need to handle a brush with such short hair.

The season ended in early November. We went one and four. The one game we won I had to miss because of my cardiology appointment. It was at that office visit that Eileen Marshall concluded my heart's leaks and squeaks would need a surgeon's touch to cease, after all. It would be safe to wait another year or so, but it would have to be done to protect my lungs from the constant slosh of extra blood flow. We drove home in sad silence that seemed all the more oppressive for the fall foliage around us, dressed up in gaudy colors, reds and oranges and yellows. A leaf now and then would fall onto the windshield of our moving car and be pressed to the glass for an instant before shooting away. The bugs had put tiny holes in some. I wondered out loud if I'd find a message there in the leaves if I studied the patterns. Mother said no, it's just the insects. Father drove in silence. Cassidy, in the front seat with him, said, "My Ma used ta read tea leaves at the bottom of her cup. Lot of good it did her. I wouldn't be lookin' for any leaves with messages, missy. Just read your books."

The next day, Tina and I collected a bucket of leaves from her backyard. We sat with them in her kitchen, holding them up to the ceiling lights one by one. On most there were just five or six random holes. Some, though, looked like parts of the constellations I had studied. There were half a dozen with holes exactly like Cancer the Crab, and a few that could have been the body of Pegasus. I found what I was really looking for near the bottom of the bucket. Two leaves with punctures forming the stellar outline of Corona Borealis, the Northern Crown. They were big brown oak leaves, each with a neat semicircle of eight holes. We glued them onto two of Tina's plastic headbands and put them on. We sat regally at the kitchen table gluing the rest of the leaves with assembled holes onto pieces of stiff construction paper. I told Tina about the book I was reading with Cassidy, the one with all the Greek gods and myths. I told her how Princess Ariadne, who was the sister of the Minotaur, wore the golden Northern Crown when she married Dionysus. It was Cassidy's favorite story.

"Who is Dionysus?" she lipped.

"Dionysus was the god of beer and whiskey." Cassidy had told me that when I had asked him the same question. "Have you ever drunk beer? My mommy drinks it. It makes her b-burp!" I considered the question for a second before answering. "No, never tasted it." It was not a lie.

"Let's make cocoa," Tina mouthed.

"Good," I signed.

"And who's Minotaur," she asked, handing me the milk. I slipped three fingers into the opening of the plastic handle.

"He's a man who is part bull. He got made with the wrong parts so he has a bull's head and big sharp horns and a tail and the rest of him is a man. He's very bad, and he kills people who get put into the place where he lives, which is like a giant puzzle where nobody can find the way out. But someone does and that's who kills Minotaur."

"Someone brave," she said aloud.

"Someone very brave and very smart," I echoed back, impressed by the lack of stumble over the difficult s and b. "His name was Theseus. Ariadne showed him how to find his way out of the puzzle, but I could find my own way out. I would count my steps from turn to turn in the puzzle, and count the turns, too. All I would have to do is remember the numbers of steps for each turn, and I would find the door. I could do just what Ariadne did and help Theseus slay the Minotaur."

She stirred in the cocoa and put the cups in the microwave. "Who made Minotaur?" Tina lipped.

I hadn't really thought about who had made him. Cassidy had answered my questions about him so quickly, so matter-of-factly, I had assumed the Assembler had done it a long time ago when He was just starting out putting people together. "God did it when He was younger."

"When he was in kindergarten?" she mouthed.

"Preschool," I said with a knowing nod. It was too big of a mistake for kindergarten.

Jeanine was born on Thanksgiving Day of my kindergarten year. I woke in the morning to the stirrings of my animals in the gray shadows on my ceiling. I said good morning to them all, though the clown still slept, and went down to the kitchen. I found Cassidy frying bacon and singing a song about fairies on the misty mountains. He sang that a lot when he was happy. I heard it in the car whenever he took me places. Now he yelled it to the meat in the frying pan.

"AceyDee," I said over his voice. He startled so much the spatula in his hand whacked the coffee pot.

"Jess, lady, you've got yourself a little sister!" His eyes were bright against the gray stubble on his face, like twin moons over an old mowed field. "Came out in the middle of the night." He waved the spatula over his head like a flag and smiled as big a smile as I'd ever seen him make. "Your daddy had me come over ta sit for you when . . . when the baby started comin', at around midnight. Little Jeanine was born at four thirteen. And everyone's in fine form, your mom, Jeanine, the old man himself. I talked ta your daddy an hour ago. We're goin' over there after we eat and do the dishes." He turned to worry the frying bacon. I turned and went back to my room. I woke the clown and complained.

The route to the hospital had become as familiar to me as the menagerie on my ceiling during the day and the constellations at night. There were eleven turns, three rights, then reciprocating left-rights, until we entered the parking garage. Then it was unpredictable how many additional turns up ramps we would need to make. But we had done the ride so many times that I knew it by heart. In the year before Jeanine was born, as we drove along our neighborhood streets, I'd count the number of empty garbage cans on sidewalks on Wednesday mornings or raised mailbox flags the other days of the week, and multiply that number by the sum of FOR SALE signs, hoping one day to arrive at four hundred ninety, which was the magic number I'd learned in my Christian Doctrine classes, that "seventy times seven" number, but never even got close. . . . But that day, that trip with Cassidy to meet my new sister, I could not concentrate on anything. I tried counting. There was actually little challenge to it—Thanksgiving Day had neither mail nor garbage service, and hardly anybody tried to sell a house this close to the holidays. I tried keeping tally of it all but quickly lost interest. There was something deep inside my brain trying unsuccessfully to come to the surface. After the second turn, my nose lost the sweet scent of spilled whiskey and the talcum of cigar ash that incensed Cassidy's car. The thumping Irish music he played melted away in my ears until only the high notes flying off the fiddles found their way in, and on Wisconsin Avenue even these receded to silence. The clear fall sunlight had winterized, crystallized in the late November sky. It seemed to seep through a gray veil of high clouds and to sift down onto the sidewalks and streets like a dull dusting of lead.

I sat next to Cassidy, seeing nothing, as he drove down the empty boulevard. Seeing nothing, hearing nothing, smelling nothing, but somehow feeling hot in the brain, simmering some emotion, some thought, like a stew that needed time to cook.

We parked on the street. He held my hand during the ten-minute walk to the elevators. He knelt down on one knee after I'd pressed the Up button, and he smoothed my hair. He straightened the collar of my blouse. He smiled and said, "You're the big sister now, girlie." His face was shaved smooth. I wanted to ask him if it would be possible for Mother and Father to leave Jeanine at the hospital. We could visit her when we came down for my appointments. But the doors opened and two nurses began to walk out. He stood and we got on.

Mother sat in bed and Father in a bedside chair. Both had that look about them I'd seen before, usually at the end of long, late parties at our house when they seemed slightly stooped at the shoulders, slightly wan around the eyes from too much effort, too much talk. Jeanine lay asleep in a wheeled bassinet next to the bed, the very definition of pink, from the glowing top of her bald head to the tightly wrapped pink blanket that encased her to her toes. I stood in the doorway a second after Cassidy entered.

"Jess! Joe!" Father boomed. His voice sounded more to me like a warning to duck or jump out of harm's way than a greeting. But then he clapped his hands, stood, and ran to scoop me up and hug me to his chest. He swung me left and he swung me right in his embrace. I never before understood how strong he was or how much joy could erupt from his quiet heart. Had I been a bell in his arms, I would have clanged loud enough for Easter Sunday and Christmas combined.

He carried me to Mother, who took me next to her in bed. She put her hand on my head and kissed me twice. "Jess," she said amid the noise of Father and Cassidy jabbering over the baby, "this is Jeanine, your new sister.

She was born in the middle of the night." She reached out and pulled the bassinet to the side of the bed. "She weighed seven pounds, and she's twenty inches long. Twenty inches, Jess. Tiny, just like you when you were born." She lifted her up onto her lap. Jeanine *was* little. She had a little fat face and two tiny ears. Her nose was squashed so much I could hardly see her nostrils. Her eyes were closed. Each upper lid was darkened by plum-colored tattoos, and there was a smear of glistening ointment along the lid margins. I was certain at first glance the Assembler had forgotten to attach a neck between her round head and her chest. Her face seemed to end in a plug of fat below her chin. It would be okay with me if she had no neck, I thought. The rest of her lay cloaked in pink mystery.

"Would you like to hold her for a bit?" Mother asked. I swallowed and said yes. Father and Cassidy watched at the bedside. Mother molded my left arm into a crook to support the neckless head and placed Jeanine against me. The weight of her, all seven pounds, felt good, like I was holding something precious to me that had been lost and now had been found. I could feel the heat of her body come through her blanket, and the rapid, shallow excursions of her breathing reminded me of holding rabbit pups at the pet shops where I'd go with Cassidy. Each quick flick of breath was as if she was excited about life, or scared, just like the rabbits.

"Don't be scared, baby," I said to her. "Chewww'll ah-bya okay." I touched the top of her head. The bones were firm and bumpy under the skin. My index finger rode the ridges softly up and down. Her head was nothing like Jeremy's from preschool. All at once she opened her eyes and cried. It scared me so much my whole body spasmed.

In response, her little body tried to jerk inside her swaddling blanket. Jeanine opened her mouth wide and wailed,
and she arched her back. At the full extent of this stretch,
I saw her neck. It wasn't much of a neck—short and square
and squat—but it was, unmistakably, a neck. My eyes fell
into the pink cave of her mouth. There were no teeth,
just the smooth, even ridges of her gums. The Assembler, apparently, had remembered. "I'll take her now, Jess,"
Mother said. I moved her to Mother's proffered arms. She
rocked her softly and said, "Baby, baby, little bitty baby,
shh-shh-shh."

Father helped me off the bed. He talked with Cassidy
a while, and then Cassidy asked Mother some questions.
He all of a sudden had an unlit cigar in his mouth. He
chomped its end tight between his teeth so the length of
the cigar rose to the ceiling at an angle to his face. I couldn't
pay attention to what they were saying. Mother had rolled
Jeanine into Cassidy's arm, and I was afraid he might drop
her. His face lit up in wide smiles. His eyes got as big as
a cow's "You did good, Kate," he said. Then, looking at
me, he added, "Again." He hefted Jeanine and rocked her
a little and touched the tip of her flattened nose. "Looks
like you been in a brawl, girlie. You gonna be a scrapper
like your sister? Eh?" He winked at me and then stared at
Jeanine. I just stood there next to the bassinet trying to
sound out her name as it was spelled on the card taped to
the plastic sidewall. She had a number in her name. I was
glad for her. But no amount of reassembly could arrive at
four hundred ninety. The best I could do watching Cassidy
beam like a shaft of light in a dim room was the number
five hundred twenty-two. Multiply nine by the sum of the
letters in her name—fifty-eight—and that was what you

got because it was fifty-eight less than five hundred eighty.
Not four ninety, but close.

A nurse came in to take Jeanine's vital signs. I watched
her blow up the cuff of the blood pressure machine. "Not
too hard," I told her.

"What, hon?" the lady asked, crouched over the bassinet with her head turned to the side to see me.

"Ana too hahr," I repeated.

The nurse looked at Mother and shrugged. I flexed
the first two fingers of each hand and struck the knuckles
against each other in an up-and-down motion. "Hahr," I
repeated.

"She'll be gentle," Mother said with a reassuring nod.

Jeanine started to cry again. When the nurse was finished I walked to the bassinet and pushed it back and
forth, counting aloud with each to-and-fro motion. The
cries quieted at number fourteen and ceased entirely at
thirty-five. I went on to seventy, because she was seven
pounds. "You're my best little helper," Mother said with
her hand lightly resting on the opposite rail of Jeanine's
bassinet. "Thank you," she added when my arms were
finally at rest.

"Can you come home now, Mama?" I asked.

"Not tonight. But tomorrow morning. And today when
you get home, there will be a surprise for you. And Daddy
will be home tonight. Just wait." She put her arms out for
me and I went to her. She squeezed me almost as tightly as
Father had. Her neck smelled sweet with soap and sweat.
"You need to go with Cassidy now to find out what the
surprise is."

I replay that scene of first meeting Jeanine very often
now*. I find it interesting that what I did just before

leaving—so important to me at the time to answer the
question bubbling below the surface of my consciousness—I would completely forget once I'd done it, and that
I'd go to my death without the slightest residue of its memory. But I watch it now*. I stick my hand down the side of
Jeanine's swaddling blanket and extract her arm. It is solid,
fat, heavy as a branch. She cries when I get it out. Not a cry
of pain, but surprise. I hold her by the wrist and gently pry
open the hand. I touch each finger, one by one, beginning
with her pinky and go to four. When at last I reach the
thumb, I hold it loosely for a moment. It is no bigger than
the stub of a crayon. "Five," I announce. Then I kiss it. I am
surprised by this each time it plays.

Surprising, too, is the look on Mother's face. There is
patience in it, and a weary concern, and, yes, around the
mouth, the slightly curled hint of a smile, as if she had
anticipated my doing this, had wanted me to do it, and was
pleased I had taken the initiative to answer the unasked
question of Jeanine's assembly for myself.

I put her arm down and look at Mother. I point with the
index finger of my right hand to my right earlobe and then
to my lips. Mother shakes her head and says slowly, so the
words hardly needed reforming, "No, not deaf."

"Jeanine," I say, but her eyes have closed and her mouth
seems to be in a puffed pout. "You'll be okay." I know she
hears me. I see her eyes flutter. They rove under her plum
tattoos like the moles mounding the soil in our yard. It
shocks me to think how large those tunnels must be, how
much loamy air they must hold.

I was quiet the whole ride home. I kept seeing Jeanine
in Mother's arms and then in Cassidy's. And their faces full

of that awful wonderment adults can express, a mixture of surprise and fear, of recognition and mystery. Cassidy asked me if I wanted McDonald's for lunch. "Not hungry," I signed. Well, really I shook my head no and signed "hungry." You need thumbs to sign "not."

My surprise at home was Nana and Ned. They were already working on Thanksgiving dinner when we got there. Nana was tying up the legs of a pimply turkey and Ned was peeling potatoes. When he had finished with one it was smooth and white as a carton egg and just as small. The kitchen smelled like cinnamon and sugar from two pies baking in the oven. The radio played music so loud my hearing aids began to whistle and buzz. Ned wiped his hands on a towel and gave me hugs and kisses. Nana was next after she washed her hands at the sink. They talked excitedly with Cassidy, but because of the background noise, I couldn't follow any of it, and I didn't watch their lips. The pale puckered skin of the turkey held my stare as I tried to see a pattern in the tiny bumps—a whorl suggested a rose, but I couldn't be sure. All I heard was the Irish music screeching in my ears. It was sharp and hurt my head. I left the three of them in the kitchen—Ned and Cassidy had a toasting taste of Irish Mist in their hands—and went to my room and lay on my bed.

I told the clown about baby Jeanine and the number in her name. I told him Cassidy liked her and so did Mother and Father. And that she would be coming home tomorrow morning. He could like her too. It was okay. She had thumbs and ears that worked. Everybody could like her, Nana and Ned and even Tina when she came over to play.

The clown's face didn't change in the pewter light coming through the window. He stood silent and grave in the etchings of plaster and listened to me repeat, "And she has thumbs and hears. And her heart probably has no holes. And she has a kidney where I don't. Her blood pressure was normal. They took it and I watched. You can like her, too. The Assembler made her perfect." I thought, but didn't say, how the unfairness of that act made the Assembler seem even more imperfect to me than when he forgot my thumbs and ears, botched my kidney and my heart. And I began to wonder why He was like that. Why even what He did well had the spark of the imperfect in it.

A shadow swept across the clown. No wisp of birds this time, but Cassidy opening the door. "I'm goin' home for a bit, kiddo, ta clean up, but I'll be back for dinner later on." He saw my blank stare and the trace of tears in the corners of my eyes. He stood in the doorway, leaning into the room the way he always did before he left after reading to me in the evenings. But now he didn't leave. Instead, he came to my bedside and knelt on one knee. He took my hand in his and shook his head. His whiskey breath was familiar and reassuring. "Jess," he said, "I can't look at Jeanine's face without seein' your dark, dark eyes shining. It's you she reminds me of when you was little. Jess, listen ta me. No baby's cry'll take the air in this house without me seein' your shining black eyes. Nothing will change for the worse for her bein' around." He put his hand on my head and made small circles with his palm. "I love you, Jess. Me and your ma and daddy and Nana and Ned. And that's the God's honest truth, it is." He took his hand away and punched my shoulder. "It is."

I made a fist and extended my index finger. I pointed at him and moved it in a clockwise circular motion just as I arched my eyebrows up. He nodded and returned my sign.

"Yes," he said solemnly, "always." Then he added, "Jess, you'll be okay." He took my hand out of the air and kissed my fingers. From his pants pocket he took the gold paper band from his White Owl. He slipped it on my index finger and repeated again, "You'll be okay." He patted my hand. I nodded back, and he left.

The light from the window leaped back into the room as he closed my door. The clown's eyes flared.

*

Why put Jeanine in my life, I wonder now*. To accept her in the face of my rejection by my schoolmates? To do unto her what others have not done unto me? To learn that my missing parts gave me space to accommodate that bulky feeling toward a new sister? To see that the only way through my imperfections was to forgive people who could not accept them? Perhaps her life says to me: give up the bone of your pride, forgo the hand of your retribution. Is that it? Sounds like Ezekiel. Ezekiel could be it.

6

TRANSUBSTANTIATION

It takes something unsettling in life to finally settle it. For me that was the first six months of Jeanine's presence. She came home, as foretold, the day after Thanksgiving. Nana and Ned took me to the hospital that morning to help bring Mother and all of her flowers home. And Jeanine. We borrowed Cassidy's car. I carried out the red carnations Cassidy had sent, thinking they would look nice in my room, in the sun that came onto my desk in the afternoons. It frightened me when I watched Mother in a wheelchair on the way to the cars. Only sick people rode in wheelchairs. Mother held Jeanine in her lap, wrapped tight in a new blanket so only her face showed. Her cheeks were plump as baby pumpkins and just as ruddy orange. Their bright, glowing color made Mother's face look sallow and pasty. A nurse pushed her along the hallway to the elevators. Not even Ned or Father was allowed to do it. Only the very weak, the frightfully sick, needed that kind of care, I thought. What had Jeanine done? What had gone wrong? That afternoon, when Nana had hugged

Mother, they both began to cry. Nana had to go into the bathroom to fix her nose and dry her eyes even before she got to hold Jeanine. But afterwards she was all wide smiles and laughing, so I had forgotten the tears. But the wheelchair ride made me remember. It looked as though the baby had stolen the life from Mother's face. And she lay there in Mother's arms, the culprit, innocent and asleep, and poisonous as an orange mushroom.

Everyone walking the hospital hallways got out of the way of Mother's wheelchair as if they were worried Mother had some serious illness, too. Some people even left the elevator when it came so we could all get on together. Jeanine slept as the elevator went down and my stomach went up into my throat. Sometimes her fat little lips moved in a pucker like there was something sour in her mouth. I wanted to put my fingers in there to feel around. Maybe there was a tooth I hadn't seen. I wanted to feel far, far back to find out if she had a uvula. I planned on doing it during the ride home while I sat next to her in the backseat. It would only take a second because I would lick my fingers first to make them slippery.

We put all the flowers in Ned's car. We filled up the trunk and then most of the backseat. Three helium balloons painted with pink storks butted futilely against the rear window. Mother strapped Jeanine into my old car seat in Father's car and got in the back with her. Nana joined Father in the front. "Ride with me, Jess," Ned said patting the passenger-side seat in the front. "I'll buckle you up."

I heard him say to Father, just before they entered their cars to start driving home, "I replaced the hardware on the crib's collapsible side rail this morning, Ford. Can't be too careful about those kinds of things. I'll show you when we get there." Father said thanks and started his engine.

It was my old crib they were talking about.

We started driving. "Best not to suck your fingers, Jess. It'll make your belly swell," Ned said. His right elbow was inches from my shoulder. A quick turn of my head to him, and he might knock the teeth out of my skull. I took my wet fingers out of my mouth, hardly aware they had been there. We made it to the third turn, a right, before I started sneezing. The thick fragrance in the air had a metallic tang to it that tickled the back of my throat. There were a lot of double-parked cars in front of Saks and Neimans, but I was too disconsolate to count them. I did count the sneezes. Fourteen. And Ned's laughs at my ongoing distress. Five. I didn't even care to think about his warning of belly swelling.

At home, Jeanine cried every two hours. Mother fed her in my old rocking chair in the guest bedroom that now belonged to her. Ned and Father got my old baby carriage up from the basement and squirted Three-In-One-Oil on it until Ned announced it was "good as new." I helped Nana put flowers in every corner of the house, and sneezed. The red carnations went to Mother's room. I sneezed some more. It didn't take long for everyone to stop saying, "God bless you." Eleven blessings, in fact, for twenty-seven sneezes. The commingled odors of florist shop and hardware store filled my throat and nose with a nasty fizz.

Intermittently, Mother appeared as if out of nowhere throughout the long, boring afternoon and evening. The first time, I was smearing mayonnaise on bread, helping Nana make turkey sandwiches for lunch. The kitchen was the one room Nana and I hadn't fouled with flowers. My hour-long sneezing fit had subsided, but my nose was an annoying, dripping faucet. All at once I could smell that familiar hospital smell and turned to see Mother standing just behind me. Her clothes reeked of glue or almost-rotten fruit like the sheets and disinfectants of every hospital room I had ever visited. She put her hand on my shoulder. I dropped my knife onto the tabletop, put my arms around her waist, and began to sob. "I hate her! I hate her, and she made you sick! Take her back to the hospital! I hate her!"

Mother put her hand on the top of my head and stroked my hair. She let me cry until I wet her dress with my tears. They washed away the hospital scent enough for me to smell her skin. That and the gentle press of her hand finally halted my tears. "I'm not sick, Jess. I'm fine. Just a little tired. And you don't hate Jeanine. You're the big sister. I need your help with her. Especially after Nana goes home. Will you help me take care of Jeanine?"

My face was still buried in the warm wet spot of her clothes. I nodded my affirmation silently and in the process rubbed my nose against her. It felt as good as scratching an itch. I nodded again and again.

That night after I went to bed, I heard Jeanine cry every few hours. The first time I knew when Mother had gotten to her room by the dim light that appeared in the gap at the base of my door like a faraway dawn. Enough brightness leaked in to extinguish the fluorescent stars on my ceiling. I went to Jeanine's room. Mother was rocking her and breast-feeding her. "Can I help?" I signed. Mother at first began to shake her head no but quickly changed her mind. "Would you get me a glass of water?" she said. I let her have the water in my own plastic Snoopy glass. She drank it down right away. "Wow. Thanks, Jess. I was really thirsty. Get on back to bed now. You need your sleep. And thank you again for your help."

In bed I turned up the gain on my hearing aids. Jeanine woke at two a.m. and four thirty a.m. Again and again her weak light eclipsed my ceiling stars. It was the way of things, I think now* as I remember how I eclipsed my Mother's blinding sun the day of my birth. It's all visible on reel one, the shadow I cast between my mother's legs as the beam fell on me, pink and wiggling. Eclipses come and eclipses come again.

That first night home with Jeanine, Mother drank two more glasses of water. She looked much better to me for all the fluids. Through the night it seemed Jeanine's pumpkin glow faded and Mother bloomed pink.

Tina came to my house Saturday to play and to spend the night. Her mother dropped her off. Before she left, she came inside to see Mother and Jeanine. She brought a present and a plate of chocolate chip cookies. She and Tina stood by the crib and watched Jeanine breathe and sleep. Mother had fed her just a little while before. I offered to wake her so they could hear her cry, but Tina's mother said that wouldn't be necessary. They stood and watched her breathe as if they were watching an unimaginably difficult feat, Hercules clubbing the heads of the Hydra, perhaps. Their eyes went big when Jeanine sighed, letting out a soft humming noise that ended in a mouse squeak. Her mom took Tina's hand and said to Mother, "She's a treasure, Kate. You're very fortunate to have Jess and Jeanine both." Mrs. Dalton's warm right hand went to my cheek and touched it like a match to a wick.

The rest of the afternoon Tina and I played in the yard
or in my room. We watched Mother feed and change Jeanine twice. Tina ran from the room when Jeanine started
passing a stool on the changing table, shouting as she ran,
"N-No! N-No!" Mother looked at me and smiled.

We ate dinner when Father came home from work.
Then Cassidy came with a movie. We sat on the couch
eating cookies and watching *Shrek* with Ned and Cassidy.
They laughed more than we did. Ned ate five cookies. I
counted.

Mother tucked us in. Tina slept on the green cot that
stayed in the garage unless Nana and Ned stayed and Ned
snored. This night, the cot went right next to my bed.
When the lights went out, Tina could see my ceiling glint
with stars. It was her first time spending the night. "Those
are my constellations," I said pointing up in the dark.

"What are c-consellay-s-shins?" she asked.

"That's when God places stars in groups to make things.
Like a puzzle God puts together in space. Right up over us
is Pegasus. He's a horse with wings. See over there, those
stars that make his wings?" I traced the wings with my
extended finger even though it was too dark for her to see.
"And over there is the Crab and there is the Archer, Sagittarius. See his arrow? It's aimed right at the Crab!" I drew
my hand half across the heavens to demonstrate. It made
me feel like the Assembler must feel all the time, His hand
sweeping across the galaxies to point things out.

"Where is Minotaur?" Tina asked with a hint of concern
in her voice.

"He's not made of stars. He's made of bones and horns
and skin, not stars."

"Oh."

We watched the stars silently for a few minutes. "One of them is blinking," Tina said. I felt the stir of air as her invisible hand rose to point to the star that fell from Aquarius's water jug. "But sometimes it stops."

"That's Aquarius, the Water Bearer. That's me."

"Why you?"

I almost answered with my February birthday. Then all at once I remembered the previous night. "Because I bring water in the night to Mother when she feeds Jeanine. She gets very, very thirsty."

"Oh."

"Three times in the nights."

"That's what I would do for my Mom but she can't have more babies. Just me and no more."

I thought to offer her Jeanine, but the realization of what that would mean for me—that I could no longer be Aquarius in the night—prevented me.

"I see two lines near the blinking star."

"The ocean," I said. "Daddy painted it. You only can see it in the dark."

"The ocean in the sky," she said.

"Yes." I heard Tina yawn, and then she was asleep.

When Jeanine cried at two, I brought water. And again at five. That second time, Mother asked me how many times was I going to do that, bring her water in my cup? I told her the number. She kissed the top of my head from where she sat rocking and saved the last sip in the plastic glass for me.

I have watched the tapes many times, carefully counting the water trips. There were two a night for almost four months; one a night for another five; intermittent night calls for the next four when Jeanine was teething. I was

up to four hundred sixty-three. Then I died and there was
no one to bring water. Now* I watch Mother with Jeanine in the dead of night in those weeks after I was buried.
Jeanine cries now* not for milk, but for comfort from the
sadness that everywhere surrounds her at home. Mother
comes to her room bearing more. Mother cradles Jeanine
in her lap on the rocking chair and cries until her tears run
dry. She is so thirsty, and no one comes. She sobs dry sobs
with Jeanine in her arms, and no one comes. I would give
anything—even these new thumbs of mine—to bring her
water again in the dark. Even just once. There was something sweet in the bottom of the plastic glass, in that last
sip she always saved me. I never wasted a drop.

*

The tapes. Cassidy and Nana and Father, their love
reborn through me. Maybe so. But as I watch my mother
drink in the darkened room, holding Jeanine to her breasts,
it is enough for me to think that my whole purpose in life
was to bear water to Mother in the nights. It was enough
purpose for several lives. A purpose I would have shared
with the Lexis and Doreys of my world if time had let me.
Because I am Aquarius. I see that. That is enough. I am
Aquarius. That is more than Isaiah, more than Ezekiel. I
brought water. Like Moses in the desert.

Starting at age four, I had Confraternity of Christian
Doctrine class every Sunday following the nine o'clock
Mass. It was held in the classroom in the rectory's basement that smelled faintly of bacon cooking and sewage
overflowing, as if the ventilation had been improperly
installed, air coming down into the bowels of the building

both from the rectory's greasy kitchen and its ancient bathrooms. There were twelve of us in that class. A nun from
St. Anthony School taught us. She sat me in the first seat
of the middle row, right in the center of the room, just a
few feet from her desk. It was to make sure I could read her
lips and hear her voice. The first year we mostly colored
Bible stories in a book with crayons. The next year we
also read some picture books—Moses in the reed basket
was my favorite—and learned some songs. Some of them
I'd already learned by listening to Cassidy sing in the car
or when he put me to sleep. "The River Is Wide" was my
favorite. Sometimes I put baby Moses on that river in my
mind and watched him cross in that reed basket. There
were no reeds in Bethesda, Maryland; otherwise I'd use
some to make a boat. From studying the pictures in the
book, it didn't look that difficult to do.

Sister George was fat, and she had a little brown mustache. When she laughed—and the kids in the class made
her laugh all the time—she sounded like a clockwork
cuckoo. Every time I heard it, almost every Sunday for two
and a half years, I had to look at her face to see if something was going to pop out of her mouth, do a little pirou-
ette, and slip back inside. Once, sensing what I expected,
she stuck her tongue out at me and winked. She surprised
me so much, I jumped. I loved her and the smell of cinnamon on her breath. She ate buns every Sunday morning.

When I was six, my third year in her CCD class, we
began the serious religious training needed to make First
Holy Communion. In September we learned the prayers
for confession. In October Sister gave each of us a Children's Missal to use at Mass. It had a soft black cover and a
pink ribbon glued to the spine to mark our place. A month

later Father Murray, the assistant pastor, came to hand out copies of the Baltimore Catechism from a brown box he blessed and sprinkled with holy water right in front of the class. Father Murray had pink skin like a cheap rubber doll and white hair that looked like cotton candy. Even his eyes were pinkish in the center. They reminded me of pig eyes from storybooks.

"Why did God make you?" he asked me as he offered me my catechism. I was the first because of where I sat. We had been studying the answer to that question for the last four Sunday sessions. It was the second question we learned, the one right after "Who is God?" We all knew the answer by heart. It began to play in my head—God made me to know Him and love Him in this life and to be happy with Him in the next—but I knew a better answer, a truer one. It had made Cassidy laugh when he heard me say it at supper. So I proudly presented it now to Father Murray. "He just likes to make stuff. He's like my granddad, Ned. He can't stop tinkering. Sometimes Ned forgets a nail or a screw. So does God." I held up my hands and nodded knowingly.

Father Murray started to withdraw the proffered book but stopped to look at my face. I saw his eyes go to my ears. Then he studied my still-extended hands, their eight outstretched fingers twitching in expectation. At last he withdrew the book and held it next to his chest, right over his heart. To Sister George he said, "I think this candidate is in need of further preparation. Perhaps it would be best if we put her off for another year." The nun's face drained of color so quickly, so completely, it seemed her mustache grew thick and dark. She put her hands on her hips— or where her hips should have been under her pleated reddish-brown habit—and glared.

I felt sick in the pit of my stomach. My face burned and my palms got sticky.

The eleven others in the class managed jumbled but apparently acceptable versions of the correct answer and received their books gracefully.

Not so graceful was the argument Sister and Father Murray had in the hallway. I didn't think you could fight with a priest. Mother had told me that when I wanted to know why Cassidy didn't often go to church with us on Sundays. But now, through the closed door of our classroom, the noise of their voices came into the room loud and sharp. After a few minutes of shouting, Sister George stuck her head in and asked me to come into the hallway. Father Murray stood with his arms folded across his chest. His skin was like a sunburn at the beach, it had turned so red. His head was tilted back as if he'd just taken a whiff of the contents of an old bowely diaper and had withdrawn to loftier, sweeter air.

"And why did God make you, young lady?" he repeated with a tone that mixed superiority with impatience. From where I stood I could see right up his nostrils. His cartilage was bent far to the left, and he had not a single hair in his nose. Those passageways looked like twin caves, naked and barren. More evidence, to me, of the Assembler's passion for imperfection. Or at least for variety.

I hesitated. Sister George nodded slowly. "Tell him what you've learned, Jessica. It's alright. Just tell him what you know." She put a hand on my head.

What I know, I mused silently. Here is what I know. "I have constellations and a sea on my ceiling. And animals and a clown there, too. I have Mother and Father, Nana and Ned, baby Jeanine and Cassidy. These are the things He made because He's the Maker, the Assembler. That's what He does. That's His nature. To assemble. But He forgot my ears and my thumbs and the hair up your nose. Or He didn't forget, He just wanted to leave them out. Whatever He makes, He does it just to make *Himself* happy. That's why God made me. I make Him happy." After a pause, I added, "That's what Cassidy thinks, too."

I felt Sister's hand grow heavy on my head before she removed it. Father Murray raised an eyebrow. It looked like a pale quarter moon rising in the sky of dusk. "Joe Cassidy? Is it Joe Cassidy, now? Is that the Sadducee you learn from? Joe Cassidy?"

"Joe Cassidy."

The priest dropped his arms and squared his shoulders. "I will not allow this candidate to go forward until I've met with her parents. I'm sorry, Sister, but this now borders on heresy." He bent to retrieve his box, squared his skinny shoulders again and turned sharply away. I could see the dark wet circles of the sprinkled holy water like a pox on the light brown cardboard.

"What's heresy?" I asked Sister George. Her maroon robes trembled like a bowl of black cherry Jell-O. All she did was shake her head and look sad.

The meeting was arranged for Monday night. Mother and Father didn't want to tell Cassidy the real reason for it, but they needed him to babysit after supper. They told him, instead, they were going to an organizational meeting for all the parents of children preparing for First Holy Communion.

Cassidy was happy to stay. We fed Jeanine a bottle and I burped her on my lap. She was almost a year old by then, and felt heavy as an anchor on me. She had already learned the signs for "more" and "good" just by watching me. So I tried teaching her how to say "Mama" and "bottle" and "book." "Bo-awk," I'd say over and over. "Bo-awk," holding *Goodnight Moon* between my palms for her to see. It made Mother laugh when Jeanine answered with a sound that wasn't right. When Jeanine sat on my lap, she liked to stroke the slippery plastic of my left ear's hearing aid. Her fat fingers would slide lightly over its arc, stop for a second, and slide back again, over and over, until she fell asleep. The movement caused me to hear a sound like the tumble and crash of the big breaking waves at the ocean, one after another, building, collapsing, crashing, retreating. She had Neptune's hands, with fingers that sloshed the sea. It was beautiful.

That night she fell asleep doing just that to me. Cassidy carried her upstairs. We changed her diaper and put her in her crib. He boosted me up high enough to wind the pony mobile I had let her have. We left her door partly open to hear her if she cried.

We had just settled on the couch with a plate of chocolate after-dinner mints and *The Golden Treasury of Myths and Legends* when I remembered the word.

"AceyDee, what is heresy?" He laughed so hard I could see his whole chocolate-covered tongue.

"Heresy, Jess, is somethin' you never need ta think about. It's for old folks, like me."

"Father Murray said I border heresy. He told me yesterday." Cassidy swallowed his candy fast and turned on the couch to look at me.

"He told you what?"

"That I border heresy."

"Why would he say that?"

"I gave him the wrong answer in class. He asked me the second question in the Catechism and I gave him my own answer. He didn't like it."

"Why did God make you? That's the second question, right?"

"To love Him and serve Him in this life so I can be happy with Him in the next. But I didn't say that. What's heresy?"

"It's sayin' something—well, probably it's believin' something—that's contrary ta the Church's teaching. What'd you say ta him in your answer?"

"That God made me to make Himself happy. That He just likes to make stuff. People and stars and babies. He makes them just the way He wants. Just to make Himself happy. He made Father Murray with no nose hairs. That makes God happy. A nose without hair where every other nose has it. It even makes me happy." I thought for a second, shrugged my shoulders, and added, "Or maybe He just forgot to give it hair and He's saying, 'See, it doesn't even matter. I'm still happy.'"

"Are your Ma and Pa meetin' with him over the heresy just now, Jess? Is that why they're out ta the church?"

"Sister gave me a note."

He was quiet for a while, just sitting with the big book on his lap and his eyes narrowed to slits like the eyes of Cleopatra's asp.

"Jess, don't ever let a man of the cloth convince you otherwise about God and what He is, what He done and why. Just don't. Anything you say about Him and His ways is as good as what those old, dried-up Pharisees have ta say. Especially Father Murray and that Father Larrie. They're nothing but mouse farts in black sacks."

"He told Sister I shouldn't study anymore for my First Communion. He said I wasn't ready."

"We'll see about that," he said. I began to open the book.

"What's a Sadducee?" I asked him, just then remembering the word.

"Someone who don't take any crap from a Pharisee," Cassidy said. He looked off into the distance for a second, then down at the book. "Grendel," he said low and rumbly. "Let's read what happens ta Grendel."

Beowulf reminded me of Theseus. I guessed both were Sadducees, like Cassidy.

I was in bed in the dark with my stars when Mother and Father returned. Even with my door closed, their voices were loud. "I will, too, Ford. I will, too! I'll settle with Murray and then go on ta Larrie. I will!" Jeanine woke and cried for a minute and their voices faded. On my ceiling the constellations shone. They made me happy, the Horse, the Crab, both Bears, the Water Bearer. The joy I took from their existence convinced me I was right about God. Somehow, the stuff He made, stars and people, even Minotaurs and Grendels, made Him happy. Sometimes He was a show-off.

It was my short brown hair that finally got me expelled from the preparations for First Holy Communion a month later. Initially, Father Murray relented, at least a little bit, and let me continue taking instruction with the class. Provisional time, he called it during that meeting with Mother and Father and me later that week.

"Provisional, provisional time," he intoned from behind his big black desk. I counted three crucifixes and seven

likenesses of the Blessed Virgin Mary. He seemed to keep
his head bent, reverently perhaps, in the presence of all
that religious symbolism, but really maybe so I couldn't
look up there again. What he meant was another wrong
answer, another lapse into shadowy theology, and I would
be switched to a different and younger CCD group, forced
to wait out the year singing and coloring. No white dress,
no lace veil, no patent leather pumps, no red rose wrist
corsage for me in May.

Every week he came into the room, skinny, pale, and
pink as raw bacon, and asked his questions. Sister had
drilled the answers into us the week before.

Who is God?

What is sin?

What is grace?

What is confession?

Who is man?

I did fine, always the first to be asked, the first to answer,
the first to chant the responses: the Maker of Heaven and
Earth, of all that is seen and unseen. (He made my unseen
thumbs, or my thumbs unseen. But I held back.) Sister
smiled. Father Murray nodded gravely, hoping for more.
I stilled my lips.

It is an offense against the law of God. Venial sin is
lesser, mortal is grave. (But truth was never a sin. Timmy
was ugly. He was that, and fat, as I was deaf and shy of
bones. No sin in any of that, I thought. But I held back.)
Sister nodded. Father nodded. I nodded.

It is a sharing in the very life of God. Sanctifying. Sacra-
mental. (But it was actual grace I prized, the grace in being.
It was this I gave God, this grace from me to Him. What
Maker doesn't take the life and soul of all He makes to His

heart? It's what makes the Maker happy. But I held back.) Sister's face was beatific, the priest's soft as snow.

It is when we confess our sins to a priest and ask God's forgiveness. (The hardest one, but I fought to contain myself. I prayed for grace. I was almost seven. I had been full of forgiveness since the moment of my birth. In the cold of the delivery room, with blue fingers, only eight, in the silence of the new breath in me, I had forgiven my doctor, had forgiven my God, for what I was, was not. I was proud of this. It was my first act of faith, my first creation, a forgiven God. But for Father Murray, forgiveness bent only in a single direction. My tongue was still.) Very good, said the nun. Yes, added Father Murray, his first word to me since provisional, provisional.

Man is a being created in the image and likeness of God. (The easiest one for me, because it explained so much about the Assembler, about me. If all men are created imperfect yet reflect the image of the Assembler, then He, too, surely must share in those same imperfections. Why else would He be so quick to forgive? Why else would we?) Yes, he said, we are all God's children. More words that came without a smile.

Then, the following week, came transubstantiation. My undoing. It was the sixth Sunday in Provisional, Provisional Time. Sister George showed us the drawings of the priest consecrating the bread and the wine. She told us how that became the Body and the Blood of Jesus. Still looks like bread and wine, tastes like bread and wine, but the priest changed it into something entirely different, in a second, with some few words of blessing. Now the bread wasn't bread, the wine wasn't wine. The power of the priest's blessing prevailed over the power of nature. I was fascinated. Transfixed, with the idea. The power of blessing over the power of nature.

That Sunday night and every night that week, I stood on the side of the tub and fixed myself in the mirror with my gaze. I could have worked on my too-small chin to enlarge it like Mother's, or on my too-wide eyes to draw them closer like Father's, or on my flopping ears. Instead, I extended my hands and fingers before me and blessed my reflection. "Platinum blond hair," I intoned with the same grave authority I'd heard from the altar each Sunday. I moved my hands like the priest at Mass, slicing my fingers through the brittle, reflected air. "Below my ears and soft as cats' fur," I concluded my blessing.

I had hoped—no, expected—to wake and see the silver-yellow hair grown magically in the night. At four a.m., I watched Mother's face as she accepted my water, hoping to see the surprise in her eyes. I returned to the bathroom and tried again. A new hairbrush I bought at the drugstore with Nana's birthday money, a bright white one never before used, lay on the sink ready to stroke the long shiny strands to the blessed count of a hundred. I slept. Morning came and my mouse-brown hair sat like a mop on my head.

I was saddened by my old looks that first morning. Later, after school, I talked to Mother about what I was doing, and to Father over supper and to Cassidy between stories. Mother thought it was sweet, Father foolish, and Cassidy, a start.

"But you don't need different hair now, Jess," Mother said peeling potatoes at the sink. "And when you're a grown-up woman you can grow it long and color it at the hairdresser's."

When, an hour later, I passed Father those same potatoes, albeit in a different state of being, now mashed with
butter and sour cream, I asked him simply if transubstantiation would work on my hair. If I wanted it long and platinum blond. "Jess, we're not much on that sort of foolishness
in this family. Hair is what hair is, is what I think. You've
got perfectly fine hair for a young girl. Don't go thinking
about dying it. In time it will naturally go to a shade lighter
just like your Mom's. Some of that gravy, please."

As she handed him the boat, Mother's eyes were fixed
on mine.

Cassidy considered my question at length before reply-
ing. "I don't see a change just yet, Jess. But it takes a priest
years of trainin' before he gets the hang of it. I say keep
tryin'. What's the harm in it?" He opened the book.

"Was the Minotaur transubstantiated?" I asked as he
flipped through the colored pictures on the pages. "Did he
start out as a bull and make himself half man? Or a man and
make himself half bull?"

"I don't think so, Jess. It's just the way he was made right
from the start. Maybe he's meant ta show there's some bad
parts in all men. All people." He looked at me as I fingered
my hair where it came to the tops of my ears. "Could be
a touch lighter, now that I study it. Hard ta say really.
Where'd we leave off?"

"Jason has just taken the Golden Fleece."

"So he has. So he did."

Beginning that night, I added dimples to the blessing.
I'd wanted them since Jeanine had been born. She had
them and they made her look cute. What was the harm in
trying? My fingers flashed and flew in the mirrored light,
cutting away the unneeded flesh of both my cheeks, as,

standing on the rim of the tub, I prayed the blessing for the loss of substance.

By Saturday night, though, a new thought had overtaken me as I stared at my familiar face in the mirror. Perhaps my hair had become as lustrous as that shiny silvery blond mane I wanted, but I just couldn't *see* it. Just like the bread and the wine. It wasn't a change you could see. Perhaps the *nature of my hair* had changed, but its outward sign remained the same. I sensed in my heart at that moment the full understanding of the mystery at hand and went armed with it to Sister's class the next morning.

As always, we practiced our answers with her, in singsong unison, before Father Murray opened the classroom door, walking stiff as Moses's staff, as if there were nothing more important in all the mystical world than reaching the Mount Horeb of a desk at the front of the room.

We stood and said together, "Good morning, Father Murray." He smiled and gently touched the cross of his handheld rosary to his thin lips. "Good morning, children. Please take your seats." Sister extended a hand toward us and we sat. "Well. Now you've had a full week to learn transubstantiation. I'm sure it will be an easy morning here then." He walked to my desk. "Jennifer," he said. I stood, only because his slitty pink eyes were fixed on my face. "What is meant by 'transubstantiation'?" His eyebrows rose a quarter of an inch. He repeated, "Transubstantiation." The word was slow in coming out of his mouth, like a long train coming out of a tunnel.

I swear I didn't mean to say it. But it was the sight of his nose hairs—I mean, the absence of their sighting—that spurred me on; the dark, devoid cave in the center of his face that pushed me. That and the error in my name, as if to him I had been transubstantiated into someone else entirely, a Jennifer. I thought all at once, "Maybe he does have nose hairs. Maybe he transubstantiated that hair-naked space into a garden of dense black growth, but no one can see it." He was a priest, an old priest, after all, and well practiced in these things, an expert on transubstantiation. So I answered in a way I thought would impress him about my depth of understanding.

"I have platinum blond hair. And it's long and soft, way past my ears. I did it every night last week. In the mirror in my bathroom, standing on the side of my tub. With my hands and a blessing." I moved my hands in well-practiced slashes through space. "That's what transubstantiation is. Changing things into other things. I bet you really have nose hair. You transubstantiated it, so it's really there but we can't see it. Transubstantiation. The power of blessing over the power of nature." For effect, I fluffed the dagger ends of my new long locks with my fingertips. "Do you like my dimples?" I smiled coyly.

Father Murray's face flashed. He started to point a bony finger at me but lowered his hand and took a big step back. "What?" he managed to say after a few deep breaths. "Hair and dimples? Transubstantiation? This is the kind of heresy that sends people to an eternity of Hell, Jennifer!" His voice rose in pitch.

"Nobody goes to Hell," I said with certainty. "Cassidy told me that. It doesn't make sense that God would send anyone He made there. Even the Minotaur or Medusa. Especially the Minotaur. It wouldn't be fair because that's how the Assembler—uh, I mean God—made them. Imperfect in just the way He's imperfect. So He's got to forgive. And Cassidy says Hell doesn't even exist."

The priest's breath stuck in his chest. Finally, he let it out. A little line of sweat had broken out on his neck, just above his white collar. "Oh, Hell exists, young lady. I assure you it exists. And it exists just for people like that drunkard Joe Cassidy. And you can tell him that the next time you see him for a discussion of theology!" He dug at his pale neck with the side of his thumb.

"But what about God's forgiveness? He always forgives. He said so. And I forgive Him." I held up my hands for the priest to see. "So we're even."

Father Murray bent low so his face was just opposite mine. Slowly, so the words were separated by great gulfs, he said, "Not. If. You. Go. To. Hell. There. Is. No. Forgiveness. In. Hell."

Two or three of the other children had begun to giggle. A girl in the first row smiled and said, "Jessica's going to Hell," but Sister clapped her hands three times to get our attention. Even Father Murray rose from his crouch to look at her.

"Thank you, Father, for coming this morning. Perhaps we shall continue next Sunday. Time to sing some songs, children. Say good-bye to Father Murray." She walked to the door and held it open. He left at a brisk pace. She slammed the door missing his retreating left heel by inches.

Since he was associate pastor of St. Anthony's Church, Father Murray's decision was law. I was not allowed to make my First Holy Communion the coming spring. I was sent back a class to relearn the dogma that had eluded me. He would follow my progress carefully before deciding to let me begin again on the route to that sacrament the next fall. He was worried, he told my parents, that my "mental capacity" was diminished to such an extent that I may never qualify for Communion. And he warned them, keep me away from unsavory, heretical influences. Pagan influences. The Minotaur. Medusa. In Heaven! "What kind of Heaven does she see," he nearly shouted, "if it's populated by monsters of myth and legend?"

Cassidy was steamed when he heard about it. He tried to get an appointment to meet with Father Murray but was denied. He managed to get Father Larrie on the phone. Father Larrie listened patiently, but wouldn't meet with him either. Father Larrie merely said he would look into the question of my suitability for Communion training.

At the dinner table that Sunday night, Cassidy kept repeating, "diminished mental capacity" and then shaking his head in bewilderment. He told Father when they started clearing, "I'll diminish their goddamn teeth, I get in a room with them alone. Like I shoulda done nineteen years ago, Ford, over Joey. They were a pair of jackasses young and are a pair of jackasses old. Diminished mental capacity, those dried-up old bastards."

"Joe," said Father, nodding in my direction.

"I mean it, Ford. The time of reckoning has come."

That night we read the myth of Perseus and Medusa again. And Pegasus and Andromeda. Later in bed they were there with me, shining down from the plaster sky. Except for Medusa the Gorgon. She was dead by Perseus's arm and Hermes's sword. Good. God, give her a new head in heaven, right from the box. I went to sleep seeing her gleaming hair blowing in the wind as she stood on the ocean's perch. The hair was like silver strings, but soft like cats' fur.

First grade was an easy year, except for CCD and soccer again. We went two and four. Timmy twisted his knee. Not playing soccer, but walking to the oranges and Gatorade table at halftime. Lexi became goalie for two games while he healed and ate potato chips with his parents on the sidelines. We won them both. Her body bath replaced Timmy's creosote in the air. I watched her more than the action on the field. Her hair was platinum blond. Long and gleaming like the night moon's silver trail on the sea that led Odysseus home.

She told me to turn around, face the play, thirty-seven times during those two games. She had hair like Pegasus's tail.

I left my regular class and went to third grade for reading and math every day. I learned cursive at home from Father and Cassidy. I couldn't draw to save my life, but I was good at naming colors. I would always spot the gray in greens, the teal in blues. I just couldn't draw a sailboat.

Spring came and went. Jeanine was walking and talking. She stopped learning new signs as she learned to speak. Cassidy read to her, now, at seven thirty while I did my homework. Then it was my turn at eight. If he couldn't come, Mother or Father read to me. I followed the words with my eyes. Sometimes I couldn't stop my hands from moving. Usually I just made the signs for the story we were doing. But sometimes, my hands moved like they had in the mirror of my bathroom when I tried mastering transubstantiation. I didn't say it to anyone, but sometimes I wanted the myths and legends to be real. To come alive. Right off the page, out of the brilliantly colored pictures. My thumbless hands were hungry for magic.

In late summer, just before second grade was to begin, we drove to Florida to visit Nana and Ned. We drove for two days, stayed with them for three, and then drove two more days back home. Jeanine slept and then cried, or sometimes cried and then slept, in the car seat next to me, unless I read to her or she was eating. I read her nine books eleven times each on the way down. She received three new books as travel presents from Nana and Ned, and I placed them in rotation for reading on the way home. Most of the time, Mother, who sat in the front seat next to Father, dozed off before Jeanine's eyes had fully closed. Then I placed my pillow against the door window so she could sleep with her head supported. She had announced her pregnancy the night before we left. Father stood behind her, smiling with his hand on her shoulder. Jeanine cried when she heard the news. To be fair, at almost two, Jeanine had taken to crying at the drop of a hat. Or the ring of the doorbell. Or the smell of pepperoni pizza. Cassidy told her he was buying us ice cream cones one hot Saturday afternoon and she started crying.

It was hotter in Florida in early September than in Bethesda, Maryland, in the height of the summer. But Florida had better clouds. They were bigger and whiter and faster than our clouds. We'd all go to the beach in the morning before the day got too hot. I couldn't get wet above my waist because of my hearing apparatus, so most of the day I sat in the shade of a red-striped umbrella and read, or lay on my back watching the clouds sail by. Most were too round and fat to be anything but clouds, but often in late morning, as the breeze off the ocean stiffened, some of them were torn into strips and bits. These I could piece together into familiar shapes—boats, animals, major gods

of antiquity, a can of mushroom soup. The wattle neck of
Father Larrie.

Nana and Ned had a dog, a golden retriever named Jed.
They let me take him for walks in the evenings, along the
beach, all by myself. Jed could get wet and swim whenever
he wanted, and if I threw a stick into the surf, he'd charge
right in and get it. When he came out and ran to me with
his mouth clamped on the wet wood, he shook his yellow
coat till it reminded me of Lexi's hair when she ran with
her ponytail untied. Except Jed sprayed me with sandy sea
water that smelled faintly of gasoline, whereas Lexi was
dry and all Jean Naté.

I walked the beach those late afternoons, scanning the
surf for Aphrodite rising up on a cushion of white foam.
Every porpoise playing in the evening waters seemed her in
disguise, smiling at me at the top of her leap. I was tempted
to hold out my hands and move them in a blessing through
the air, but I had promised Father, so I didn't.

On my last afternoon walk, the west wind was high.
The sound of the wind-driven water was bright green
whisperings in my ears, hollow and luminous like the low
notes of a sad song. That music brought me to the water's
edge. I stepped in a few paces, and the coral foam gripped
my ankles. The gurgled green song of the sea grew louder
in my ears. The foam then was to my thigh. The water was
warm and soft like the music in the wind. I bent slightly
and brought my face to the skin of the sea. A swell rose
to meet me. I kissed its lips. I felt the tug of the receding
waves pull at me. I stepped once, twice, three times further out. The music softened to a golden voice made weak
by the sight of beauty. I looked to my yellow bathing suit
darkened to my chest by the sea. The song now was the

whisper in a shell. I covered my ears with my hands. The whisper was light as a feather, soft and shiny and alive. A wave moved past me and seconds later began its strong retreat. My right foot rose from the sand, drifted forward an inch. The whisper in my ear was a sad, certain yes. I will dive into the sea and swim out, far out, to the whispering song, I thought. Then I felt a creature scrape past my back. Frightened, I turned. Jed began to bark and growl as he paddled around me, placing himself between me and the wind and the waves and the whisper. His bark was loud and guttural, wet and incessant. The whispered song of the sea was stilled. I turned and walked to shore.

We drove home to Maryland the next morning. Mother helped me write a thank-you note to Nana and Ned for the fun time they showed us. I tried to draw a likeness of Jed on the reverse side of the card, to thank him. I tried to make him look like he was barking, but the way I rounded his lips made him look more like he was singing.

School began again. Second grade was easy. I went to fourth grade twice a day for math and reading. Our soccer team went five and two. Timmy decided not to play. Father would not consider my quitting the team. I looked at Lexi less and less but smelled her just as much. I did not practice transubstantiation. My second tour of provisional, provisional time went well. For some reason, it was Father Larrie who sat behind the desk now each Sunday when he came to ask the stupid questions. I answered well. Father Larrie smiled at me sometimes. Once or twice, I even thought he would have smiled if I had made a mistake.

Mother's belly swelled as the months went by.

Jeanine's second birthday came. Cassidy came to the party we had for her, the day after Thanksgiving that year, with eyes whiskey-wet at noon. When we sang her "Happy Birthday," he barely lifted his voice. The rest of that week he only read to us once. His face was like the ocean running out from the sand, roiled and angry and rough.

7

THE COMFORT OF SILENCE

Cassidy continued to drink heavily. Some evenings he called on the phone to tell Father he wasn't coming for supper or to read books with me or BJ, as Jeanine was being called. But even on those nights he'd sometimes arrive, haggard and stumbling, coming like a blind man into the kitchen and banging his hip against the Formica table as he tried to negotiate his way to his chair. Then he listed left or right on the rough whiskey sea inside of him and mumbled on about his bad day at work, the heartless weight of Christmas mail, the needless parcels needing to be weighed and postaged, the dull folks buying ten-dollar money orders to give to their kids as presents. This last gripe he repeated again and again. He was moved, temporarily, to the loading docks. He refused the coffee Mother offered and the food we were eating. Sometimes Father tried to convince him to sleep the night on the living room couch rather than drive home. If Father threw a bottle of rye into the bargain, he stayed. On those occasions, I saw him in the morning before I went off to school or out to play. Usually, there was a tumbler of whiskey in his hand even at that early hour. His eyes were red and tinged with yellow in the whites like a poorly beaten egg, and his breath was wormy. His breath those mornings when I went to hug him was the primordial air itself, the mushroomy wick of what tunnels below.

"You okay?" I signed each time. Yes, he'd answer flatly, sipping his rye. Finally, three days before Christmas, he said nothing in reply to my question. Instead he broke into tears. Whether he did it purposefully or not, I don't know, but the way his left hand went to his wet eyes and slid down his cheeks seemed to be the sign for "sad" or "sorrowful." The death in his breath blew at me. The whiskey in his right hand trembled.

"Joey?" I mouthed slowly. I knew it was. I had heard Mother and Father talking about it over the past few days. He looked at me with startle in his face. "Sorry," I signed, rubbing my fisted right hand in circles over my heart. I placed my hand on his wrist. He went to take another sip but I held on tight. He jerked his hand free and began to say something. His face seemed full of pained apology, but he fell into silence. There was comfort in that silence, it seemed, like the comfort of the confessional's private whisper that I'd practiced twice in CCD class. He blankly looked past me, through me and past me, and signed, "Joey and more." The fingertips of both hands banged together twice, and then twice again. More and more. Some whiskey dripped onto the tabletop, forming the number eight as two pools merged. I remembered the gravestones with the identical dates of death. Today was the anniversary.

"Joey and Rose Mary?" I finger-spelled. "Twenty years today?" He went to drink and caught himself. He brought the tumbler back down on the top of the coffee table with such force the loud *bang* made me turn my head to see if he'd shattered the glass.

"That," he signed, "that and more." There was nothing but hopeless, vacant space in his eyes. And our resorting to unspoken communication, to sign, seemed to expand that void to engulf us both. I didn't have the heart to brush my right index finger down over my left palm to ask the question, "What?" Instead, I put my arms around his neck, locked my fingers, and pressed him as hard as I could. I felt his torso lean to the table and his arm reach for his drink. "You will be okay," I said into his ear as perfectly as I could. He put his glass down, gently this time, and tied me up tight with his arms. He kissed my cheek and cried. Kissed it again and was quiet.

He held me like that until Mother came in with BJ and sent me and her back to my room to play. "You will be okay" were the last words I said to him. He had gone home half an hour later when I came downstairs, and I was dead only twelve hours after that.

Here's how I died: My voice, my imperfect voice, died first. My throat grew so tight, so constricted, I had no air for my dysmorphic words. My breath was blocky and thick, so difficult to move beyond the beefy tissues of my throat, I spent every joule of my body's energy pushing the frozen bellows of my chest. Soon my arms grew limp, too weak and too tired to form a sentence, a phrase, a word in sign. I sat in my chair in my room hearing at first the dull hiss of the cool-mist vaporizer Mother shot my way. My leaden arms drooped at my sides like the stems of a dying plant. My mouth hung open. My chest caved with each impossibly stridulous breath until I thought I felt my breastbone kiss my spinal column. My ears, my drilled ears, died next. At ten that night the hiss softened to a gentle breeze like the one that ruffled the canopy of the trees in high summer. And that sound slowly waned to become the longingly hollow, caressing susurrus of a seashell. The sound was familiar and frightening. Mother came in with a cool cloth and spoke. I heard nothing. I saw her lips move a little but nothing seemed to drop to my eyes, my lips. I remember the look of panic on her face. The sound of the sea in the shell ceased. A last difficult breath smelled richly of fungus and damp.

That's how I died: as silently as I was born.

*

Then I was here* and the movies began.

It is not a good thing to have here* in heaven, the last memory of your mother's face full of panic over your death.

I see the death, I see the panic, and it seems I know nothing of my existence, have learned nothing from the exercise of the tapes. The tapes are as deaf and dead as my ears in the womb, in the tomb. They teach me nothing. I am no Isaiah, no Ezekiel, no Moses. Only a girl with no thumbs whose life was bookended by silence and despair. The meaning of my life? It is not to be found in the tapes.

I see the panic on my mother's face. Mercifully, I cannot hear her screams.

PART TWO
ACT OF GOD

8

NIGHT ADVANCES

There is a police investigation of my death. It is a routine procedure when a child is brought in dead by the rescue squad. I was dead for six minutes when they arrived at my room. Father's attempt to give me rescue breathing was futile. He knelt by my bedside with his dry lips on mine and blew as forcibly as he could while Mother called 911 and, later, did chest compressions, just as she had learned in her Red Cross CPR class. My blood surged under the frantic weight of her palms, but it did no good. My blood was brown by then, brown and thick as sludge. My upper airway was obstructed and none of Father's furious air went beyond my vocal cords.

The EMS techs arrive. One of them manages to insert an endotracheal tube down my airway, which relieves the obstruction, but by then it is much, much too late. Five minutes, to be exact. Cassidy could make you cry if he sang that long, and five minutes without oxygen makes you dead. They try to restart my heart. They push drugs down the tube into my lungs and into a vein in my arm. It does no good.

Mother stands near my bedside staring blankly during this time, her frozen gaze directed to the dark outside my window. Her face registers no emotion but shock. It seems to darken, to take on the color of the night. Her mouth is open a fraction of an inch and, if I look closely, I can see my own fixed the same. It is the tube that parts my lips; shock, my mother's. Neither of us blinks. Our eyes are offered to the dry air of the house, our vision to the advance of the night. Her hair is swirled wildly as if a great wind had coursed through the room, whipping her long strands where it will. But it is from the position she held those eleven minutes working over my breastbone with the palm of her hand. My hair is too short to be disheveled.

Father creeps closer to the working men as their nine minutes of effort spin out. It is not so much shock on his face as bewilderment. His slow encroachment on their space seems like the action of a curious child who wants to understand what he is viewing from too far a distance. Just another few feet closer and it will all make sense, he says with his baby steps.

The men are still breathing for me with their black Ambu bags and banging on my chest and squirting drugs into my vein as they load me onto a stretcher and bring me downstairs to their truck for the ride to the emergency room. Mother and Father follow behind in their car. Mrs. Sampson from across the street stays with BJ, who sleeps through it all.

In the emergency room, my hearing aids gleam under the intense light from the overhead lamp as Dr. Arthur

Jamison pounds my chest with the fury of an angry man in a brawl. Another doctor shines a light into my eyes and shakes his head. "Fixed and dilated," he says.

Jamison gives my breastbone a last frustrated shove and announces, "Ten forty-two. Let's call it." A nurse closes off the IV drip; a respiratory therapist detaches the Ambu bag from the tube in my airway. I am officially dead.

But even in death I still fascinate my doctors. Jamison places both gloved hands on my head and rolls it from side to side so he can inspect my ears and their hardware. "Huh," he manages. He reaches down and takes my right hand into his. He squeezes the thumbless spot near my index finger and moves his hand up the length of my forearm, pressing every inch or so for the missing bone. "Huh," he says again. He pulls his gloves off with a snap that sounds like the whip of the animal trainer at the circus. He leaves to find my parents.

I am surprised Mother and Father don't cry right away in the emergency room when Jamison tells them I am dead. Perhaps their immediate tears would have buffered their anger over what was to happen. Perhaps, if they had fallen into each other's arms and sobbed in pain, they would have spent themselves emotionally too much to grow angry over what was to come. There are only a few seconds between the doctor's terrible declarative sentence, "I'm sorry, Jessica didn't make it," and the next about the police needing to clarify the events of the evening. Father, in those few moments, does put his arm around Mother and tugs her closer. And Mother does take a deep breath and pauses. Is this the advance of tears? Perhaps. And perhaps if Dr. Jamison had waited just a moment longer they would have come, the tears. Was he so busy he could not wait? Was he, at thirty-six, already so jaded about the death of a child? Or was it the death of *this* particular child, this two-"huh" deformed child, that propelled him through the event so tranquilly? Nothing on the tape clarifies this for me.

He says, "I'm sorry, Jessica didn't make it . . . and the police have some questions for you both. We'll let you see her first."

It's then, just there and then, that both their faces look as if they'd been stabbed through the heart.

"The police? Why the police?" a wounded Father asks. "What for?"

"They'll explain it all. Everything. Just answer them honestly."

Mother takes a half step forward. "What is the. . . ," she starts, but Jamison is already turning away, leading them to my cubicle, my corpse. Number Sixteen, the cubicle, a number with no particular resonance.

"The nurses did their best to clean her up. But we have to leave the tubes and IVs in place until after the autopsy."

The next nine minutes of the tape break my heart. Me on the gurney. Mother and Father holding on to me, embracing me, sobbing over me. The pain pouring out of them, and there is nothing I can do. Minute after minute, their arms unfelt around my shoulders, my thighs. Their faces buried in my chest, ruined breaths puffing my pajama top numbly until it is too wet to rise again. Mother kissing the tips of my ears so softly, that even if I were alive I would have to strain to feel it.

But the seed of anger, of recrimination, had been planted before they spilled their sorrow. The seed of anger scattered in the ripped furrows of their souls. And more seed to come. What is that parable about the Kingdom of God and the sower of seed? Yes, more to come, sadly, even with kind Dr. Burke.

The nine minutes are mercifully finished. Burke walks in. He zips open the curtain and stands there looking uncertain and unfit for the job at hand. It is midnight. Night advances like the Kingdom coming. "Kate . . . Ford. I am so sorry," he begins. They look up with faces flushed and streaked with tears, their hands unable to lift from my body to be shaken in grief.

"How . . . how could she die so quickly? It was just a cold this afternoon. A runny nose, hardly even a sore throat. What . . . how is this possible?" Mother doesn't know what else to say. She is just now leaving her disbelief that the events of the past hour were real, that her child is dead. She can barely take her eyes off the plastic tube taped to the left corner of my mouth half convinced I will awaken and pull it out.

She steals a quick look at Burke. He shrugs his shoulders and looks away. At the first viewing of the tape I missed the significance of Burke's unstudied reply: "I wish you had called. Maybe . . ." That's all he says, "I wish you had called. Maybe . . ." But now I see how those words strike like darts at my parents, work their way deep into their too-fertile memories, waiting the drenching rain of vengeance.

*

"Vengeance is mine!" the Assembler likes to say to me. "No, it's not," I tell him. He never argues the point. He knows too well the stories His Son told. The Prodigal Son. The Tax Collector. The Woman at the Well. In the end, it's people who own vengeance, who will not pardon the injustice. He forgives, forgets. Forgives.

He is a detective from the DC Police Juvenile Homicide Squad, and looks it. His tan suit jacket is shapeless and wrinkled. A small yellow encrustation of yolk from the morning's breakfast special streaks down his left lapel in a zigzag pattern. At a quick glance, it might be a metal insignia pin of some private club—the Blitzkrieg Club, say—but upon further inspection it's clearly egg yolk. It matches in color and texture the yellow dots that stipple his blue tie. He drinks black coffee from a cheap paper cup and coughs with each swallow. He mutters in short bursts when others are speaking as if he is a bomb with a quirky fuse. As if he wants to remind you, he might go off at any instant. And he is young looking, with a face that hasn't gone to the trouble of forming a crease or wrinkle even after a decade and a half of dead children.

But it is his heart that is rucked and seamed by the endless flow of babies' blood down the years, and by the erosion of joy his memories carve. Heads caved against fireplace brick so red it was hard to see the blood but not the creamy mash of brain; limbs stiffened by an epoxy of ooze from hundreds of cigarette burns; tiny necks snapped by a shake and shout—"STOP CRYING!" Oh, they were made to stop, alright. Sprung joints, splintered bones, carved skin. And in the face of all this mayhem and death, the charade of denial by the parent, the babysitter, the sibling. Oh, it's never them. Never. Except when it is. And to Officer Mattingly these fifteen years, that was pretty much always.

Mattingly sits in a chair in the consultation room of the emergency room, a brown clipboard resting on a desk.

"First," he says with the coffee cup just under his lower lip, "I'm terribly sorry for your loss. It's gotta be tough for you both." He sips and swallows and coughs. "But if you'd bear with me for a few minutes here, I just got to go over the last hours of the decedent's life. Forms to fill out for the ME's office. Won't take too long. Been a long night for you already. Gotta be tough for you." He sips and swallows again. He times his cough to coincide with the click of the cup's bottom hitting the desktop. "So, why don't we start with you, Mrs. Jackson. What happened?"

Mother sits next to Father on a bench across the room from the detective. The distance seems odd to her. She has the sense she is a member of a theater audience who has just now been singled out by the lead actor to join the performance. It is at once reassuring and unsettling. She stares at the floor, momentarily unable to formulate a beginning thought. "Like, how was she this morning?" Mattingly suggests.

Mother's ears do not register the detective's prompt. Her brain is filled instead with the sight of me embracing a weeping Joe Cassidy, comforting him over the lifetime sadness of his loss of son and wife. Cassidy, she thinks, we haven't told Cassidy. Startled at this realization, she looks to Father seated next to her.

"Ma'am?" Mattingly adds. "This morning. How was she?" He writes a note in the margin of his Parental Interview Form: *12:31 a.m. 12/23/04. Decedent's mother reluctant to give her account of day's events. Looks to decedent's father for ? prompt.*

"This morning? This morning Jess was fine. She woke late—school was out for Christmas break—went over to her friend's house to play most of the day. Came home before it got dark. Then she was a little sick but, you know, ate supper and talked about her day at Tina's."

"A little sick, ma'am?" Detective Mattingly says looking up from his jottings.

"Like a cold. A runny nose, little scratchy throat. She coughed once or twice during the meal but we—"

"Kid coughed, kid coughed," he mutters and writes. Then he coughs.

"—but we didn't think much of it. Then she went up and had her bath and put on her pj's. That was—"

"Who did the bath, ma'am? You or the father?"

"The bath? She did the bath. She was independent in her bathing and whatnot."

"Seven year old," he mutters. *Bath, alone.*

"Seven but independent," Mother stresses, looking to Father for his approval. "I don't know what you want me to say, Detective. What now?" I can hear her voice rise in pitch.

"Well, ma'am, it's past bath time and she's okay. What happens next?"

"I . . . uh . . . I don't know, exactly. She was in her room, reading, and I was getting our other child ready for bed. BJ. And Ford, Ford was doing the kitchen cleanup."

"Father does dishes."

"When did you see her next?"

"Next was after I got BJ down. It was probably near eight or so. She was making this noise . . . She didn't look sick or troubled by it. But she sounded . . . you know, like a seal every time she coughed. Like a seal barking. The first time I heard it, I even laughed. At her sounding like a seal—"

Laughed at the kid. Sound like a seal.

"—and I went and looked in our home health care book and they suggested a cool-mist vaporizer and then Ford went into her room and heard it. Her cough. So, then . . . Ford went out and got a vaporizer at CVS, and I sat with her for a while as she was reading and I . . ." Mother stops and lets her tears fall again. She sees me in my chair struggling with the big Greek words in *D'Aulaires' Book of Greek Myths*. Heph-aes-tus, Mother remembers pronouncing for me, syllable by syllable. "I helped her with some of the big words." Mother blots her tears with the Kleenex a nurse had given.

"Anything else, ma'am?"

"I felt her forehead, and she didn't feel warm. We had Tylenol in the cabinet, but she didn't feel like she had a fever. And then, then Ford came back and I set up the humidifier and—"

"Ma'am, vaporizer or humidifier? Earlier you said 'vaporizer.'"

Mother looks at Father and shrugs. Father opens his mouth to speak, but Mattingly holds up his pen like the baton of a symphony conductor and says, "Wait your turn, Dad. You'll get your turn. Right now I want to know what Mom remembers."

"I don't know. I don't remember what it said on the box. I just poured water in the hole and plugged it in. I aimed it at Jess's face where she sat reading."

"*Aimed it. Daughter's face.*"

"What?" Mother asks, sounding confused and exasperated. "What?"

"And next what happens?"

"I think . . . she seemed to get a little better. That coughing noise slowed down some for a while. But then at eight thirty or maybe nine, she started another noise with her breathing. Like a crowing sound when she inhaled. Just when she inhaled. But she was sitting there in her chair, just reading and didn't have a fever. I asked her if she had a sore throat or a pain anywhere, and she just said no. So I left her to—"

"*Left the kid,*" Mattingly mutters and makes a note on his forms.

"—to do more housework. With Christmas coming and all."

"*Christmas. Christ, Christmas.*" He shakes his head.

Mother stops her recounting and stares at the floor. She sees me breathing, the hollow at the base of my neck growing deep as a cave with each inspiration, my neck muscles straining like wire pulleys, my nose flaring like a breathless horse in a race. "I wanted to give the mist some time to work," she whispers.

I want to comfort her, to reach out to her and reassure her.

"So now it's what time? Nine? Nine thirty?"

"Maybe closer to ten," Mother says with a flat voice.

"*All the way to ten.*"

"I came into her room with a cool cloth to freshen her face. She . . . she was vacant, her face was vacant. She could barely breathe. Her arms were limp. And her legs. I called her name. I called it again. She didn't recognize me. Or hear me." Mother covers her face with her hands and closes her eyes in the futile hope the vision will fade.

"Go on," Mattingly says tapping his pen on the desk.

Mother uncovers her face and says, slowly, "I shouted for Ford. I went to our bedroom and dialed 911. I went back to Jess's room. Ford had her on the bed and she . . ." Mother buries her face in her hands and weeps. Father encircles her with his arm, wrapping it lightly around her shoulders, and he cries, too. Mattingly sips from his coffee, and, finding how much it has cooled, swallows half the contents of the container in five gulps. He coughs and waits.

"Then we did CPR," Father says.

"Not your turn yet, Dad. Still listening to the wife's version."

"This is not a *version* of the story, Detective. This is a recounting of the events of the night. I agree with everything Kate has told you about the day. At least that part of it I was there for." He takes his arm from around Mother and sits straight in his chair. "So it is too my turn. We lost our daughter tonight, Detective, and we'd appreciate a little compassion and understanding for the pain we are going through."

Compassion. "So, I haven't heard anyone mention a call to your doctor yet. She did have one, didn't she, a pediatrician?" He scans the sheet of paper on his clipboard for my name. "Jessica did see a pediatrician, right?"

"Of course. Dr. Burke. He was here an hour ago. You missed him."

"Well, with all due respect, sir, *and compassion,* the question is why didn't you call him when the girl got bad? And if you want, you can go first on that one and then the missus."

"Because until the last few minutes, Jess didn't appear to be troubled by any of the symptoms she was having. The cough, the noisy breathing. She felt fine. The book even mentioned that about the croup. How it's rare after infancy and usually is more of a nuisance than a serious illness in the older child. We didn't think we should bother Dr. Burke after hours with a call."

Didn't bother, Mattingly writes. "Ma'am?" he asks.

Mother sits, mute and crying.

He takes pictures of my body in Cubicle Sixteen before he follows Mother and Father home. Mrs. Sampson is sitting on the couch in the living room when they come into the house. She cries in Mother's arms when she hears the news. Mother's belly is so distended by her pregnancy, Mrs. Sampson can barely get her arms around her. Her plump hands start to pat Mother's sides, then grab folds of her coat and desperately hang on as sobs shake her body. Detective Mattingly asks about Jeanine. "Not a peep," Mrs. Sampson says. She wipes the smudge of tears from her cheek, puts her hand on Father's shoulder, promises them her prayers, and leaves.

Mother leads the way upstairs, walking ponderously as much for her advanced gestation as her overwhelming sadness. Mattingly tries to pass her halfway up, but Mother stops and turns and stares at him. "First the sister's room, ma'am," he says. Mother takes him to Jeanine's room. The detective turns on the overhead light and looks around. He leaves the light on as he leaves.

In my bedroom, he takes pictures for the death scene investigation. My chair, my bed, my new vaporizer, my desk, even the cover of *Greek Myths*. It lies on the floor where I had dropped it before Mother found me. "This the book she was reading?" Mattingly asks Mother. She nods and Father whispers, "Yes." They embody a church-like reverence in my death room. "Weird," mutters Mattingly, stepping over the book to get to my bedside. His thick body throws the book cover, a drawing of Helios, the sun, in shadow for a moment. Mother bends to retrieve the book and holds it to her breast with both arms crossed. "No medicines given to her during the day?" the detective asks as he takes close-ups of my bedding. "No stuff for colds and coughs?" He coughs.

"No, none. As we told you earlier," Father says.

Mattingly bends low and checks under my bed. He sorts through my dresser drawers, photographing the contents. He enters my bathroom and empties the garbage can into the sink. He finds an empty toothpaste tube and eleven Q-tips. "What'd she need all these for?" he asks without turning around to see if Mother or Father is watching him from the doorway. They are. His camera memorializes the wax from my ears.

"Jess wore hearing aids. She needed to pay special attention to her ear . . . hygiene," says Mother. "They were to clean her ears," she finally manages to restate. She feels that, at last, she has been able to answer knowingly.

"Clean as a whistle."

Mattingly looks through the contents of my vanity. "Anything removed from here?" he asks. His camera catches my hairbrush, ear syringe, toothbrush, powder puff, Avon skin cream, giant box of unused Q-tips, and a Mars candy bar at rest on the shelves. "Did you know she hid candy in here?"

Mother looks at Father. "No," he says. "We never checked her bathroom for candy."

Sweet tooth. Greek myths. Mars bar.

"No," Mother says, almost smiling at the thought of me hiding candy. "We didn't."

"And your bedroom would be where?" Mattingly says, checking the clarity of his last two digital images.

"But she never was in there," Father volunteers.

Mattingly finishes his review. "Where?" he says walking past them.

Mattingly leaves a little after two in the morning. Father signs a form listing the items Mattingly takes for analysis: the used Q-tips, my bedsheet and bedspread, a sample of

water from the vaporizer's reservoir, the discarded toothpaste tube, and my uneaten candy bar.

His camera contains thirty-eight digitized images of
my room. For all the years of practice in the rooms of the
dead, he missed what was most important, most reveal-
ing, for it was all above him in the heavens of my stucco
ceiling. A glance at the sad clown would have told him
the story, a look at Aquarius brimming a bucket of tears
would have been enough. But he did not see. He looked
down, always down. The Assembler likes to say, "Look
up, look up to the mountain whence comes your deliver-
ance. From on high, He comes." I have no quarrel with
that one.

"Sorry again for your loss," he says when he is departing. "We'll figure it all out."

In their stunned graciousness, both Mother and Father
tell him, "Thank you."

"*Mars bar*," he mutters going down the steps. Above him,
the billions of stars blink in the black night.

At first they sit in the kitchen, each lost in a grief that
separates them. Mother rests her head in her left hand. Her
face is pale and sagged as dough. She stares at my drawings on the refrigerator door, the poorly rendered boats,
jack-o'-lanterns, Jed the dog, and some just-completed Santas, a collage of my last six months of life. Father watches
the fruit bowl on the table's center, an orange on the bottom of the pile showing a blot of blue mold on its shiny
skin. As exhausted as they are, neither considers sleep.
Mother replays the memory of finding me semiconscious
in my chair. She creeps backwards in her mind from there,
identifying points where she could have acted differently.

The noisy inspirations. The barking cough. The early struggle to get air in. The failure of the mist to produce continued improvement. She sees Dr. Burke standing at the entrance to my death room in the ER. "I wish you had called . . ." She winces at the words. Father watches the mold and thinks he can detect the faint musty fragrance of rot in the air. He remembers the awful failed breaths hours ago. All his force unable to lift my chest a fraction of an inch. All his fatherly force, undone. He closes his eyes. He feels again the fracture of the seal his lips made on mine, the pressure of his expiration so great it breaks the bonds of his kiss-of-life. He feels weaker than ever before in his life. There seems to be no breath left in him.

"I should have called. I should have called Dr. Burke right away when I heard that cough." Her voice is weak and thin, and she begins to cry again.

"Kate," starts Father, and then he falters. "Kate," he says again. "No. We did what anyone would have done. Don't say that. You're not to blame for this." He reaches his arms across the table and takes her hand in his. "Kate," he says again, trying to penetrate her tears. "Kate, don't. No."

She says, "It just all happened so fast. One minute the coughing. The next—"

"Kate, don't," but he's crying now, too. "I should have called. When I needed to get that damned vaporizer, I should have called and asked what else should we do."

Get up! Get up! I shout to the film as I watch them. Go to her and hold her. Weep together. Weep in the yellow kitchen light together and in the night dark of your bedroom together. You were my parents and you loved me. That is enough. That is all and enough. Weep, embrace each other for that. It would be good, the bath of your tears.

Instead they sit opposite, hands in hands, crying, remembering what Burke said, what they didn't do. Blaming themselves.

Dawn is slow to come. Night lingers, wanting more. It has an appetite for sorrow. It feeds on guilt.

Outside, the stars take advantage of the dark and shine more brilliantly.

*

I see through my death how much they loved me. Still love me in their separate and sprawling grief. I have returned to that thought as the meaning of it all. Love. Just their love for me. I have seen enough. Please, let the tapes stop. I am ready to let it all go.

I am dead. I am gone. I was loved. What more can there be? Let their love be the end of me.

9

THE BASEMENT TAPES

Benton Ridgely, the medical examiner for the District of Columbia, finds it easier to dictate as he works on the deceased than to take notes and reduce his findings to words later. A foot-controlled dictation system makes this practical. "The body is that of a seven-year-ten-month-old girl. She is well nourished and well developed. She apparently lacks thumbs. She is dressed in a Snoopy pajama top and bottom. On her left index finger is a paper cigar band. Twin hearing aids sit behind her pinnae, attached by tan wires to her mastoid antra and middle ear clefts. Evidences of medical treatment include an intravenous device in the right antecubital fossa and a five-millimeter endotracheal tube taped to the left corner of her mouth. Her chest is covered by two monitoring pads. There are needle puncture marks in both antecubital fossae and the dorsa of both hands. A urinary catheter exits her urethra.

"The integument demonstrates dependent lividity but is free of scars, bruises, tattoos, and identifying marks. The hyoid bone is intact. Palpation of the cranial vault discloses no edema or depression. There are no palpable fractures in any bone. The thumbs are aplastic. Her teeth are in good repair. Her tongue and palate are intact. The uvula is absent.

"The thoracic cavity is entered using the standard Y incision. The lungs are pink and spongy. The heart is dextro. The pericardium is smooth. It strips easily. It contains five cc's of clear, serous fluid. The heart is removed in the usual fashion. It is attached to a main pulmonary trunk and aortic arch in the normal position. The aorta is seen dividing into . . ." He lifts his foot from the pedal that activates the recording system. He uses his gloved fingers to push aside the connective tissues and tiny lymph nodes in the very center of my chest, my mediastinum, to obtain better exposure. "What is this, little girl?" he asks me, though he couldn't know that one day* I would be watching and listening. "This isn't supposed to be there." He snaps off his gloves and opens the folder containing the faxed medical record from Sean Burke. He scans the section on "Cardiovascular" to see if he had simply read too quickly before starting the dissection. Then he flips to the section marked "Radiographic Studies." He reads the reports of my last two echocardiograms. "ASD, VSD. Nothing else," he whispers to me. He dons new gloves and extends his incision to mid-neck level. He retracts nodes and thymus. He traces the course of the vessel from aortic arch to the base of the neck. "Oh, shit," he says shaking his head. "Oh, holy shit."

He removes his gloves again and calls the number for outpatient pediatrics. As soon as the receiver is lifted, he begins to yell, "Don't put me on hold! Don't put me on hold! It's Ridgely in the autopsy room. Get me Sean Burke, immediately. It's a matter of life and death. Well, it's at least

a matter of death." That always did the trick with the secretaries. A little humor from the autopsy pit. They always
moved pretty quick on that.

"Sean," he says when the pediatrician is on the line,
"you better get down here. And bring Marshall with you.
I found out what happened to your little Hilgar girl. You
gotta see this."

I see from their faces the displeasure they experience in
visiting the morgue. The room is old and dark, perpetually
cold and damp, and were it not for the commingled odors
of ethyl alcohol and methane, it could be the crypt of a
church.

Eileen Marshall holds a handkerchief across her nose
to ward off the odors. Burke, a drained look on his face,
stands right next to my head. I can almost feel the warmth
of his breath on my face, it seems. But the good news is I
can't feel a thing. Which is really very good because the
medical examiner plunges his hands into my chest like he
is trying to catch a guppy in a tub of water. "That's what
killed her," he says with a nod to the structure now perfectly visible amid the ripped tissues of my chest.

"Aberrant right subclavian," mumbles Eileen Marshall.

"An A for the cardiology lady. Aberrant right subclavian
artery. It comes off as a separate branch of the aortic arch,"
Ridgely points with the blunt end of his scalpel, "courses
up and over here, and winds its way all the way to here,
where it dips behind the trachea. It's as fat as a worm and
goes almost up to her throat. No wonder she obstructed
her airway with a little croup. Trachea was already fifty,
sixty percent compressed from behind." He lets the information settle. "Trouble is, my friends, it wasn't detected

in life." He releases the tissues. They barely move toward their original anatomic position. Such is their stubbornness for the truth. "That's the trouble, my friends."

Eileen Marshall removes her hand from her face. Her eyes dart left and right before she speaks. Even then she does not look directly at either colleague. Her eyes course from one face to the other, to my chest, to the floor, to the metal-shaded lamp hanging over my table like a hanged man, without fixing on any of it. "I'll have to review her echoes. I don't see how something that big could have been missed. . . ." The silence in the room calls for more explanation. She adds, "But, I mean, aberrant subclavians aren't part of her syndrome. I mean, who could have suspected?" She clears her throat and finishes, "I'll have to check her echoes."

Burke's face is blank enough that it might be pure shock he feels, like Mother's at my bedside as I died. But the way he sucks in his lower lip and narrows his eyes, the quick lock of those eyes on Ridgley's, tells me he feels more. Anger. Sadness. Worry. "Let's do that," he manages to say.

"Anything else for us?" Eileen Marshall asks. Her arms are folded across her chest, warm and full of blood's hot life. My chest is hollow as a cave now, and just as cold.

Ridgely thinks for a moment before answering. "Yeah. She was wearing a ring on her finger. From a cigar. Now, who does that anymore? All those young kids with real gold rings and this one, paper. How do you figure?"

"Any more *medical* findings, I meant," she says peevishly.

"Nope. Just that," and he points with his finger at the worm from my heart. "Full written report in about two weeks, after we get the toxicology and histopathology back."

*

For reasons He won't share with me, the Assembler now* presses me to view the Cassidy tapes. The ones from before I died were so difficult to sit through. And the ones from after, well, I'm just not sure how they will make me feel. I think He wants me to see something there, something that will revive my interest in piecing the parts of my life together so it makes sense in a bigger way. Something that will take me further than what has become my belief since I viewed my death and its immediate aftereffects. That my life made sense ultimately and simply because I lived and was loved. I lived a life of happiness and sorrow, of acceptance and rejection, of fullness and incompletion, and of forgiveness, all wrapped in the love of my family.

When I tell Him I want to stop this exercise, this Cinema Purgatorio, He says to me again, "What has been hidden from the wise has been revealed to the blind!"

But not now*, not yet*. There are the Cassidy tapes to watch. When I finally agree to them, He smiles and replies, "Ah, yes, I'll get them. They're in the basement." It seems to take forever* before He returns with them. Perhaps He thinks I need the time to ponder? Or has He lost His way? "Make straight, make straight the way of the Lord!" I want to joke. But I don't. His feelings are easy to bruise.

Cassidy is off the morning before my death, just as he had been each December twenty-second for the preceding twenty-one years working for the postal service. Mother sent him home from our house with a mug-full of coffee. He laces it with glove-box whiskey in our driveway, again at the first stop sign down the street, and again when he parks in front of his house on Macomb. He tries to wash and shave but abandons his razor before he's done his chin and left cheek. By day's end, which is also my life's end, he looks mangy and piebald in the face, like he has a cancer. But now, as a shaggy coat of flu mucus begins to form on my throat, he walks through his house room to room, stopping to contemplate the living room couch, the kitchen table, the padded rocker in the spare bedroom, the funeral holy cards stuck in the frame of his bedroom mirror. Two of these he pulls away and reads. "Joseph (Joey) Delaney Cassidy Jr. entered eternal light and rest 12/22/1984." He mumbles from memory the prayer on the card's other side. He repeats the process with Rose Mary Ferraro Cassidy's card. His voice is drunk with whiskey and sorrow. He wipes a tear from his left eye before replacing the cards in the frame.

He turns sharply to leave the room, loses his balance to whiskey's pull, and falls onto the corner of the bed. He starts to get up, his arm going to the mattress as if to push away, but suddenly he stops and sits staring at the mirror. He sees his slumped-over frame, his gray uneven stubble, his red, sunken eyes. He sees the third funeral card, and for the first time in many years, he lets himself remember the last morning, the last good memory. Rose Mary leaving their bed for the six a.m. feeding, then bringing Joey back with her to snuggle warm next to him while she showers; the smell of him, of her, almost the same smell; her body glimpsed naked in the mirror of the bathroom vanity before she steps into the shower, her breasts swelled up like life itself; the noises Joey makes from mouth and ass; his joy in it all; the sound of water cascading down his wife's body; Joey then asleep next to him, the soft spot on his head sucked in with each tiny breath. Then there was his Ma in the kitchen putting out the breakfast. The bacon and eggs and potatoes. A good breakfast in case they get caught long at the doctor's for Joey's two-month checkup and Rose's second postpartum visit. Her words to him as she puts down his plate of food, as Rose Mary enters the kitchen in her robe and black hair so wet it drips. "You never know. At the doctor's office, you just never know." Rose saying, "Good morning, Carina," and his Ma smiling back with that woman's smile a man can never penetrate. "No counting calories this morning," his Ma saying as she scoops bacon grease on the yolks of their eggs sizzling in the pan. Rose, after she's certain Carina is engaged with the eggs, grabbing her breasts through the terry cloth and saying, "No one I know is about to complain." Her look, a smile a man can penetrate.

Then he's at the door readying to leave for work. Then the words, "I'm leavin' the cab money. Won't cost much, Ma. I'll get to those old brakes of yours this weekend. Replace the brake hose, flush the system. If you can remember it, a call after Joey's visit just to fill me in, OK?" And he's out the door to his own car, bringing the morning smells of the kitchen in his clothes.

The rest flashes by in bursts. The police car's red lights beyond the post office window. The ride to the hospital, passing the scene of the accident, his mother's old Chevy broadsided by a pickup truck at the intersection of Wisconsin and Reservoir. The eerie quiet in the halls of the emergency room. The corpses of his son and wife on separate gurneys. His mother unscathed, weeping, weeping in a chair, unable to stand, unable to say anything.

The corpses, separated by space, untouching, alone.

*

It is a tape within a tape the Assembler has brought. To see a young Cassidy, his baby and wife and mother, vibrant and alive, and in a flash, to see the two youngest dead, is too much for me to bear. And there appears to be no clue in the sad footage for my own needs. Or what He thinks must be my needs. I continue to watch, knowing full well how it is to lie limp and dead on a hospital gurney. I am broken, heart and soul.

Cassidy stares at the funeral Mass cards on his mirror. He closes his eyes and lies back on the bed. He sees Father Larrie at the wake sitting opposite his mother, knees to knees, holding her hands as she cries in the corner of the room with the caskets and flowers. Her face holds as much wild terror as deep sadness. Father Larrie is a new-minted priest then, his hair brown and wavy, his eyes shining with the blue of Mother Mary's hope and love. Carina Cassidy is urgent, nearly hysterical, in her cries and in her words between them. Her face bursts with need. Larrie nods, whispers, "Yes, yes," and retrieves his stole from the side pocket of his black jacket. The vestment goes around his neck. If you didn't know better, you'd think he is preparing to leave for the cold walk to his car. The stole is long and ends in dark purple rectangles that dangle almost to the floor. The purple is the color of the bruise on Joey's forehead in the ER, the only mark on his dead body. Cassidy wants to turn away from the scene when he makes this connection, but there is something in Larrie's demeanor that won't let him. It is the way he leans forward toward his ranting mother, the half turn of the head so that she's whispering directly into his right ear, the slow nodding he does like a man completely convinced, fully certain, about what he hears. The nodding, slow, so slow. He releases her hands and they immediately come together in the pose of prayerfulness. His mother's face is fixed on the priest's, as expectant as before but now calm. He turns his head to look at her. His hand makes the sign of the blessing in the air. Cassidy hears the first few Latin words, *"Absolvo te . . . ,"* and turns away, not knowing if it's sadness or anger that makes him go.

There is a hospitality room at Leary's Funeral Home. Leary's is an Irish establishment and the hospitality room is stocked with bottles of good Irish whiskey the mourners bring. But Cassidy doesn't touch a drop the two long afternoons and nights of the wake. He takes condolences from family and friends and drinks warm soda from a plastic cup. He comes and goes from wake to home in his car, alone, while Nana and Ned chauffeur Carina. Before the concluding prayers on the second night, Father Larrie tells him to see after his mother. "She's suffering mightily for your coldness and distance. Comfort her, Joseph," he says in the hallway. Cassidy is astonished the priest would even think to approach him after the row they had over the two coffins. But he does, his blue eyes a little cloudy from fatigue and his face a little shiny from sweat. There are a hundred people present for the service and the heat is intense.

"It's for me ta decide how ta go on, not for you, Father. She's the one who drove, who's responsible for their deaths. That's not somethin' I'm likely ta put behind me." He turns to go but the press of the standing crowd locks him in place.

"She's received the absolution of the Church, Joseph. With a penitent heart she has come to Christ and He has forgiven her. She asked me to tell you that. She has no debt to God in any of this sadness, and now you must forgive her also." His face is set so hard, Cassidy feels like punching it.

"Well, all the absolution in Christendom won't put breath back in my wife or my son. That's what it will take for me ta give her forgiveness. Their lives returned."

"Joseph, you risk the loss of their loved memory. That memory which you share with your mother. You risk losing that and your mother's love. You won't get through this with hate and retribution. They will eat the love out of you. Only with love and forgiveness will you get through. Replace your stony heart with a living heart, the Bible says to you, Joseph. Your heart will not live, truly live, unless you go to her in forgiveness."

"Well, you're wrong there, Father. I'm livin' off anger and hate right now. If I don't have that, I don't have nothin'. Nothin' at all but emptiness. I left her the cab money. She killed them and that's the way it will always be for me."

"Joe," the priest begins, but Cassidy finds a gap and slips away. "Put away . . . ," he says to the retreating figure, but his words fall unheard into the din of the room. I read his lips, though, as he finishes, ". . . anger. Put on mercy."

The funerals are the next morning at St. Anthony's. Cassidy refuses to sit next to his mother. Nana holds her, weeping in the front pew the entire service. It is no better at the cemetery. Cassidy does not return to his home for the reception. He drives instead to Rory's Place and gets drunk in his mourning suit.

The next day he packs up his clothes and the few mementos of his wife and child and moves out. He drinks to stupor again that night. And the next.

At first it is Ned who provides him care and attention. He comes every morning with hot coffee and buttered rolls to his basement apartment on Rollins Street to see that Cassidy is up and out for work. For weeks, he rouses a hungover Cassidy and gets him moving, never stooping to lecture his young friend on his drinking but only telling him what he thinks is the secret to being a man: a man goes to work. No matter what, a man wakes and washes and works. Cassidy curses and grumbles, but he showers, drinks the coffee, and goes to his counter at the post office with crumbs on his shirt. The work starts to put a wedge between his anger and his day.

For a few months, it seems enough. But when spring comes with its cruel, green reminder of his April wedding day, Cassidy's grief is reborn, and the violence begins. The county police let him go the first time—he'd punched a fellow patron at Rory's Place when that man let his disdain for married life be known to those seated at the bar with him—but they take him into custody for his second offense, smashing the windshield of Father Larrie's car with a stone hurled from two hundred feet away. But before the hearing takes place, Nana intervenes. She asks the priest whether it is better for Cassidy if he loses his job and goes to jail, or does something useful with his talents. He had been a high school standout in baseball, the shortstop on the team that went to the Maryland state championship game his senior year, she tells him. Why not drop charges in exchange for Cassidy's agreement to coach baseball teams in the Police Athletic League? And let Ned replace the windshield? In the space of the few seconds it takes for Larrie to consider the request, he sees Cassidy standing on the corner two blocks from the rectory parking lot as

he, Larrie, drives onto the street. He sees Cassidy bend-
ing to retrieve a rock. He sees Cassidy's arm in a throwing motion. He sees himself in the car, smiling, thinking,
"Never in a million years from such a distance." Then he
sees the rock coming at him in a straight line like it's on a
string. He sees himself still smiling when the rock smashes
his windshield with a noise like a gunshot. Father Larrie
blinks, and he sees the wisdom in Mae O'Brien's request.

Nana's suggestion was shrewdly calculated, and proves
even more successful than she'd hoped. Cassidy grumbles
at first, adamant not to do anything the priestly ass had
agreed to. But he finally sees the wisdom in Nana's argument, that he would lose his job and perhaps even go to
jail, if he didn't take the offer. So, reluctantly he begins
coaching junior high students. And loves it as much as
his charges love him, even a stubbly-bearded, hungover,
Saturday morning him. Especially a stubbly-bearded, hungover him. He has a flair for the game, true, but also a way
of dealing with boys on the cusp of adolescence that is
something to see. He makes the wind sprints, the games
of pepper, the endless fielding of hard grounders and tow-
ering fly balls seem like the most important things in the
universe for his players to do. His teams win and win and
win. And in the winning, he wins the admiration of their
parents, many of whom are members of Montgomery
County's police department.

In the months and years that follow, those brown-suited
enforcers of the county's laws have a difficult decision to
make when they arrive at Rory's to find Joe Cassidy at the
giving end of a sound beating, or at the receiving end of
one: do they jeopardize their own sons' futures in baseball by hauling their coach into jail, or call Ned and Mae

O'Brien to come pick him up? Nana is amazed at the power of baseball. The basement tape ends.

Eileen Marshall is childless and, for the past three years, unmarried. Mercifully, unmarried. She comes and goes as she pleases now. There is no longer a man who needs things—a meal, a conversation, a friend, a lover. She is free to work late, eat late, retire late, without having to offer an excuse or an explanation. Especially this time of the year with all those tedious Christmas parties that rise up like speed bumps, slowing her down as she tries to forge on ahead. "But you have to come with me," Ray would plead about some partner's gathering. "I can't show up alone." And for those four constraining years she did go with him.

And hated him for it. The chitchat, the talk of trials won, of *strategy* that won them, of billable hours, of rain makers. And the food, always the same, always eaten standing, eaten with the fingers. But that is over now, finished. And good riddance.

Which is why there is nothing unusual about the lady cardiologist working late in her office the evening of December twenty-third, when everyone else is out having a good time. Even the janitors have grown used to that—they know to collect her trash the last of their shift.

She has retrieved the metal canisters containing my echocardiograms from the film library and has brought them to her office to review. There are two studies done in the newborn period, and then a study from each of my yearly evaluations. She reviews the first and sighs relief when there is nothing arising aberrantly from the aortic arch. The second newborn study likewise is clear. Even more relieved, she spools and plays the echo from age one.

And there it is, partly hidden among the plumper pulmonary vessels, but clearly visible, a gray-black wisp coiling into the chest. It is even more apparent on the next three echoes, the artery growing in size and definition as the rest of my body does. The diagnosis is clear and clearly missed.

"But it is not supposed to be there!" she says aloud to herself. "It's not part of Hilgar's. It has no *right* being there!" She thinks of the statistics. A one in one hundred thousand chance of Hilgar's and a separate one in ten thousand chance of the aberrant artery. The chance of both occurring in the same individual is one in a *billion!* She takes comfort in the numbers. "I should not be *required* to search for something as rare as that! Her death was out of my hands." She ejects the tape from the projector and sits looking at the grayness of it. "Gray," she says aloud as she taps the eraser of her pencil on the echo's empty metal canister. The hollow, tiny sound is like the beat of a drum. The silver-gray film from the viewed echoes sits on her desk in a jumble like a nest of snakes. There is a knock on her door.

"Housekeeping," says the tremolo voice of Henrietta. "Housekeeping, Dr. Marshall."

In that instant she ceases her drumming. "Come in, Henrietta," Marshall says. "I've been doing some Christmas cleanup. You can take this stuff away. Take it all away." At the last moment, she retains the second ·of the two newborn echoes. She first thinks to keep both but argues against the idea. Verisimilitude, she understands, will be her *strategy*. Tapes are often lost. Even the very first one is gone. Only one can be found in that god-awful film library. Those filing clerks can be the height of incompetence.

On top of the tapes goes the uneaten remnant of her working supper, the glutinous mashed potatoes and gloppy creamed corn soaking the silver celluloid tape, darkening it, making the snaky tape look old, old as the hair of Medusa.

Before leaving that evening, she replaces the sole surviving echo on its proper shelf. In the morning she will ask her secretary to place a written request for all my echoes; she will raise a stink when only one can be found. Very verisimilitude and very discoverable should a suit arise, she thinks as she walks to her car. All that will remain of the lost studies are the dictated reports in the chart and her own imperfect memory of what those images showed. She thinks of her actions as a Christmas present to herself, one she fully deserves. It is a present that will prevent her from suffering the unpleasantness of a lawsuit over a matter so unfair to the treating physician, the discovery of the rarest of rare constellations of anomalies in an already blemished child. No need to get trounced over a slipup like that. Ears and heart and voice and artery and bones and kidney. Who knows what else lay beneath her skin? A mess. The girl was a mess. A mess *no one* should be responsible for.

Cassidy is too hungover the morning after my death to notice that Father has not come to work. Instead, he swallows aspirin and drinks black coffee while he waits on a long line of holiday-impatient customers. He manages a few tablespoons of instant noodle soup during his lunch break and has just decided to dash to his car for a quick pick-me-up when the manager calls him to his desk phone. "Joe, it's Jackson for you. He's got some bad news. Real bad. You better sit down." Cassidy's hand shakes when he reaches for the phone. But it's been shaking all morning long. His face is gray-green in the cheeks and black about the hollows. His eyes are rimmed with red and look cold and lifeless.

"Ford," he half whispers. "Where are ya?"

"Joe, I'm home with Kate and BJ. It's Jess, Joey. It's Jess. She's dead." Cassidy moves the phone a few inches from his ear. The cries he hears are like spikes in his brain.

He waits for the sounds to stop. "What? What are you sayin' about Jess? She's dead? She died?"

"Last night, Joey. She got sick last night and just . . . just couldn't breathe. We did mouth to mouth, everything. But she was all obstructed in her windpipe. By the time EMS got here it was too late. She was dead. They're doing an . . ." but he breaks off again into sobs. The manager can hear them where he stands at the window. He walks to a stunned Joe Cassidy.

"Gimme that, Joe," he says taking the phone from Cassidy. "You get over there. Help 'em out."

Cassidy goes to his Taurus. Somehow his hand is steady when he inserts his key in the ignition. Still, he reaches for the glove compartment before shifting into drive. "Another casket," he says when he sees the pint tucked away. "How in the name of Christ will we be able ta bury another small casket?" The whiskey warms his throat, burns his belly, all the way to my house.

My parents are sitting in the parlor with Father Larrie when he arrives. At first no one stands when Cassidy enters. Mother and Father sit and stare at him blankly, as if he has been gone a long, long time and they hardly remember him. It is Larrie who stands, who speaks first. "Joe," he says as he walks down the length of the couch to provide

Cassidy space, "sit." He gestures to his vacated cushion. Then Mother stands and goes to him and Father quickly follows. The three who love me join their grief with an embrace. Cassidy cries the hardest, and I know his tears are for more than me. No one speaks.

Finally, they sit and Mother says, "They think it was the croup that took her. Her windpipe just closed over and she couldn't breathe. We tried everything we knew, but . . ." Mother sounds exhausted. She recounts my last hours. Her sentences are all short sighs. Cassidy drips his tears on his shirt, not even bothering to wipe them with his hand as they course down his cheeks. He doesn't speak what they already know, what no one has stated: that he was in his home, in his room, passed out from the drink when I died. Home passed out drunk when he should have been here, reading to me. He remembers what I said to him, the last I said to him, "You will be okay," and shakes his head in disbelief. He stays with them for an hour, through the phone calls, the people dropping off food, BJ waking from a nap.

When he leaves, Father Larric walks out with him. "Joe, we've had our differences, you and I over the years. . . . That's the God-honest truth. But I'm asking you, don't be putting the burden of guilt on either of those two over her death. They've borne enough of that already. It's mercy and compassion that's needed now." The priest had said little while they sat in the parlor, and this is the most information he's parted with since Cassidy arrived. At first Cassidy is prickled that the priest would look to direct his actions. It seems an unfounded affront to the obvious love that all three of them had for me. He is about to protest that no such thought of blame could ever enter his mind, when Larrie continues. "And the same goes for blaming yourself.

I know from . . . from CCD how close you were to that girl. What she meant to you, even if I can't accept your approach to holy dogma. But you loved her and that is enough. Don't go laying on the blame there either. Cherish her memory. Guilt and blame will only tarnish it and serve to separate you from it and from those who share it. That's like another death when you cut yourself off from that. I'll not be repeating any of this unless you bring it up, Joseph." Surprisingly, the priest offers his hand. Surprisingly, Cassidy takes it.

"I'd like to do a song at her funeral Mass," Cassidy says. Larrie's eyes widen. "'Amazing Grace,'" Cassidy continues, "before the Kiss of Peace." Larrie considers the request. "That would be within the rules. Okay, then, 'Amazing Grace.'"

Cassidy can't bring himself to say, "Thanks." He just nods and gets in his car.

*

Later*, the Assembler comes by to collect the day's* tapes. I tell Him I am shocked over Father Larrie's wisdom, insight, and concern after all I had heard about him from Cassidy, after all of his meaningless questions in CCD class. I expect one of His stock and cryptic replies, such as "Many were the Prophets in Israel in those days, but God's word came only to Larrie." Instead, He regards my new thumbs and inspects them with His Artistic Eye. "It takes longer for some to understand than others." He leaves for the basement, and I do not see Him for days*.

Nana and Ned arrive later that day. There is another wash of tears. My family goes out in the evening to select a casket. Cassidy stays with BJ. They begin to read *The Golden*

Treasury of Myths and Legends. Cassidy sings BJ to sleep. He tucks her in and goes to my room, where he sits and cries in the dark. He looks up to the ceiling. There are more stars than ever before, from the refraction of the light through his tears.

On Christmas Eve, two days after my death, a caseworker from Child Protective Services comes to the house to interview Mother and Father and to do a site visit. She is a matronly black woman close to Nana's age. She wears a bright orange turban around her hair and a white-striped black caftan. She comes well armed with forms. Before she talks with either Mother or Father, she walks through the house noting items on her list with the concern a surgeon has for his stitches. There is no fire extinguisher in the kitchen, no smoke alarm in the basement, no flashlight in the cabinets, and Mother's prenatal vitamins are within easy reach of a child on the kitchen counter. The temperature of the hot-water heater is set dangerously high. The Mister Yuk sticker on the refrigerator is mostly obscured by my old art. No one can see the telephone number of the Poison Control Center. A mouse has left a pellet in the drawer containing the aluminum foil. There are no covers for the electrical sockets in Jeanine's room.

When finally the three sit together in the parlor, Ms. Smith begins by announcing that she has met with Detective Mattingly. "Frankly, with such a preventable death, he is required to investigate your fitness as parents. As that pertains to the incident involving Jessica, it's in his bailiwick. But we at CPS have a duty to protect the interests of your younger child, Jeanine. That's the purpose of this visit. And just where would Jeanine be now?"

"She went to the mall to see Santa. My parents and a friend took her a little while ago," Mother says. There is no strength in her words. They seem to leak out of her mouth like a stanched stream of water. Two nights of sleep deprivation, a day and a half of self-recrimination, guilt, and drowning grief have taken their tolls on both my parents, so much so that neither is offended by Ms. Smith's remark concerning their fitness as parents. They are arriving at that very same conclusion themselves. Mother sees me limp and staring in my chair. All she had thought to bring was a damp facecloth

"I will need to see her before I leave. Is there any way to contact the grandparents and have them return?"

Father looks at Mother with a shrug. "We don't use cell phones in the family, so I don't see a way of getting to them short of one of us driving over to Macy's." He lets his head drop as if he is ashamed.

"Well, then, let us begin with these questionnaires and see where that takes us. Maybe they'll be home by the time we finish."

The interview drags out over two hours. They are each asked questions about their education, jobs, family relationships, personal histories of violence suffered and delivered, income and spending, drug and alcohol use, diet, religious affiliations, medical and psychiatric histories, use of emergency rooms. They are culling their memories on this last topic when the front door opens, and Cassidy carries BJ into the room. Nana and Ned follow close behind. Cassidy stands just to the side of the couch where the caseworker sits, and sways. BJ sees the stranger in the room and begins to cry. "Zokay, Zokay, BeeChay," Cassidy slurs. "She's nice lady in orage hat." Mother stands and snatches

BJ out of his arms. She fixes Cassidy with a glare. He looks like a lashed puppy, his eyes droopy-lidded and his mouth lax. The caseworker stands, smiling thinly, and says, "I'm Beatrice Smith, caseworker from Child Protective Services of Montgomery County. And you are . . . ?"

Cassidy sits in the kitchen with his face buried in his hands. Ms. Smith has left. Mother has stormed off to BJ's room with BJ and Nana. Father and Ned have gone to the church to see about the funeral service. In the unlit space behind his eyes, Cassidy sees a single vision and hears again a sole shrieked sentence. It is Mother's face, wild-eyed with terror, wet with tears, yet somehow set sharp in anger, too, some hot spray coming out of her mouth as she screams: "They can take BJ away from us because of you! They can take BJ away from us because of you!" He feels a turning in the pit of his stomach. He barely gets to the bathroom before the retching begins. It is the caseworker's broad smiling face he sees as he leans over the toilet and suffers the assault of the day's shots at the bar and the pulls from his glove-box bottle. The smile never fades as she asks him question after question and dutifully records his slurred answers. "Oh, God!" he moans just before he vomits again. "Oh, holy God!"

My wake waits until the evening of December twenty-sixth. My autopsy prevented a wake the day after I died, and the rules of the Church forbid funerals and wakes on Christmas Eve and Christmas Day. I am given only a single evening session for the mourners to come because Leary's is overwhelmed by the log-jammed dead of the holidays. Only an evening in my casket in that room with all those flowers and pictures of me and family and friends. Dozens come, sign the book, find Mother and Father and express their sympathies, wander about marveling at me playing soccer, standing in the waves at the beach, splashing in the bathtub as a baby, reading on Cassidy's lap, eating cotton candy at the circus. Then they approach my casket and kneel on the hard rubber kneeler. I am dressed in my Communion dress, ironically putting it to good use earlier than expected. The dress is pleated white taffeta and my black rosary beads are wrapped around my eight fingers. If the mourners look closely, they can spot my White Owl ring on the index finger of my left hand. Most never see it because they don't want to look at my hands. But it is there. It was returned to Father along with my hearing aids when he signed the hospital papers releasing my body to Leary's. My parents had never seen it on my hand before because I only wore it on special occasions, and even then, only in my room. I had put it on the night of my death because of what had happened with Cassidy that morning. The loud bang of the whiskey glass on wood echoed in my ear all that day, and I put it on.

"Wood hath hope," the Assembler tells me when I think about that incident. "A tree, if you cut it down, shall spring a shoot from the root and shall live!" I don't know what He's talking about, but I sometimes still feel Cassidy lean against me, hear the second clunk of the glass on the wood, this one a gentle sound, like a dying echo. I ask Him, "Did You ever feel the power go out from You?" "Wood hath hope!" He replies.

It is Cassidy who tells them the history of the paper ring, and they put it on my finger before the viewing starts.

The doctors come to me in death as they came to me in life, with a mixture of duty and curiosity. They drive over from the hospital all together, Burke, Garraway, Marshall, Stein, and O'Neil all in the same car. Burke and Garraway are the most affected by my death, though for different reasons. Burke hugs Mother and shakes Father's hand and repeats, like a mantra, "We will miss her so," to everything either one of them says.

"So nice of you to come."

"We will miss her so."

"She loved going to see you in your office."

"We will miss her so."

"Thank you for your care all these years."

"We will miss her so."

Stein and O'Neil say, simply, "I'm so, so sorry," and leave it at that. Marshall cries in Mother's arms, whispering, "And we never got the chance to fix her heart. But maybe it was all for the best." Garraway kneels at my casket before approaching my parents. He makes the sign of the cross and closes his eyes. His height makes him look like he's peering down on me from heaven itself. Then, slowly, he bends. His lips brush my fingers a last time. The third, fourth, and fifth black beads of the rosary's third decade briefly sparkle with his breath's moisture. He smiles when he spots my ring and taps it with his finger.

Other than my family and Cassidy, he is the only one of the multitudes to touch me. The Assembler lets me feel it, those soft warm dabs to my fingers like some tiny bird at play.

He greets Mother and Father. He says at first how sorry he is for their loss. Then, how privileged he was to have known me and them. And finally, he says what none of the other doctors have ventured to say. "You were the absolutely best, best parents she could ever have had. And I really mean it."

The tape ends there with Mother breaking down into tears and going to Father's arms. They seem weak and tired, those arms, as they surround her.

The Assembler insists I watch Basement Tape #14. I pass a second eternity* waiting for it. It is Cassidy at the wake. Helping put my ring on. Helping to settle photos around. Talking with friends and coworkers about me, my life, his life with me. Laughing at some of this, crying too. Cassidy in the hospitality room pouring stiff ones into plastic cups, working hard not to slur his words, not to stagger and sway, darting his eyes around the room for the lady in the orange turban. Wondering who is caring for BJ tonight, trying to remember to ask Father that very question, willing to volunteer to drive home to read her to sleep, but in the thickening alcohol fog, forgetting and forgetting again. But he does not forget, cannot forget, the nights decades earlier in these same rooms, the two coffins, the swamping twin miseries of heartbreak and anger. He feels almost at peace here and now, at peace that he must confront only the sadness, and the sadness of just one death. It is like a gift he has gotten from me.

During the short ride back to the hospital parking lot, Garraway asks where the autopsy stands. Burke answers, "So far, just the aberrant subclavian causing partial airway obstruction so that a little croup was catastrophic."

"How'd we miss that?" Garraway asks, sounding far away.

"I don't know that we *missed* anything," Marshall replies. "I've requested all her prior echoes to review. I'll let you know what I see. It is an unrelated anomaly, you know,

the subclavian. Not something one would expect to find."
Marshall thinks the geneticist looks a trifle haughty, and
must blame her for the mistake in the girl's management.
She adds, trying to take the fight to him, to make him
doubt the thoroughness of his own evaluation, "God, it
makes me wonder what else there was missing from that
poor girl. She was like a walking time bomb. And she just
went off."

Garraway is about to tell her he has my echo from age
two, just before the kidney surgery, and that he was going
to review it with her in preparation for the case report he is
writing, but Stein interrupts his train of thought. "Anyone
for a beer and a burger? I'm starving."

Marshall is the only one to opt out. Too much to do.

I receive Basement Tape #15. It is one of the briefest
recordings of events I have seen to date*. Cassidy is sitting
on the examining table in the same ER room where I was
pronounced dead. It is near midnight of the evening of my
wake. He is drunk. He nods off twice waiting for the doctor. Each time, his body slumps off the plastic surface of
the examining table, and he is jarred awake. He mumbles
something inaudible. I cannot see his lips well, and even
if I could, the drunken laxity of his facial muscles would
inhibit my reading ability. The Assembler has chosen not
to overlay the tape with Cassidy's internal voice. Cassidy
is nodding off again when the curtain parts and an Indian
doctor enters.

"Well, what can I do for you tonight, Mr. Cassidy?"
he says, sounding precise and dignified. He has a young-
looking face but graying hair that's so long in the back it
covers the collar of his white coat.

"Drunk," says Cassidy, touching his index finger against his breastbone three times so there is no mistake as to *who* is drunk.

"So it would seem, sir."

"An' tamorra I can't be drunk. Mus be a pill for that. Gotta be."

The Indian doctor strokes his chin. "Tomorrow is a special day, is it?"

Cassidy nods so forcefully, he loses his balance and almost tumbles again. "Tamorra I gotta sing at the fun'ral. Jus' lemme have a pill." He holds out his hand. It swoops and rises and falls like he's trying to catch a butterfly. He quickly brings it to his side and sighs from the effort.

"Would you consider taking the treatment for more than a single day? Would you be interested in seeking sobriety, sir?"

"Doc, I ain't. Jus' tamorra through the fun'ral z'all I ask. One pill. Two. Nothin' more." He closes his eyes and his head spins like a top. He opens them and is surprised to see a doctor standing before him, rubbing his knuckles.

"I could write you a script for Antabuse and you could fill it first thing in the morning. But I cannot administer you a dose now. It would cause you marked gastric distress if you take it with alcohol in your blood. You would be afflicted with the most pernicious retching, sir. So, a dose in the morning should do the trick." He folds his hands together as if in prayer and then rubs them again. The word "pernicious" sticks in Cassidy's mind like a pin.

"Zokay. Zokay, Doc. I'll jus' take it now. I can't trus' myself ta take it in the mornin'. Jus' gimme it." Again he holds out his dancing hand.

"If I treat you now, you would need to stay here under observation and intravenous fluid therapy until the vomiting subsides. Is that acceptable?" All this to sing a song at a funeral, he thinks. The Irish.

"Yeah, sure," Cassidy says. He stills his hand and offers it to the doctor.

The tape is edited at this point. What remains is a haggard Cassidy forcefully emptying his stomach contents into green basins that look like half moons six times over the ensuing hours, saying, "Oh, Christ Almighty," after each episode. He leaves at five thirty a.m. with two additional tablets and a script for a month's supply. "Just in case," the doctor says as he hands him the discharge papers.

Tina and her mom are at my funeral Mass. Even a few parents of my classmates come. Ms. Smith the caseworker is there, too.

Tina is frightened and holds her mother's hand as they walk past my casket in the vestibule, where it sits next to the baptismal font waiting for the service to start. After they pass, she turns to look at it again and says without a single stutter, "I think she can hear better now. She can hear me and speak to me better now, but I can't hear her anymore."

"Maybe sometimes you might hear her whisper in your heart."

"Will she tell me why she had to die? At Christmastime?"

"Maybe someday she will."

"Why did she have to die, Mommy? It's Christmastime."

"I know, baby. No one knows why now. Maybe someday we'll know." She squeezes Tina's hand and Tina squeezes back. They slide into an empty pew.

"Mommy, there's BJ!" She points excitedly to my sister in Mother's arms at the back of the church, squirming to reach the white handkerchief sticking out of Ned's jacket pocket.

"I see her," Mrs. Dalton says.

The organ music plays louder and the ushers push me down the center aisle. Mother, Father, BJ, Ned, Nana, and Cassidy slowly lead the procession of the rest of the family. They step into the first two pews as Father Larrie ascends the sanctuary steps to the altar. He turns and greets the congregation. "On behalf of the Jackson family, I would personally like to thank you all for coming to this celebration of the Mass of Christian Burial for Jessica Mary Jackson. We are here today to celebrate Jessica's uniting with her risen Lord and Savior, Jesus Christ. In the midst of all the pain and sorrow her passing has brought, we take comfort in our faith, her faith, that life is not ended in death but merely changed. We believe in our hearts that she now is fully alive in Christ. So we start what is our celebration of her life and her new life, as always, in the Name of the Father, and of the Son . . ."

The service is not long, under an hour. Father Larrie's homily is brief. It makes Mother and Father, Ned, Nana, and Cassidy cry. I had not realized that through the steel bars of that priest's many rules, there still beat a heart that could feel. "She brought joy to her family and her friends. Vexation for her willfulness to her teachers. Admiration from them because of her perseverance. And clarity about God's complex design for humanity because of her setbacks that did not set back her spirit. In short, she was like all of us hope to be."

Before the Kiss of Peace, Cassidy leaves his pew and walks up the steps to the lectern. The black suit smothers his frame. The jacket hangs loosely over his stooped shoulders, his pants cuffs drag at his heels. His eyes are hollow and seem to have retreated into their sockets. His guitar is next to the altar boys' seats. He retrieves it and begins to play. His hands are shaky at first and he misses a note or two as he starts the introduction to "Amazing Grace." But before the voice comes in, he abruptly switches tunes. Out come the sweet slow notes of "Dark Eyed Molly."

> *Deep and dark are my true love's eyes*
> *Blacker still is the winter's turning*
> *As the sadness of parting proves . . .*

Father Larrie is standing behind the altar. His mouth falls open a fraction at the switch. He moves his arms a little in protest. Then he thinks, "Let him have his way with it. It's harmless and maybe it'll do the family some good." He closes his mouth and reverently hangs his head. The music is lovely and sad.

I feel it in my marrow up here* when I hear that song Cassidy sings, the thumping and buzzing alive in my bones.

Especially in my thumbs I feel it. I feel it all.

In an eternally* repeating epiphany, I realize how close those words are to Cassidy's promise to me in my room after BJ was born. He sings from the lectern:

> *No fiddle tune will take the air*
> *But I see her swift feet a-dancing*
> *And the swirl of her long black hair*
> *Her smiling face and her dark eyes glancing*

The song ends with the triple refrain: *"Then who's to know in the morning after, That I long for her dear dark eyes."* Tears drip silently in the congregation while he sings. At the close fifty people take to blowing their noses. It goes on for over a minute, the only sound now in the church. Finally, Father Larrie continues the service. "Peace be with you," he says looking over to Cassidy. "Peace be wit' you, too, Father," Cassidy says into the microphone. Though the congregation mumbles this same reply in unison, their noise doesn't drown out Cassidy's response.

After the service we drive to the cemetery. It is a normal winter day, cold but not bitter, tranquil but with an occasional puff of wind, overcast but with jagged spots of blue suddenly appearing above. The robins hop on the straw sod and sometimes fly off, frightened. Their shadows are still like arrows. It feels good to be buried on an ordinary day. There are more prayers at the grave site. Then the mourners walk slowly to their cars, and four men I never knew lower me down into the earth.

Tina is right. I hear everything. The sound of earth clumps on my casket like the pounding of an eternal drum. I think, now* or then*, it's hard to say, there should be a constellation, the Drummer. The drum should be long and rectangular and made of polished wood and ring loud enough to wake the dead. Even the deaf dead.

The earth, surprisingly, smells sweet and clean, of pine. Death has exhaled the wormy whiff in me.

The Assembler provides me with the long tape of the reception at our house after my interment. It is generally known up here* that He likes to memorialize parties—there are hours* of footage of bar mitzvahs, seders, communions, confirmations, birthday parties, wedding receptions, baptismal gatherings. He says to me when I ask why, "Wherever two or three are gathered together in My Name . . . ," but I really think there is another reason. It's as if He can't ever get His fill of simple human joy.

I sit through the long film. It's much like all the other affairs my parents have had at home, but larger, warmer, louder, and more ironic given the mix of tears and laughter in the rooms. The sunlight through the windows seems on a switch, coming and going through the afternoon in shafts of clean brightness that fall on tables and floors in ever-changing geometry. There is so much food, Nana sets up tables in the kitchen, dining, and living rooms. No one needs to circulate much. They just arrive, find a place to sit or stand, and begin eating, drinking, and talking. The dozen children who are there chase each other through the rooms, sometimes making chains by holding on to the dress or sweater of the child in front and behind. It makes the adults smile to have to move aside for the twisting onslaught of twelve linked kids. Mother and Father keep busy attending to the ice and drinks, putting out new trays of food that seem to magically appear on the stove top or on the old glass table on the back porch. In all, there are five pans of baked ziti, two hams, a twenty-pound turkey, casseroles that pair meat and potatoes, chicken and broccoli, tuna and noodles, a Dutch oven full of baked beans, breads, rolls, and two platters of cheese. Each room has a bar and the bottles come with the guests.

Cassidy takes condolences on his loss and congratulations on his song in equal measure. He sweats even before the house is stoked with body heat. He blinks hard every few seconds as if he is trying to clear his clouded vision.

He turns to regard the lineup of whiskeys on the tables and blinks again. He moves to the kitchen and receives instructions from Nana, this platter, this casserole, this tray of rolls to here or there. Then there is nothing more to do but stand and talk. He stares at the bottles between greeting the mourners. He watches as they refill their glasses. He looks at his watch. It is almost one o'clock.

His stomach is in a knot and he feels the tug of the bottles. They slosh when people pour and set them back down. It makes him dizzy to watch the liquids rock. He can smell the contents of the plastic cups passing by—Jimmy Shehan's bourbon, Murphy's rye, Ivey's rum and coke. The table is against the living room window. The sun emerges from behind a cloud, and the browns in the bottles seem to glimmer, seem to burn. He taps his shirt pocket that holds the plastic vial they gave him in the ER. He shakes his head. The surfaces of the whiskies are like burnished gold skins in the sun, and he longs to kiss them all.

"It is time," he says out loud to no one. He steps to the table and reaches for the Seagram's.

In the kitchen doorway, BJ cries in the arms of Aunt Miriam. "Come on, BJ," she says, "I'll get you a Coca-Cola." BJ continues to wail. Through the chatting knots of people she sees Cassidy. "AceyDee!" she yells, extending her arms toward him. "AceyDee!" Cassidy turns to grimace a smile at her as they make their way to him. He sees, beyond the doorway, the broad back of Beatrice Smith. She stands in the kitchen dressed in a black pantsuit, but there is no mistaking her. She wears the same orange turban as the day they met. The way she stands, he can't see her face. He remembers it, though, and a shiver passes through him.

"I want Coke," BJ proclaims as she throws herself into his arms and Miriam leaves to find Mother. My sister's hands play with Cassidy's ears the way they used to play with mine.

"Let's make it two," Cassidy says. He sits her on the edge of the table while he pours out the contents of a can into two cups and adds ice to hers. She reaches for her cup and misjudges, pushing it dangerously close to the table edge. Cassidy's hand saves it. "Careful, little lady," he says, handing it to her. He reaches into his shirt pocket and takes out his vial of two pills. He twists off the cap, shakes a tablet into his hand, looks at the brown bottles and then at BJ two-fistedly slugging down her soda, and pops it into his mouth. He sips his Coke and swallows. The sun unlights the bottles, and the dull ache he didn't know he had disappears from behind his eyes. He is replacing the cap to the container when he hears her voice behind him.

"Perhaps not the safest place to seat a child, Mr. Cassidy, on the edge of the *bar*. There's the glass and the possibility of a fall." Cassidy places his medicine on the table and hoists BJ into his arms. He turns, and the caseworker's eyes are on the contents of his plastic cup.

"I was just gettin' our drinks and being real careful about it, too." BJ has finished her Coke. She drops her empty cup onto the tabletop and reaches for Cassidy's. He obliges her with a sip. Ms. Smith's eyes narrow. "Coke, Ms. Smith. Just Coke." He stops there for a second's consideration. "You don't suppose I'd give a child liquor, do you now?" She gives him a look of derision. He steps away from the table. She sees the medicine container and empty Coke can. "Would you mind dropping that prescription into my shirt pocket? My hands are kind of full and I wouldn't like anyone gettin' inta *that* at an Irish funeral reception." He nods at the vial. Ms. Smith picks it up and reads the label before putting it in his pocket. BJ says, "More, AceyDee. More."

"Today, little one, even if our friend doesn't approve, you can have all the Coke you want." He turns away, sets down his cup and opens another can. When he turns back, Ms. Smith is gone. "We showed her somethin' today, kid. We sure did." He drains his cup and adds more.

It is almost dark by the time the last of the mourners leave.

"Spend the night, Joe?" Mother asks Cassidy. "Be good to be together on a night like this. And all those leftovers." She has noted his abstinence today, and she is touched by his sacrifice. She has noted, too, Ms. Smith's demeanor become less judgmental as she witnessed the outpouring of support and love from so many family and friends. Mother feels less threatened by the "system" as Ned calls it. Ms. Smith has already mentioned the possibility of Mother and Father taking parenting classes. The thought of doing this eases Mother's guilt a little, as if in taking those classes she would be doing a kind of penance for a sin confessed. But she fears for Cassidy alone in his home on my funeral night. She worries that what he managed in the light of day he likely would not manage in his mother's old dark home, alone, as night advances.

Cassidy looks at her face. She looks neither tired nor sad, though he knows she must be both. All the doing of the day has placed her somewhere between those two emotional poles so that neither shows. He knows she does not need his company this night and that she asks for it out of concern for him.

"Not tonight, Kate. Thanks, but no. I got some things ta attend ta."

"Like what?" Mother asks, not really wanting to hear the truth.

"Like things," he says evasively.

"Like things. Let me make you a plate for later at home."

"No beans," he says.

The same physician enters his ER cubicle this night. Cassidy is relieved. He had practiced his history during the hour's wait to be seen, but he is not sure of what to say. It is becoming more and more difficult for him to think straight. His hands are shaking whenever he tries to use them. And those sweats take over his skin and make him shiver.

"Good evening to you, sir!" the physician greets him. Cassidy notes for the first time how large and white his teeth are. They seem to gleam in his mouth. "How are you, sir?"

Cassidy holds out his fingers. They twitch and shake until he pulls them back and sticks them under his armpits. "Haven't had a drink since before I came here yesterday. But I'm getting a case of the shakes. The cure I know about I don't want ta take. I'm wondering what your cure might be. There must be a pill or somethin' I can take ta settle my nerves."

"Very good man!" the ER physician says. "Very good! We'll fix you right up. Take the edge off, sir. You will see." Dr. Vinik extends his hand; Cassidy takes it. "But there will be some difficulty for a week or two, even with the pills, Mr. Cassidy. Night terrors, irritability, difficulty concentrating. Perhaps you would consider a short leave of absence from your employment? I would be most happy to write you a letter. A week, two at the most. Then you will be in fine form, sir."

Cassidy shakes his head no. "It's where I go, Doc. The post office. Gotta work, regardless."

"Yes, of course," says Vinik softly.

Cassidy thinks the doctor looks disappointed. He can't look into Vinik's fallen face any longer, so he lets his eyes rest on the doctor's name tag. Zacharia Vinik, MD, he reads. Tough name to go through life with, he thinks. "You know, maybe I'll take that note, Doc. Just in case."

Vinik beams a smile. "Good man!" he exclaims. He offers his hand again. His teeth gleam.

Nana and Ned decide to stay. First, there's the meeting to discuss the autopsy findings. Burke expects that should be in a week or ten days. Then there's the new baby due to arrive in late January. The normal life of a family tries to reassert itself.

Father returns to work at the post office two days after my burial. His supervisor tells him to stay out until after New Year's, but Father doesn't have the heart to roam the house room to room remembering his life with me, as he does the day, all day, after my funeral. He stops at my chair in the kitchen and strokes its white-painted wood as if it's a saint's bony relic. He remembers the fights over me eating squash, my fondness for bananas, the mashed green peas spread by my hands through my hair when I was a year and a half. He sits next to my reading seat in the living room on the slipcovered couch marked through the years by spills of chocolate milk, juice, and soda. He presses the spots to see if one is still damp, like the sand at an oasis. He trudges to my bedroom where he cries looking at my sky. He takes my blue floating duck from the tub and carries it with him through the remainder of that winter day, full of gray sky and shadowless streets beyond the windows. At dinner he places the duck next to his water glass, and no one thinks to ask why. He returns to work the next day hoping it will relieve him of reliving all the memories because they are the conduit to the pain that feels to him as if his heart has been struck by a hammer.

The post office is a-hum with customers, and it helps him to help them with postage, zip codes, and dimes. He sees his life now as inconsequential as the help he gives, stamps, tiny numbers, ten-gram coins. He can take comfort in tiny things. The few families who bring their children with them manage to queue in other lines. He is grateful for this. He doesn't know what he would tell them if they came to him, but he thinks it might be to say to treasure the small things, the trivial and seemingly mundane. But even this balm has splinters of glass that impale him, for he goes from this thought to the next: and take every illness, every symptom of every illness, gravely "If only . . . ," he says aloud to an old man buying stamps.

Mother and Nana walk in the mornings when BJ is at school. Because her due date is only three weeks away, Mother can't go very far. They often make it only two blocks south, to Wisconsin Avenue, where they stop on the corner, face each other as pedestrians go by, and relive the events of that night, and of the wake and funeral. Nana cries as often as Mother. Each day at least two passersby stop to offer help. Their tender concern makes Mother cry all the more. "The people, these strangers, they offer me help without even knowing who I am. And I did nothing for Jess that night." Nana hugs her there, right on the corner, and says into her ear, "You were her mother, Kate, and you loved her so well, so dearly." Their noses are raw and red from cold and crying.

In preschool, BJ wets her pants each morning and is surprised when none of the aides tells her she is a bad girl. She refuses to take her nap and is allowed to color instead. She breaks a whole box of crayons pressing down too hard. No one scolds her. At home, someone holds her in their arms every waking second. She forgets I am dead and wants to know when I'm coming back. Her question during dinner causes Mother to leave the table in tears. Father goes after her. Ned shows her how to make a pyramid out of baked ziti. It makes her laugh. Then she smashes it with her spoon and cries.

Ned buys an old snowblower from the newspaper classifieds and begins its overhaul in the garage. For hours he is alone with his wrenches and bolts and nuts. He remembers the summer before, when we made sand castles at the beach and when he taught me to ride a two-wheel bike in the parking lot of his church. It was so hot that day the asphalt was soft as fudge, but we practiced until I could coast twenty feet downhill. He promised me a big surprise for Christmas that very afternoon. He turns from the gearbox of the snowblower and sees the red bike he and Nana shipped up as their gift. It leans against the wall, its multicolored streamers dangling from the handgrips, still and limp.

His eyes tear over. He smashes his Allen wrench against the gearbox and wages war against rusty bolts.

Cassidy is the least in tune with his grief, and it hurts him to sense this. It is the effect of the drugs. Or, more precisely, the effect of a lack of one drug—alcohol—and the generous oversupply of another—Valium—for the shakes. He sleeps fitfully through the nights, visited intermittently by frightful dreams of son and wife and mother and me, and by halcyon visions of the same. He wakes every hour or two with demons or angels in his brain and wants to drown them all in drink. Then he remembers Ms. Smith, sips tap water and washes down another pill, and sleeps until the visions bloom again. He tries to return to work, but he is a zombie. He makes errors counting change for every other customer. He handles the tape dispenser as if it were a sledgehammer.

After work he drives home and sits in his idling car for an hour, taking inexplicable solace in the engine's fitful hum, his thoughts like the morning light just before the first true light, flitting disjunctively in bits and pieces. When he visits BJ and Mother and Father at night, he has little to add to the bleak dinner conversation. He nods off reading to BJ. He knows he is sad, but the jumble in his brain can't fit the pieces of his emotion together. Sadness looms in his head like the horizon's black storm clouds that refuse to coalesce, open, and release a flood. The storm's relief doesn't come.

He wonders, finally, if it is another effect of his shorted-out brain, that he *wants* to feel the rock heaviness of sorrow in his heart. He *longs* for it.

The next morning, he drives to work and shows the manager Dr. Vinik's note. It's written on a prescription pad in letters too tiny for Cassidy's bleary eyes to read. "Take what you need, Joe. A week, two, whatever it takes. Call me anytime you want to talk." Cassidy wants to cry, wants to blubber like a baby. The tiny letters, his boss's concern, everything so sad. Dry-eyed, he walks past the queuing customers and drives home.

When BJ takes ill with a low-grade fever and cough on New Year's Eve Day, Mother calls Burke, and he sees her in his office. Father leaves work to join them for the visit. BJ is not sick at all—in fact, she feels so well she refuses to leave the house until she gets to wear the Rudolph the Red-Nosed Reindeer suit she received for Christmas. No amount of urgency on Mother's part can convince her otherwise.

"A touch of the flu, nothing more," Burke says after looking her over. As they dress BJ in preparation for leaving, Burke mentions that he has been in contact with Ms. Smith and that together they are trying to work things out. Neither Mother nor Father has a response to that. At the door, he repeats again about BJ, "Nothing more than a little flu."

His diagnosis does nothing to placate my parents' concerns. BJ sleeps in their bed the next few nights. Of the three occupants, only she sleeps well. Mother and Father keep vigil in the dark, separated by twenty-nine pounds of sleeping flesh that splays its limbs out broadly in a child's abandonment of the concept of space. They listen to her noisy breathing, her few coughs, each remembering the sequence of sounds that tolled her sister's death, my death, each trying to match that memory to this moment.

"I'm glad we took her in," Mother whispers in the dark.

"Good to know it's only the flu," Father whispers back.

Mother hesitates as BJ shifts position, jutting her left leg so it pushes on Mother's right. "And now it's on record that we called right away and took her in. I mean, they can all see that we . . . we care. Are careful."

Father takes a deep breath and quickly pushes it out of his lungs. "Yeah. That too."

Mother waits for more before saying, "You don't sound all that convinced."

"I'm just starting to get mad, is all. It's starting to get to me, all this investigation stuff. Smith and Mattingly. I'm starting to think we've been, I don't know, unfairly pegged as bad parents. And now Burke and Smith whipping up somethin' for us to do. And, like today at Burke's, what did *he* do? Nothing. Not even some cough medicine. And BJ didn't sound any different than Jess when she started off. Sounded the same until just before the very end. So what would a call have accomplished? I don't know. I wish we had called, but . . . I don't know." He stops for a minute thinking of Detective Mattingly. "I should have told him to go fuck himself, that Mattingly, the night he was here. Not 'thank you,' but 'fuck you.' And now the goddamn caseworker and her parenting classes. I don't know. It all makes me so pissed. I want to tell them all to go take a flyin' leap."

Mother sits up in bed and reaches her hand across BJ to lay it on Father's chest. In a voice more a whisper, less a moan, but both, she says, "Ford, no. Ford, no. Don't go there. They got the system and they got us in it. If we do anything to resist, to try to block them . . . They got us in it, Ford." Father lies quietly. She presses her hand down on his ribs. "They could take BJ away from us. Smith said as much." Mother's voice is husky, and then she begins to cry. "We just lost Jess and they could take BJ, and I would die, Ford. Jess and then BJ, Ford." She pulls her hand away.

Father throws off his covers and walks around the bed to Mother. He sits next to her in the dark and finds her hands. "No one is taking BJ," he says aloud. "That's my promise to you, Kate. I'll hold my tongue. I'll do it for you and for her and for this little one." He puts a hand on Mother's round belly. "I'll be mad, but I'll be quiet." Mother puts her arms around his shoulders and pulls him next to her. There is so little room, he is half on and half off the bed. Her face lies on the side of his neck. He can feel her warm tears, and he can feel her head going up and down, nodding her acceptance of his promise. He can hear BJ's breathing. He looks to the clock on the nightstand. It is not yet the New Year.

Cassidy comes for New Year's Day dinner. He is calmer than in the previous tapes. Five days distant from his last drink, he feels that the agitation, the sense of his engine racing that took hold of him those first few days is waning. He drinks Coke and plays songs for BJ and Ned while the others cook and set the table. Twice he forgets the words to songs he's sung since childhood and receives prompts from Ned. His confusion makes BJ laugh and yell, "Again!" for the stumbled song.

The house is warm and fragrant. There are football games to watch. They eat at two. At three Cassidy proposes a visit to my grave. Just to say hello, he says. Everyone is eager to go, but Mother doesn't think it a good idea to expose BJ to the cold and blustery day. She has sung and played and colored in her books all day but still has a low-grade fever and a cough. Ford quickly agrees with her. Cassidy shrugs his shoulders. "Okay. You all go, and I'll stay with the Red-Nosed Reindeer. Besides, I already visited there this morning."

They leave him and BJ home and bring flowers for my grave. They put them next to Cassidy's, all the colors so fresh and bright on the winter sod, it somehow seems cruel. They say three Hail Marys and cry. When they return home, BJ is napping on the couch. Cassidy is talking with Father Larrie, who has stopped by for a visit.

I have asked. There is no tape of Cassidy's visit to my grave that New Year's morning. Nor of Cassidy and Father Larrie visiting. The tape He gives me shows them all sitting over dessert and coffee as it grows dark outside. BJ waking from her nap, being frightened by Larrie's white collar. Going to Cassidy's lap and eating so much pie from his plate, her stomach hurts and she cries again. Nana taking her up for a bath. Cassidy producing his vial of Antabuse, showing it around, taking one when it comes back to him. No one saying anything. Mother and Father and Larrie staring at each other, nodding.

*

He makes me mad, sometimes, the Assembler. What is so important here for me to see? Why not Cassidy at my grave, instead? Why not Cassidy and the priest, talking? What am I supposed to see in this tape? What's the point?

"The pies," He says. "Pumpkin and pecan. I thought you'd like to know."

That second night in their bed, BJ is less noisy but still as flung in sleep as the limbs of a tree. Father almost falls from the bed, she has taken so much room. Mother sleeps better that night, the problem of Cassidy, the problem of Father's anger, the threat to BJ resolving. Father lies awake until nearly four, listening and remembering. His heart pounds even as he is thankful for the two quiet female forms lying next to him. But his gratitude cannot suppress the memory of his grievances. Finally, he tries to recall every piece of information about geography he has ever learned, and he falls asleep naming rivers.

BJ is fully well the following day. She sleeps next to Mother and Father that night, and the next, before being returned to her own bed. She cries an hour that night, angry over her relocation. Father sits outside the door of her room, reading and listening to the sounds coming through the opening.

Ms. Smith schedules a follow-up visit for January fourth at noon. Father arranges to leave the post office during his lunch break so he can be home. Ms. Smith arrives early at ten forty-five. Mother is upstairs changing when she comes to the door. Nana answers the bell and lets her in. Ms. Smith has interviewed Nana before but decides to ask more questions while they wait for Mother to come down.

"I've now had a chance to discuss this matter with BJ's doctor and Jess's many physicians and to review their files, Mrs. O'Brien. I'm surprised you didn't mention that your own brother died at almost the same age as Jessica and that he had some form of her syndrome. Why was that, do you suppose?" They are seated facing each other in the living room. Nana's spine straightens and she pushes herself back from the edge of the chair.

"I suppose because it's a genetic syndrome is why they both had it. That's why we went to see Dr. Garraway. He explained it all."

"That I know, Mrs. O'Brien. I spoke with Dr. Garraway myself. No. What I meant is why didn't you tell me about any of this when we spoke the first time I was here?"

"I didn't see how any of that related to your looking into Kate's ability to take good care of her children. Which is what you said you were here for." Nana's tone is clipped. She has not blinked since the dialogue began.

"You don't think your attitude toward a handicapped sibling while you were raising your own daughter might have . . . colored her thinking about children with special needs? "

"It was never an issue in my house when I raised my children. Billy—he died years before any of them came along."

"True, perhaps. But it *was* an issue in this house, wasn't it? How to deal with a handicapped child? Certainly that was something that loomed large here. Am I correct?"

Nana has become too angry to answer. They sit in silence for half a minute staring at each other. Mother enters the room. She has promised herself to be patient with the slights likely to come her way during the meeting at noon. She is not prepared to see Ms. Smith sitting on her couch at eleven in the morning, nor to see the look of distress on her mother's face.

"Ms. Smith," says Mother frowning a bit. "You're early!"

"I wanted the opportunity to see how the home looks. I was just about to walk the rooms with my check-off list when Mrs. O'Brien and I started to discuss your . . . uncle, Billy. Shall we go?" She rises in her green and blue patterned caftan. Her orange turban looks like the setting sun at the beach. Mother and Nana lock eyes. "No," Mother signs, and hurries to catch up with Ms. Smith.

All of the deficiencies of the last visit are remedied. Ms. Smith makes note of BJ's visit to Dr. Burke. They sit again in the living room. Ms. Smith refuses a cup of tea.

"It's unfortunate Mr. Jackson is not here for this meeting. But I'm sure you will fill him in. We at CPS feel there has been some progress in the home setting. It is safer and better organized. And you did appropriately bring BJ to her physician when she took ill. And family friend Mr. Cassidy seems to be making an effort to deal with his alcohol addiction. On the other hand, there may well be some unresolved issues in the family over such things as the rights of the handicapped, appropriate use of off-hours medical assistance, child nutrition. Enough concern for us to recommend the parenting classes we discussed last time. Don't think of this as punishment for something you did. Far from it, these classes are merely a practical way to shore up whatever . . . gaps there are in a family's understanding of child rearing. The classes are offered at the County Department of Health, three days a week. The series runs twelve hours. That's six classes, each two hours long." She pauses there to see if Mother needs clarification. Mother sits mutely. The film captures the bounding pulse in her neck. It pushes the hollow in the base of her throat from shadow to light, shadow to light. Nana sits, staring at the water rings on the coffee table. Ms. Smith continues. "We think that if you and Mr. Jackson complete this curriculum successfully, we can close the book on this . . . chapter of your family's life." She pauses again to solicit questions before concluding. "Then all you must confront is the conclusion of Mr. Mattingly's investigation and, hopefully, you can get on with your lives."

Mother's eyes fall to the carpet. The sadness in her heart over my death has been crowded these past days with guilt over her part in it and with the fear of losing BJ. For a second she wonders what would fill her heart if both these terrible emotions—guilt and fear—were to leave. Would there then be room for joy? For love? Acceptance?

She wonders, too, if the fear were to go from her heart, whether the sadness would grow too strong, overwhelm her, bring on the black days and blacker nights. Or would the guilt rule all, paralyze her heart, bring her sense of "motherliness" to its knees? What kind of mother lets her child die like that?

There is too much uncertainty to see her future clearly. But the certainty of her present torment—a spirit steeped in the poison of an unholy trinity of sadness, guilt, and fear—prompts her to say to the woman in the orange turban, "When's the earliest we can start?"

Ms. Smith leaves just before noon. Nana goes up to her room. Mother hears her crying when she passes her door carrying clean towels for the bathroom.

*

I am gaining humility through this exercise. I play but a small part in the events that determine the life of my family. Cassidy's repentance is not entirely of my doing. He gives up the drink, he heals his heart, as much for the love of Mother and Jeanine and Father as for love of me. My parents grieve the threatened loss of Jeanine as much as the real loss of me. I begin to see my life as a small part of something grander, more elegant: the intertwined nature of the souls of man. What am I in all this? The yeast? The dough? Both? Perhaps my humility is incomplete, but I ardently think: both.

10

COLD, THEN HOT

There are five other couples in the class. Mother and Father are the only Caucasians. They gather in a room with wooden folding chairs and a single, long, collapsible table. At the end of the table is a pot with tepid water, a jar of instant coffee, and Styrofoam cups. HELP YOURSELF! says the sign in hot-pink marker written under a smiley face. Nobody does. Behind the table sits Shaniquia Russell. She sits before a box containing six blue folders, the handouts for the participants. Ms. Russell is young and petite and has a tattoo on her forearm. The printed words NOT GONNA HAPPEN make a circle around a fist. She has an open face, a crew-cut hairdo, and silver hoop earrings.

Mother and Father are the last to arrive. The wall clock reads seven forty-one. They are eleven minutes late. There were two flights of stairs to walk in the building. They take in the impatient looks of a few of the participants. "Hey, Mamacita," says a man who looks like he can't be finished with his teenage years yet, "get the Papi to drop you off out front so we can start on time. You crawl like the turtle when you walk." Father notices his tattoo. It is a blue skull that shines through the stubble of his shaved head like a reflection off murky water. The woman sitting beside him laughs and throws her head back. She is pregnant but not nearly as far along as Mother.

"Sorry," says Father to the woman behind the desk. "Had a little trouble finding the place. Then, all those stairs." They take seats in the rear. Two of the men haven't opened their eyes since Mother and Father entered the room. They appear to be dozing in their chairs. Ms. Russell rises and distributes the folders, one to each of the men. When she arrives at the chair of the first sleeping man, she stands silently at his side and waits. In half a minute, the female member of the couple shakes his arm. "Leon. Leon," she whispers as if Ms. Russell shouldn't know she is waking him. "Wake up." Leon opens his eyes. "Fuck you do that for?" he says jerking his arm out of her grasp. Then he sees the group leader. He looks away to the front of the room. She offers him his folder. He takes it without looking.

The second sleeper has been roused by his mate before Ms. Russell arrives. He receives his folder and promptly drops it to the floor.

"Pick it up," Russell says.

"When I'm good and ready, I will," he replies, staring at her.

Shaniquia Russell bends and retrieves it and carries it with her to her place at the table after she has distributed the rest of the folders. The man's wife or girlfriend gives him a stare that could freeze water.

"I am Shaniquia Russell and I am the liaison educator for the Department of Public Health of the county. I will lead these next two weeks of sessions on parenting. I will assign reading from the packets I just distributed. I will administer a written quiz to start each session. You fail even one quiz, you fail the class. Take heed. If you don't have the readings, borrow someone's and copy it." She stares at the folder dropper for half a minute. "This is where we go around the room, giving our names and what we do, and why we are in this group." She consults a list on a paper. "Esmeralda and Alberto Rivera. Esmeralda?" Esmeralda stands like a schoolgirl before a nun and begins.

Three couples are in attendance because of suspected child abuse. Leon and his girlfriend are in this group, as are Esmeralda and Alberto and Eduardo and Lucida. One attends because it is a requirement of his recent parole from prison, where he served eighteen months for assault and battery. His son was born while he was "away." This is Robert Hill, the folder dropper. His girlfriend, Erika, is newly pregnant. It is she who accounts for their presence. When it is Robert Hill's turn to speak, he merely adds, "My line of work is in the services industry. That's what I provide, services. And there ain't no way they sendin' me back to prison over this." He sweeps his hand over the seated group. "I know how to be a daddy." Carlos, the boy who spoke to Mother, is seventeen, "a carpenter, just like Jesus." He is already the father of two children. His attendance is mandated by the juvenile court system if he is to remain out of detention over gang-related activities. His girlfriend, also seventeen, proudly tells the group she has lived away from her parents' home for a year. She helps her aunt clean houses.

Mother and Father present last. Mother begins from her chair. "I am Kate Jackson. This is my husband Ford. I'm a homemaker. He works for the postal service. We're here because our oldest child just . . . She died at home from something and then CPS came and looked us over and thought . . ." She tears over and Father takes her hand.

"What, you kill the kid?" Carlos taunts. "I do that and they put me in jail, man. You do it, man, and wham! They send you to school. Bullshit, man. Bullshit." His girlfriend laughs again. Father glares at him and he glares right back.

The curriculum for the first evening includes a review of nutrition during pregnancy. Many of the pages in the handout are simply unembellished drawings of composite meals that provide optimal nutrition for the developing fetus. It's as if a drawing of a bowl of oatmeal or a turkey sandwich should stick in the memory while the written description on a page should not. Mother gives Father a look of surprise at the simplicity of the information; he returns a shrug. They sit through a discussion of snacks: potato chips, sugary drinks, fried pork rinds. Father whispers, "Fruit bowl," and Mother nods. Ms. Russell asks for a show of hands: Who drinks during pregnancy? All the women's hands rise but Mother's. Marijuana? Ms. Russell asks. Erika begins to bring her hand above her head, but Robert Hill takes her arm by the elbow. Russell begins a discussion of the effects of drugs on the fetus. She directs the class's attention to page six of the handout, a picture of a newborn baby suffering a seizure from drug withdrawal, its tiny pink limbs stiffened straight, its spine arched to form an impossible C shape, its mouth open in a cry. "You do drugs, your baby does drugs," she says, looking at Erika. Mother stares at the picture. "Oh, Ford," she whispers. My father shakes his head and sighs. He covers the picture with his hand.

There is a ten-minute break at eight thirty. Mother and Father stay in their seats and pretend to be interested in looking through the nutrition lesson in their folder while the rest of the participants leave the room to descend the stairs and smoke outside in the cold night air. Just before eight forty, a shadow falls on the picture of a green salad. "Hello," says the man called Eduardo. He offers his hand and Father takes it, not surprised it is cold, but very surprised it is soft. "Don't pay them any mind," he says nodding toward Carlos and Erika retaking their seats. Father nods. "We done nothing wrong, either," Eduardo continues. "Baby fell from the couch." He touches the back of his head three times. "Laughing like crazy at something and falls. Now we're here." He shrugs his shoulders and walks to his seat.

The final hour is a review of infant nutrition. Breast or bottle. Feeding on demand. The introduction of solids. Burping. Mother's eyes close over briefly near the end. Shaniquia Russell calls her name. Mother startles awake and Erika laughs.

They are the last to leave. Mother walks slowly down the dark stairs. There is a single lightbulb illuminating the landing between the first and second floors. Father says the place should be condemned.

The car is a block away parked in the shadows between two streetlights. As they walk, the wind penetrates their cloth coats. Father opens the door and Mother gets in. As he is unlocking his own door, Robert Hill appears at his side. Father removes the key before he turns it and has the quick hope that Mother will lock her door from the inside.

Robert Hill holds up his hands as an assurance of his peaceful intent. "Didn't mean to scare you none," he says. "Just wanted to borrow your folder, is all. Bitch took mine.

I need yours." Father had tucked his folder under his arm as they walked to the car. It is still there, the blue cover barely visible in the dark against his black coat.

"Well, I need it too," he says. "Come to the post office on Macomb tomorrow and I'll give you a copy." He turns and begins again to use his key. In a deft movement, Robert Hill pushes Father against the car, wrenches the folder from under his arm and begins to walk away. Father recovers his balance and takes a step after him. "Ford! Stop, Ford!" Mother screams, half out of the car. He turns to her and, in the car's dome light, sees the fear pressed into her face. "Don't," she says pointing to Robert Hill walking away. "Just take me home." Father looks at the retreating form of Robert Hill. His stride is a loping jitterbug, a sort of victory dance in the dim light.

"I'll find you on Macomb, Mr. Postman," he sings from half a block away. "Mr. Postman," he repeats joyfully again. "Don't go writin' no letters to anyone about any of this. Lot can happen to a nice car parked on a dark street hereabouts. Mr. Postman."

Father wants to quit the classes. He wants to call Beatrice Smith in the morning and complain about the lack of safety, the threats and intimidation, to which they have been subjected. Mother begs him not to. "Five more classes, Ford. Just five. Then we're done with it. Done with it all. We can go on, mourning Jess, loving BJ and our new one. Like Dad says, pick up where we left off. Please, Ford, five more classes." She puts her hand on his shoulder. They are in the foyer of their house, hanging up their coats. They are finally warm. The house is quiet. It is well after ten and all are asleep.

"Well, going to the sessions won't do us any good if we don't have our manual. What are we going to do about that? The quizzes and readings and all." Father wants to fight the "fucking system," play hardball, be a man. Increasingly he feels that what they did the night of my death was what any parent would have done. It has taken almost two weeks of remorse and self-recrimination to arrive at this brightening clarity: she was hardly sick at all and then she died. *How* could they have known what to do about that? *Who* in the world could have known what to do about that?

Mother says, "We'll call Ms. Russell in the morning. Get another folder from her. Or find one of the participants in the phone book and copy their pages. Dad and I can do it while you're at work. Please, Ford. Five more evenings." Her face is transparent and stretched out the way the sky appears just before dark. Her tired eyes flare with a little remnant of energy. He realizes he has never once in these years of marriage said no to a serious request from her. Nor would he now. "Five more sessions," he says wearily. "Five."

"Yes," she says, "five."

Shaniquia Russell does not return the message they leave on the phone-mail system of the Public Health Department the next morning. They leave another at noon. That, too, is unproductive. When Father finally reaches a secretary, he learns no one has access to the list of participants for the parenting classes and, even if they did, privacy law would prevent its disclosure. There are dozens of R. Hills and Robert Hills in the Montgomery County phone directory, and just as many Riveras. They realize no one else was identified by last name. They leave more messages throughout the day on Tuesday. Shaniquia Russell does not return them.

Tuesday night at dinner, Mother allows they are certain to know the answers to the questions to be faced the following evening at the next session simply by virtue of their parenting experience. They knew all about nutrition when it was presented, didn't they? So shouldn't they be able to pass a quiz on other general topics on parenting? Father chews his chicken and says, "I hope so."

The post office is unusually quiet in the late afternoon of the next day. Father has worried since awakening what would happen if they did fail the quiz this night. He knows it would then be too late to come forth with any of his legitimate reasons for quitting the sessions—the robbery of his folder, Kate's advanced pregnancy, the unsafe environment. No, if they fail the quiz, they thereby fail the course and thereby announce their unfitness to be parents of BJ and thereby . . . "Thereby," he mumbles with a shake of the head. He looks up and Robert Hill is standing at the counter in front of him.

"Mr. Postman," he says. Father looks at his hands. One rests, palm side up, on the counter, holding nothing. The other holds the blue folder. He looks at Robert Hill's face. It holds meanness and contempt.

"Mr. Hill."

"I'm bringin' you the folder. Read it real good for tonight, now. Pages eleven to twenty-three inclusive. And thank you for the loan."

Father extends his hand to receive it. "And two twenty-dollar rolls of stamps while you're at it," Hill says. Father hesitates but then gets the stamps. Hill takes them and hands Father the folder. He turns and leaves. The walk is the same.

Father has no cash with him. He borrows forty dollars from Cassidy to reconcile his drawer. "Forty dollars,"

Cassidy says blankly. It is his second day back at work after his leave of absence. He's done well but the strain of the day—all the weighing of parcels, all the numbers, all the counting out of change—has drained away his mental energy. He opens his wallet and stares at the bills. He removes them all from the billfold and gives them to Father. Father takes two twenties and returns the rest.

Outside the entrance to the post office, Robert Hill sells the stamps for twelve dollars a roll. "Services industry," Father says, watching him through the plate-glass window.

While Nana cooks supper, they huddle at the kitchen table and review the folder's assigned pages. Mother had been correct. None of the reading material contains anything new. It deals with the normal visits to the pediatrician's office during the first two years of life. It lists the important features of the physical and developmental exams that the physician will be especially concerned with, reviews the immunizations that are given, and lists safe and effective approaches to "the crying baby" and "the willful toddler."

"Jess never cried much," Mother says at the table. "She was so sweet-tempered."

"She let her sister take care of that," Father says. At that moment BJ lets out a loud wail from the living room where she plays Old Maid with Ned.

"No!" yells BJ. "N-O-O-O-O!"

It's bath time and BJ has voted against it. Mother and Father laugh, their first real laugh since my death.

BJ's shouts grow fainter as Ned carries her up the stairs. They hear the report of one well-placed kick against the banister. They both laugh a second time at that, and then

Mother cries. It is more a brief shower than a storm; her hands stay calm on the tabletop. "It's all so mixed up inside me. The sadness with Jess still so heavy. But the new baby inside me kicking like a new hope, and the fear about BJ, all of it so sharp in me. It's . . . I don't know. It's . . ." She wipes her cheek with her finger. "There seems to be just too many parts for one thing. Am I . . . Is it . . . ?" Father thinks her face is that of a child awakened by a bad dream, straining both to remember and to forget. He takes her hand, and Nana comes over from the stove to stand behind her. She places her wet hands on Mother's shoulders. No one knows what to say. They all have too many parts to construct one single, simple emotion. They hear the upstairs pipes clunk as Ned turns on the bathtub tap.

"Cold and then hot," Father says. Mother cheers a little at this attempt to focus on the here, the now, the practical.

"Cold and then hot," Mother echoes. They haven't read that in a book anywhere. They just know how to fill a tub safely.

Father deposits Mother in front of the building and finds a parking place two blocks away. Mother walks the flights of stairs alone. Her back aches with each step, her breath quickens with the effort. But she is grateful none of the other participants enters the building and makes his way up the dark staircase with her. The conference room door is locked. She checks her watch. It is ten after seven. At the far end of the hall, light—the only light—shines out of an open doorway. She can hear music coming from there. Heat is pumping out of the radiators along the wall, and Mother feels warm. She removes her coat and hangs it on the conference room doorknob. She walks the length of the hall hoping to find Shaniquia Russell. Mother's thought is that Shaniquia could open the door, switch on the lights, maybe be made to understand a little more about Mother and Father and their situation, something more than the awful and incomplete confession the last time. Possibly even become their ally. The room at the end of the hall houses four work cubicles. Shaniquia Russell is alone and sits at her desk eating Cup Noodles soup with a plastic spoon. Mother gently knocks on the doorframe. Ms. Russell looks up and Mother says, "Ms. Russell. Good evening. We got here a little early and were wondering if you could unlock—"

Shaniquia Russell holds up a hand as a signal for Mother to stop. Mother complies. "I'm eating my supper now. Go back down and wait." She returns her attention to her soup. Mother walks slowly back to the locked door. Her coat is gone. Carlos and his girlfriend walk into the hall from the stairwell. "Ma-Ma-Ci-Ta!" he says with a sneer. He casts his eyes around to be sure Father is absent. "After you push that fuckin' baby out of your pussy, you know what? You come see me and I will put another one inside of you. You like that? A little fuckin' gift from Carlos." The girl's laugh frightens Mother as much as the young man's threat does. He steps to Mother. She can smell a sickening mix of stale sweat, cologne, and cigarette smoke clinging to him. He smiles and delivers a sharp jab to her belly. The shock of it doubles her over and steals her breath. She feels the baby shift and squirm. There is the feel of wetness between her legs. For a second, she thinks her water has broken. Still bent over, she steps back. She smells the odor of urine in the low air and knows what liquid the punch has produced. Anger, relief, embarrassment wash over her. From the stairwell come the sounds of foot scrape and echoing words. Then she hears the boy and girl both laughing, and it is only anger she feels.

After Father arrives, she goes to the ladies' restroom to remove her underwear and blot her dress dry. Her coat is jammed in the toilet.

There are ten questions to the quiz. It is the first order of business. Mother and Father work through the questions quickly and easily. They are the first to finish. Father carries their answer sheet to Ms. Russell. On his return, Carlos glares at him and tries to trip him as he passes. "Hey! Man! Watch where you stepping," Carlos yells. He is the last to turn in the quiz and then only after Ms. Russell has started counting to ten. At ten, she will accept no more papers returned. "Why you have to make it so hard on me?" he tells Shaniquia Russell at the three-count. "It is not fair you don't test me in Spanish. I think you violate my rights. I should read these in Spanish." He waves the paper in the air. "Yeah," says the girlfriend. "We gonna sue."

"Eight," says Shaniquia Russell, and Carlos is on his feet and moving fast to the table in the front of the room.

They spend the remainder of the session on pediatric poisonings and how to childproof the home.

"Hey, gringo, this how you did it with the kid? A little poison? What did you use, man? Come on, share it with us. We all good friends now. We won't tell nobody. Was it the rat poison? Huh? Did you put it in her milk, amigo? Come on, Papi, open up. This is like question number eleven: What'd you use, man?"

Even Shaniquia Russell pauses, looking like she would like to know, too.

Mother stares at the floor. Father feels his heart pound in his chest and something soft and weak in his heart grows hard as rock. He knows he won't be able to suffer this abuse much longer. Four more sessions, he thinks. Four. No, he thinks. No.

The next morning Father calls Dr. Burke's office to find out if the autopsy results are ready. Burke is tied up with a heavy clinic load and can't come to the phone. The receptionist takes Father's name and number. At five o'clock, shift's end, he has heard nothing. He calls again. A taped message informs him the office is now closed. Father is irritable at home that night. He makes little dinner conversation. He reads to BJ in the evening without intonation. Mother is exhausted and retires at eight thirty. Father declines Ned's invitation to help him with his garage project and takes a long walk in the cold instead.

The next morning, Friday, he phones Burke again. He is asked to leave another message. He tells the young-sounding receptionist, "It's about our daughter's autopsy report. I just wanted to know if it's finished. If Dr. Burke has received the report. We are supposed to get a copy and then have like a final meeting."

"I'll let him know," she says. "Thanks for calling!"

"Wait," he interjects before she hangs up, "where is the report coming from? I mean, who issues it? Maybe they would be the best place to check on its status."

"Well, that would be the medical examiner's office. Would you like that number?"

Father dials the number robotically, convinced it will be another dead end. "Benton Ridgely," the speaker says smartly into the phone. "Medical examiner."

Father is doubly surprised it is the medical examiner himself who answers. He was prepared for another secretary, a wait on hold, more time to practice his words silently again before they died silently in his head. But there is no time to do that now. "Yes. Sir. This is Ford Jackson. Jessica Jackson's father. The girl you did an autopsy on just before . . ." Father has to stop to compose himself. His voice is wavering, his silent practice undone by his ears. The words coming out of his mouth sound too distanced, too coldly clinical, for the emotional weight they carry, and they collapse in his chest. He takes a deep breath and is about to continue when the medical examiner speaks.

"Mr. Jackson. Let me express my deepest sympathies on your daughter's death. I low very sad. And how difficult it must have been for you and the family to witness her . . . passing. With her airway already partly compromised by that aberrant blood vessel, well, even a cold could have closed it over enough that she couldn't breathe. I'm so, so sorry for your loss."

Father is stunned. He tries to form a sentence in reply. "Well, ah, well, thank you for your kind words. But I . . . we didn't know . . . hadn't heard—"

"Mr. Jackson. It's all right. Just take a second. I got all day."

Father tries again. "I don't really know what you're telling me. A blood vessel and her airway? I was just calling to see when you would be finished with your investigation so your report would be issued. We're supposed to meet with Dr. Burke to discuss it. And we hadn't heard anything from him."

"Well, I sent him . . . no, I faxed him the final report on Monday. I thought you had already seen it, and maybe were calling for me to clarify something. I'm sorry. I didn't mean to overwhelm you with the findings like that, but I thought you already knew. I'm sorry."

"No, it's okay. But explain it to me again. Jessica had what?"

"She had . . . Everyone has two large arteries that branch off the top of the heart. They are called subclavian arteries. They are large and normally bring blood from the heart into the upper extremities. The arms. Well, in Jessica's case one of them came off the top of the heart at the wrong spot. It then had to run all the way across the upper chest from the left side of the body to the right, so it could go into the right arm. It's usually not a big deal unless it runs behind the trachea. Which it did. The trachea is . . . You know what the trachea is, Mr. Jackson?"

"I do. It's the main windpipe into the lungs."

"Right. So this large blood vessel ran behind the trachea and pressed in on it from the rear, making the diameter of the airway much, much smaller than it should have been. So the real problem happens when there is something that causes *additional* narrowing in the diameter of the trachea. Like what happens in croup. And any new narrowing produces marked and immediate increase in resistance to airflow. It's a law of physics. You know, it's not hard to breathe through a regular straw, but narrow that opening just by half and you can't. Like trying to breathe through a cocktail straw. Impossible. That's what happened to Jessica in her bedroom that night. Her airway narrowed quickly and unexpectedly to the point where she couldn't move air. It was a totally unexpected problem. And totally undiagnosed until the autopsy. That's what I told Burke. And Officer Mattingly."

"Mattingly has the autopsy report, too?"

"Monday. I talked to both of them Monday."

"And he—"

"He should be ending the investigation into Jessica's death. Cause of death is natural. That's what I wrote on the autopsy report and the death certificate I issued. Laryngo-tracheo-bronchitis (croup), mild. Airway obstruction secondary to aberrant right subclavian artery, severe. I have it all right here. You have a fax machine?"

"I do," says Father. He becomes breathless and light-headed as he recites the ten digits of the post office's fax.

"But you have to review this with Dr. Burke. There's a lot in here for a layperson to grapple with. You'll see. Meet with Dr. Burke. He'll take you through it."

"We will," Father says. He wonders why Mattingly hadn't called to inform them of the investigation's end, to remove that weight from their backs. Or Burke. Burke who knew about the parenting classes they were attending on threat of CPS action. Burke should have called, he thinks. He had all week. He had my messages. He should have called.

"And Mr. Jackson," says the medical examiner.

"Yes, sir."

"You should . . . There is . . ." He stops for a moment. "I'm real sorry for your loss and everything that happened. Just wanted you to know that."

"I appreciate that. Your report at least will . . . will help us understand what happened."

"Yeah, that it will."

Father has the sense Benton Ridgely wants to say more but can't.

*

The Assembler brings more tapes. "You are troubled by what you see, yes?" He asks.

"Aren't You?" I snap the tapes from His hands. Oh, the advantage to having thumbs. I turn away, but He's still there* in front of me.

"Honestly?" He asks.

"It's a sin to tell a lie," I respond.

"Lies can be their own truth, as a path is part of the destination. I am not troubled in the least by My creation." He looks at me with those big "Thou" eyes of His. Today* they are blue.

Father calls Ned from work after he's read the fax twice. He asks him to come to the 7-Eleven near home to talk at three. "Three?" Ned asks. "Yeah," says Father, "I'm getting off a few hours early today."

"What's it about?"

"The laws of physics." Benton Ridgely said it was the laws of physics behind what happened. And Father knows only one person who might understand them, if only a little.

"Physics," Ned says flatly. "Sure. But why can't we talk physics in the garage. That's where I keep it."

"You'll understand," Father says.

"It'll cost you a Slurpee."

"Deal."

They buy two hot teas instead and stand talking near the racks of magazines that offer everything from *Automotive Digest* to *Zodiacal Review*. Father gives Ned a copy of the autopsy report and lets him read through it before they start. When he is done reading, Ned says, "Whew. Some complex stuff here. What do you suppose all that stuff about feeling her bones is about? Even her neck bones."

Father looks at him with his face set and angry. He blows on his tea. A puff of steam rises up and dissipates in the air. "Same reason Mattingly and CPS were on us afterwards."

"Oh. No." Ned shakes his head in disbelief.

"Yeah. They took the tack that we might have abused Jess, beat her." He pauses, then says it. "Killed her."

Ned shakes his head again. He looks over the summary paragraph at the end of page three. "Says here the cause of death was natural means, secondary to airway obstruction from an aberrant right subclavian artery and superimposed mild croup. I take that to mean they no longer have their suspicions."

"That's what the medical examiner told me. Thing is, these guys—Burke and Mattingly and Beatrice Smith—they all knew about these findings Monday. Monday, Ned. And no one contacted us. Would have saved us a week of worry. Would have saved us two trips out to those shitful classes. But no one did. They just went on letting us feel guilty, lettin' us pay the price for something we had no part in. And I'm wondering why they would do that." He blows on the tea again, and takes a tiny sip.

Ned's eyes narrow. "Ford, I know where this is going. Says here Jess had an anomaly that no one knew about. Not us, not Burke, not anyone. And that's what closed off Jess's airway when she got the flu. You're thinking—"

Father interrupts. "I'm thinkin' they missed it. They flat-out missed it. Either they didn't do the right tests or they missed seeing it on all the goddamned tests they did do. All those expensive X-rays and echo studies and CAT scans, something this big just has to show up."

"That's the law of physics you want to talk to me about? The limits of resolution of sonar waves and X-rays? Ford, I don't—"

Father holds up a hand. "No, Ned. Two other laws. One is why no one can breathe through a cocktail straw. That's what the medical examiner said to me to explain what happened to Jess and her airway because of this thing in her chest." He nods to the report in Ned's hands. "Like breathing through a cocktail straw."

Ned scratches his head. "Well, not so hard a concept. Resistance to flow in a tube goes up by the fourth power for every decrease in diameter. So, you decrease the diameter by half, resistance goes up sixteen times. It doesn't go up twice, it goes up by a factor of sixteen. Even plumbers know about that one. I can look it up in my books when we get home, show you on paper, but that's the essence of it." He studies Father's face. There is something in it he hasn't ever seen before. It's not smugness, or haughtiness, but it's close. "You said there's another law you want my help with."

"Yeah. The law of gravity."

"Gravity?"

"What goes up must come down."

Ned looks from the report to Father's face and back to the report again.

"Meaning?"

"Meaning, I'm getting even with those bastards for what they did. Their mistake is what took Jess from us. Then, as if that weren't bad enough, they put it all on us. I'm going after them, Ned, and I asked you here to get your support.

Kate's going to be reluctant to do it. But I want to take those guys down for what they did. Will you help me?"

Ned thinks for a minute. "And how will it help if you do succeed in this? How will it help you grieve Jess's death? It certainly won't bring her back. And the money, if it's money from a suit you're talking about, the money would be tainted. Every nickel of it stamped with her loss. You'd get no joy out of any of that. I'm just saying, Ford, this paper exonerates you all. Let it all go. Just go on. Make a fresh start with BJ and the new one, keep Jess's memory in our hearts. And just go on."

"It's justice I'm looking for, Ned. Justice and fairness. What they did was wrong. All of it, wrong. I mean to make it right." He looks away to the racks of magazines. "They broke your daughter's heart, Ned. And mine and yours and Mae's. There's a price to be paid for that. Are you with me?"

"I'll start with you, Ford. I may not end with you, but I'll start with you. We're all subject to the law of gravity. We need to keep that in mind."

Father sips his tea. It's cool enough now to gulp.

It is a strange tape I now* watch. It shows Dr. Burke reading Father's phone message late Thursday morning. I can see the note. "Father of d'csd pt wants info on autopsy/death meeting. F. Jackson," followed by Father's home and work numbers.

The secretary has pulled my old chart and paper-clipped the message to its cover. Burke opens the folder and turns to the autopsy report. It has already been filed in my chart and initialed by Burke. The header shows the date and time the fax was received: January 7, 2005, 10:31 a.m. He wishes now he had called Father when the report had first arrived on his desk. And, what upsets him is that he's not sure, really, why he didn't call. He's tempted to lay it at the feet of sadness. He's sad about my death. Sad it happened, sad my life is over. But sad, too, the autopsy showed a serious deficiency in his team's workup of my anomalies. Sad—and this truly saddens him, and troubles him that it does—it really *wasn't* my parents' fault, my death.

Sad and troubled about the unpleasantness to come when he would finally sit with my parents and discuss the findings.

Sad it would be with Eileen Marshall that he would share this experience. Sad he holds such a smart colleague in such low regard for her aloofness from patients, her calculating coldness, her shallow manipulation of parental feelings. He hears her say to Mother at the wake, in a voice choked with tears, "And we never got the chance to fix her heart," when she *knew what was behind the girl's death.*

He thinks: But you did have the chance to study her heart, find out what was wrong a dozen times. And you missed it. The one cardiac finding that really mattered, you missed, Eileen Marshall. If we had known about that blood vessel, the family would have been instructed to get to the ER at the first hint of something going on in the airway, a cough, stridor, increased work of breathing. Had the family taken her in, the ER would have intubated her, bypassed the obstruction. She'd be alive today, at home on Christmas break, playing with toys, lost in the wonder of the time of year. She'd be normal, he thinks. "Normal," he mouths. "Jessica Mary Jackson, normal," he says aloud to the chart. And he smiles a brief smile out of the slew of sadness he has assembled in his mind.

I am shocked when he slips the autopsy report out of my chart and carries it to the reception desk. "Cindy," he says to the young girl filing charts. "Would you please start a separate temporary file for all of the materials that come in about this girl's autopsy report?" He hands her the fax. "I'd like to keep them all in one place so I don't have to thumb through the entire chart when I need to reference those materials. You can start with that," he adds, nodding to the pages he has handed her.

"Certainly, Dr. Burke," she says.

As he walks away, he initials the phone message and jots: "no rpt in chart yet. 1/10/05."

It is beneath him. Beneath the good Dr. Burke.

Ned and Father drive from the 7-Eleven to Burke's office. It is almost four thirty on January eleventh. The return of the sun since the winter solstice has added a few minutes of light to the end of the day. The sun sits bright just above the milky blue horizon in the west. Father feels better inside than any day since my death. He is doing unto others what they have done unto him These were the very words of the Assembler when he handed me the Friday tapes. I didn't know what He meant then, but now I do.

They go to the reception desk and ask to see Dr. Burke.

"Do you have an appointment?" the young girl asks politely. Father recognizes her voice.

"Yes," Father lies.

"Patient's name."

"Jessica Mary Jackson," Father replies.

The receptionist types into her computer. "I'm sorry. I don't see her on our roster. Are you sure it's for today? Maybe . . ." She suddenly appreciates there is no child with the two men. "Is this for a child or are you here for counseling?"

"The child is dead. And we're here to find out why," says Father, loud enough for the two mothers queuing behind him to hear.

"Please have a seat in Waiting Room One, and I'll let him know you are here. Mr. Jackson?"

Father nods. "We'll wait right here, thanks." Ned and Father step a few feet to the side and stand watch for Burke. He emerges from the corridor leading to the examining rooms a few seconds later. He looks worried and tired. He offers his hand. Ned shakes it and Father refuses it, choosing instead to pull his shoulders back, raise his head, grow stiff-spined. "Mr. Jackson," Burke says. "Let's slip into an empty exam room where we can talk privately."

To me, the chaos in the office late on a Friday afternoon in the busy flu season is palpable, even on the tape. Babies getting weighed cry on scales, toddlers fight nurses over shots and throat cultures, older children in the waiting rooms squabble over the stand-up toys while mothers pretend to be amused. But Ned and Father neither see nor hear any of this. Their minds are focused like lasers on the script they discussed in the car.

"So," says Burke after he closes the door to Room Eighteen. "What can I do for you?"

Father hands him a copy of the autopsy report. "First thing you're gonna do is call Beatrice Smith and tell her you advised us, based on this report, to quit the parenting classes she registered us in. And then you call Mattingly and tell him to go fuck himself."

"Ford—" begins Ned.

"This the autopsy report?" Burke interjects looking at the first page. "Huh, I haven't gotten my copy of it yet. Let me peruse this." Burke's face is like a young boy's now, open and guileless. Father knows it's a ruse.

"Benton Ridgely faxed it to me this morning. He said you got your copy faxed this past *Monday*. So don't act all surprised. You know what the medical examiner found. He found that we didn't cause Jess's death. That you and your team never found a major anomaly in her chest. That's what killed her. That's why she died. Because of *you*, not *us*. *You*." Father points with an index finger. It shakes with rage.

"Mr. Jackson, wait a second." He picks up the phone from its cradle on the wall. "Beth? Beth, would you please bring me Jessica Mary Jackson's chart? We're in Eighteen. Date of birth, February, ninety-seven. Thanks." He turns to Father again. "Mr. Jackson, I do know about that lesion. Dr. Ridgely called me to the autopsy room to see it the day after Jess died. But that's not the same as knowing in its entirety the results of his evaluation. And I assure you I hadn't seen this report until you handed it to me. Please, give me a minute to read it." The door opens and my chart arrives. He hands it to Father while he reads the autopsy. "Please, check through Jess's record. If there is a report there, it's something never brought to my attention."

Burke reads and Father checks through my chart. He sees his phone message of the prior morning with Burke's notation. He flips through the pages. There is no autopsy report. The emptiness of the chart drains energy out of him like a storm growing weak. It seems Burke hadn't received the report, that maybe Burke is in the clear about the past five days of their purgatorial life after all.

Burke looks up from the page. "Mr. Jackson, I'm glad you came by this afternoon. What I read here is exactly what I hoped Ridgely would find. Jess's death was a natural, unpredictable event. I agree fully with your request concerning the police investigation. I will call Officer Mattingly as soon as we finish up. And, yes, I implore you, do not attend any further parenting meetings. They are not anything you and Kate need to sit through, now that the reason for Jess's death is fully clear. I will call Ms. Smith and explain it all. What we need to do now is find a time for us all to meet and fully review these autopsy results. For me, the sooner the better. I can clear my schedule during the noon hour this Monday. And I'm pretty sure I can get the major players in Jess's care to attend. We'll go through this document page by page, explain it all. Answer all your questions. How's that?"

Father is mute. The ebb of his anger has met the flow of his sadness rising up in a tide of memory, me limp on my bed, his breath failing us both, our lips unsealed by forces both too weak and too strong. He looks to Ned and shrugs his shoulders. Ned says to Burke, "We'll all be here at noon Monday." Father wants to say good-bye but something is stuck in his heart. The ebb of his anger is somehow not complete. He *wants* to be mad, to have something with which to push back the sorrow. Anger gives him breath. Sorrow drowns him.

They leave the office and walk to the car. It is night.

Father's anger refloats during the ride home. He and Ned at first sit silently in the car, immersed in their new thoughts—Ned that there be found some middle ground in Father's search for justice; Father that if Burke's not to blame for Jess's death, then the cardiologist Marshall must be. He muses about the lost fax and is almost feeling apologetic about his belligerent confrontation of Burke, when he remembers what Benton Ridgely had told him. That he had conversations with both Burke and Mattingly Monday morning, stressing his written conclusions that my death was the natural result of my anatomy and mild croup.

Father says to Ned, "It's a ruse, Ned. It's a bullshit ruse that Burke is trying to pull on us. Medical examiner told me today he talked to Burke on Monday about the autopsy results that he was faxing. Burke knew all his findings and conclusions right then.

"So even if that fax did get lost, he knew it all. So why then doesn't he call us up? Why doesn't he *call the medical examiner up* and tell him to resend, that he never got it? You know why? Because he did get it. He got it and didn't want to deal with it because it put the blame square on them, Burke and Marshall and the lot of 'em. I think that fucker was hoping we'd be so cowed by CPS and Mattingly that when he finally got around to telling us what was in the report, we'd just be happy to be done with it all. That we'd just walk away, meek as lambs. That's what's goin' on here, Ned."

"Ford, you don't know that for sure. That's just speculation. Faxes get misplaced and sent wrong all the time. You know that. He's a busy doctor taking care of lots of sick kids day in, day out. Maybe he was just waiting for that report to arrive to move into action. Fact is, we don't know, Ford. We can't know."

"Ned, no. No. The only thing I got to know is this: Whose side are you on? The family's or his? He didn't know about that artery and he should have. He knew the autopsy stuff and did nothing to help us. That's all the knowing we need to do."

"To be fair, Ford, I know he took good care of Jess for all those years. I know he cared about her. And about you and Kate. That's got to count for something, those seven, seven and a half years. You got to hold them up next to all this stuff now and be fair."

"Ned, I'm going to tell you this, but you're not to let Kate know you know."

Ned looks at Father and nods, just a slight twitch of the head.

"Those parenting classes. They weren't . . . benign or anything. They weren't just an inconvenience to our evenings at home. One of the guys in that class threatened sexual violence on Kate. And Ned, he punched her. He punched her in her pregnant belly. I had dropped her off so she wouldn't have to walk from where we had to park, and she was alone with this guy and his girlfriend. First they took her winter coat and stuffed it in the toilet. Then he threatened her and he hit her. She thought her water broke right there when he struck her. Kate was so scared she couldn't sleep all that night. Up and down, all night long. That's the kind of thing Burke could have prevented by deciding not to hide the results of the autopsy. And another guy in our group assaults me on the street after class, steals our binder with the reading assignments. He comes to the post office two days later and extorts forty bucks from me to get it back. That's on Burke, too. But we're not going there anymore, Kate and me. We're not because I decided to take action this week, find out what we should have known Monday. So I ask you again, Ned, whose side are you on? You got to decide."

Ned's face flushes at the thought of his pregnant daughter, my mother, made to suffer the affront Father has just revealed. Such a violation of decency, he thinks. He turns to look at Father. The new look on his face, first seen at the 7-Eleven, is manifest again. It's tainted with anger in the creases by the eyes, but it is a face of something else. Not haughtiness or smugness. Something else. It's the

face of the judge who has already decided the case and
passed judgment even if the evidence has yet to be fully
presented. Self-righteousness. A face nauseatingly full of
self-righteousness. Ned doesn't much like what he sees.

"Ford, I'm with the family on everything. You know that.
But I'm not *against* anyone, either. Let's start with that and
let it all play out. Fairly. For everyone. Us, Burke, Marshall,
the rest. Fairly."

"Deal," Father says loudly as they pull into the driveway. But his word sounds empty again.

There is a sense of gaiety in the house later that night.
But first Mother reads the autopsy report, the conclusions
only, and cries. She can't read beyond those first few lines
because her eyes have scanned the rest of the first page
and noted the words "body," "lividity," "thoracic cavity,"
"glistening," and "aorta," and they freeze. Involuntarily,
her hands shake and the word "aorta" seems to burst into
blurred, spurting letters. Father takes the report from her,
places it on the kitchen table and steadies her hands in
his. He tells her of their meeting with Burke, that they
have been absolved of any complicity in my death and,
as a consequence, are advised to quit the evening classes.
She is so relieved by the double dose of good news, she
picks BJ up and holds her against her chest for as long as it
takes for BJ to start to protest, which is about ten seconds.
Her tears cease in these few moments, and she closes her
eyes against the glaring white pages on the table. The family lingers over dinner, savoring every bite of the baked
cod and boiled potatoes. Nana does not cook meat on
Fridays, even now. They good-naturedly chide Ned over
his failed attempt to rejuvenate his old snowblower; they

compliment Nana on her cooking; they tease Father over the drip of butter on his shirt. No one teases BJ, but they do get her to sing the new songs she learned in school that week.

Cassidy is not there and no one mentions his name. They are too happy to be free of their guilt, of their investigations, of their false penance performed to protect BJ. It is the first night BJ does not ask where I am. All four adults notice that. All four go about the rest of their evenings—the dishes, the bath, the reading, the TV shows—and marvel inside their hearts, BJ is getting through it, getting better.

Cassidy is not there and no one mentions his name.

11

BASEMENT TAPE #16

Cassidy swallows two Valiums and half a glass of water at seven thirty. He has sat in the gloom of his living room on the couch that was his grandmother's watching the ghosty TV and picking at a piece of stale pizza since he came home. The TV's reception is particularly bad tonight, all the images blurred and doubled.

For twenty minutes, he has the recurring idea to rummage through the junk drawers in the kitchen for an old pair of 3-D glasses, thinking it will clarify the forms. Inexplicitly, the screen comes sharp and clear, the images tighten. He sits watching the crisp forms for a minute. His left hand slowly rises to his face. Tentatively, he feels around his eye sockets for the glasses. Now he knows. He did not leave the couch.

The ancient timer switch his mother used turns the corner lamp on at eight thirty with a loud *click!* He takes the light coming into the flicking gray-dark room as a signal for his bedtime.

The Valiums tumble into his hand, slowly go to his mouth. He drinks water again. The last two in the vial. He shakes it to be sure, then holds it up to the light to watch the amber plastic turn warm and molten. He shakes the empty container again, then replaces the cap and shakes it a third time. Satisfied, he holds it to his chest and flops back lengthwise onto the couch. He doesn't close his eyes. They close themselves. He lies there trying to calculate the number of days since his last drink. He sees numbers that seem friendly, like kittens. The numbers call a vision of me to mind. "Four crows," he sees me say, "attempted murder." He thinks he smiles, but in the act of bringing his hand to his lips to check, he sleeps.

The light clicks off at eleven. The TV plays through the night. He has found the best way to chase away the dreams.

The next morning he wakes to find the empty Valium vial on the floor. He shakes his head, trying to remember when he last dosed himself. The Valium was to last for four weeks, Dr. Vinik told him.

It is gone in less than two.

He takes an Antabuse pill from the other vial that sits on the table and swallows it down with the inch of water still in his glass. He makes coffee and drinks it and waits for the unpleasantness to come.

But it disappoints.

Yes, there is the knot in the lower belly and his mouth does partly overflow with saliva that tastes like rusty metal as that knot tightens and relaxes and tightens, and a slight nausea creeps up his gullet to his throat where it deposits its sour juice that makes him gag. But then it stops.

Today there is no retching, no residual nausea, no sweats, no panting for breath, no stars in the black of his brain. He moves his bowels and is at peace. The swirl of the water carries it all away in a moment of remembering.

He showers, and for the first time in four days, he shaves.

His hand is almost steady. It quivers only until the razor is against his skin, then stops. There are no more nicks and cuts. Afterward, looking in the mirror, he convinces himself there is a little light in the dark center of his eyes. A thin sheen of luster only, but light.

As he begins to dress, he is amazed: his stomach growls. And growls again. "Hungry," he says with disbelief. For food.

He has a box of Cheerios but the milk has gone sour. He eats the cereal by the handfuls right from the box. Like a pregnant woman with the morning sickness, he muses.

He thinks of Rose Mary. He thinks of Mother.

He thinks of me.

His hunger leaves, chased by sadness and oats.

He goes upstairs and brushes his teeth. He gets his car keys and drives. The cemetery first, then the house. We are all in our own graves, and he addresses us all, me and Joey and Rose Mary and now his mother, Carina. His voice is flat like the land in winter. Nothing rises in green between the graves. But there is a summer softness to his words, like the chords in his music. He plays his voice until it is choked. Then he stands on the hard ground ignoring the cold.

At our house, no one is home.

Burke is the only one who frets over the meeting planned for Monday. Eileen Marshall, Vincent Garraway, and Pat O'Neil agree to come. They enter the date and time and place into their PalmPilots and go about their weekends unencumbered by the prospects of confronting a family grieving the loss of a child.

For Garraway and O'Neil, their detachment is both practical and ethical. They routinely deal with children afflicted with conditions that bring early death. They would deny the callus on their hearts from the rub of these many deaths, but it is there, hard and horny. And it is good it is there. Without it they could not go on bringing their care to other needy families, many of whom will not suffer this early loss. And, just as importantly, both feel absolved of any error in my care. Neither was charged with the evaluation of my cardiovascular system. Neither contributed to Eileen Marshall's missed diagnosis.

Vincent Garraway takes his wife to a movie Saturday night, a comedy, and his kids bowling on Sunday afternoon, also a comedy, if you were ever to see him bowl. He's an ostrich doing ballet when he rolls that ball. He laughs Saturday night at the punch lines and Sunday afternoon at the gutterballs.

Pat O'Neil is on call for ENT for the weekend. At three in the morning Sunday, he treats a four-year-old for epiglottitis, an infection of the flap covering the trachea that can be just as rapidly fatal as was my airway infection. He rushes from home and bed to the hospital with unbrushed hair that looks like Woody Woodpecker's, sees the child with compromised respirations on her gurney in the ER, and intubates her then and there, saving her life in about twenty seconds. He carries his fatigue with him like a badge all day Sunday, feeling tired and sluggish, but special, heroic. He sleeps soundly Sunday night, arising Monday morning feeling utterly refreshed, and godlike.

Friday night Eileen Marshall dictates a scathing letter to the administrator in charge of the sonography library, lambasting him for negligence in securing the echocardiograms that had been entrusted to his safekeeping. It is the last piece in the paper trail she has diligently constructed about the missing studies of Jessica Mary Jackson. Saturday she shops for shoes. Sunday she goes to church and takes her mother out to dinner, then gets a full night's sleep.

Burke suffers guilt and confusion in equal measure throughout the weekend. He does not feel guilty over my death—Eileen Marshall is the only member of his team who can interpret the images from an echo—but he feels guilty that he attempted to sidestep the difficult emotional work of dealing with its aftermath. And his aversion to that process is what confuses him. He wonders if he lacks the gene for empathy. He wonders if there are others like him, physicians who are tireless in their dedication to the complex care of children, even of those children with the most tenuous of grasps on life, on "normalcy," but then who are entirely divorced from the circumstances after their deaths. It is as if he doesn't value death, as if death is all loss, and one's involvement in death is like throwing good money after bad. He doesn't know why he is like this; he wishes he wasn't, and it saddens him he is, but he'd just like them all to go away when the child dies. He did his best, always does his best. But with death, end of contract. No more service. Time to start over, fresh, alive, newborn.

If you don't call them back to answer their questions about a dead child, he likes to think, eventually they will stop asking, grow quiet for a time, grieve their loss, reattach, have another baby, remember his good care, and make an appointment.

It was not the first faxed autopsy report he conveniently misplaced, thinking, maybe they'll call the ME and get him to answer the questions.

His stomach bothers him all weekend. He leaves his son's basketball game early Saturday afternoon with a headache. He cuts his finger carving a roast chicken Sunday night. There is blood everywhere before he realizes it. The white meat is inedible.

He's awake in his study reading journals until two a.m., not tired for sleep. Finally, in bed at two thirty, he says to the night air, "The dead. The damn dead."

There is not a single star on his black ceiling.

Cassidy learns about my autopsy results Saturday night at dinner. He understands the words well enough—the blood vessel obstructing my breathing, the croup closing off the airway unexpectedly—but Saturday he has difficulty getting his reawakening brain around the emotions that seem to pour out of Mother and Father, Nana and Ned. They are relaxed and happy one moment in celebration of their innocence. They are sad and weepy the next because they grieve my loss, because my body sits disassembled onto three printed pages with headings such as "Thorax," "Abdomen," and "Integument." And they are angry and vengeful the next about Burke's lies and Marshall's error. Cassidy feels nothing but a creeping sadness inside his heart as sobriety begins to operate in the absence of Valium's numbing suppression of his brain. Things in his head seem to be returning to normal, whatever that might be. He gets hungry. He gets sleepy. He awakens from a nap refreshed. He remembers. More, he remembers and then wants to forget. He laughs, he cries. He is content in his sadness.

Sunday he attends Mass with my family. His eyes close over at the homily. Behind his eyelids he sees me look up from the pew where I sit next to him. My finger goes to my nose and twists. He sees himself nod and smile at me and mouth, "Yeah. Boring." He laughs aloud and Nana takes his arm. He opens his eyes with a start. He begins to whisper, "Sorry," but stops and gives the sign he'd just seen in better times. Nana shakes her head, but she smiles.

That night after dinner he starts reading *D'Aulaires' Book of Greek Myths* to BJ. They sit in her room for an hour. His voice is inflective and strong. It scares her, the parts about Cronus and the babies. It makes her laugh, the stone wrapped in baby's clothes. She does not want him to stop. She cries in her bed when Mother intervenes.

He is invited to the meeting with Burke. "No," he says. "I think I'll pass." It is enough simply to be sad.

Burke's conference room we habitually used always seemed small to me, even when I was very young. There often wasn't enough room for everyone to sit on chairs around the table. Sometimes residents or students stood lining the walls like minor gods attending Zeus on Mount Olympus. But on the tape of the autopsy meeting, the room seems even smaller than usual. I think it's because Burke tried to arrange the chairs so that the physicians would be well separated from the family. The four chairs for Mother, Father, Nana, and Ned are bunched together and there's hardly room for shoulders and arms, legs and feet to exist individually. The body parts touch and seem to merge. The same goes for Burke, O'Neil, Marshall, and Garraway at the other end of the table.

Before they sit, each physician approaches my family to shake hands and again extend condolences. They all say the same things—how are you doing now with all of this? Is it getting any better? Such a beautiful wake—though Garraway asks Mother about her current pregnancy and promises to visit her and the new baby in the hospital. "And I'm sure it will just be a social visit," he says taking hold of her hand.

When the meeting starts, Burke holds up a copy of my autopsy report. "I know everyone here has seen this. So I'm not going to go through it organ by organ unless someone," and he nods to my family's end of the table, "needs me to. Instead, I want to get down to the main issue coming from the study of Jess's body after death. She had a vascular anomaly—an artery that arose from the heart in the wrong place and went behind her windpipe, partly blocking it—and no one knew about it.

"I want to know why that was the case. And I'm sure the family feels the same. I don't read echocardiograms, so I have no idea whether one of those should show a vessel like this. That's why Dr. Marshall has come today, to shed some light on this issue. So, Dr. Marshall. Eileen. Please."

Father is pleased that Burke is tackling the issue head-on. It is exactly the question he and Ned had formulated for Marshall when they talked over their strategy for the meeting. Okay, Burke, he thinks. Point for you, but I'm still watching for lies.

Eileen Marshall stands. In her hand she holds what she thinks is the one extant echocardiographic study of my heart, as well as a second patient's echo. She goes to

the door, opens it, and wheels in a portable echo player.
"I just wanted to show the family two tapes. The first
one"—she grunts trying to flip the switch that opens the
spool holder—"is from a child of about one with the same
lesion Jess had. Aberrant right subclavian. The second is
Jess's echo." She sets the first tape. The screen lights up and
begins to display gray shadows and squiggles that seem to
float and jump like fish. "Dr. Burke, the lights please." She
advances the tape as the room goes dark, and stops. "This
is the other child's heart." She points with the tip of her
Bic pen. "And this is the arch of the aorta, at the top of
the heart where the major arteries branch off. Now, you
can see here this shadow," and she manually advances the
spool while pointing to a gray blur that seems to appear
out of a stormy sea of gray and black. "That's the aberrant
right subclavian artery." She rewinds the tape and plays it
again so the vessel reappears. She rewinds a second time
and replays.

"Now, to be really certain it is an aberrant RSCA, you
need to do an arteriogram, but this is what we see on an
echo to suggest its presence. Now," she says, removing the
first study and replacing it with mine, "this is Jess. Same
views. Same machine. Same magnification. Look here."
She sounds to me like a magician preparing the audience
for a sleight-of-hand trick: now you see it, now you . . .

"There's the aortic arch off the top of the heart." Her
pen makes a nice sweep from dark chamber to a half-moon
grayish structure. "And then, nothing here. Nothing. Her
aberrant subclavian artery is not visible. I'm not saying it's
not there. It *has* to be there. But it simply is not visible.
Possibly the size, possibly surrounding structures compet-
ing for the sound waves, who really knows, who will ever

know, but it's not there to see." She is facing the screen looking away from my parents. "Again." She replays the study. "Not there, just not there for us to see." She removes the tape of my heart.

The room is black but for the grainy gray light from the machine. She stands in the dark, above the light, invisible to the seated viewers, smiling.

Burke stands, fumbles for the light switch and throws the room into brightness. Everyone blinks. Father is speechless. More than speechless, thought-less. He simply is unprepared for this display of . . . of innocence. He thinks: She looked for it. It's not there to be seen. What is anyone to do? What?

Burke reads the blank faces of my family. Time to wrap this up, he thinks. "Dr. Marshall. Thank you. I . . . we . . . Medicine is both an art and a science. Sometimes it fails by art. Sometimes by science. Here, technology failed us, failed Jess. But the sadness is the same, no matter the cause." He shoots a quick glance to the echo player. He shakes his head side to side like a scold to a naughty child and returns his gaze to my family. "Is there anything else? Any part of the autopsy we can clarify for you? Terminology? The anatomy? The conclusions are self-evident. Jess's death was an act of God, nothing more, nothing less." He hangs his head and stops.

Mother has tears in her eyes. It is the sadness of her loss and the joy of her innocence again at work. She wants nothing more than to walk out of this conference room and go home to remember me, her dead child, to love BJ, her live one, and to await her coming labor. Nana and Ned both are satisfied with the explanation they have just heard, and they are relieved the book can be closed now,

once and for all, on the question Father pressed all weekend, the question of justice.

Father stands, though his shoulders slump forward, his
spine seems to bend. "Thank you all for coming," he says in
a half whisper. "We really appreciate it." He shakes hands
again with the four departing physicians. Eileen Marshall's
hand is cold as ice.

He walks alone to get the car, to spare Mother the steps.
"Act of God," he tells himself over and over. "Act of God."

Brian Joseph Jackson is born two days later. The labor
is short and comparatively easy. Mother is not even tired
the morning after, even though Brian Joseph's arrival has
kept her awake until the sun has also made its appearance.
He weighs eight pounds and one ounce and has ten fingers
and ten toes, two normal ears, and the heart of a racehorse,
according to Burke who spends five minutes in silent concentration listening to that internal canter. Nana and Ned,
BJ and Cassidy arrive late morning to visit. The chorus
of "oohs" and "ahs" meets BJ's rebuttal kicks and screams
when it is time to leave. She wants to stay with Mother
and voices her displeasure, no, her "hate" for everyone else
in the room, especially the stupid baby boy who sleeps
pinkly and peacefully in his blue blanket. Cassidy cajoles
her with the promise of "winter ice cream" and the gift of a
new box of crayons. She leaves holding his hand, demand-
ing the "big, big box." They are calling her Jeanine now.
"BJ" is handed down to Brian Joseph, at least until he's old
enough to choose "Brian" or "Joe." All is right in the world.

Then Garraway arrives.

Garraway arrives at noon carrying a briefcase. He exam-
ines Brian Joseph, and declares him "normal." After Burke's

careful exam, Garraway's proclamation sounds to Mother and Father like the priest's last blessing at Mass. They half expect him to walk to the doorway, turn and say, "Go in peace." But he lingers by the cribside. They exchange a few words about me. Garraway recalls our first meeting in the nursery. Then he opens the briefcase.

"I found Jess an interesting example of Hilgar syndrome, especially her highly accelerated cognitive development. So I've written her up as a case report. I'm sending it in to the *Journal of Pediatrics* for publication. I thought you might like to have a copy of it for your scrapbook on her." He hands Mother a manila folder. In it is a five-page document titled, "Hilgar Syndrome and Cognitive Development: A Case Report and Review of the Literature."

Mother looks at the neatly typed pages, going through them hoping to see a photograph. There is nothing but words and tables and numbers. "Thank you, Dr. Garraway. I'm not sure we'll understand the medical words in here, but it's good to know there was something to learn from Jess's life." She looks to Father, who nods.

Garraway's face grows somber at that. His eyes lose the little crinkle of lines at their edges. Color drains from the port wine stain on his forehead. He just stands there a moment then reaches again into his briefcase. In his hand he holds a round metal container. He hands it to Father. "There may be one last thing to learn from Jess. I don't know. But this is a copy of her two-year echo. I borrowed it from the sonography library a few months ago when I started writing her case report. But I never needed to use it. Now, it seems, it is the only echo still existing except for the neonatal study you saw Dr. Marshall play on Monday. All the others are lost. I checked. How or why, I don't know. No one knows I have this spool, or that I made a copy for you. My duty to Jess wouldn't be complete if I didn't let you know of its existence and give you a copy." He looks at Father and then back to Mother. "Seven, eight echoes lost. I don't know." He shakes his head. "I don't know if there is something left for Jess to teach us with this study or not. I hope not, actually. But I wanted to give you the opportunity to answer that question for yourselves." He snaps the latches on the briefcase shut, one by one. He goes to the door and turns to them. "If you're ever asked how you came into possession of this tape, you can tell them it came with the case report from me. The original echo I'm going to refile in the library. Today." He considers saying that it, too, will probably disappear, but feels he doesn't have to. Instead, he says, "It's my last duty to Jess. I think she would have wanted me to discharge it. Put all the pieces of her life on view." He turns and leaves.

At first Father is not infused with anger. He feels too shamed by his gullibility—no, his stupidity, for that. On Monday, he never thought to ask about the other echoes done through the years. He allowed Marshall to take him in, make a fool of him. If he had questioned her then on the other studies, he would have learned of their disappearance. That alone would have heightened his suspicions. But, no, he sat there in the dark, *in the dark*, weepy-eyed and forgiving, and let her get away with her ruse because he was who he was, a mid-level postal clerk with a year and a half of junior college. And she was who she was, the brilliant cardiologist with enough paper framed on her office walls to wrap a three-hundred-pound box of weights. So before he gets angry he says matter-of-factly to Mother, "We'll find the smartest goddamn malpractice lawyer in the city and we'll get her. We'll get them all. Act of God, they said. Bull. I'll show them an act. An act of man."

Brian Joseph begins to cry a hunger cry. Mother looks at his plethoric, wriggly form under the blue blanket, then back to Father. She nods.

*

My heart breaks. I love you, Vincent Garraway. But why did you puncture their peace with the truth? I have seen the truth, and you know the truth. But they would be happy and whole and healed if left in the lie. Why ask them to find the answer in the life of Jessica Mary Jackson? Or was my entire life somehow about "the truth"? What is my truth, Dr. Garraway, and why must it bring pain? Again.

Nothing I have seen in these tapes provides me even a tiny clue. I remember the first tape with the photo of Mother holding me, a newborn, and roses in her arms, her Christmas message to the world. Now* I cannot escape the sadness of my breaking new-knitted heart as I watch them both consumed with vengeance, and mindless, forgetful rage. It is a new photo I see: every rose is wilted black, every thorn thick as thumb.

The tapes seem more useless than the hands of my birth. I am worried that, through Garraway, Mother and Father will find the answer to my life, one that only causes more anger and bitterness.

PART THREE

WHAT MOST MAKES US HUMAN

12

THE ASSEMBLER OF PARTS

It is the advertisement in the *Washington Post* that convinces Father to make an appointment for a "free consultation" with an attorney at D'Woulfe and D'Woulfe. The ad reminds Father of a postcard. It is rectangular in shape. In its center is a picture of Brandon A. D'Woulfe, an elderly, serious-looking man wearing a plain dark suit and a short beard. He stands, arms crossed at his chest, before a gathering of fifty people, all of whom smile while they hold up settlement checks. The caption printed in bold letters below the photograph is a single word: "Justice." The firm's address and phone number are in the upper left corner. The zip code is in bold. Father has talked to many friends about finding a malpractice attorney. None of his acquaintances has ever used one. He has read through the yellow pages twice, each time analyzing the information to settle on a firm, but all the write-ups seem identical, unrevealing.

But D'Woulfe's zip code is in bold. The postman in Father likes that. The firm attends to detail. Plus the man's eyes fix you as if they know something prophetic and unimaginably painful about life. Your life. Even his stare is bold. Father decides he likes that, a lot.

The office of D'Woulfe and D'Woulfe occupies the entire seventh floor of a metal and glass building just south of the expensive department stores I used to see on Wisconsin Avenue during trips to the hospital. Mother and Father are served coffee in china cups. They sip it slowly. It tastes like the coffee they've had in restaurants on anniversaries or birthdays. There is a plate of cookies on the silver tray bearing cream and sugar. "Galettes," says the receptionist setting down the tray on the glass-topped table. Father bites one and the crumbs seem to disappear in his mouth before he can crunch them, like buttery ashes on his tongue. Mother raises her eyebrows in exclamation, as if to say, "What in heaven are galettes?" Through the picture window in the waiting area, they can see the care-free cursive of Bloomingdale's and the sedate seriousness of Saks Jandel.

Father is at first disappointed with the man who enters to greet them. He is tall and young and clean-shaven and wears red, white, and blue suspenders over a starched white shirt. The letters BAD'W are written in blue thread on his shirt pocket. Father is taken aback by the man's eyes. They seem altogether too closely spaced in his narrow, elongated head. He has none of that look of strength and experience Father thought he'd seen in the advertisement. He is hoping the man is simply an assistant or a secretary. And the monogrammed initials, perhaps nothing more than part of a corporate uniform. Like the UPS people.

"Brandon D'Woulfe," he says as he offers his hand. "And you are Mr. and Mrs. Jackson? Yes?"

"Yes," says Father. Mother smoothes her blouse collar before taking his hand. He looks so well dressed, so proper and dignified, she thinks.

"Welcome," he says. "Please come with me. We can talk in my office. Leave your coats. They'll be fine." Brandon D'Woulfe turns and leads the way. The receptionist smiles at Father's perplexed look as he walks by her desk. She mouths, "Junior." His eyebrows register her remark. He wants to smile back in thanks, but his head is too full of words, facts, dates, and contradiction to do so.

"Please, have a seat," the younger D'Woulfe says gesturing to a leather couch against the wall. He occupies the sole chair opposite them. A low table sits in the space between them. He waits until the creaking noises have quieted before he says, "So, I want to know the details of your problem. I will sit and listen to you until you are finished. I will not interrupt. I will record everything you say. I will ask you some questions. I will review whatever materials you have brought. I will discuss your case with the senior member of the firm, my father, Brandon A. D'Woulfe, Sr., and I will let you know where we propose we go from there. Agreed?"

Mother nods. Father clears his throat as if to speak, and nods.

"Alright. Who would like to tell me the story?" He presses the record button of the machine on the table.

"This here is the autopsy report. And this is the echo tape," begins Father as he hands D'Woulfe the "materials" he brought. "Jessica was our firstborn. They killed her, the doctors did. Then we were made the scapegoats. Then the autopsy proved us innocent. But then they tried to cover up their mistakes by getting rid of the evidence. We don't think any of that is right." He stops. His face is flushed and his eyes are narrowed in their sockets like he is seeing too much sun on snow. He waits a few seconds and adds, "We want justice." The only sound in the office is from the machine. It seems to breathe in a wheezy, struggling way.

When it is apparent that Father is finished, B. A. D'Woulfe, Jr. says, "Alright. That's a good start. But go back to the beginning now. Tell me the *whole* story of what happened to Jessica Mary. Everything."

Mother is touched the lawyer has used my full name. Before Father can begin again, she starts. "Jessica Mary was born with Hilgar syndrome almost eight years ago. She came out of me with no thumbs, but that didn't matter. She had her life, and she had us. That's what matters." Mother spins out the story of my life and death. She talks, uninterrupted for half an hour.

What Brandon A. D'Woulfe hears makes him happy. Exceedingly happy. Wait until the old man hears about this one, he thinks after my parents have left and he returns to his office to make written notes from a review of the audio. He works until midnight getting the timeline, the players, the medical facts straight. He keeps his secretary working until ten typing the transcript of the interview. He sleeps on his office couch until five, showers and shaves and puts on clean clothes but still his signature suspenders. He works over coffee highlighting the transcript in yellow from five thirty until seven a.m.

He's in his father's office at two minutes past seven, waiting for him to arrive for the presentation.

It's going to be a blockbuster of a case.

He can feel it in his bones, which resonate with a distinctive tickle to the internal "Ka-ching! Ka-ching!" of the insurance industry's cash register. Oh, how his fingers twitch, how his thumbs hum! At five past seven, he can bear it no longer. He hooks his thumbs under the suspenders and does five sets of ten repetitions against the elastic bands. His thenar muscles are screaming in pain when his father enters the room at seven minutes after seven. It is January twenty-second.

Even Cassidy is anxious about the phone call they all await from the firm of D'Woulfe and D'Woulfe. He eats supper with the family the night of the consultation and listens to Father describe the three-hour meeting. He thinks it is fair and reasonable to sue if the facts are as Father insists. But he himself has a sketchy recollection of the events from the time shortly before I died until a week or so ago. He remembers me in his arms the morning of my death. And the words I whispered in his ear. He remembers singing at my funeral. Looking at Jeanine pouring chocolate milk onto her smashed sweet potatoes and yelling, "Gravy, Mommy, gravy!" he remembers the face of Beatrice Smith, and even now a chill of fear rattles his spine. He remembers Father Larric shaking his hand and exhorting him to lay aside his blame and his guilt. He remembers how easy it was for him to do just that even as the sadness coalesced and bore down on him like a storm. He thinks it was the acceptance of that storm that eased his heart of other anger, other blame. He remembers now how sweet sadness can feel. The rest of the days are conflated with withdrawal dreams, the hauntings of his past, the phantasms of his future without me. When Brian Joseph cries in his crib upstairs in my old room, he is startled from his minute steak and his miasmic rememberings.

It takes him a few seconds to recall the birth of the boy who will go on to choose "Joey" as his appellation, who will attend college on a baseball scholarship, and who will never once in his life drink to excess. "Brian Joseph," he says to Mother who is already pushing back from the table to go to him. Cassidy's face is full of certainty, as if it is he who must remind her of the new birth. "Yes," says Mother with a slight nod. "Brian Joseph." It is as if an agreement has been concluded between the two of them, ending some uncertainty.

Cassidy holds the baby after Mother has fed and changed him upstairs. The dessert is being served. He smells like a bottle of good rum to Cassidy, caramel and vanilla and the salt sea. He kisses the baby's forehead. "Yo-ho-ho," he says to the wide-eyed boy.

Later that night, after Jeanine has been fed the story of Cupid and has succumbed to the length of the day by the creak of the rocker and the velvet in his voice, he tells Father, "Ford, whatever I can do ta make it all come out right, I'll gladly do."

"Kind of you, Joe. We'll keep that in mind."

The next morning, Father watches the clock on the far wall of the post office as he sets up his counter slot. In his worldview the gears of justice grind slowly. He envisions hours, days perhaps, of tortured deliberation on the merits of their case at the office of the attorneys. The debate of pros and cons. The caveats. The loopholes. The finer points of the law. He imagines three, four lawyers in the firm's library surrounded by leather-bound books piled high as walls on mahogany tables, scouring the law for the way, the truth, the light. He imagines yellow legal pads full of scribble, one of the pages neatly divided by a thin red line down its very center. A sort of exodus for truth and justice. The page, a yellow sea divided by the attorney's hand. "Drown them all," Father mumbles as Cassidy unlocks the front door.

Before the first customer can enter, he hears the manager sing out from his office. "Ford, you got a call. An attorney. Take it in here. I'll leave ya alone."

"Mr. Jackson?" Brandon A. D'Woulfe, Jr. says over the phone. "We're going to take your case. We'd like you and your wife to come in again, this time to sign our standard contract and some authorizations for release of records. We think you have a case, a real good case. And we feel, given *all* the circumstances, the sooner we go forward with it, the better it will be. Could you come sometime this afternoon or evening? It won't take but a minute. Then we'll get Jessica Mary's records and send them out for expert review. Within a month, the suit will be filed. By Passover, they'll be begging to settle. Shall we say six?"

"Six would be fine," Father says. "Kate and I will be there."

"Excellent. And, please, jot this down. The key code to the gated parking lot is W-O-U-L-F-E. The lot is heated. Cold out there."

"Thank you, sir," says Father. "Kate and I appreciate that." He remembers the bleak cold of the street where he parked to attend the parenting classes. Anger and relief compete in his heart.

"No problem," says D'Woulfe. He is doodling on a tablet of yellow paper. It has the summary of points made by his father at the morning meeting. Four lines that read: "Sympathetic plaintiffs," "Understandable medical issues," "Medical fraud," "Settle for policy limits." He adds his own commentary to this paternal wisdom and writes, "Punitive damages—fifteen million."

"See you at fifteen," D'Woulfe says to end the call.

"Sir?" Father asks.

"I meant, six. See you at six."

"Yes, sir," says Father. He hangs up the phone and calls Mother, misdialing twice out of excitement.

Brandon A. D'Woulfe, Jr. turns his eyes again to the memo, reading, "The Jackson case will settle not because of the medicine but because there's fraud on the part of the docs. The hospital will pay up to protect its reputation. So fraud's the angle to take in the discovery phase. Bang on it like a kettledrum.

"Name everybody who touched the kid, and the hospital. Work up a damages claim that goes heavy on the kid's lost future wages. Like forty years at 100K per. And add another half mill for loss of consortium, pain and suffering, blah, blah, blah. That ought to scare them into surrendering the policy limits on the cardiologist and the hospital. Settlement figure I have in mind is four mill.

"Send the file to Freidman, the cardiologist in Boston and to Bill Chester, our peds guy at Hopkins. In your letter to them, tell both there's a rush on the review. Let them charge a premium. I'd like to get this case filed in a month.

"Last. Badger, as slam dunk as this case is, DO NOT try to hit it out of the park. They're gonna come back at us with limited lifetime earnings capacity b/c/o her set of handicaps if you do. Then we're in a brawl that will take years to sort out, expert by expert. Just go at them hard over the fraud thing, and take the policy limits.

"Dinner? This week? This month? B. A."

It is this closing inconsistency that kindles his thinking. January has but one week to run. To dine with his father "this week" or "this month" is a distinction without a difference. It sets him to wondering what else might be wrong with the old man's logic.

Certainly not the part about the hospital's eagerness to settle because of the specter of fraud. No, that's a given. Or the probable strategy of the defense to try to limit the economic damages by suggesting the child's handicaps would have constrained her vocational opportunities. No, a jury would certainly consider those arguments. And four mill for a quick case with forty percent going to the firm, well, that's not bad for a couple months' work drawing up the complaint, filing the suit, getting the depos of the treating docs and parents done. But there is something in the case that gnaws rat-like at him, because he thinks that, with just the right manipulation, juxtaposition, reassembly, it could be an altogether different case, a big, fat, juicy one. Say fifteen mill. Say twenty mill. He repeats that out loud, "Twenty mill." He likes the sound of it.

He reads over the memo again as he waits for the mother and father to arrive, digging and pawing at the nugget in the case. It's in there. He can feel its solidity beneath the surface. He's the Badger.

It is a great relief for Mother and Father to hear Brandon A. D'Woulfe, Jr. say that there will be no cost to them for his firm to litigate their claim unless the outcome is successful. Until then, the firm will bear all the costs including the fees of the experts, which, the young attorney says with great earnestness, may run upwards of forty thousand dollars if the case goes to trial. No, as the contract he hands them stipulates, all costs will initially be borne by D'Woulfe and D'Woulfe. Whatever monetary settlement is won will be proportioned forty percent to the firm, sixty percent to the claimants. Only then will the costs of bringing the claim be taken out of the family's share. "So you see," he says, "there is no risk to you and your family. For instance, if we receive four million dollars in settlement, the firm retains one million six hundred thousand and you get the rest, two million four hundred thousand, out of which you pay the experts' fees, the court costs, duplication costs, postal costs, those sorts of things. Let's say they all come to fifty thousand. That leaves you with a net of two point three five million." He lets that last word hang in the air like the peal of a Sunday church bell. "Mill-y-on," he repeats for effect. "If all that's clear, please, both of you sign and date the last page above your names."

Mother looks at Father. Her face does not hide her fatigue. She is but a week postpartum. Brian Joseph calls for her breasts every hour and a half through the nights. Father has tried bottles of milk so that Mother can rest, but the hungry baby will have none of it. Fatigue has eroded some of her eagerness to join Father's cause to set my death aright. So she regards Father's face and simply says, "Ford?"

"It won't cost us a thing," Father says. "And it's what we got to do. For Jess." He doesn't hesitate a bit. He signs his name and adds the date and hands the paper to Mother. She signs but even her cursive is grudgingly slow. "It won't cost us anything," he repeats when he takes the contract from her.

They also sign a dozen form letters requesting a release of my medical records to the law firm of D'Woulfe and D'Woulfe. Brandon D'Woulfe explains the next step—a formal review of my records by their experts and then the filing of papers that will commence the legal proceedings. He offers his best guess of the timeline—a month to file the case, three or four more for discovery, and then either settlement or trial by summer. Mother nods. Father makes notes.

"May I offer you some tea or coffee?" he asks.

Father checks his watch. "No, thanks. It's getting close to seven and we best be getting home. Our new little one will be wanting his dinner about now."

"Shame you can't stay. I'd like to learn more about Jessica. Pity." Even before he stands to lead them to the exit, his mind is racing, unlocked by the word he last spoke. Pity. Yes, pity, the missing element in his father's construction of the case. The central theme of damages should not be the economic losses of a life of well-paid work by an intellectually capable but physically handicapped citizen. That truly would be worth three or four million. But there is a different, much more lucrative calculus of the case. The approach to take is to make little Miss Jessica entirely *pitiable*. In her hearing and speaking and eating and walking and ass-wiping, as pitiable as a human child can be made to seem. So pitiable she seems barely to break the threshold of humanness. Her garbled words, some animal dialect. Her motor ears, some robot assembly. Her gamboling gate, Neanderthalic. Her claw-hand touch, alien. All for the jury to see. He knows already how his closing to the jury will sound. "And what did the defendant doctors do to this poor unfortunate child, this innocent, simple gift of a gracious God? They judged her not worthy. Not worthy of the care you or I or yours or mine might have expected as one's just due. Just due.

"But Jessica Mary Jackson, *not worthy?!*" He will shake his head in amazement and disbelief before continuing. "Their wanton act of negligence was their judgment on poor Jessica that she didn't deserve the special life she was given. Because she was different from the rest of us, they turned away. They turned away and let her . . . strangle to death. Like a criminal hung on the gallows, or a wild animal caught in a steel trap. But Jessica Mary was no criminal, unless the way her imperfect hands stole her parents' hearts is criminal. And no wild animal, either, unless the spirit in her that clung to life through the pain of her surgeries and the rejections of her peers, is animal.

"And, ladies and gentlemen of the jury, I know you will not turn away from little Jessica now. You will not join those mighty judges of worth, those doctors sitting smugly there in good clothes and comfortable seats. You will not turn away from the duty you now have to her. They are guilty of her death. And her death is no small thing. Punish them for thinking it is a trifle, a nothing. Punish them for extinguishing the pure light of love that was there in her and in her family with her. Return a verdict for twenty million dollars. Teach them a lesson. Teach these doctors, these healers, these demigods, a lesson in life. They sure to God need it."

Father waits for B. A. D'Woulfe to unlock the front door with his key. Mother stands at his side. He thinks the attorney looks otherworldly, lost in some complex legal place weighing the good, the bad, on the scales of justice. Father is glad he has retained this firm, this man. Justice, he thinks, justice.

"It would help me a lot if we could spend some time together so I can get an in-depth feel for Jessica, the person she was. Maybe review some photos and her schoolwork, her art, any videos you may have of her, and talk with you at length about her accomplishments. And, of course, her limitations. It is of utmost importance to put forth a full and complete picture of any plaintiff but especially a young child so the jury can form a relationship with her. So that Jessica is not some abstraction we merely talk *about*, but is instead a real person whose presence in the courtroom is *felt*. So I was wondering if we could meet again, at your convenience, on days when you, Mrs. Jackson, might have some help with your new baby at home?"

Father has Friday off. They will bring their pictures of me and all my refrigerator art and the video of our beach vacation. And Brian Joseph, too, if he persists in refusing the rubber nipple.

And their memories. They are happy to bring their memories. For the first time since my death, they see their memory of me as a sacred part of who I was. As real, as palpable, as clippings of my hair kept in a plastic pouch or the shriveled umbilical cord pressed between the pages of my baby book. Their memories, now, are not all painful, any more than touching the cut locks from my first haircut is a source of pain. They will bring their memories, troves and troves of them. They will come now with brave smiles and only occasional tears.

Badger writes a memo to his father. "B. A. Met with the Jacksons tonight. Signed the contract and release of records requests. Seems, though, the kid might not have been as bright as they first let on. They're coming back Friday with videos, school stuff. Art. Then I'll be able to judge this wrinkle better. Have a thought I'd like to run by you about the damages angle if what I get from the family corroborates this wrinkle. Working lunch tomorrow? Next day? LM know. B. A. Jr."

Father turns onto Wisconsin Avenue. The last of the evening traffic herds by in headlamp shafts of brightness. If all the streetlights along that corridor were to be extinguished at once, Wisconsin Avenue would pulse with silver light like an enormous wriggling glowworm in the dark.

"I think we should be glad we found this firm of attorneys for our case. That young D'Woulfe, he seems to know what he's doing. He's smart. And thoughtful. I looked at his face when we were leaving, and I swear I could almost hear the gears in his head grinding on about Jess, and us, and the case. And in a week, two tops, he'll know Jess as well as anyone. I think we're lucky, Kate. And it isn't costing us a thing."

Mother's eyes are closed, though she is not sleeping. "Do you think he could do that with Jess? Get to know her so well that he could make people on the jury—just a group of strangers—see her as she was, love her the way we all did? Do you think he could really do that?"

"That's what good lawyers learn to do over a career. That's their duty to their clients, to present them and their case honestly and completely. So, yeah, I believe he can." He turns his head to steal a look at Mother. Her eyes are still closed. The warmth of the car, the drone of the engine, the sense of confinement in a space, are making her sleepy. He turns back to the road and traffic. Her face, his face, are more shadow than skin in the silver light of traffic.

I watch and listen and loathe those empty words, words that seem the hollow echo of what had been spoken on the same stretch of road eight years earlier as we three drove home from my first outpatient conference with the doctors. "I think we will be real glad to have the doctors we have for Jess. They all seem to know what they're doing," Mother had predicted. And now Father's prophecy.

Jeanine is sleeping in my old room now. Mother and Father had never gotten around to taking the changing table and old rocking chair out of her room after she outgrew the need for diapers, breasts, bottles, and burps. So it seems the best solution is to put Jeanine in my room and hand over her room to Brian Joseph. They wheel the old crib up from the basement. The pony mobile is still clamped to the headboard and plays as loud and clear and quick as ever. Jeanine fusses the first few nights, but my nocturnal ceiling soon catches her imagination. Father or Cassidy sit with her in the dark, after bath and books, and tell her about the constellations.

She is Sagittarius, the ninth sign of the zodiac. She learns to count to nine in the dark at Cassidy's teaching well before little Brian Joseph takes his first bottle at ten weeks. She bids me goodnight most nights—well, not me really, but the constellation Aquarius—just as Father or Cassidy is at her door to leave.

Ned, Nana, and Cassidy all volunteer to join Mother and Father at the attorney's office for the upcoming meeting. Each is eager to join his memories with the others' in constructing my essence. But D'Woulfe forbids it, telling Father by phone it would sully their case if he met with any potential witnesses other than those who brought the case, namely, Mother and him. He will hear what the others have to say about me, but that will occur when the defense deposes them, or at trial if they are called as witnesses. "You can tell me anything at all about Jessica and her family, but I have to hear it from you right now, not from them. Ask them for reminiscences that seem to make Jessica . . . special." The word drips out of the phone like drool. "That's going to be the key to unlock the case. Jessica, one of a kind. Unique. Unmatched in all of God's creation. Remember her that way, bring her to life that way, and we all win. We win it all. A special, special child."

*

I ask Him, bluntly, just how many more tapes must I see? I rattle the canister holding the tape He's come to collect, realizing how similar all His tapes are to my lost echocardiograms. I rattle it louder. If the point is that life goes on, that people linked together in love can heal their hearts, He has shown me more than enough. Cassidy is sober. He suffers his sadness over my death without the intinction of anger or vengeance, and the purity of his pain has spread to his past. More and more he can miss his child and wife, suffer that loss, without the need to bury his mother in blame. More and more he comes to believe he erred in not making peace with her. There had been so much love among them all, he sees clearly now, it was almost alive, a living thing, that love. He sees now that his blind, unforgiving anger toward his mother accomplished nothing less than the death of whatever love remained after their passing.

He often hears the words Father Larrie spoke the morning after my death. They come at odd times—frying hamburgers at the stove, dropping cans in the trash, searching for matches in kitchen drawers: cherish her memory.

Don't let guilt and blame tarnish it.

That will only sever your connection to her and to those who keep her alive in their memory and love.

He thinks it the most sensible thing he's ever heard a priest say.

Cassidy is sober and sad and full of memory and hope. But my parents' anger demands the compensation of justice. Though it seems their right, I would rather they had no need of justice over my death. Still, what they do seems the proper venting of their justifiable emotion. Their anger unsettles me, but justice will vent that anger, be their vengeance, and they will go on, and away from Brandon D'Woulfe's complex maze of malpractice law.

I see all this clearly in the tapes. How many more must I watch? I ask Him this. No, I demand it of Him with my double voice, my throat and fingers, pitched and poked. He carries a book in His hands. I recognize the Catechism. "Who is man," He asks pompously. The tone of His voice—very Moses the Prophet—at first suggests there will be phrases to follow, to complete the question. I expect something like, "Who is man that he should eat of the fruit of the Tree of Life?" Or some such pronouncement. But, no, He rests his Charlton Heston voice a moment and then repeats, "Who is man?" He waves the Catechism. It is His subtle hint that His question and its answer reside there, known to me.

"Man is a being created in the image and likeness of God," I mouth. It is the third question in the book, I know full well.

"And so *should* it be," He intones seriously. The Catechism becomes a tape. Then the Assembler mimics me, rattling His tape like a box of unused bones.

There are days—and weeks and entire months—when B. A. D'Woulfe, Sr. thinks his only son would have made a better used-car salesman than personal injury lawyer. It's not in the way he dresses—no, he has the lawyerly look down pat, from the width of his pants cuffs to the width of his suspenders to the brief whiff of his cologne. And it's not in his work habits, for the Badger is known to burn the midnight oil, to cut no corners. And it's not in his intellect, for he knows the law and how to use it uncannily well. No, sadly, it's in his face, for he has that *erasable* look, a "now you see it, now you don't" sneer, which emanates from his rodent eyes and pointy chin. You look at his visage and *expect* a lie. Or if not a lie, at least a shaded half truth.

He says with his face, every car on his lot is cherry. Garage-kept. One owner, little old schoolteacher. Never driven over fifty miles an hour. He preys on hope. The hope to believe. So the senior partner thinks, What's he got on his Etch-A-Sketch mind about the Jackson case? It's a case made in heaven. Clear-cut negligence, medical fraud, readily apparent injury. Hell, the death of a child. What more could Badger want from it? More money? Well, more money is *always* nice, but they're rolling in money already. Last year alone, verdicts and settlements of over seventy-five million. So no big deal if the kid's not bright and wasn't going to go to Harvard, and they have to pare back their economics. All right, three mill instead of four, the settlement value. That's one point two mill to them. For what, sixty hours of work between getting the complaint filed and sitting in on six, seven depositions? That's two grand an hour compensation. He thinks of his own father, David D'Woulfe, making pastrami sandwiches in the deli he owned in Brooklyn. A dollar ninety-nine, including a whole dill pickle. The old man was happy to clear two bits on each transaction. Two grand an hour now for me, he thinks, not so bad.

If not money, what then, more fame? Hardly. The firm's
already the best on the East Coast. Badger could never
improve on that with a single wrongful death case. So if
not money or fame, what then for the Badger? Chutzpah?
Ego? His coming of age? Yeah, well, maybe. Trying to
show the old man what the kid's really made of. Could
be. But who was that guy who flew too high, got too close
to the sun? Daedalus, he thinks. Remind the Badger about
Daedalus. He makes a note on his legal pad and leaves his
office for the meeting at Clyde's Restaurant.

They order the same lunch out of habit, cheeseburgers
and fries and a side salad. Badger will attack with ketchup,
his father with mustard and mayonnaise. They drink black
coffee before, during, and after the meal. NutraSweet for
the elder, sugar for the younger. Neither will touch the
salad.

The senior D'Woulfe flaps three packets of sweetener
to settle their contents before he rips them open with his
teeth and adds the powder to his cup. He stirs with the
folded empty paper packets. "So. What's going on with
the Jackson matter? You mentioned wrinkles. I don't like
wrinkles."

"I don't either. But maybe the kid was less educable
than I heard at the first interview. I'm thinking she must
have been, with her deafness and speech impediment and
all. Parents are back Friday for an extended interview and
they're bringing her stuff from school and whatnot. But I'm
thinking it's not so much a wrinkle as an opportunity." He
lets that sink in as he gulps his coffee. He's gone over this
pitch eight, nine times since the idea crystallized yesterday
evening. He *knows* he can sell the idea. His father's face is,

as always, a poker stare. "So I think this. We *embrace* her limitations. We *embellish* her imperfections. She becomes not the next brilliant architect or lawyer who happens to have a handicap—come on, they're a dime a dozen these days. Instead, she's this barely human being, this sort of thalidomide *creature* with claw hands and no voice and megaphone ears and no friends and hardly a life to speak of." He pauses a second before saying it. *"But she's loved."* He lets the words sink in, find their way through the hard shell on his father's heart.

"By her family, see, she's loved. Hell, everyone loves her." He flips both hands in the air to suggest a world of love. "She's as lovable as a sheepdog. Why? Because she really *is human.* Sometimes, it's what barely breaks the surface that we see most clearly. And she does. Break the surface. Of human- ness. But barely, like a fish half coming out of the water. Weak, wretched, repulsive, ugly, deaf, mute, hands like the creature from the black lagoon, an almost monster, but people love her anyway, just like a full human. Especially her family. Those good simple folk, our clients." He raises his cup to drink. Poker face has become "you're bluffing," the slight rise of his gray brows and the display of a little more cloudy eyeball. "So. You're thinking, all right, why? Why go the dumb-dumb route?"

"Should I be?"

Badger nods affirmatively. "Here's why. If we make her a scary sea monkey but one who *feels* this love of peo- ple, here's what we arouse." He waits while the waitress refills their cups. He notes with satisfaction that the old man doesn't grab for the sweetener right away. He thinks, I got him. Then he thinks, NutraSweet, bladder cancer. Then he remembers a fact from his undergraduate study of psychology: behind the fear is the wish. His father coughs into his napkin and Badger continues. "We arouse pity. Pity. We arouse the jury's goddamn, monstrous, sweet pity." He tings the rim of his water glass with the nail of his thumb. "Pity," he repeats. The fading ring of the glass sounds like the bell at the end of a round of boxing.

The food arrives. The old man scans the table for mustard. His hands go out into the air, palms up, in a gesture that wordlessly says to the young waitress, "Can you spare it?" after he utters the single-word sentence, "Mustard?" His face is screwed into a sour scowl, a face like mustard itself.

"Right away, sir," she says.

Badger notes she's young, a college kid trying to make a buck. And pretty. Sort of Italian face, dark brown hair, nice body, good legs. A runner, probably, he thinks.

"And what does pity get us? Now that it's *aroused*, what does it *provide*?"

Badger pauses until the waitress gets to the table with the Gulden's. "Twenty million dollars," he says. His father is looking into the cleft between the top and bottom of his hamburger bun, assaying the thickness and melt of the cheese. Badger looks up to the young woman and smiles. "Forty percent for us." She smiles back.

"And just how does pity get us twenty million?"

Badger squirts ketchup from the squeeze bottle into his bun's interior, and smiles again at the waitress. Her name tag says "Angela." "Thanks, Angela," Badger says. Then he looks into the face of his father. Gone now are all the veneers. He sees an old man with an old man's face, saggy and gray and covetous as Midas. "That, Father, is the beauty of this all. Pity is guilt's one and only offspring and protector. It is pity that guards the guilt in people, and it is guilt, Father, that guards the gilt." He rubs his thumb against his index and middle fingers. "Twenty million in gilt." The ketchup bottle sucks air after Badger replaces it on the table. The sound is like a roar from the crowd. A knockdown, he thinks.

The senior D'Woulfe chews his burger. "Inflame the jury's pity and in so doing stoke their guilt?"

"Exactly."

"Their guilt over what? That is the missing part for me, Badger. They pity the girl with the basement humanity, that I get. But of what are they guilty?" He wipes the corner of his mouth and studies the yellow stain on his white napkin.

"Her death. They are guilty of her death."

"Not if they're not named in the suit, they're not."

"Universal guilt is what they've got. The guilt of everyone, all people, when they're put before the Jessica Jacksons of the world. The urge to turn away in disgust and revulsion over her very monstrousness. Turn their backs on her, on those like her, out of primal clannishness that is always separating the 'us' from the 'them,' the worthy from the un, the beauty from the beast. Dad, when I get done with the folks on the jury, they'll know that in their hearts they are just as guilty, just as heartless, as the folks who killed her, the defendant doctors and hospital. And Dad, in punishing these medical sacrificial lambs, they will be *expiating* their *own* guilt. Don't you get it? They crucify the docs to make up for their own sins. Twenty. Twenty million and not a penny less for their absolution." Badger hangs his head in reverence to the act of forgiveness he proffers the jury.

The senior D'Woulfe chews and thinks. His son sits across the table apparently deep in meditation. With his head bowed, he doesn't look quite as rat-like. There is a center of solid gold in what the kid has said, he thinks. The docs, those heartless bastards, just turned their backs on the kid preferring to see the monster in her rather than the little girl. Maybe the same reaction the jurors already have had in their own lives, or would have had if little Miss Thumbless had gone to school with their darling little brats. Get them to acknowledge their own prejudice and then wham-bam-thank-you-ma'am, it's a twenty million payout. He does some quick math. Six thousand six hundred sixty-six dollars an hour. 6666, he sees on his retinas. It's beautiful. "Badger, I got to admit. It's a good approach. But are you sure the kid was *that* bad off? I mean, she was in second grade, for Christ's sake. A lot's riding on you making her pitiable. A second grader, public school, I don't know. You sure you can dumb her down like you say?"

"Dad, trust me on this. I've met the parents. Not the sharpest knives in the drawer. Postal worker dad. Stay-at-home mom. I can get them to help me put this kid together so she's as stunted and ugly and stupid as a wombat. But lovable and sweet and a girl child. It's all in how you arrange the pieces.

"And Dad, here's the best part. I saved it for last. You're gonna love this. The defense is going to be our strongest ally in doing what we have to do to this girl." The old man purses his lips as if he's not buying it all of a sudden. He knows defense attorneys are no fools. "Listen. We write up the complaint leaning heavy on the lost wages angle. Get our health economist from Jersey to plug in some pretty big numbers figuring the kid's an architect or an accountant. They say she was good at numbers and puzzles.

Whatever. So we go heavy on that end of the damages, and it forces the defense to cut her off at the knees, make her look as defective, as retarded as they can. *As we want.* And, see, what we do is we let them. During the discovery phase, we let them make her into a monkey's ... aunt. We tell the family to go easy on her abilities when they get deposed. That we'll make it up with their trial testimony. But the thing is, at trial we don't. On my direct, I talk only about the events of the night she died. Just the night of her death. And that I make come out like the death of Christ Almighty Himself. A death of one weak and innocent and a death that's unmerited and full of love and heartbreak. Then the family's scapegoating at the hands of the guilty ones. Oh, man, this'll be fun!

"Then the defense gets to cross-examination. What can they do but mitigate damages? So, in front of the jury, they go hard at her academic potential, try to make her sink back into the primordial mud. The family thinks it's okay to go along with this, 'cause their turn is coming afterwards to set the facts straight for the jury on my redirect. But my redirect promise is a double cross. They think I'm going to rehabilitate her but I never go to the lectern to do it. Sure, they'll be sore. They'll be sore until I give them their check for sixty percent of the twenty mill." He takes a bite of his pickle. His lips curl to the sour acidity. To his father, he now looks like a rat with a smile. "Trust me. This is a case made in heaven. Made in heaven." The waitress is at the table refilling their cups. He takes his business card from his jacket pocket and hands it to her. "Just write your phone number on the back and bring it with the check. Angela." He watches her legs as she walks away. Made in heaven, he repeats to himself.

The old man stares at his son and chews his lunch. He is reluctant to embrace the idea, he knows, because it's his son's. He asks himself what kind of a father does that to a son? Give the young man his head, he tells himself. Let him take the lead. He's got the defense working his case for him. That's real good. Like me in the old days. Twenty million. Eight for the firm. Let him go with it, he thinks. Worst-case scenario, the jury doesn't buy the guilt thing and they return a modest award, reduced from the demand because of the kid's limitations. Say two and a half million. He does the mental math. Yeah, let him fly with it. "Lunch is on me," he says.

"Deal," Badger replies. "But I get the waitress."

Badger watches as his father scans the waitress standing by the bar printing their bill. His eyes go up and down. He looks at his son and says, reluctantly, "Deal."

Son and father have gone their separate ways—Badger back to the office, D'Woulfe senior to sit in on a deposition in another case— before the latter remembers about Daedalus. He's glad, now, that he had forgotten. Let the boy take the lead. Let him rise and fly and soar.

The attorney is excited by, of all things, my artwork. He declares my sailboat "perfect." The mast is crooked because the crayon slipped twice. The sail appears to have a deckle edge. I did it in the backseat of Father's car as we bumped along a beach road in Florida. The bow of the boat seems to have a double point to it, but not like a catamaran, more like the letter *W*. I was in a hurry to finish, I remember. The clouds were out, and I wanted to study them as they sailed by. The tiller I made tiny. I wanted more room for Jed the dog to recline. The work in general lacks perspective such that it appears the boat is in the act of sinking into the blue sea. Even that begs the question of just what is a dog doing out sailing alone? "Perfect," he says again when Father announces it was one of my last creations, done in the early fall before my death, at age seven and a half. "And this?" he asks. "This is a smiling donkey?" In his hand he has my Christmas drawing I did for Nana and Ned.

"No," says Mother a little defensively, "that's my parents' dog, Jed. We visited them in Florida a lot. Jess really liked Jed. She did that to give to my parents as a Christmas gift when they were to come up. But she never got to."

"I see," the attorney says somberly. His heart is leaping for joy. "Very interesting material. Special stuff." He sorts through the pages my parents have brought. Stick-figure people. "Circus clowns," Father explains. A huge set of interconnected circles. "Elephant," says Mother. "Of course," the attorney says. My parents announce the themes and identities of the remaining drawings. Our house, appearing bleak and haunted, Tina shouting the printed word "STOP" from an open mouth almost the size of her whole head, BJ rendered in the same manner in the midst of one of her wails, the word "NO" written on her forehead, Cassidy with a big red smile and big red eyes, and a self-portrait I did just before my seventh birthday. I stand akilter with my arms extended, my eight fingers splayed like peacock feathers and just as brilliantly colored. My hearing aids are much too large for my ears. They look like telephones stuck behind them. "Oh, this is the best!" the attorney says, nodding in approval.

"She always struggled in art. She could read well beyond her grade level and was a whiz with numbers, but

she never could learn to draw. Partly because of the difficulty of holding the crayon. Right, Ford?" Mother asks. She
remembers me working at the kitchen table on my art, how
my tongue would pop out between my lips as if it wanted
to see the magic being created. Magic, she muses. How
my head would turn to get a different view of the work in
progress. But it never seemed to matter. What came out of
me through my fingers was rude and imperfect, no match
and certainly no mirror for what I saw with my eyes. She
remembers my eyes, how they drilled into her with their
eternal biting blackness. "But let me tell you how special
she was in math," says Mother with pride in her voice. "She
taught herself to count and to write . . ."

"Well, we'll get into that a little later, Mrs. Jackson. I just
want a little more insight into the . . . weaknesses Jess may
have had. Clearly, her gift for art was, shall I say, modest.
But that is all to the good. We don't want the jury to see
her as too perfect. Too perfect becomes unreal, and hard-
ens hearts. So let's find her flaws and *celebrate* them. We're
not afraid of the truth about Jess. It's right here in front
of us. She was imperfect. And aren't we all, in some way?
Beautiful but imperfect. Let them laugh at these attempts
at art, if they want. It won't hurt our case. It will only help
it. So what else? What else besides these drawings makes
her come to life for the jury? Makes them know who she
really was? "

Mother and Father sit quietly on the couch and think.
They tell him the story of my transubstantiation debacle.
He writes the name of Father Murray on his notepad and
next to it, the word "witness." They tell him my history of
athletic ineptness. Next to Mr. Lester's name, he writes,
"witness." Father has brought tapes of my soccer games and

my last Florida vacation. "Oh, this is good!" he chortles
as I lurch around after a ball. "Oh, how precious!" he says
to them during the five full minutes the camera catches
me at the beach. I lie motionless on my back in the pink
shade of the big red beach umbrella, hardly ever blinking
my eyes, and stare up at the sky. I am studying the clouds,
but you can't know this by seeing the video. My face looks
vacant, devoid of higher consciousness. It is the look that
came over me whenever I tumbled and tore cumulus clouds
to make them fit together as gods and goddesses, their
friends and foes, animal species I had seen.

Zeus was in the heavens that day, to the west, just
above the horizon, walking on the water in the way of
gods. With the perfect sight of heaven now*, I can see the
clouds reflecting off the corneas of my eyes. Even now* I
can make Zeus from those tiny dots, with a tumble and a
twist and a turn. Even now*, I am a maker of gods. But the
eyes of the Badger are not so keen. He looks at my eyes
caught on the film. A slant of light briefly crosses them
from the wind shaking the umbrella. I see Zeus dance in
that second's breeze. The Badger sees dollar signs light my
globes.

"The jury must see all of this, hear all of this, if they are to
know Jessica as you do. It is our task to see they do, it is our
task and solemn duty to her memory." He hangs his head
for a moment, apparently lost in reverence at my memory.
"Anyone a Coke?" he asks when he snaps his head up.

Father has one. It comes in a glass with ice.

They return weekly to conference with Brandon A.
D'Woulfe, Jr. They bring report cards from school, a list
of books on my shelves and desk, the names of classmates,

teachers, and aides. A list of my favorite foods, of all my dislikes. The names of my soaps, lotions, and toothpaste.

They devote hours to a minute-by-minute review of the events of the day of my death. The attorney compares their memories to the notes made contemporaneously by the EMTs, the ER medical staff, and Detective Mattingly. He wants to rectify any seeming contradictions. He constructs a timeline from the moment I awoke that day until the ambulance sped away with my moribund body. He watches the faces of Mother and Father as they give their accounts to learn their flash points, the way to open their hearts to the stab of grief, using words that have sharp emotional edges. Mother cries each time she talks about the damp cloth she brought to refresh my face. Her voice cracks when she quotes what Burke had to say in the ER, "I wish you had called." All the lawyer need do is ask what room I was in when they were brought to see my dead body. "Cubicle Sixteen," either answers and the tears start. Father chokes and weeps when he reveals, for the first time, the vaporizer he purchased was on special at CVS that night. He bought it and was pleased to save seven dollars. He cries whenever D'Woulfe asks him its brand name. "Breathe-Easy," he says, and bawls. The attorney is pleased, very pleased, with the tears that will soften the jury's heart.

But it is Father who gives him what he really is looking for. It is the scene that will nail the jury to their hidden guilt like Christ to the cross: Father never has the breath to finish recounting his failed rescue breathing as I lay blue on my bed. He starts his description of his mouth on mine, his deep, deep inspiration, his gale of air out, and he must stop for his panting. He pants, gasps, ever hungrier for air, and wets his lips and drips his tears, and pants again, before he can go on to tell how his lips exploded, uselessly, on mine. He pants, and cries, and wipes his eyes, and sighs. It is bee-you-tee-full, thinks D'Woulfe.

The Badger makes note of it all. Their tears are the nuts and bolts, the nails and screws, of the whole case, he thinks. Their tears attach their love to their deaf deformed child. He is so happy.

The reports from the reviewing experts arrive in late February. It is all D'Woulfe had hoped for. He shows them to Mother and Father. He waits silently while they read first the cardiologist's report, then the pediatrician's. Father has become better versed in the medical issues of my case through a review of my hospital records. Mother continues to be an outsider to the medical jargon. She understands little of either report, except for the conclusions. Freidman, the cardiologist, concludes that a large right aberrant sub-clavian artery is clearly visible on the echocardiogram done when I was two. He concludes it would be below the standard of care for any cardiologist reviewing the film not to identify that large and potentially dangerous structure. Chester, the pediatrician from Hopkins, states unequivo-cally the treating doctors failed to provide proper anticipa-tory guidance to prevent airway obstruction. Further, such guidance would have in all certainty saved my life had it been followed the night in question.

"It's an open-and-shut case," the attorney states. "Medi-cal negligence and resulting injury. Malpractice. All that's left to decide now is damages. How much was Jess's life worth. That's what they'll be coming after you about when you are deposed. They'll want to show that Jessica's life was of little value. And I mean that in economic terms. That her lifetime earnings would have been trivial because of her disabilities. You know, *I know*, better than that about Jessica. And trust me, her real value will eventually become apparent to the jury. Trust me on that. But our strategy must be to wait to show them that until the end of trial. So it's there, fresh and stuck in the jury's mind and memory when they go back to deliberate the case. But until then, until the very end, we let them have their way with us. They ask you during your deposition, how was Jess in school? You answer, Okay. She was okay with numbers. But she struggled in a lot of subjects. Art. She had no ability with art. She did have to repeat a grade, go back a class, in her religious studies. The concepts proved too hard for her at seven. Then let them take that stuff anywhere they want. Let them. We'll get her straight in the record just before the jury goes out.

"They'll come at you about her speech impediment. But you just answer, simply, *we* could understand her. Sometimes it was hard for strangers and her teachers to know what she wanted to say, but we had no problem. Then they'll hit you over the head with her hands. About them. You know, what'd it do to her activities of daily living and that sort of stuff. You say, well, she needed help with some of it. Blowing her nose, toileting, grooming. Buttons. Grooming. Use the word "grooming" if you can. It conveys . . . a lot in it."

"But," Mother interrupts, "she was fully independent in all that. We didn't need to help her since she was three or four years old for most of it. And by six and a half, she did all of it by herself." She turns on the couch to look at Father. She is uncomfortable with what she has heard from the mouth of their attorney, making Jess less than what she was. She wonders what Father thinks. Father looks to the carpet. He thinks the lawyer must know what he's doing. He thinks, I know what I'm doing in my job, he knows in his. We got to trust him. He knows. He knows how to get justice.

D'Woulfe regards Mother, and he nods knowingly. He looks as if he is readying to explain the mystery of transubstantiation to a first grader. He hopes his sincere explanation might effect blind acceptance, if not understanding. "True, true, Mrs. Jackson. Absolutely true. But here is our problem. The jury *wants* to hear this about Jess's physical limitations. They want to hear it because in their hearts they *already believe it to be true*. If we at first say otherwise, it will give them cause to disbelieve *all* of what we say about her later. For them to believe us about what matters most, about what we'll present to them at the very end, that Jessica was *blessed* with a mind, an intellect, that would have carried her far in life, they must also believe us about her physical limitations. And trust me, Mrs. Jackson, I know a thing or two about prejudice. People—good, decent, everyday people, the kind who sit on juries—are prejudiced when it comes to the handicapped of our society. They prejudge them, Mrs. Jackson. Those jurors will have judged Jessica Mary with her electric ears, her garbled speech, her thumbless hands, as being *physically* different, materially less perfect, than they. Defective, Mrs. Jackson. I hate to use that word, but defective is what the jury will preconceive about her." He proffers the palms of both hands, beseeching like a priest at Mass, before finishing. "If we at first paint her otherwise, we have lost the jury. We have lost the case."

Mother shakes her head. "But none of that changes the fact that you're asking us to not tell the truth about our daughter. She could do all her own care. People did understand her when she spoke. She was gifted in reproducing sounds. And even without thumbs, she did well with her ASL. What you say we should say just isn't the truth. Ford?" She looks at Father again.

"Mr. D'Woulfe, Kate's right. None of this really applies to Jess. Not really. There's got to be a way to get the jury to understand without making them doubt us."

Brandon D'Woulfe lowers his hands and raises his eyes upward. "How shall I explain this?" he says to the white paint on the flat ceiling. "What is the best way?" He looks down to his shoes, then up to Mother and Father. "Here is the problem. Prejudice is a lie. A grave, grave lie.

"We know this.

"And we know, too, that the jury is guilty of that lie. That is the awful truth. But our focus in these proceedings is not to confront this lie of theirs. *They* are not on trial here, after all. Our focus is to confront the far greater lie, the deadly lie, the one that sealed Jessica's fate. The lie from the physicians and the hospital about their *sacred duty* to the health and well-being of people. All people, strong and weak and perfect and imperfect. We can prove *their* lie and make them pay for their heartless error. We can have justice in all this. But *not* if we confront the lesser, common lie of the jury. That is not our goal, in the first place, and it is our stumbling block, in the second. What I am saying is this: You will not be *lying* when you give this testimony. You will simply be choosing *not* to confront the lie there in the jury box, but to confront, instead, the lie that sits in suits and good dresses at the defense table.

"Devote your future life to confronting society's prejudice, in Jessica's name, if you want. That would be all fine.

But *do not forfeit justice* for the sake of some other cause. You will not be lying. You will simply be choosing to confront their lie with the truth at a later time and place." His hands rise again and slash the air in punctuation. "You will *not* be lying."

Mother's head is spinning, listening to the words that seem unanchored in anything but the thin, corporate air blown from the mouth of their attorney. Lies not lies, truth not truth, my life, my being, somehow exchangeable with another's version of it. She tries, but fails, to remarshal his explanation. The words "prejudice" and "sacred" and "truth" seem to ping from the sides of her confused mind.

She sighs, hoping a cleansing breath will make it all clear. The room spins a little instead.

Father says, as if awakening from some dream of the past, "They did talk about switching her big toes to her hands to make them thumbs, so she'd be able to grasp things and do her ASL better. They never did that, but they thought it would improve her abilities to hold things and to make her signs. We could answer with stuff like that. That would be all true, and would be admitting she had problems. Kate?"

Before Mother can answer, Brandon D'Woulfe interrupts. "Now that's the most powerful and insightful memory I've yet heard about Jessica. Absolutely you should use that in your answers. It's exactly what I had in mind. Show the jury the specifics, the tiny dots of her life that make up her picture in the aggregate. Toes for thumbs, that's like two tiny dots on the connect-the-dots portrait we are going to show those jury folks. You just put down the dots, one at a time, and I'll connect them up at the end. Just you wait and see." He thinks to himself, Oh—my—God! Wait till the jury hears this! A girl with toes for thumbs. Gotta be worth another million. Maybe a million *a toe*. "Kate, do you see how this could go? Just remember the bits and pieces of her handicap struggle. Lay them out for the jury to see. They'll see one thing at first through the eyes of their prejudice, then I'll change it, reconnect the dots, make it the truth of Jessica Mary Jackson at the end. Do you, Kate? See how this could go?"

Out of confusion as much as embarrassment over that confusion, Mother says she does. She says yes to the new-changed me that she will swear to. Yes to the girl who needed her teeth brushed, her bottom wiped, her snaps snapped, her back dried. Yes to the girl with the snarled voice of a dog, the low-wattage brain of a monkey. Yes to it all. Yes.

And Father, too. His yeses, her yeses, all in the cause of justice. Yes, yes, yes to one created in the image and likeness of Brandon A. D'Woulfe, Jr., the Badger to his father and friends.

The complaint is written. The suit is filed.

My parents' depositions are taken. I am remade in paper and ink, in question and answer, in omission and half truth. Metal clips in the left upper corners of the manuscripts assemble my new, papery parts in proper order.

The depositions of defendants are taken. More lies and half truths. Burke and Marshall are videotaped when they testify. Eileen Marshall cries, she is so enraged the film library has lost all my other echoes. "They prove beyond any doubt her vascular anomaly was undiagnosable in life. Just as the one extant echo demonstrates." Burke is doubtful I would have gone beyond high school, given my many physical limitations. He bangs his fist on the table to underscore how upset he is that my parents didn't call the night my croup began. "If only they had called," he says mournfully into the camera in response to D'Woulfe's question, "Do you contend the parents are in any way guilty of contributory negligence in the death of Jessica?"

"So the answer to my question, then, is yes, you do so contend?" D'Woulfe retorts.

"Move to strike. Calls for legal conclusion on the part of the witness," says Burke's attorney.

"Let me ask you this, then, Doctor. It seems you are saying a phone call to you buys a trip to the ER that night, and that would have made the difference in survival? She goes to the ER, gets treated that night, and she's okay? Is that your opinion, sir?"

"It breaks my heart to say it, but, yeah. A trip to the ER that night, and she's outside now in this beautiful winter weather playing in the snow. God, I wish they had called me." He hangs his head. The camera catches his smile.

Winter becomes spring.

Spring grows weary of May's hot spell. Summer comes early with a bumper crop of shade.

The plaintiffs' experts are deposed. The lone, lost tape of my echocardiogram is entered into evidence at Freidman's deposition. The defense attorneys object. They abruptly discontinue their examination of his credentials to have an emergency meeting with the judge over the admissibility of the new evidence. The judge learns the tape came from my parents and was, in turn, part of a gift from one of the treating doctors months ago. He chides the lead attorney from the hospital for not inquiring as to whether the family had any such evidence in their possession when he deposed them. The judge thumbs through their transcripts. "Total of seven hundred pages of questions and answers here, counselor, most of it about the girl's limitations and not a one about medical materials in the parents' possession. And now you want me to exclude this tape from evidence? No, sir. You all are going to have to live or die by what's on this here tape. This meeting is adjourned."

Freidman and Chester go forward with their testimony. Within days, the hospital offers to settle the case for 1.2 million dollars, a generous figure given the disabilities afflicting the unfortunate plaintiff, the attorney for the hospital states. D'Woulfe and D'Woulfe demand 4.5 million dollars, or the hospital can take its chances in front of a jury, and try to defend itself against the double accusations of malpractice and medical fraud. The demand is half a million dollars over the policy limits of the named defendants. The defense attorneys convene before the hospital's board of directors. They vote unanimously to pay up. The risk to the hospital's reputation drives the decision. No one is happy to pay such a large sum, but in the end, it is the best strategy. They decide, too, not to renew Eileen Marshall's contract come the new academic year.

But Brandon A. D'Woulfe, Jr. rejects the offer of four point five million, a sum he had demanded just days earlier. "The family wants justice," he tells Bridget Conley of Medical Center Legal Affairs.

"Meaning?" she says into the phone. She is angry but not shocked. Nothing from the mouths of the plaintiff attorneys of the world shocks her any longer. Thirty years of doing this work has seen to that.

"Meaning twenty million."

"See you in court, counselor," she spits back. "You're all living in a fantasy world. Twenty million for a handicapped child! No way. Your problem is you think you can turn her into a pile of gold like Midas, just because you touch the case. Get real. Our offer stands until close of business tomorrow. Then, there is no settlement offer.

"Twenty million. The kid couldn't even find her way out of a connect-the-dots drawing. I've seen the exhibits from the mom's deposition. Go back to the parents and explain this to them. Close of business tomorrow, or we make the kid a stewed vegetable in front of the jury, and then you'll see what you get." She hangs up and Brandon A. D'Woulfe laughs.

The trial is set for the week of August eleventh. The tape goes to black.

*

Before I can gather my disgust at the assault on the truth of my life, He is before me holding another canister. "This is the last one. The grand finale," He says. "You want to see it? It will answer your every question." *The Time of Trial* sits in the palms of His hands. Reluctantly, I nod my head yes. But I do not laugh at His little joke. He has no thumbs today*.

13

THE TIME OF TRIAL

When the D'Woulfes signed the lease for office space ten years ago, they immediately undertook renovations guided by a single principle: that the preparation of key trial witnesses was the most essential ingredient in securing a plaintiff's verdict from the jury. And the key to preparing their clients was *desensitizing* them to the intimidating nature of the courtroom environment: the lofty judge's bench, the coldly removed jury box, the opposing tables of warring attorneys with their files in big boxes like barricades, and their egos in smart suits like armor, all participants focused laser-like on the lone man or woman who takes the seat on the bare-bones witness stand, whose only comfort is iceless water in a paper cup. The D'Woulfes had come to see the physicality of the courtroom as the great equalizer—housewife, neurosurgeon, husband, physicist, garbage collector, art collector—everyone equally brought low by that space, sometimes so low they forgot their names, their facts, their well-practiced lines, *their cause* and babbled on instead about being sorry they ever started the process that led them to the present Golgotha, crucified by the truth of the halls of justice. This, they would not allow of their clients.

They constructed an exact replica of a courtroom in the very heart of their office space. And more—they had it built like a stage that could easily be reconfigured to mimic the design of the courtroom wherein the trial would actually be held. Father and son had bragged at the American Trial Lawyers Association meeting time and again that they "owned" three Latino carpenters, and that these men were more important to the firm's financial success than any five young associate attorneys from the Harvards and Stanfords of the country. They put their star plaintiff witnesses on the mock witness stand day after day during the two-week run-up to the trial and sweated the worry out of them.

Some days the D'Woulfes marched in their associates to man the lawyer tables, and the secretaries and paralegals to sit in the jury box, and they put black robes on the security guard and handed him a gavel. The witnesses were examined and cross-examined and recrossed. They suffered "Move to strike!" and "Objection, non- responsive, Your Honor," and "Counsel, please, approach the bench," and computer failures and bathroom breaks. They were told how to dress, how to sit, how to answer, how and when to cry, what kind of tissue to use to blot those tears. When it finally came time for their clients to testify live at trial, the jitters were gone and the story, the D'Woulfe version of the story, spun flawlessly out of their mouths like the lines of a play.

And there was a second advantage to these preparations, these rehearsals. They seemed so much like *theater* to the witness, so evocative of the idea of "play" and "fiction," that the half truths became untroubling to mouth. After all, this was just practice, they'd think. Day after day, the raising of the almost-shaky hand for the oath, the same sequence of questions, the same always-perfect answers full of feint and false hesitancy and practiced sobs and sighs, as they claimed this or that did or did not happen. The daily, twice daily, thrice daily recounting of myth and mutant truth made it true to them, as true as any play they'd ever seen was true.

For the duo of D'Woulfes, their efforts were simply another spatial reorientation, this of inner space, moral space, whose walls and floors and ceilings they could unbolt and press closer together, or farther apart, or higher, or lower, or remove entirely, to fit their need. As in a play, they could make the actors seemingly stand on air. Indeed, they felt they *owned* the air, *created* the truth.

Mother and Father begin their rehearsals at the end of July. Nana and Ned return from Florida to help with Jeanine and BJ. Cassidy is additional help in the evenings when Mother and Father need to meet with D'Woulfe to review their testimony in preparation for the next day's "dress rehearsal."

Neither Nana, nor Ned, nor Cassidy has any part in the proceedings. The defense decided against deposing them since none was present the night of my death and because they believe the testimony they have elicited from Mother and Father has clinched their case about the limited monetary damages my death merits. In the few weeks following the filing of the claim in March, all three had lost interest in the matter. Mother and Father had their attorneys, had good experts, had a good case, would in all likelihood settle, and life would go on, they all thought.

The few times one asks about the slow grind of the gears of justice, Mother or Father answers matter-of-factly, "It's getting there. It's all coming together."

Brandon D'Woulfe provides Mother and Father with a list of questions every evening they meet. Each is identical to a question asked months earlier at their depositions. They spend two hours reviewing their answers, reformulating them as needed, fleshing them out to perfect form. They thumb their transcripts repeatedly, searching them for phrasing and fact and inconsistency until they look like heirloom Bibles with dog-eared corners, marginal notations, and tattered edges. When they have done enough of an evening, D'Woulfe releases them always with the same admonition. "Please review your answers in the morning. We start in the courtroom at ten." And so after Jeanine is off to school and Nana has BJ in the stroller, they sit on the edge of their bed where they made me with no practice at all, and practice unmaking me.

At ten they sit in mock court and testify or wait their turn at the plaintiff's table at the side of the confident Brandon A. D'Woulfe, Jr. They even learn from him the face one should wear as one hears the sad or sweet words of a spouse in reply to a question such as, "And at bath time, how was she? Did Jess enjoy her baths?" He tells them, "There is a time for laughter, a time for tears, a time for mourning. Just like the Bible says, there is a time for everything. So, Ford, laugh a little when Kate says Jess liked to splash like a frog in the tub. That's a happy memory. And for God's sake, let out a sigh the jury can hear when she starts in on her Mattingly answer. They'll know what's in your heart," and he points to the seven secretaries reading the newspaper or filing their nails in the jury box. "It was your time of trial back then. That time is over. *Now is the time of justice.*"

He weans them from their depositions. He allows them to carry the transcripts to their seat in the witness box for the first week of preparation. They are free to page through them to help with the formulation of the answers to the more complex questions. Then, he forbids them access to those printed words. Instead, for the next five days they must lay the manuscripts down on the plaintiff's table, walk away from them to the witness stand, and dredge all the answers from pure memory. "Please, Mrs. Jackson, if you would, tell the jury about the quality of Jessica's speech. And feel free to comment on her sign language. I'm sure without thumbs that must have been tricky. And wasn't she due to get some toes put on her hands to help overcome her problems? Well, let's see, Mrs. Jackson, seems I've just asked you three questions in one. So you just go ahead and put them together with your answers any which way you can." Mother stares at the transcript on the table across the room. Her long and cohesive answer, she knows, comes from testimony given on pages 19, 37, 69–71, and 211–219. She finishes, flushed and excited, and thinks, "I know it all by heart."

I watch in dismay and disgust. "Chewww'l ah-bya okay," I had said to Cassidy. He understood me. They all did. Mother's changed heart is deaf as stone.

"Well done," D'Woulfe tells Mother as she steps down and Father rises to take her place. "Very nicely done." He sounds to me like Mr. Lester, the soccer coach, complimenting a child on a kick.

The trial is to commence at ten a.m. on Tuesday, August eleventh. On Sunday afternoon, August ninth, D'Woulfe calls Mother and Father at home just as they are at the door in the act of leaving for his office. "Today, I want you to leave your depositions home. Today and tomorrow will be final rehearsals for our Tuesday opening. No props, no aids, whatsoever. Just leave them home. You'll be okay." They are in the foyer by the front door speaking on the portable phone Cassidy brought. They place their transcripts on the hallstand, and go.

Which is how Cassidy comes to read them.

Ned and Nana are out with Jeanine to the community pool. Brian Joseph has been fed. The breast milk and baby rice cereal prime him for a nap like Thanksgiving dinner. Cassidy is alone in the house, and bored. The paper has been digested, the sports on TV are lackluster. He walks to the foyer to find the phone. He sees Mother's transcript. He thinks it would be nice to spend an hour with me through the medium of Mother's memory. The months since my death have turned one by one, from winter to spring to the light-drunk days of summer. His memories of me now are more sweet than sad. Time has blunted much of the sorrow, sharpened much of the joy. So he carries the booklet to my old room, now Jeanine's room. The light streams through the western window. No constellation is visible, but he knows the stars are there. In the swales of the shadowed plaster, he can see my menagerie. The clown, the faithful clown, seems to frown.

He sits on the chair and flips through the transcript. The compendium of questions and answers goes on for over three hundred pages. Everywhere he turns, Mother has underlined and highlighted and starred and double-starred answers. There is marginal scribble on every page, much of which references other pages in the transcript where she has divulged more information on the question at hand. Not since high school has he seen anything so well studied as these pages.

He reads from the beginning. By the fourth page, he is troubled. Misspoke. Kate must have misspoke, he mumbles. Mother's testimony is that I often fought going to school, that I was reluctant to do my studies, that I essentially lived in my own quiet locked-in world. A fantasy world, really, she remarks in answer to a question, with stories of gods and goddesses and with imaginary animal friends It is where I preferred to stay, away from people and reality, in a world of my own fashioning, childish and sweet but unreal. Cassidy cannot understand her confusion of fact. The Jess he knew loved the academics of school. Friends were hard to come by, true, and there was a lot of teasing, yes, but he knew a Jess who gladly went to learn math and reading and who readily engaged the physical world. And this Jess lavished her energy on her story life, drawing ideas from her books to fire her imagination. His Jess didn't live in a fantasy world. She created one to visit as she wished, as do all children in their love of mystery and enchantment. She *used* it for her own enjoyment, but she did not hide in it.

He reads on, about my ears and my voice and my hands and my heart. "No!" he cries aloud, "No, Kate, this isn't right! This isn't Jess. This isn't her." He reads further, and sinks further into confusion and distress.

He goes downstairs and takes Father's testimony. He sits on the couch in the parlor and discovers again the alien, mutant Jessica Mary Jackson grown from Father's memory, dressed in Father's words. He is shocked and sad, wounded. And angry. Very angry.

He reads undisturbed for over an hour. There are far too many pages to review them all, but what he reads makes him tremble with rage. He begins to wonder if it is the prospect of money that has induced them to do this to me. But he rejects this thought. Ford is a man who gives away dimes. Kate, a warm woman he has known all her simple, kindhearted life. "Vengeance, then, is it?" he wonders aloud. But how could this possibly serve vengeance, this reconstruction of their daughter into a less perfect being? He does not know; he cannot find his way from point A to point B, from their omissions and half truths to their purpose in it. His confusion intensifies his rage, and he is consumed with a single thought—that whatever their motivation, what they will do to my memory and to their ability to love and cherish it, will be a poison in their souls. No amount of money, no punishment for the guilty, will be antidote to the poison about to enter their lives, he thinks. They will hate themselves, they will hate each other for what they are about to do in court. Their vengeance will not be sweet. It will be venom. They must be made to see this, be made to stop their plan for trial.

He lays the transcript on the coffee table and sits on the couch in the quiet house staring off into the mid-distance. Memory, he thinks, should heal the pain of loss, not inflame it. Haven't they all been witness to this? How could they not have seen? Or seen and ignored? D'Woulfe and D'Woulfe's phone number is listed on the front cover of the transcripts. He dials it. A phone recording announces the office is closed. He looks at his watch. It is only three thirty. He thinks the blame, the fault, might lie in greater part with their attorney, that Brandon D'Woulfe they are always talking about. He thinks D'Woulfe must have had a hand in the transformation of me in these pages of black and white. How else could they have done what they did? He waits ten minutes longer and then begins to pace the house. He is eager for the sound of a car in the driveway, the scrape of shoe on stairs, the creak of the front door. The house is quiet, inside and out.

He waits another ten minutes. He is desperate for confrontation. He cannot suppress the anger he feels at all three of them, the lawyer and Ford and Kate. He dials the firm's number again with the same results. Finally, he decides. He searches the transcript for D'Woulfe's address, and finds it easily.

He retrieves the spare infant car seat from the hall closet and brings it to his car. He struggles to clasp the seat belt around it, and curses. He slams the car door shut and scrambles up the front stairs, missing the top step by a fraction of an inch. He stumbles forward into the doorjamb. He curses again and proceeds up the hall stairs to Brian Joseph's room. The baby lies peacefully on his back, asleep. The fan on the dresser turns the air, and the air turns the pony mobile. It sways and circles in the current.

A moment of practical clarity intrudes on his anger. He rushes downstairs to the kitchen and removes a bottle of pumped breast milk from the refrigerator. He warms it in the microwave and returns with it to BJ's room. He takes a paper diaper and the small canister of baby wipes and puts them and the bottle into the carryall Mother uses. He goes to the crib and gently lifts Brian Joseph.

The baby wriggles and stretches and moves his head side to side and settles in Cassidy's arms. "Shh. Shh," he says to the baby, and he takes him to his car.

He walks carefully, purposefully, with the baby in his arms and the blue carryall slung over his shoulder, but even so, he misjudges the last of the brick stairs and lands unexpectedly hard on his left foot. The baby wakes and begins to fuss. "It's okay, BJ. Just takin' a little car ride. Quiet down now. We'll be on our way real soon." He puts the carryall on the car roof while he tries to strap BJ into the car seat. It is the first car seat the family ever used, my old baby car seat, and he is no longer familiar with it. He at first makes a jumble of the straps. He can't remember where the arms go, where the legs. He is tempted simply to tie the straps around the baby's middle. It's a short drive, only a few minutes, he offers as argument. But he rejects his own bad advice and persists until finally Brian Joseph is made to fit. But he is wailing now, mad to have been awoken from sound sleep, uncomfortable in his wet diapers and on the cusp of hunger. Cassidy stops for a second to reconsider.

But it is only a fifteen-minute trip to the attorney's building. That's okay, he thinks, I'll change him when I get there. He'll be okay.

He closes the door on the bawling baby and walks quickly to his seat. He starts the car. I can hear the deep rumble in the old engine. The vibrations massage the cry out of my brother for a moment. Cassidy breathes a sigh of relief and begins to pull away from the curb. Out of the corner of his eye, he sees the blue carryall fall from the car roof to the street. He brakes hard. The jolt startles Brian Joseph and he cries again. Cassidy can see his red face and open pink mouth in the rearview mirror. "Not a good idea," he says to the reflection of that face. "In fact, a

stupid one, kid." He parks, retrieves the carryall and brings
Brian Joseph back inside the house.

An hour later, Nana and Ned return with Jeanine.
The rage that boils out of Joe Cassidy as he shows them
the transcripts and summarizes what Mother and Father
have sworn to, frightens Jeanine. She begins to cry, and
Nana holds her in her lap, torn between hearing what
Cassidy has to say, and taking the frightened child into
the other room. She stays. Cassidy goes on and on about
the testimony he has read. He leaves for the law office
at five.

Nana and Ned sit on the couch, each immersed in the
questions and answers that seem to them to pertain to some
other child entirely, a child born on the pages of myth and
legend rather than to flesh and blood.

There is little Sunday traffic on Wisconsin Avenue. The
city has suffered the retreat of many to the beaches and
mountains, so the roads are mostly empty.

Cassidy is as angry as when he first encountered the
transcripts. His review for Nana and Ned refuels his rage.
His hands shake holding the steering wheel. The dull
sheen of the sun on the metal of his car's hood puts an ache
behind his eyes. He tries to control his breathing, tries to
slow it and steady it, but it comes in rapid gulps and his
head spins. He can feel and hear the squeezing surge of
blood in his ears.

His eyes fall briefly on the glove box. He knows it is
empty, has been empty these past eight months. Almost
enough time to have a baby, he thinks. He approaches

Rory's Place. There are parking spaces right out front. The word "baby" lingers in his brain. He parks.

He studies the glove box again and then turns to regard the awning-shaded front of the pub. Through the window he sees the haphazard array of tables and chairs around the bar. A baseball game is on TV. In its sallow glow, patrons sit with glasses and bottles and cigarettes lost in the smoke and shadow. He closes his eyes and squeezes the steering wheel until his fingers play sharp notes of pain. He holds the pain for a minute, savoring it. He opens his eyes, starts the car, and drives away. Now he's angry *and* he's worried. He is desperate to reach D'Woulfe's office before Mother and Father leave. He wants all three of them together to hear what he has to say. And if that D'Woulfe gets in the way of it, he's got a punch in his lawyerly face just for him. He speeds southbound down the empty avenue. He makes the light at Wisconsin and Calvert, and the next and the next. A driver pulls his parked car onto the street fifty feet ahead of him, and he must slow and change lanes. The green light at Denton turns amber. He accelerates and gets through the intersection as the light turns red. He switches back to the right lane moving fast. There are only four blocks left. He scans the few cars traveling in the opposite direction, hoping not to see Father's maroon station wagon. The light at Reservoir goes amber. He accelerates and the Taurus's engine pings and groans. The light is red before he ever gets to the crosswalk. He looks left. The cross street is empty. He looks right. The white SUV seems to come out of the western sun and slams into his car, caving both passenger doors and sliding Cassidy's Taurus across the northbound lanes, where it comes to rest against the brick wall of the Georgetown Public Library. Cassidy's head has

spiderwebbed the side window, leaving a bright red bloom
of blood at the center of the filigree of cracks.

It looks like a rose window from a medieval cathedral.

But Cassidy can't see this; he's unconscious. He cannot
see, as well, the old car seat impaled by a jagged lance of
door metal.

Eleven minutes later Mother and Father pass the scene
on their way home. Cassidy has already been evacuated
and is in transport by ambulance to the University Hospital
ER. But they are so engrossed in rehearsing their answers—
Mother has just sadly recounted Burke's insensitive words
in the ER—that they note merely a slight slowing of the
few cars driving in front of them and two DC police cruis-
ers parked with lights flashing in front of the public library.

"Ah, my most excellent friend, Mr. Cassidy," says
Dr. Zacharia Vinik as the EMTs wheel the stretcher into
the trauma room. "Get neurosurgery stat," he intones to
his nurse, "and hang a bolus of mannitol. We need a head
and a c-spine CT. And add a blood alcohol level to the
admission bloods." He throws Cassidy's wallet to the pale
medical student at the foot of the bed. "See if you can find
the next of kin," Vinik says.

Cassidy's lips are parted almost an inch by the endotracheal tube in his mouth. He looks to me the way I looked
the night of my death when they breathed for me with
those black bags. But his tube angles up jauntily away from
his face.

A different day, a different hospital room, it would have
been a cheap cigar tooth-bit in his mouth, a celebration of
another birth, another life. But today, a plastic tube for air,
for breath. His parted lips almost seem to smile.

I note, too, he has a collar around his neck affixed at the scene by the EMTs to stabilize his spine in case it had been injured in the crash. The collar is white and not even the blood from his scalp wound has marked it.

That is how I know he will not die. He looks just like a priest; he looks just like a new father, too alive to the joy of the moment, its spirit and its flesh, for anything as jarring as death. As I watch with this realization, his right arm rises as if in benediction, startling me. Then his right leg begins to twitch and the extended arm jerks rhythmically. "Seizure!" yells the nurse. "Dr. Vinik, in here stat! He's seizing!"

*

He comes to stand before me. He should be in shadow; He should be dark as sorrow. Instead, He's light itself. "It's happening," He says with excitement in His voice. "The future. Your creation."

I turn my eyes from Him, but the light is everywhere. Except in my heart.

Catastrophe befalls those I love most dearly. My parents, weak and changeable and full of anger, now at the turning point in their life's understanding of who I was. Cassidy on a ventilator, needing emergency surgery for massive head trauma, the consequence of his protective love of me and my memory.

The light is everywhere, but it drives darkness deeper into my heart. The blackest of thoughts grow there: my missing fingers and stone ears, my wormy heart, my nubbin kidney, were somehow not even defects *for* me, but were lures instead, means to bring forth even more sorrow in the world. My life made me not a new Moses, not Ezekiel, not Isaiah. I'm the Minotaur reassembled, love affixed to hate, joy to sorrow, good to evil.

To my healing past he sews a raging, hateful future. He makes me a monster, and I cannot find forgiveness for what He has done. I cannot forgive myself for letting Him do it through me. To forgive the prodigal God who made this— evil coming from good, hate from love, vengeance from justice—is too much.

He hears my dark thoughts, but the glow of a thousand supernovas never dims. *"Your* creation," He repeats loudly.

I turn my eyes back to Him but He is gone. And gone with Him is the light.

It is for the best. Darkness would be my only solace now*, but it is a torment instead: the film plays on in it.

Mother cries, Father shouts, Nana sits, sad. Only Ned seems in control of his feelings. He stands in the kitchen with Jeanine's arms wrapped around his neck, her legs around his waist. He pats her back and whispers in her ear. When he puts her down, she walks quickly out of the room. "Ford, stop your shouting. You too, Mae. You're scaring the kids. We can talk about this quietly, civilized. No need for yelling."

Father stops his ranting. The moment he and Mother had stepped into the house, Nana had accused them of lying under oath, of turning me in an "ugly, stupid monster" with their untrue words. What Nana said made Jeanine cry, and Ned picked her up in his arms and held her. He whispered in her ear, loud enough for everyone in the kitchen to hear, "Jess is fine, Jeanine. She's just not here. She's happy and the same and she is no monster. Nana was just talking." That's when Mother broke into tears.

Father speaks again, his hoarse voice just loud enough to hear over the sound of Mother's sobs. "Brandon D'Woulfe explained to us why it was important to testify like we did. That it wasn't lies, as such, just not . . . just not doing something the jury wouldn't buy because of their . . . their prejudice. And then he would redo us all at the end. Make Jess come back together again as she was. As she really was. That way we'd win against the biggest lie, the one those docs committed when they let her die like that. Mae, I'm telling you, this is D'Woulfe's strategy, and he said it wasn't a lie. We'll win the case and it will all come out right." He looks at Mother and holds up his hands. "Kate, tell her it's as I say."

Mother stares at him for a moment, then looks to Nana and Ned and back again to Father. "Ford," she says slowly, "yes and no." Before she can go on, the phone rings.

"Cassidy, probably," Nana says. "He left an hour ago looking for you at the lawyer's. Hot. Very hot." She shoves the portable phone into Father's hands. He shakes his head, sighs once, and speaks, "Hello? . . . Speaking."

Mother, Nana, and Ned watch Father's eyes narrow as the caller goes on. After a minute, Father says, "We'll be right there. Oh, God. We'll all be right there." He puts down the phone and buries his face in his hands like a child ashamed of what he's done. "He's in the ER," he says from behind his hands. "Car crash. His head. It's smashed.

They're going to do surgery, but they don't know . . . They don't know if . . ."

Nana grabs him by the elbow and pulls hard at an arm. Her face is drained of color, but her words are red hot. "This!" She holds out the transcript of Father's deposition with her other hand. "This is what you've done!"

All Father can do is take away his hands, look at Mother, and say, "Kate?"

Before Mother can speak, Nana shouts, "No! This is what you *both* have done!" She shakes the pages so violently they blur.

I close my eyes. I will see no more. But my new perfect ears hear the pages flap loud as Harpies' wings. My bones rattle.

*

"I am done with the tape," I tell the Assembler when He reappears. "You can take it away." I try to avert my eyes from His brightness, but there is no evading it. My eyes seem made of it. It presses on them like the sea on fish. And now*, for the first time*, the scenes of my family's drama play out in the light. I look without looking, see without seeing. Mother and Father leading the way into the ER, walking quickly along the central corridor toward the nurse's desk, then turning left and right and left again in the maze of hallways, Nana and Ned, each carrying a child, eight, ten feet behind them, as if distance were an accusation. Each child is crying. Each adult looks ready to.

"What do you see?" He asks.

I have had enough of His theater. "This was never about putting the pieces of my life together to see its meaning, was it? All these movies don't reveal a thing about any of that, do they?" I know I sound angry, but I no longer feel solicitous about His feelings.

"What do you see?" He asks again patiently, unmoved by my grief.

I have no choice about seeing. The images are the undimmable light of my inner world. Now* Dr. Vinik is leading them to Cassidy, talking about the CAT scan findings, the plan for surgery. The risk of death. Brain damage. Vegetative state. He draws the curtain to Cassidy's room, stands aside to let them enter. "I doubt Mr. Cassidy will know you are here," he says. "But, in these matters, one never truly knows what a patient senses. So be gentle. Be strong."

"I see more sadness and anger than I can bear," I tell the Assembler. "And it's my fault. And it's Your fault. And it is all wrong."

"No, what do you see?" He asks a third time.

The images burn in brightness. I see my family gathered in a knot at the entrance, each reluctant to approach Cassidy's side. I see their fearful faces, their wet cheeks, their wild eyes. The cool light from the fluorescent bulbs bathes Cassidy's face the bluish color of old snow. An IV drips tiny clear drops. A machine bigger than I ever was whooshes air. Before I can answer again in my anger— "Nothing. I see nothing."—Nana steps across the threshold into the room, Jeanine in her arms. She goes to the bedside and touches Cassidy's shoulder. Jeanine laughs. The child who cries at anything laughs at Cassidy in a hospital bed, his head bandaged, his eyes closed, his face lax. Before the echo of that laugh fades, his left hand twitches. Those broad fingers with thick yellow nails rise

off the bed, try to touch the source of laughter. Or it's
another seizure. I cannot tell. But Nana moves her hand
from Cassidy's shoulder to his rising wrist. "It's us, Joe,"
she says. She looks toward the entrance. "All of us. We're
here." His hand comes to rest in midair then slowly lowers
to the sheet. She pats it twice, straightens, carries Jeanine
back to the entrance.

"It's AceyDee," Jeanine says gaily. At this announce-
ment, everyone is completely still for a few moments, as if
they are considering the truth of her statement. Then Nana
moves. She extends her free arm around Mother's shoulders and pulls her close. "It's alright," she whispers "Whatever it is, it will be okay." Father leans against Mother, puts
his arm around her. "I'm sorry, Mae. We never meant—"
But Ned has joined the scrum, BJ in his left arm, and he
interrupts. "Ford, we're with you and Kate on this. It's all of
us here together. It's going to be okay."

Mother snuffles her drippy nose and wipes a teary eye.
Father rumbles, "I Im-hm," and pulls her tighter. Ned clears
his throat. Jeanine says again, "AceyDee." Baby BJ breathes.
Then there is silence as heavy as gold.

I am about to repeat my denial, to tell the Assembler,
"Nothing. I see nothing," when I notice the silence. It is
unlike other silences, or perhaps like every silence, for
the ventilator whooshes like a noisy bellows, the moni-
tors beep and ping, the patients and doctors in adjoining
spaces talk, a man in a distant room shouts for a nurse, BJ
breathes again, noisily through his nose. But in their souls
too there is silence, as real and expandable as space itself.
It is a stillness amidst the tug of the world's noise like mine
at birth, at death. It is beautiful.

"You see," the Assembler says.

I do. I do see. I see forgiveness in that inner silence. I see the love they have for each other, and I see it come together, healed and whole. I see love made perfect by forgiveness, as a hand by a thumb. And I see there can be no forgiveness without loss, grief, chaos. Without His chaos, my chaos, there is a hole like a cave in love. Only through chaos can forgiveness exist, can forgiveness touch everything with healing, the past*, present*, future*, all people, all creation, the Assembler Himself. Only through imperfection can forgiveness make love perfect.

"I see," I tell Him. "I do see."

He takes my hands. Never before has He touched me. But now He takes my hands in His. They are big, soft, warm hands, hardly those of a carpenter or a tinker or a mechanic. More the hands of a mother. More the hands of a postal worker. He brings my hands to His lips and kisses them. He slowly breathes on them. It is as if mountains move under my skin and deserts bloom. My new-made hands grow full. The hollowness at the base of the new thumbs He gave me solidifies, warms, fills in. The cave in my being is gone. This sense of fullness somehow unleashes all the stored memories of Mother in my mind. They flash by now* in God's instant; and those of Father and Nana and Ned and Cassidy and Jeanine and Tina and Burke and Garraway, and, and, and, and

He makes me full of my life.

In that instant*, He makes me full of my life the way a woman at term is full of life. It squirms for room inside me. All the caring, smiling faces; all the sneering, jeering faces; all the songs and sweet words, the sighs and whispers and insults; all the voices at once slurred and perfect, full of air and water, light and shadow, sugar and salt; all the stars in

the night skies of plaster and black eternity; all the animals
stuck in stucco and running the beach sand; all the gods
and goddesses, heroes and monsters, alive inside me. All
growing and stretching and kicking with the possibility of
love, the *necessity* of forgiveness.

Something inside me tightens. All my bones become
one bone.

I am full of joy that I am and that I love and that I am
loved, that I forgive and am forgiven.

He releases me with a last caress of my thumbs, but
my hands, my being, continue to register His touch. "That
which most makes you human, also makes you divine," He
tells me.

I know in my fullness what He means. He does not
mean my thumbs. Forgiveness is all we know of God, and
in the end, it's all He cares to know of us.

Then, He is gone. He has taken the tape, the last unfin-
ished tape. I have seen enough. No, I have seen it all. What
was hidden from the wise, I remember Him telling me at
the very beginning*, has been revealed to the blind.

14

NOW*

I know their lives on Earth now* without seeing, without the constraint of time*. Images, information can come at once, or at length. Cassidy makes a slow recovery. His brain has been injured—subdural bleeding, neurosurgery, weeks in the intensive care unit—but he lives. His right side is paralyzed for a year. But the post office welcomes him back. He weighs packages, doles out stamps and change, uses the tape dispenser to secure boxes, all with his left hand. He walks with a limp and a lurch like some big ape, his body dodging left, then right, then left as he tries to go in a straight line. His guitar sits unused in his closet these months. With time and physical therapy, strength returns to his arm and he can thrum his notes. He sings with a slight droop to the left corner of his mouth. Surprisingly, his voice is the better for it. The slight weakness in his vocal cords intensifies his lower range. When he sings a lullaby to Joey, as they now call my brother, the density of his song throws a blanket of sleep over the tired baby that takes him full through the nights. Mother is happy for this. She is expecting again. Irish twins, their many friends tease, what with that little Joey still a baby. She is expecting again and needs the rest.

Mother and Father tell Brandon D'Woulfe not to take the suit to trial. They cut him off in mid-sentence as he tries to wrap his words around their decision. Either settle it or drop it, they tell him, and hang up the phone. He does settle it. All the hospital offers is expected defense court costs. D'Woulfe takes his forty percent of the eighty thousand dollars. Mother and Father use their share to renovate the basement. They put in a shower and fix a bedroom and add windows. Cassidy moves in. He sings every night. Nana and Ned visit a lot. They tape his songs, often downstairs in the basement where the sound booms off the bright grass-green of the painted cinder block walls, enlarging in its echo. It sounds as if there's more than one singer down there. Later, much later, Father will play one of those recordings at Cassidy's funeral because no one, no one, sings "Dark Eyed Molly" like Cassidy.

Father distributes quarters now* to the meter-needy in line at the post office. "Whoa! Who needs quarters? Quarters for sale! Twenty minutes on Uncle Sam. Come and get your quarters!" He never charges for quarters. He holds the record, most free quarters, unbroken to this day*.

Cassidy takes a little nip at night, most nights. Just one before the meal. Rye, rocks. One is enough. He sips it slow. When Mother and Father are not watching, he lets Jeanine or Joey or, later, little Carina dip their fingers in. "A toast ta your big sister, Jess. Her life," he says before they drink their glass, knuckle by knuckle.

I know that this is true. My tongue, my throat, burn in the hallowed light of every full evening where all is forgiven. And my thumbs, my thumbs shimmer. They are perfect.

ACKNOWLEDGMENTS

A writer is needy.
A writer needs critical readers. Mine are special. Kathy Carter, Barbara Dagenais, Mary Mason, Suzanne Aro, Mary Ann Hillier, Caroline Wellbery, Chris Gilson, Katie Gekker, Mariah Burton Nelson, Pat Hieber, and Frank Palumbo all provided invaluable critiques and guidance through the drafts of *Assembler*. Thank you all.

A writer needs family and friends who nourish the writer's life. Mine—my wife, four great children, and dozens of close friends from Northern Virginia, D.C., Maryland, Dallas, Texas, Phoenix, Arizona, New York, and Southern California—provided me every support, from encouraging words for my ears to what apparently is some fanciful concept of a writer's wardrobe, pipe and slippers included. Thank you, all.

A writer needs an agent. Mine, Sorche Fairbank, is the best. She provided sure-handed guidance, steady resolve, and unerring insight from start to finish. Thank you, Sorche.

A writer needs an editor. Mine, Cal Barksdale, is brilliant. He found the dim and unjoined stars in my writing and showed me how to make them shine and where they fit. Thank you, Cal.

A writer needs a first-believer. Mine, Barbara Esstman, was first to see what lay inside the imperfect sentences of my earliest draft and graciously urged me on. Thank you, Barbara.

And last, but possibly really first, a writer needs the spark of an idea. Holly and Bob Kimmitt asked me to do them a favor one Super Bowl Sunday afternoon. The sacrament of human dignity that walked across the street to meet with me became the rite of initiation, the "Big Bang," for *The Assembler of Parts*. Thank you, thank you, Holly and Bob.